Bad News
cowboy

MAISEY YATES

Bad News cowboy

HQN™

ISBN-13: 978-0-373-78853-8

Recycling programs
for this product may
not exist in your area.

Bad News Cowboy
Copyright © 2015 by Maisey Yates

Shoulda Been a Cowboy
Copyright © 2015 by Maisey Yates

This is a work of fiction. Names, characters, places and incidents are
either the product of the author's imagination or are used fictitiously,
and any resemblance to actual persons, living or dead, business
establishments, events or locales is entirely coincidental.

This edition published by arrangement with Harlequin Books S.A.

For questions and comments about the quality of this book,
please contact us at CustomerService@Harlequin.com.

® and TM are trademarks of Harlequin Enterprises Limited or its
corporate affiliates. Trademarks indicated with ® are registered in the
United States Patent and Trademark Office, the Canadian Intellectual
Property Office and in other countries.

www.HQNBooks.com

Printed in U.S.A.

CONTENTS

Bad News Cowboy

CHAPTER ONE

KATE GARRETT HAD never much belonged to anyone. And that was how she liked it.

She didn't have the time or desire to deal with anyone telling her what to do or how to act or how to sit. If she wanted to ride across the field like a bat out of hell and let her hair tangle in the wind, gathering snarls and bugs and Lord knew what else, she'd do that.

It was the perk of independence. Compensation from life since it hadn't seen fit to give her a mother who was around to tuck her in at night. The consolation prize that came for living with a father whose every word was scented with whiskey, who moved around her as if she existed in a different space. As if she wasn't even there.

But who needed warm milk and itchy tights and whatever the hell else came with being hovered over for your entire childhood? She'd rather have freedom and the pounding of a horse's hooves on arena dirt.

Or on the soft soil of the Garrett family ranch, which was what she had today. Which meant it was a damn good day. She had to be at the Farm and Garden for work in a couple of hours, so she would have to cut the ride shorter than she'd like. But any ride was better than none, even if she'd rather keep going until her face was chapped from the wind and her lungs burned.

The sun was getting high in the sky and she knew it was time to haul ass back. She grimaced and slowed her horse, Roo, turning sharply, as she would if they were going around a barrel, before picking up the pace again on the way out of the loop and galloping back in the direction she'd come.

Wind whipped strands of dark hair into her eyes and she cursed her decision to leave it loose. So maybe nobody yelled at her for letting her hair get tangled, but in the end she had to comb it out and that was always a pain.

She would braid it before work. Because when she'd gotten her horse ready to be put away, she wasn't going to have time to get herself looking pretty. Not that she needed to be particularly pretty to man the counter at the Farm and Garden.

She would settle for not looking homeless.

She slowed Roo as they approached the horse barn, and she dismounted, breathing hard, the early-morning air like a shot of ice to her lungs on every indrawn breath. She led the horse inside and removed her bridle, then slipped on a halter and looped the lead over a hook. She didn't even bother with tying a quick-release knot on Roo when they were at home. She knelt down and loosened the girth on the saddle before taking it off completely, along with the bright blue blanket underneath. In spite of the chilly air that marked the shift from summer to fall, Roo had worked up a sweat during the ride.

She pulled the towel off a nearby rack and wiped Roo down, making sure she was dry and that the saddle marks were removed. Then she took her bright yellow pick out of the bucket and ran her hand down Roo's leg, squeezing gently until the horse lifted her foot. She picked out any rocks and mud that had collected during the ride, humming softly as she did. She repeated that step on the other three legs and was nearly finished when she heard footsteps on the ground behind her, followed by her oldest brother's voice.

"You're up early, Katie."

"I wanted to get a ride in before I headed to work. And if you call me Katie one more time, I'm going to stick this pick in your eye."

Connor only smiled at her threat, crossing his arms over his broad chest, his wedding band catching her attention. In the seven months since he and Liss had gotten married, it had stayed shiny. It was some kind of metal designed to break if it got caught on anything, since ranch work was dangerous for men wearing jewelry.

She liked the reminder, though. The reminder that he was happy again. Connor had spent way too much time buried in the depths of his grief, and Liss had finally been able to lift him out of it.

As an added bonus, Liss had allowed Kate to wear jeans and boots to the wedding. Which was more than her future sister-in-law, Sadie, was letting her get away with for her and Eli's upcoming mammoth nuptials.

"Sorry, Kate," Connor said, his smile getting wider.

"You're cheerful this morning," she observed, finishing with Roo's last hoof before straightening.

"I'm pretty much cheerful all the time these days."

"I've noticed. Which is more than I can say for your wife."

"Her ankles are swollen. It's all my fault," he said, but he didn't look at all abashed. In fact, he looked rather proud. Love did weird things to people. It was kind of strange being surrounded by it like she was now.

Watching both of her older brothers fall fast and hard.

And she was just alone. But then, she was kind of used to that. And she liked it. She wasn't beholden to anyone. It was secure. It was familiar.

Anyway, it made for a lot of free time available to ride her horse.

"Yeah, she makes a good case for staying far away from marriage and pregnancy—" Kate tucked a strand of hair behind her ear "—what with all the complaining."

"Suits me just fine if you stay away from it for now," Connor said. "Nobody's good enough for you anyway."

"I don't know about that. But I haven't met anyone with the balls to keep up." That wasn't strictly true. It was more true to say she hadn't done any serious looking.

Really?

She gritted her teeth and ignored that thought.

"That doesn't surprise me. What time do you get off?" he asked.

"Pretty early."

"Are you coming out for poker?"

She was usually invited to the family game these days, after years of them behaving as though her presence stifled conversation. No matter whether she was three, thirteen or newly twenty-three, Eli and Connor looked at her like she was a child. Of course, Sadie and Liss weren't much better.

And Jack was pretty much the worst.

She ignored the slight twist in her stomach when she thought of her brothers' friend.

"Isn't it my night to bring dinner?" she asked.

He leaned against the barn wall. "That's one reason I was making sure you're coming. If not, I was going to have to cook something."

"By which you mean opening a frozen pizza box?"

"Yes. Because that is the extent of my skills and if I ask Liss to cook anything right now, I'm going to end up with a ladle shoved up where the sun don't shine."

Kate winced. "Well, out of concern for your…that, I promise to bring dinner."

He pushed away from the wall. "Excellent. See you tonight."

She hesitated before asking the next question. But she did need to know. "How many of us will there be?"

Connor screwed up his face, clearly doing mental math. "Six counting you."

So that meant everyone was coming. Which wasn't all that remarkable. It was more common than not. Considering that, her stomach should not have felt the way it did when she took an extra-sharp barrel turn while riding Roo.

"I might bring fish and chips from The Crab Shanty."

"You don't have to do that. It's expensive. And greasy." He paused for a moment. "You realize that expensive was the negative and greasy was the positive."

She waved a hand. "I'm sick of pizza. I'll spend my money however I damn well please. Anyway, I still have some cash from my last win." The purse for the last amateur barrel racing event she'd won hadn't been very big, but it had been enough to continue giving her the luxury of working part-time at the Farm and Garden while she kept honing her skills.

It was too expensive to jump into the professional circuit without the ability to back it up.

"Fine. Spend your money on seafood. In which case, I'll take the lobster, thanks."

"Liss isn't the only one who might stuff things in places, Connor. I'd watch it."

He reached out and mussed her hair, like she was a damn toddler. Or a puppy.

"Watch it, asshole," she grumbled.

"Sorry, did I break one of the eggs in that bird's nest of yours?"

She scowled. "I hope your wife punches you in the face."

"That isn't a far-fetched hope."

"Excellent," she said, knowing she sounded bloodthirsty. She felt a little bloodthirsty.

"I hope you don't plan on treating your customers the same way you treat me."

"No, I perk up for actual people."

"I don't really care how evil your mood is if you bring food. And money to lose."

"Shut it, Garrett. You know you aren't going to get any of my money."

Connor's smile turned rueful. "No. Because Jack is going to end up with everyone's money."

The outright mention of Jack's name made her skin feel prickly. "Well, that's true," she said. "I don't know why you invite him."

Connor looked mystified. "I don't think anyone does. He just shows up."

"Ha. Ha." Kate scuffed her boot through the dirt, leaving a line behind.

"I have to get a move on," he said. "These cows won't castrate themselves."

"Damn lazy beasts. Also—" Kate held her hands up and wiggled her fingers "—no thumbs."

"Right. It's thankless work. It's also the only magic trick I know."

She narrowed her eyes. "Magic trick?"

"I'm off to go change bulls into steers. With the help of my lovely assistant, Eli."

She snorted. "Yeah, well, enjoy that. I'm going to give thanks that I'm not on ranch duty today."

"See you tonight." And with that, he turned and walked out the alley doors.

Kate grabbed her brush out of the bucket, then tossed the pick back in. She straightened and ran the bristles quickly over Roo's hair before taking the end of the lead rope and guiding her into her stall.

She unhooked the rope and patted Roo on the nose before scratching the white star on her forehead. "See you later," she said, unable to resist dropping a kiss on the horse's nose.

A day that started with a ride and ended with a poker game surrounded by her family could only be a good day.

And the presence of Jack Monaghan didn't matter at all.

IT WAS A strange thing knowing that whenever a random expense came up, he had the means to handle it. After spending most of his childhood in poverty, Jack Monaghan was still getting used to having money. Not just in his pocket but in his bank account. In stocks and bonds. He even had a savings account and some set aside for retirement.

If someone looked at his finances, they might think he was responsible. Stable. Because on paper, he looked good. A person might be tempted to draw the conclusion that Jack was a steady, staid family man.

Yeah, that motherfucker would be wrong.

But Jack didn't care either way. Because today his tractor was broken, and he was headed over to the Farm and Garden to get a replacement part and he didn't have to beg anyone for a loan.

He killed the engine on his F-150 and got out of the truck, walked to the front door of the store and pushed it open. The little bell that was strung overhead signaled his arrival and a dark head popped up from behind the counter.

"Hey there, Katie," he said making his way across the store.

The youngest Garrett narrowed her brown eyes, her glare as penetrating as a rifle bullet. "What are you doing here, Monaghan?"

"I'm a paying customer, twerp."

"Did you just call me a twerp? Because I have the right to refuse service to anyone." She flipped her braid over her shoulder, her expression remaining fierce.

"Yeah, that would go over real well with your boss. Especially since I'm here to drop decent money on a freaking carburetor."

"We're probably gonna have to order it. You could always go to Tolowa and pick it up at one of the bigger stores."

"I'd rather get it here. Keep my business in Copper Ridge."

The corner of her lips turned up in a bad approximation of a smile. "That's appreciated."

"It's okay, Katie. I know you don't appreciate much about me."

"If you called me something other than Katie, I might."

"I just called you twerp and you didn't seem to appreciate that, either."

"Maybe if you pulled your head out of your ass and realized I was a grown-up and not a child, we wouldn't have so many problems." She crossed her arms beneath her breasts—which he knew she had; he wasn't blind—and cocked her hip to the side.

"We don't have problems. You have problems. *I* am fine." He pulled a piece of paper out of his pocket that had all of the relevant make and model information for his tractor. "Well, except for a carburetor problem." He handed her the paper and she took it from him, studying the information before scrunching her nose and turning to the antiquated computer on the counter.

The monitor was practically the size of a hay bale, big and square, off-white. Like something they had used back in the junior high school computer lab.

"Doesn't that thing drive you crazy?" he asked, indicating the machine.

Kate frowned, entering numbers in slowly before turning to look at him. "Why would it drive me crazy?"

"Because it's so outdated I'm surprised you can't hear gears turning inside when you give it a command."

"It works fine."

"Isn't it slow?"

She blinked. "Compared to what?"

"Do you have a computer?"

"Why would I need a computer?"

He looked at the completely earnest and completely confused expression of the younger sister of his two best friends in the world. Kate was pretty enough even if she didn't choose to make the most of her assets, not a bit of makeup to enhance her features, her hair rarely in any configuration other than a single braid down her back. Invariably, she wore slightly baggy T-shirts or flannel button-up tops tucked into either a pair of Wrangler or Carhartt jeans.

Kate dressed for functionality, not decoration.

He had no issue with that. Kate was... Well, as women went, she was more functional than decorative, so it fit.

"I think most people would say they couldn't survive without one," he said.

"Well—" Kate flashed him a smile "—look at me. Surviving and shit."

"Good job." He tapped the counter. "Now let's see if you can order me a carburetor as handily as you can survive."

"Watch it, Monaghan," she said, still typing numbers into the computer. "I am bringing dinner tonight, and I don't have to bring any for you."

"Oh, do we have the option of excluding people from dinner now? I'll remember that when my turn comes around."

Lately, Kate was usually prickly as a porcupine when he was around. He was never sure why. But then, he seemed incapable of leaving her be. He wasn't sure why that was, either. She brought out the devil in him. Of course, the devil in him seemed to live real close to the surface.

It hadn't always been like this. Sure, they'd always hassled each other. But beneath that, he'd known where he stood. Somewhere in the vicinity of her brothers. Both of them had had some pretty shitty home situations. His mother stressed, angry and resentful of his presence. While Kate's mother had been gone, her father a slobbering drunk.

Eli and Connor had done their best to take care of her, but when they'd needed help? He'd been all in. Making her smile had been his goal. Because she'd been so short on reasons to smile.

An only child, he'd had no one around to take care of him. To cheer him up when he'd been smarting from a slap across the face delivered by his mom. He'd had the Garretts. And he'd soon realized that the void he'd felt from having no one to take care of him could be filled by offering Kate what he'd so desperately wished for when he'd been young.

Somewhere along the way they'd lost some of that. Something to do with her not being a kid anymore, he supposed.

The bell above the door rang again and Alison Davis walked in, carrying a white pastry box with a stack of brochures on top. "Good morning, Kate." She offered Jack a cautious smile, tucking her red hair behind her ear and looking down at the ground. "Good morning."

"Hi, Alison," he said, softening his tone a bit.

Though she'd left her abusive husband a year and

a half ago, Alison still seemed skittish as a newborn colt. Maybe that was just him, too.

"What brings you by?" Kate asked.

Alison appeared to regroup in time to focus on Kate. "I wanted to bring you a pie. And also to ask if it would be all right if I put a couple of advertisements for the bakery here in the store. I have two new employees, both women who just left men who were… well, like my ex. I'm happy to have them working for me, but now I need more business to match the expense. One of them hasn't had a job in fifteen years and no one else would hire her." Alison let out a long breath. "It's hard to start a new life."

"I'm sure," Kate said. "Yeah, I'll take a whole stack of those ads. I don't think Travers will have a problem with it. But if he does, I'll tell him he's being stupid. And then he'll probably change his mind because he's pretty cool."

"I don't want to get you in trouble," Alison said.

Kate snorted and planted her hands on her hips. "Nobody gets me in trouble unless I agree to be in trouble."

"I appreciate it." She set the bakery box on the counter and took the brochures off the top of them. Then she lifted the lid, revealing the most perfect meringue he'd ever seen in his life. "Lemon meringue," she said. "I hope you like that."

"I do." Kate took the pie and moved it behind the counter. "I gladly accept. I promise to refer customers to you, too. If anyone comes in with a pie craving I can send them right down the street."

"I appreciate it. Really I appreciate what everyone has done. I thought when I quit the diner, Rona would be mad at me. But instead she decided to order all of her pies from me now that I'm not making them there."

"That's great!" Kate smiled.

Yes, she seemed perfectly capable of being nice to other people. So it was him.

"I have a few other businesses to go to. And I don't want to distract you from your work."

"Great—just leave the brochures here on the counter."

"Thanks, Kate." She offered a shy wave, then turned and left the store.

Jack watched her go, then turned his attention back to Kate. "That was nice of you."

"I am nice," she said.

"To some people."

She scrunched up her face. "Some people deserve it."

"Oh, go on, Katie. You like me."

Kate looked at the computer screen, a slash of pink spreading over her cheeks. "I like my brothers, too, but that doesn't mean I don't want to punch them in the face half the time."

She was blushing. Honest-to-God blushing. But he didn't have a clue as to why.

"That embarrassing to have to admit that I'm not the worst person in the world?"

"What do you mean?" she asked, looking back at him, her dark eyes glittering.

"You're blushing, Garrett."

She pressed her palm to her cheek before lowering it quickly. "I am not. What the hell would I have to blush about around you?" She turned her focus back to the computer screen, her expression dark now.

"You wouldn't be the first girl I made blush."

"Gross."

"Are you bringing that pie tonight?" He thought it was probably best to change the subject, because something about it was making him edgy, too.

"I don't know. I might hide it back in my house and keep it all for myself."

"You can't eat a whole pie."

"I can absolutely eat a whole pie. And will."

"Better idea. Only you and me know about the pie. Save it, and I'll come back to your place with you."

Kate blinked rapidly. "No."

"What?"

"I don't think it's a good idea for you to come to my house. I mean, I think we need to share it."

He wasn't sure why it was so difficult to find a topic that didn't make her mad or…weird. Jack never had problems talking to women. Women liked him. He liked women. The exception seemed to be Kate. And seeing as he'd known her the better part of her life, he couldn't fathom why. Usually, their banter was pretty good-natured. Lately, he wasn't sure that was the case.

"Your total is one ninety. That includes shipping," she said, the change in topic abrupt.

"Great. When do you expect it to be here?"

"Should only take two days."

"Even better." He reached into his back pocket, took out his wallet and handed Kate his debit card. "I might actually swing by the bakery and pick up another pie on my way home."

"Yeah, I wish there was more I could do to help. For now, all I can think of is increasing my pie consumption. Which I'm not opposed to. But there has to be more that can be done."

Ideas started turning over in Jack's head. His brain was never still. Not unless he was on the back of a bull intent on shaking him loose. Or riding his horse so hard and fast all he could hear was the pounding of hooves on the ground. In those moments he had what he imagined was tranquility. Outside that, it never happened.

"If I think of anything, I'll let you know," he said. He was already determined that he would think of something.

The printer whirred, spitting out a receipt that Kate tore off and handed to him. "You're all set. Someone will give you a call when it's in."

"Great." And then, for no other reason than that he was curious whether or not he could make her cheeks pink again, he tipped his hat, nodded his head and treated her to his patented Monaghan smile. "See you later, Katie."

He didn't get a blush. He didn't even get a return smile. Instead he got a very emphatic middle finger.

Jack laughed and walked out of the store.

CHAPTER TWO

"I COME BEARING FISH! And chips. Well, French fries. But you knew that." Kate pushed her way through the front door of Connor's house holding two large white takeout containers. One held the fried fish fillets, and the other the fried potatoes.

"I'm starving." Kate rounded the corner and saw her sister-in-law, Liss, standing in the center of the dining area with her hand on her rounded stomach.

"You're eating for two," Kate said. "Or so I've heard."

Liss screwed up her face. "That would make sense. If I knew I was gestating a ravenous wolverine rather than a human child."

Kate laughed and walked over to the table and set the cartons down. The only other thing on the scarred wooden surface was the big green Oregon Ducks ice bucket her brother put his beer in. Well, beer and soda now, since Liss was pregnant and Connor barely drank anymore.

"Although, if it isn't a wolverine, it just means that I lack restraint." Liss groaned. "I can't pass Rona's without going in for a milkshake. And I can't pass The Grind without getting an onion cheese bagel. I'm a cliché without the pickles."

Connor leaned in and kissed his wife on the cheek.

"You're having a baby. You can be a cliché if you damn well please."

Kate's heart squeezed tight as she watched the exchange between Connor and Liss. Connor's first wife, Jessie, had been an influential figure in Kate's life. The two had gotten married when Kate was only nine, and seeing as she didn't have a mother, Jessie was as close as she'd gotten to a female influence.

Jessie's loss had been devastating for everyone. Though she knew it had been the worst for Connor. Considering that, him falling for and marrying Liss was only good in Kate's eyes. And Liss had always been a fixture around their house, seeing as she'd been best friends with Connor since they were in high school.

Having her as a sister was a bonus that Kate quite enjoyed.

"Ugh. Can I be a cliché eating French fries?" she asked, sitting down at the table and digging a Coke out of the ice bucket.

"I'll get you a plate." Connor turned and walked back into the kitchen just as they heard a pounding on the door.

"Who even knocks?" Liss mused.

She had a point. Jack, Eli and Sadie never knocked. "I'll go see." Kate walked back out to the entryway and jerked the front door open, freezing when she saw Jack standing there holding a stack of four pastry boxes. Her heart did that weird thing it did sometimes when she was caught off guard by Jack. That thing where it dramatically threw itself at her breastbone and knocked against it with the force of a punch.

"Were you kicking the door?"

"I couldn't open it. Not without setting all of these down."

Kate looked up, studying his expression. He was so very tall. And he always made her feel…little. Sure, Connor and Eli were tall, too, but they didn't fill up space the way Jack did. He was in every corner of every room he inhabited. From the spicy aftershave he wore to his laugh, low and rough like thunder, rumbling beneath every conversation.

Kate stepped to the side and held the door. "What do you have?"

"Pies. From Alison's."

"Four pies?"

He sighed heavily and walked past her into the dining room. She shut the door and followed after him. "Yes." He placed the boxes on the table next to the fish and chips. "Four pies."

Liss's eyes widened. "What kind?"

"I'm not sure. I just bought pies."

There was something about all of this that made her feel weird. A little bit weak, a little bit shaky. He'd done this for Alison, which was…touching. Definitely touching. And nice. Beyond nice of him. And a little bit curious. Because he was Jack, and he had a tendency to be kind of a self-centered asshole. So when he did things for other people, it was notable.

And strange.

And it made her throat a little bit dry. And her face a little bit hot.

"Is that going to be your solution for her?" Kate asked. "Going on a four-pie-a-day diet?"

"Obviously not," he said, sitting down at the table and snagging a beer out of the bucket.

"What solution are we talking about?" Liss asked, crunching on a French fry.

Connor returned then, setting a plate in front of Liss before setting places in front of the rest of the chairs, then taking his seat next to his wife. "Hey, Jack," he said.

"Hey," Jack replied, putting a handful of French fries on his plate.

"I brought fish," Kate said. "It's healthy. And you people are eating French fries."

"Don't worry, Kate," Jack said. "We'll get around to eating your healthy battered fried fish in a minute."

"Solution?" Liss prompted, her eyebrow arched.

"Alison stopped by the Farm and Garden today," Kate said. "She had brochures for her bakery. And she mentioned that she's hired on a couple of other women who just got out of circumstances similar to hers. But of course, it's a new business, and she has a lot more overhead now since she's renting out store space. Anyway, Jack and I were talking earlier about how we wish there was more we could do."

"So Jack was also at the Farm and Garden?" Connor asked.

"I had to order a carburetor." He ran a large hand over his jaw. His very square jaw. And she heard it. The brush of his palm over his dark five o'clock shadow. She swore she could feel the friction, deep and low in her stomach. And it wrapped itself around the general feeling of edginess firing through her veins.

For some reason the line of conversation was irritating to Kate. Possibly because it was preventing her from figuring out just what Jack's motives were where

Alison was concerned. And even more irritating was the fact that she cared at all.

For some reason a lot of little details about Jack's life sometimes ended up getting magnified in her mind. And she overthought them. She more than overthought them; she turned them over to death. She couldn't much explain it. Any more than she could make it stop.

"So you obviously stopped by the bakery and bought pies," Kate said, trying to speed things along.

"Obviously," Jack said, sweeping his hand in a broad gesture, indicating the still-stacked boxes of pie.

"It was nice of you." She was pushing now.

"I don't know that I'd go that far," he said, shrugging his shoulder before pushing his fingers back through his dark hair. "But you know I was raised by a single mom who couldn't get a lick of help out of her deadbeat ex. Stuff like this… I don't like hearing about men mistreating the people they're supposed to care for. It sticks with me."

Kate felt as though a valve had been released in her chest and some of the pressure eased. "Oh. Yeah. That makes sense, I guess."

Jack arched a black brow, his blue eyes glittering. "I know you don't think I make sense very often, Katie. But there's usually a method to my madness."

"Don't call her that," Connor said. "She hates that."

"Thank you, Connor," Kate said, feeling exasperated now. "But I'm perfectly capable of fighting my own battles. Especially against Monaghan. He's not the most formidable opponent."

"I'm wounded, Katie."

He'd said it again. That nickname that nobody else

but Connor ever called her. But when Connor said it, it rubbed the wrong way, made her feel as if he was talking down to her. Like he was still thinking of her as a kid.

When Jack said it, her skin felt as though it had been brushed with velvet, leaving a trail of goose bumps behind. It made her feel warm, made it hard to breathe. So basically the same as being rubbed the wrong way. Pretty much.

Either way, she didn't like it.

"You're a slow learner, Monaghan."

He chuckled and leaned back in his chair, crossing his forearms over his broad chest. "There are quite a few women who would beg to differ."

Her cheeks caught fire. "Shut. Up. You are so gross," she said, picking up her plate with shaking fingers and serving herself a heaping portion of fish. No fries. Ungrateful bastards not eating her fish.

She heard the door open again, and then Eli's and Sadie's voices. Now the gang was all here. And she could focus on playing cards, which was really what she wanted.

Sadie led the charge into the dining room, holding her now-traditional orange-and-black candy bowl in front of her, a wide grin on her face. Eli was a step behind her looking slightly abashed. Probably because his fiancée was breaking sacred football laws by bringing the colors of an opposing team onto hallowed ground.

But she did so every week. And every week, Connor made a show of not eating the candy in the bowl. Eli didn't eat it either but didn't make a big deal out of it. While Jack ate half of it without giving a crap what anyone thought. Which summed them all up, really.

Kate always ate the candy, too. If only because she didn't see the point in politicizing sugar.

"Fish and chips!" Sadie exclaimed. "That makes a nice change from pizza. And pie!"

"The feast is indeed bountiful tonight," Liss said, eyeing the pie. "We have Kate to thank for that."

"Excuse me," Jack said. "I brought the pie. I will have you all know that Katie has a lemon meringue pie hidden back in her cabin. And she did not bring it to share with you."

Kate lifted her hand to smack Jack on the shoulder, and he caught her wrist. Her heart hit the back of her breastbone so hard she was afraid it might have exploded on contact. His hand was so big his fingers wrapped all the way around her arm, holding her tight, a rash of heat breaking out from that point of contact outward.

Her eyes clashed with his, and the sharp remark she'd been about to spit out evaporated on her lips.

She tugged her wrist out of his hold, fighting the urge to rub away the impression of his touch with her other hand. "I didn't bring it because I don't want to share my pie with you," she said, looking at Jack.

"Selfish pie hoarder," he said, grinning at her in that easy manner of his.

And her annoyance tripled. Because him grabbing her wrist was a whole event for her body. And he was completely unaffected. That touch had been like grabbing ahold of an electric fence. On her end. Obviously, it hadn't been the same for him.

Why would it be? It shouldn't be that way for you.

Yeah, no shit.

"I am not." And she cursed her hot cheeks and her lack of snappy remark.

"I might have to side with Jack on this one," Liss said, her tone apologetic. "Or maybe I'm just on the side of pie."

"Traitor," Kate mumbled.

"Though, on the subject of pies," Jack said, turning his focus to Sadie, "we were trying to figure out if there was something that could be done to help bolster Alison's business."

"Hmm." Sadie piled food on her plate and sat down, Eli taking a seat beside her. "I'll have to scheme on that for a while."

"You have to watch her. She's a champion schemer," Eli said.

"The championest." Sadie smiled broadly.

"Scheme away," Jack said.

"You don't have to tell her to scheme," Eli said. "She can't stop scheming. This is how I ended up with an annual Fourth of July barbecue on my property."

"I'm delightful." Sadie nodded, the expression on her face comically serious.

"She is," Eli agreed.

"Are we going to play cards?" Kate asked.

"So impatient to lose all of your money," Jack said.

This was a little more normal. A more typical level of Jack harassing her.

"To me," Sadie said, her grin turning feral. Sadie, it turned out, was a very good poker player for all her wide-blue-eyed protestations to the contrary when she first joined their weekly games.

Kate opted to stay silent, continuing on that way

while the cards were dealt. And she was dealt a very good hand. She bit the inside of her cheek to keep her expression steady. Sadie was cocky. Jack was cockier. And she was going to take their money.

By the end of the night Kate had earned several profane nicknames and the contents of everyone's wallets. She leaned back in her chair, pulling the coins toward her. "Listen to that. I'm going back home, dumping all this on the floor and swimming in it like Scrooge McDuck."

"No diving in headfirst. That's a sure way to spinal trauma. It isn't that deep of a pool," Connor said.

"Deeper than what you have. I have all your monies." She added a fake cackle for a little bit of dramatics.

"Then I will keep all the pie," Liss said.

"That's my pie," Jack said.

"You have to stay in fighting form, Monaghan. Your bar hookups won't be so easy if you lose your six-pack," Liss said cheerfully.

"I do enough work on the ranch every day to live on pies and still keep my six-pack, thank you very much."

"You aren't getting any younger," Sadie said.

The conversation was going into uncomfortable territory as far as Kate was concerned. Really, on all fronts it was getting to an awkward place. Jack and sex. Jack's abs. Yikes.

"I would return volley," Jack said, "but I'm too much of a gentleman to comment on a lady's age."

"Gentleman, huh?" Eli asked. "Of all the things you've been accused of being, I doubt that's one of them."

Jack squinted and held up his hand, pretending to

count on his fingers. "Yeah, no. There have been a lot of things, but not that one."

"Anyway," she said, unable to help herself, "you comment on my age all the time."

"I said I never commented on a lady's age, Katie."

She snorted. "I am a lady, asswipe."

"I don't know how I missed it," he said, leaning back in his chair, his grin turning wicked.

For some reason that comment was the last straw. "Okay, hate to cut this short, but I have an early morning tomorrow." That was not strictly true. It was an optional early morning since she intended to get up and spend some time with Roo. "And I will be stopping by The Grind to buy a very expensive coffee with the money I won from you."

Jack stood, putting his hands behind his head and stretching. "I'll walk you out. I have an early morning, too, so I better get going."

Dammit. He didn't seem to understand that she was beating a hasty retreat in part to get away from him. Because the Weird Jack Stuff was a little more elevated today than normal. It had something to do with overexposure to him. She needed to go home, be by herself, scrub him off her skin in a hot shower so she could hit the reset button on her interactions with him.

She felt as if she had to do that more often lately than she had ever had to do in the past.

The thing was, she liked Jack. In that way you could like a guy who was basically an extra obnoxious older brother who didn't share genetic material with you. She liked it when he came to poker night. She liked it when he came into the store. But at the end of it she was always left feeling...agitated.

And it had created this very strange cycle. Hoping she would see Jack, seeing Jack, being pissed that she had seen Jack. And on and on it went.

"Bye," she said.

She picked up her newly filled change bag and started to edge out of the room. She heard heavy footsteps behind her, and without looking she knew it was Jack. Well, she knew it was Jack partly because he had said he would walk her out.

And partly because the hair on the back of her neck was standing on end. That was another weird Jack thing.

She opened the front door and shut it behind her, not waiting for Jack. Which was petty and weird. She heard the door open behind her and shut again.

"Did I do something?"

She turned around, trying to erase the scowl from her face. Trying to think of one thing he had actually done that was out of line, or out of the ordinary, at least. "No," she said, begrudgingly.

"Then why are you acting like I dipped your pigtails in ink?" he asked, taking the stairs two at a time, making uncomfortable eye contact with her in the low evening light.

She looked down. "I'm not."

"I seem to piss you off all the time lately," he said, closing the distance between them while her throat closed itself up tight.

"You don't. It's just...teasing stuff. Don't worry about it."

Jack kept looking at her, pausing for a moment. She felt awkward standing there but also unable to break away. "Okay. Hey, I was thinking..."

"Uh-oh. That never ends well," she said, trying to force a smile.

"What does that mean?"

"I've heard the stories Connor and Eli tell. Any time you think of something, it ends in…well, sometimes broken bones."

"Sure," he said, chuckling and leaning against the side of his truck. "But not this time. Well, maybe this time since it centers around the rodeo."

"You don't ride anymore," she said, feeling stupid for pointing out something he already knew.

"Well, I might. I was sort of thinking of working with the association to add an extra day onto the rodeo when they pass through. A charity day. Half-price tickets. Maybe some amateur events. And all the proceeds going to…well, to a fund for women who are starting over. A certain amount should go to Alison's bakery. She's helping people get jobs. Get hope. I wish there had been something like that for us when I was a kid."

Kate didn't know anything about Jack's dad. As long as she'd known him, he hadn't had one. And he never talked about it.

But she got the sense that whatever the situation, it hadn't been a happy one.

And now mixed in with all the annoyance and her desire to avoid him was a strange tightening in her chest.

"Life can be a bitch," she said, hating the strident tone that laced its way through her voice.

"I've never much liked that characterization. In my estimation life is a lot more like a pissed-off bull. You hang on as long as you can, even though the ride is uncomfortable. No matter how bad it is on, you sure as hell don't want to get bucked off."

"Yeah, that sounds about like you."

"Profound?"

"Like a guy who's been kicked in the head a few times."

"Fair enough. Anyway, what do you think about the charity?"

Warmth bloomed in her stomach. "Honestly? I think it's a great idea." She couldn't even give him a hard time about this, because it was just so damn nice. "We only have a couple of months until the rodeo, though. Do you think we can pull it off?"

"We?"

Her stomach twisted uncomfortably. "Well, yeah. I think it's a good idea. And I would like to contribute in any way I can. Even if it just means helping the pros tack up or something."

"When are you going to turn pro, Katie?"

She gritted her teeth, and it had nothing to do with his unwanted nickname for her. "When I'm ready. I'm not going to waste a whole bunch of money traveling all over the country, entering all kinds of events and paying for association cards when I don't have a hope in hell of winning."

"Who says you don't have a hope in hell of winning?" he asked, frowning. "I've seen you ride. You're good."

The compliment flowed through her like cool water on parched earth. She cleared her throat, not sure where to look or what to say. "Roo is young. She has another year or so before she's mature. I probably do, too."

He reached out and wrapped his hand around her braid, tugging gently. "You're closer than you think."

Something about his look, about that touch that should have irritated her if it did anything, sent her stomach tumbling down to her toes.

Then he turned away from her and walked around to the other side of his pickup truck, opened the driver-side door, got inside and slammed it shut. He started the truck engine and she felt icy spots on her face. She released her breath in a rush, a wave of dizziness washing over her.

You'd have thought she'd been staring down a predator and not one of her family's oldest and dearest friends.

Freaking Jack and all the weirdness that followed him around like a thunderclap.

She walked over to her pickup and climbed in, then started the engine and threw it into Reverse without bothering to buckle. She was just driving down the narrow dirt road that led from Connor's house to her little cabin.

The road narrowed as the trees thickened, pine branches whipping against the doors to her old truck as she approached her house. She'd moved into the cabin on her eighteenth birthday, gaining a little bit of distance and independence from her brothers without being too far away. Of course, it wasn't as if she'd really done much with the independence.

She worked, played cards with her brothers and rode horses. That was about the extent of her life. But it filled her life, every little corner of it. And she wasn't unhappy with that.

She walked up the front steps, threw open the front

door that she never bothered to lock and stepped inside. She flipped on the light switch, bathing the small space in a yellow glow.

The kitchen and living room were one, a little woodstove built into a brick wall responsible for all the heating in the entire house. The kitchen was small with wood planks for walls that she'd painted white when she'd moved in. A distressed counter-height table divided the little seating area from where she prepared food, and served as both infrequently used dining table and kitchen island.

She had one bathroom and one bedroom. The house was small, but it fit her life just fine. In fact, she was happy with a small house because it reminded her to get outside, where things were endless and vast, rather than spend too much time hiding away from the world.

Kate would always rather be out in it.

She kicked her boots off and swept them to the side, letting out a sigh as she dropped her big leather shoulder bag onto the floor. The little lace curtains—curtains that predated Kate's tenure in the house—were shut tight, so she tugged her top up over her head and stripped off the rest of her clothes as she made her way to the shower.

She turned the handles and braced herself for the long wait for hot water. Everything, including the hot-water heater, in her little house was old-fashioned. Sort of like her, she supposed.

She snorted into the empty room, the sound echoing in the small space. Jack certainly thought she was old-fashioned. All that hyperconcern over her not owning a computer.

Steam started to rise up and fill the air and she

stepped beneath the hot spray, her thoughts lingering on her interaction with Jack at the Farm and Garden. And how obnoxious he was. And how his lips curved up into that wicked smile when he teased her, blue eyes glittering with all the smart-ass things he'd left unsaid.

She picked up the bar of Ivory soap from the little ledge of the tub and twirled it in her palms as she held it beneath the water, working up a lather. She took a breath, trying to ease some of the tension that was rioting through her.

She turned, pressing the soap against her chest, sliding it over her collarbone.

Yeah, Jack was a pain.

Still, she was picturing that look he got on his face. Just before he said something mouthy. She slid the bar of soap over her breasts just as she remembered her thwarted retaliation for his teasing tonight. The way his fingers had wrapped around her wrist, his hold firm…

She gasped and released her hold on the bar of soap. It hit the floor and slid down between her feet, stopping against the wall.

She growled and bent down, picking it back up, ignoring the pounding of her heart and the shaking in her fingers.

The shower was supposed to wash Jack off her skin. He was not supposed to follow her in.

Another jolt zipped through her at the thought because right along with it came the image of Jack and his overbearing presence sharing this small space with her. Bare skin, wet skin…hands on skin.

She turned and rinsed the soap off her chest, then shut the water off, stepped out and scrubbed her skin dry with her towel, much more ferociously than was warranted.

She needed to sleep. Obviously, she was delirious.

If she didn't know better, she would think she was a breath away from having a fantasy about Jack freaking Monaghan.

"Ha!" she all but shouted. "Ha ha ha." She wrapped her towel around her body and walked to her room before dropping it and digging through her dresser for her pajamas.

She found a pair of sensible white cotton underwear and her flannel pajama pants that had cowboy hats, lassos and running horses printed onto the fabric.

There could be no sexual fantasies when one had on cotton panties and flannel pants.

With pony pajamas came clarity.

She pulled a loose-fitting blue T-shirt over her head and flopped down onto her bed. Her twin bed. That would fit only one person.

She was sexual fantasy–proof. Also sex-proof, if the entire long history of her life was anything to go by.

"Bah." She rolled over onto her stomach and buried her face in her pillow. She had arena dirt, pounding hooves, the salty coastal wind in her face, mixed with pine and earth. A scent unique to Copper Ridge and as much a part of her as the blood in her veins.

She had ambitions. Even if she was a bit cautious in them.

She didn't need men.

Most of all, she didn't need Jack Monaghan.

CHAPTER THREE

JACK ROLLED INTO the Garrett ranch just after nine. He'd finished seeing to his horses earlier and was ready to ambush Kate with coffee and a plan. It was her day off, and he knew she wasn't still in bed lying low while the sun rose high. It wasn't her way. Which meant he would have to track her down on the vast property.

But that was fine with him. He didn't have much else happening today.

His equine operation had gotten to the point that it was running so smoothly he often felt as if he didn't have enough to do. He had people who worked on the ranch seeing to all of the horses' needs and a housekeeper who took care of all of his needs. He was forging great connections in competitive worlds. Both the Western riding community and dressage. And he was very close to signing a lucrative deal to breed one of his stallions to a champion hunter jumper, Jazzy Lady.

Now that all that was falling into place and he wasn't traveling with the rodeo, he was left with a lot of free time.

His mother had said idle hands were the devil's workshop, usually before she booted his ass outside so he'd stay out of her hair. But then, he'd never had much use for worrying about things like that. In part because he never worried all that much about the devil.

He'd gone to church once when he was a boy with a friend from his first-grade class. The pastor had said something about Joshua the son of Nun. And after the service the boy who had been his friend when they'd walked into the building had decided Jack the son of Nun was a fitting nickname for him since he didn't have a daddy.

Jack had punched that little son of a bitch in the face and had never darkened the doors of any holy institution from there on after. He hadn't stayed friends with the kid, either. In fact, the only people he had stayed friends with were the Garretts and Liss. He'd raised too much hell over the years to keep many other connections.

Hell, he'd taken to it as if it was his job. And when he'd transitioned from causing trouble in town to bull riding, it had just been a more legitimate method.

And another way for him to try to get his old man to take some notice. To make his mother look at him for more than thirty seconds.

It hadn't worked. His success hadn't changed that, either.

But he had Eli and Connor.

Together they'd knit a strange and dysfunctional group that continued on to this day. He liked to think they were all a little more functional now. Well, the rest of them more than him, he supposed.

Though he had some stability now with his ranch. He might not be married and procreating like his friends, but he wasn't a total lost cause.

And he knew that in and of itself was a big surprise to most people in Copper Ridge. Oh, sure, they were all polite enough, but he knew for a fact no one wanted him dating their daughter or their sister.

Though now they were happy to have him spending money at their establishments.

He killed his truck's engine and got out, grabbing hold of the big metal thermos he always carried with him during the workday and two tin mugs.

This was a peacemaking mission, which meant he had come prepared. He shoved his truck keys into his jeans pocket and crossed the gravel lot, heading toward the newly built barn, Connor's pride and joy, with the exception of his wife and unborn child.

Just then Connor walked out of the alley doors and Jack called out to get his attention. "Morning," he said.

"You brought me coffee," Connor said, flashing him the kind of smile that up until a few months ago had been absent from his friend's face.

"Sorry. You're out of luck. The coffee isn't for you."

"I'm hurt," Connor said, putting his hand on his chest. "You're bringing coffee to another man, Monaghan?"

"Nope. It's for Katie."

Connor's brows shot up. "Uh-oh. What did you do?"

"Nothing. But I do need to convince her to help me out planning this charity rodeo day. I can use some contacts with the pro association. I've been in touch with a few people since I stopped competing. But she's in a better position with the locals."

"You could probably seduce help out of Lydia. Or just ask."

Jack thought of the pretty dark-haired president of the chamber of commerce. Yeah, Lydia would be into it, no seduction required. The charity event, not sleeping with him. He let his brain linger on that thought for a moment, if only because it had been a while since he'd seduced anyone or been seduced in return.

"Sure," he responded.

"You don't sound enthused."

"I'm not *un*enthused."

"Yes, you are."

Jack shrugged. "Not interested, I guess."

"Are you sick? Because she's female, so she's your type."

Jack couldn't argue with that. "I don't need to seduce her into helping. It's a good idea. You make it sound like women only want to listen to me because of my body," he said, arching a brow. "I'm more than just a pretty face."

"I want to say something right now...but I have a feeling I could dig myself into a hole I'll never get out of."

"You probably shouldn't say it," Jack said. "However, if you were thinking that I'm also a very sexy ass, you would be correct."

"You better wash your mouth out with soap before you bring that coffee to Kate. Or she'll probably end up throwing it in your face."

"She's not my biggest fan."

Connor offered him a skeptical smile. "Actually, I think she's a pretty big fan of yours." Jack puzzled over the words for a second before Connor continued. "You're like another brother to her. Which is why she gives you hell."

Jack let out a hard breath. "Lucky me. Do you have any idea where the little she-demon is?"

"She took Roo out for a ride. But she should be back in soon."

"Which way does she normally go?"

"She rides out through the main pasture toward the base of Copper," Connor said, talking about the mountain that the town was named after. "And she comes back around behind the horse barn."

"Thanks. I'll head that way."

Jack turned away from his friend and started walking down a dirt path that would lead him toward the horse barn and hopefully bring him into line with Kate.

The cloud cover hadn't burned off yet, gray mist hanging low over the pine trees, pressing the sky down to the earth. The air was damp, thick with salt from the sea, and he had a feeling it would rain later. Or if they were lucky, the moisture would burn away, leaving clear blue skies.

But he doubted it.

He cut through a little thicket of pines and came out the other side on another little road. This was the one that led all the way back to Kate's cabin, but if he crossed that and cut through a little field, he would make it to the barn in half the time. So he did, wet grass whipping against his jeans, dewdrops bleeding through the thick denim.

He could only say thanks for good boots that would at least keep his feet dry.

He hopped the wire fence that partitioned the next section of the property off from the one he'd just left and stood there in the knee-high weeds, staring off into the distance. Then he saw her, riding through the flat expanse of field, strands of dark hair flying from beneath her hat, her arms working in rhythm with the horse's stride. As she drew closer, he could see the wide smile on her face. It was the kind of smile he rarely saw from her. The smile of a woman purely in her element. A woman at home on the back of the horse.

He felt the corners of his own mouth lift in response, because that kind of joy was infectious.

He stood and watched her as she drew closer, hoofbeats growing louder as she did.

He could pinpoint the exact moment she saw him, because she straightened, pulling back on Roo's reins and slowing her gait. He started to walk toward her, and she dismounted, her smile faded now.

"I have coffee, so you can stop frowning at me," he said, holding up the thermos and the mugs.

She squinted, her expression filled with suspicion. "Why do you have coffee?"

"Because I want to talk to you about something. And I figured it was best to try and bait you."

Kate screwed up her face, wrinkling her nose and squinting her eyes. "I am not a badger. You can't bait me."

"Sure I can, Katie. I bet I tempt you something awful," he said, holding out the thermos and unscrewing the lid.

Kate rolled her eyes. "Tempt me to plant a boot up your ass."

He left one mug dangling from his finger and straightened the other, then poured a measure of coffee into it. "Be nice to me or I won't give you what you want."

He watched as the faint rose color bled into her

cheeks, lit on fire by the first golden rays of the sun breaking through the cloud cover, adding a soft glow to her face. "You seem to be forgetting who you're talking to, Monaghan," she said, her voice gaining strength as the sentence picked up momentum. "Boot. Ass."

"You do need your coffee. You're cranky." He held out the mug and she took it, wrapping her fingers around it like claws.

"I *wasn't*."

"Well, stop. I want to talk to you about the rodeo."

She took a sip of the strong black coffee and didn't even grimace. But then, she would have trained herself to never make a face. She drank her coffee and her whiskey straight up and never complained about the burn. Kate never seemed to show weakness, never appeared to have any vulnerability at all.

In that moment he wondered what it might be like if she did. If she softened, even a little bit.

Dark brown eyes met his, a core of steel running straight on through, down deep inside of her. Yeah, there would be no softening from Kate Garrett. "Then talk," she said before taking another sip.

"Who do you think you can get to volunteer to ride when there's no score or purse at stake? I mean, we can keep score, but it won't count toward anything. Just winning the event."

"I'm not sure as far as the pros go. We'll probably have to reach out to the association. But I know some people who can do that. You being one of them, I assume."

One thing about the rodeo he'd liked. He'd come in with no established baggage. Nobody cared that he didn't have a dad, that he'd grown up poor. His luck with buckle bunnies and his propensity to fight in bars had also added to his popularity.

But the circuit wasn't real life. It was like living in a fraternity. Too much booze, too much sex—it was all good there. It just wasn't real life.

Of course, real life was often hard and less fun. "Yeah, I've got a lot of buddies from back in those days."

"You make it sound like it was a million years ago."

Only five, but it felt like longer sometimes. "It doesn't just have to be all pros," he continued, pitching an idea at her he'd had the other day. "We can do amateurs against professionals. That would make for a fun event."

"Well, you know I would do it. And a few others might. I bet Sierra West would."

At the mention of Sierra's name Jack's stomach went tight. Her involvement in this could be a slight complication.

He gritted his teeth. No, there was no reason to consider the Wests a complication. Sure, he shared genetic material with them, but the only people who knew that were his mother, the man who had fathered him and Jack himself. As far as he knew, the legitimate West children knew nothing about it, and Kate certainly didn't.

If he were a sentimental man, he might have been tempted to think of Sierra as a sister. But he couldn't afford sentimentality. And anyway, he'd accepted quite a bit of money to pretend he had no clue who his father was. And so he was honor bound to that. Well, not exactly honor bound. Bought and paid for, more like.

"Great. Sure."

"If you don't want my suggestions, don't ask for my help," she said, her tone cutting.

"I *want* your suggestions," he bit out.

"You sound like you want my suggestions like you want a root canal."

If he was this transparent at a mention of Sierra's name, then dealing with her while coordinating the rodeo events would be somewhere way beyond awkward. Which meant he had to get it together.

"Sorry, honey," he said, not quite sure why the endearment slipped out. Because he was trying to soften his words maybe? "I do want your suggestions. That's why I came to you for help."

She chewed her bottom lip. "You really do want my help?"

"Yes."

"Why? I mean, there are a lot of people you could get to help you. People who aren't kids."

"I don't think you're a kid."

He could remember her being a kid, all round-faced enthusiasm, shining dark eyes, freckles sprinkled over the button nose. Usually, she'd had dirt on her. Yeah, he could remember that clearly. But that image had very little to do with the woman who stood before him. Her cheeks had hollowed, highlighting the strong bone structure in her face. Her nose was finer, though still sprinkled with freckles. Her dark eyes still shone bright, but there was a stubbornness that ran deep, a hardness there developed from years of loss and pain.

She cleared her throat. "That's news to me."

"Consider yourself informed."

"Now that we've established we're on equal footing—"

"I didn't say we were on equal footing. I said I didn't think you were a kid."

"What is that supposed to mean?"

"I've been pro, honey badger," he said, combining her earlier assertion that she was not a badger with his accidental endearment. "I know the ins and outs of these events. My contacts are a little bit out of date, which is where you come in, but the rodeo is still my turf."

"Bull riders. The ego on y'all is astronomical."

"That's because we ride *bulls*. Those are some big-ass scary animals. A guy has to think he's ten feet tall and bulletproof to do something that stupid."

"It's true. You are kind of stupid." A smile spread over her face. Sometimes, it turned out, Kate did smile at him. But usually only after she was done insulting him.

"I'm wounded."

"Don't waste your time being wounded. First, we're going to have to find out if the Logan County Fairgrounds are available for the date we would need it. Probably the day before the actual rodeo starts or the day after."

"You know who to call for that?"

"Yeah, but I might want to go through Lydia."

"Good call," he said. "See? This is why I asked for your help."

"Because I'm a genius."

"Sure." He shrugged. "About a couple things."

"Aren't you going to have any coffee?" Kate asked, something searching in her brown gaze now. He had no clue what the hell she was looking for, but even so, he was almost certain she wouldn't find it.

"I have to run," he said. He didn't have to run. He didn't have anywhere to be. Except for some reason he felt averse to prolonging this moment here in the field with her. "When is the next local meeting?"

"Tomorrow night. You should come."

He'd stopped going to the amateur association meetings in Copper Ridge years ago. He'd turned pro when he was twenty, using the money that the man who was, according to genetics, his father had given him to keep his mouth shut about his existence.

Sometimes it felt like his attempt at being seen when he'd been paid to disappear. A way to demand attention without breaking that damned agreement. Other times it had all felt like an attempt to bleed that unwanted blood right out of his veins, let it soak into the arena dirt until the Wests weren't a part of him anymore. But that feeling had faded as he turned that initial bit of money into yet more money through event wins and investments and sponsorship deals.

Though at thirty-three, he felt too damn old to get trampled on a regular basis. He'd felt too old five years ago when he'd quit. Not just too old for the getting-trampled part but the hard living that went with it. He knew there were plenty of guys still out there riding, but he didn't need to and he felt lucky to have escaped with as little damage as he had.

"Sure, I'll be there. I'll do the hard sell and see if anyone else has more ideas."

"Do you want to ride together?"

He nodded slowly. "Yeah, let's do that. Do you want to drive?"

"I think your truck is a little bit cushier than mine, but I appreciate the offer."

"Okay, then, I'll pick you up… When?"

"Seven."

He gripped the brim of his hat with his thumb and forefinger and tipped it slightly. "Okay, then, see you at seven."

SHE HEARD A car engine and raced to the window, her heart pushing against the base of her throat. But she didn't see anything. No truck. No Jack.

"Oh my gosh, calm down, me."

It was probably just one of the ranch hands headed out to the barn, or maybe Eli getting home from work. There were three whole minutes before Jack was supposed to show up, after all. And she was being ridiculous about it. Completely overcome by the sense of hyperawareness that often assaulted her when dealing with Jack-related things. And she would picture him pulling up, and her stomach would turn over sharply, her breath catching, and there was nothing she could do to stop it. The response was completely involuntary, and it was so strong it made her legs shake.

Anyone would think she was waiting for a date.

She gritted her teeth and closed her eyes tight just as she heard another engine sound. Her eyes popped back open and she brushed the curtains aside again just in time to see Jack's truck rumbling up the drive.

She put her hand on her stomach. "Stop it," she scolded herself. It did nothing.

She grabbed a jacket and her bag and jerked open the front door, then walked out onto the front porch as she slung both over her shoulder. She wasn't going to sit in her living room and wait for him to come to the door. She was not going to encourage her weird bodily reactions.

She scampered to the truck and flung open the passenger-side door, then braced her foot on the metal running board before climbing into the cab. She slammed the door shut and buckled. "Let's go."

"In a hurry, Katie?"

"I would like to be on time," she said, battling against her urge to bristle.

She didn't want to bristle. She wanted to be sleek. She wanted to have no reaction to him whatsoever. None at all.

"Is it still at the Grange Hall?"

"Yes, it is. And I hope you ate, because they still serve store-bought sugar cookies and watered-down punch."

"Ah yes, the official small-town meeting food."

"I don't mind the cookies. I don't even really mind the punch. I just don't know why people think they go good together."

He put the truck in Reverse, then turned around and drove back down the narrow driveway that fed into the wider main driveway that eventually curved onto the highway.

"It's one of the great mysteries of our time," Jack said. "Personally, I think overearnest meetings like this should come with whiskey."

"I would have no problem with that. But somehow I don't think the budget allows for alcohol."

"Well, that's an oversight. What has to be cut to make room in the budget for alcohol?"

"There really isn't much to cut. We kind of pay for our own stuff. In addition to paying dues to be a part of Oregon's Amateur Riders Association. But you know, support system. Training. And we do get to use the arenas of the fairgrounds a couple times a month at no extra charge."

"I guess next time I'll bring my own whiskey," he said.

"There won't really be a next time, though, will there?"

"I suppose that all depends on whether or not I'm creating a monster with this."

"You feel pretty passionately about it, don't you?" She so rarely asked him sincere questions that he seemed stumped by this one. Well, she was, too. She had no idea what she was doing. Why she wanted to know more. Why she wanted to dig deeper.

"I do," he said finally. "It feels like half the time the odds are stacked pretty high against women."

"Seeing as it was my mom that screwed everything up, I can't say that's been my experience," Kate said.

He huffed out a laugh. "I suppose in your life it was different. Not just because of your mom, but because Connor and Eli would kill anyone who hurt you. You're surrounded by people who love and protect you. There are a lot of people who aren't. A lot of kids, a lot of women. They're either abandoned and left to their own devices, or worse, they're actively hurt by the people who are supposed to love them."

Kate immediately felt stupid for her earlier comment. "Did your dad… Did he hurt your mom?"

"No. Thank God all he did was leave. But even that didn't make it easy. It just… This kind of stuff gets me. I don't want a wife. I don't want kids. Because I know myself. It doesn't make any sense to me, these men who have kids just to leave them. Who get married just to mistreat the women they made vows to. At least I know my limitations."

"You wouldn't hurt anyone, Jack." Kate's voice was small when she spoke the words.

"Not with my fist." He tightened his grip on his steering wheel.

She studied his profile, the strength in his hands, the muscles in his forearms. He was tan from hours working out in the sun, strong from all the lifting and riding he did.

And regardless of how he treated her sometimes, regardless of the fact that he had been around since she was a little girl, he was most definitely not her brother.

She swallowed hard, her throat suddenly dry. "I'm sure that you... I mean...if you wanted to..."

"I don't. So it isn't an issue."

His response, so hard and sharp, definitive, made her feel stupid. Young.

He took a hard right just before Old Town, moving farther away from the ocean and into the less quaint part of Copper Ridge. The Grange was a tiny little building nestled between a modern grocery store and the edge of a residential neighborhood. It looked as if it was built out of Lincoln Logs, and Kate imagined it was supposed to be quaint, when really, years of repainting and foul weather had left it looking worse for wear.

An American flag and an Oregon flag flew high in the parking lot, which was already filled with pickup trucks. There was no place for Jack to park, so he pulled up to the curb, put the truck in Park and shut it off.

"Maybe we should have warned them?" she asked.

"With what? You can't email them—you don't have a computer."

She snorted. "I could have called."

"You don't have a cell phone."

"I have a landline."

"You could send smoke signals."

"Jack," she said, exasperated, opening the passenger door and sliding out, not waiting for him. She went ahead and walked into the building, greeting everyone who was in attendance, already seated in a semicircle in the back room.

The front room had permanent seating and a stage for community theater. But they met in the back in a sterile environment that had a little kitchenette with bright orange countertops, a white linoleum floor and fluorescent lighting.

Long folding tables were set out with the promised punch and cookies. They looked mostly untouched.

The lonely punch and cookies weren't all that surprising. They were more of a formality. An offering of refreshment because if there was going to be a gathering, refreshments had to be on offer. The laws of small-town etiquette.

There were only two vacant chairs, and it so happened that they were right next to each other, so any hopes she'd had of getting some distance from Jack were thwarted.

Her friend Sierra waved, but there were, of course, no open seats next to her. Sierra somehow managed to exude both femininity and strength. Kate had no fucking idea how you were supposed to exude femininity. Yet Sierra managed. Her blond curls were always perfectly set; her brightly colored eye shadow made her blue eyes glow. She was the classic sequined rodeo queen. Kate couldn't even fathom trying to wear a sequin. It would just feel like trying too hard.

She wasn't the type to ride with turquoise and rhinestone.

But sometimes Sierra made her wish that she was.

Eileen, the president of the group, was reading minutes, so Kate took her seat as quietly as possible. She kept her eyes fixed on Eileen and jumped when Jack took a seat next to her. Did he have to be so...warm? Yes, he was warm. Uncommonly warm. She could feel it even with a healthy bit of air between them. And it was distracting. And disturbing.

She looked down at her hands, which were folded in her lap. But then she saw Jack's denim-clad thighs in her peripheral vision and became completely distracted by that. They looked hard. And if they were like the rest of him, they were probably uncommonly hot. Temperature-wise. Just temperature.

She forced herself to glance away.

When Eileen got to the part where everyone brought up relevant business, Kate didn't speak up, because she didn't want to speak first. And also, the dry throat.

When it finally seemed that topics had been exhausted, from a need for new barrels for the arena they trained in at the fairgrounds to shared transportation to amateur events on the West Coast later in the year, Kate opened her mouth to speak. But Jack beat her to it.

"Hi," he said, clearing his throat. "If you don't know me, I'm Jack Monaghan. I used to ride pro in the circuit, though I haven't for a few years. But I wanted to come today to talk to you about the possibility of doing a charity day at the upcoming rodeo here in Logan County."

Eileen brightened visibly. "What sort of thing did you have in mind?"

"Well, Kate and I have been talking, and she was the one who told me I should come tonight." He gestured toward her and she lifted her hand, twitching her fingers in an approximation of a wave. "We were thinking that it would be a chance for this group here to take part in some events. And I could get in touch with some of the riders I know coming through with the pro association. See if maybe they wouldn't mind participating, either. You could all compete against each other. And we would work with the chamber of commerce both here and in some of the other towns to get food donated, as well. I have plans for the proceeds to go to a couple of the battered-women's shelters and to help a local business that's been trying to get disadvantaged women back on their feet after they leave abusive situations."

"Well, provided we can secure the space, I think that sounds like an excellent idea," Eileen said. "Can I get an informal count of who would be interested in participating?"

Nearly every hand in the circle went up, and Kate's heartbeat increased, satisfaction roaring through her.

"That's a good start," Eileen continued. "We'll just want to see which day the fairgrounds might be able to accommodate us. I'm willing to do that."

"That would be great," Kate said.

She was more than happy to let Eileen use her connections with the board at the county expo.

"Kate and I will work on the roster and the schedule of events." Jack was speaking again, and volunteering her for things, things that they would work on together. She wasn't sure how she felt about that. "So you can get in touch with either of us if you want to participate, and we'll get you added to the list. If you don't want to compete, we could still use the help. We'll need a lot of volunteers to try and keep costs down. Because if it gets too expensive, we won't have anything to donate."

After that, much-less-organized conversation broke out in the room, a buzz of excitement surrounding them.

"Okay, I think that concludes official business for the evening," Eileen said above the din.

Kate stood, and Sierra rushed across the circle and to her side. The other woman spared a glance at Jack, a half smile curving her lips upward, a blush spreading over her pale cheeks. She was doing it again. *Exuding.* Sierra West was beautiful—there was no denying it. She was even beautiful when she blushed, rather than awkward and blotchy. Kate had a feeling that *she* was just awkward and blotchy.

"This is such a great idea," Sierra said. She reached out and put delicate fingers on Jack's shoulder, and everything in Kate curled into a tight hissing ball. She did *not* like that.

"I can't take much credit," Jack said. Except he really should have been taking all the credit.

"I'd love to participate in a barrel racing event," Sierra went on.

Jack cleared his throat and took a step away from

their little huddle. "Well, just give Kate a call about it and she'll add your name."

"And anything else I can do to help…"

"We've got it," Jack said.

Sierra looked confused at Jack's short reply, as though no man had ever turned down the opportunity to spend extra time with her. "Okay. I will…call Kate, then."

Jack nodded, his jaw tense. And Kate was perversely satisfied by the fact that Jack didn't seem at all enticed by Sierra's clear interest.

On the heels of her satisfaction came annoyance at said satisfaction. Jack could do what he wanted with whoever he wanted.

Though Sierra was one of her few female friends and she had to admit it would be weird if the other woman was sleeping with someone Kate was so close to.

Jack. Sleeping with Sierra.

Immediately, she pictured a messy bed and a tangle of limbs. Jack's big hands running down a bare back. Long hair spread out over a white pillowcase. Only, for some reason, the woman in her vision wasn't a blonde with a riot of luxurious curls. Instead she had straight dark hair…

Kate bit down on the inside of her cheek. "Yes," Kate managed to force out, "call me."

"Hey, some of us are headed to Ace's," Sierra said. "You want to come?"

"I came with Jack…"

"That's fine," Jack said, cutting her off. "She can go. We'll both go."

"Great." Sierra smiled brightly. "See you there."

Kate rounded on Jack, the tension from earlier taking that easy turn into irritation. "Did you just give me permission to go somewhere?"

"I'm your ride."

"Yes. My ride. Not my dad."

He chuckled. "Oh, honey, I don't think for one second that I'm your dad."

"Stop calling me that," she said, ignoring the rash of heat that had broken out on her skin when he'd spoken the endearment.

It made her angry because she was not his honey. Not now, not ever. She clenched her teeth and her fists, turned, and walked out of the room, headed out into the warm evening air.

"I can't call you honey, I can't call you Katie. I can't win," he said, his voice coming from behind her.

She turned around to face him. "You could call me Kate. That's my name. That's what everyone calls me."

"Connor calls you Katie."

A strange sort of desperation clawed at her chest. "Connor is my brother. If you haven't noticed, you aren't. Now let's go to Ace's."

CHAPTER FOUR

JACK WAS FEELING pretty irritated with life by the time he and Kate walked into Ace's. He was pretty sure his half sister had attempted to make a pass at him, and Kate was acting like he'd put bugs in her boots.

He also couldn't drink, because he was driving.

Irritated didn't begin to cover it.

He was getting pretty sick and tired of Kate's prickly attitude and now he'd gotten himself embroiled in a whole thing with a woman who was the human equivalent of a cactus.

He really needed the drink that he couldn't have.

Though maybe if Kate had one, she would calm the hell down.

"Can I buy you a drink?" he asked.

"A Coke," she said.

"You want rum in that?"

"No."

"Why not?"

"Because making an ass out of myself in front of a roomful of people is not on today's to-do list. I'm a lightweight."

He laughed. "Okay, I'm a little bit surprised that you would admit that."

"Why?"

"You're the kind of girl who always has to show

the boys up. I would think you'd want to try to drink us under the table."

She arched her brow. "I'm way tinier than you. I'm not drinking you under any table."

"All right, one Coke for you."

He turned and headed toward the bar, and to his surprise, she followed him rather than going over to the table where her friends were already seated. "Why are you buying me a drink?"

"I was hoping to trick you into getting drunk so you wouldn't be so uptight," he said, because he always said what was on his mind where Kate was concerned. Neither of them practiced tact in the other's presence.

She sputtered. "I'm not uptight."

"You're something."

Kate's lip curled upward. "Now I don't really want you to buy me a drink. I don't like your motives."

"I'm not going to sneakily give you a rum and Coke. I'm ordering you a soda."

"But it was not born out of generosity."

"Will you please stop making it impossible for me to do something nice for you."

"But you aren't doing something nice for me," she insisted. "You were trying to…calm me. With booze."

He turned, and Kate took a step back, pressing herself against the bar. He leaned forward, gripping the bar with both hands, trapping her between his arms. "Yes, Katie, honey, I was."

Her dark eyes widened, her mouth dropping open. Color rose in her cheeks, her chest pitching sharply as she drew in a quick deep breath.

He looked at Kate quite a lot. He saw her almost

every day. But he'd never really studied her. He didn't know why in hell he was doing it now.

There wasn't a trace of makeup on her face, her dark lashes long and thick but straight rather than curled upward to enhance her eyes. There was no blush added to her cheeks, no color added to her lips. It exemplified Kate. What you saw was what you got. Inside and out.

And for some reason the tension that had been gathering in his chest spread outward, spread around them, and he could feel a strange crackling between them. He wasn't sure what it was. But one thing he was sure of. He'd made a mistake somewhere between calling her "honey" the first time, days ago, and the moment he'd pressed her up against the bar.

Everything he knew about her had twisted. The way Kate made him feel had shifted into something else, something new.

If it had been any other woman at any other moment, he might've called it attraction.

But this was Kate. So that was impossible.

And then the sort of dewy softness in her eyes changed, a kind of fierce determination taking over. She took a step away from the bar, a step closer to him, and reached up, gripping his chin with her thumb and forefinger, tugging hard, bringing his face nearer to hers. "Look, Jack," she spat, hardening every syllable, "I think you need to back off."

Her skin was soft against his, her hand cool. Her hold was firm, uncompromising, like Kate herself.

Unlucky for her, he didn't compromise, either.

He leaned in, closing some of the distance between them. Her lips parted, and for just one moment he saw Kate Garrett soften. But it was only a moment. Then the steel was back, harder than ever. He waited for her to back down, waited for her to step away and hiss at him.

But she didn't. She simply stood there, holding him fast, her breasts rising and falling with each indrawn breath.

The noise faded into the background, and the people around them turned into a blur as his focus sharpened on Kate. The only thought he had in his head was that this was without a doubt the strangest moment of his entire life.

They were playing chicken—he knew her well enough to realize that. She was challenging him, and she thought he would back down.

That was fine. It was almost normal. It was the undercurrent beneath the challenge, the one making his heart beat faster, making his stomach feel tight, that was giving him issues.

She leaned in slightly and without even thinking, he took a step back, breaking her hold on his chin. Breaking whatever the hell thread had wound its way around them.

"I'm going to get you that soda," he said, knowing his tone sounded way harsher than he intended. "Go hang out with your friends. I'll meet you over there."

He expected her to argue, but she didn't. She just nodded and moved around him cautiously, her dark eyes glued to his for a moment before she averted them and made her way to her group.

He let out a breath he hadn't realized he'd been holding.

Well, that was fucking weird.

"Monaghan," Ace, said sidling over to his end of the bar. "Can I get you something?"

"Two Cokes," Jack said, resting his forearms on the bar.

Ace laughed and pushed his flannel shirtsleeves up. "Sure. You want me to start a tab for that?"

"I'll pay now," Jack growled.

Ace grabbed two glasses and filled them with the nozzle beneath the bartop. "So... Kate Garrett?"

"What about her?" Jack asked, feeling irreversibly irritated by the other man now. Because he could feel himself being led somewhere, and he didn't like it.

"You and her are..."

"What? No. Fuck no."

"It looked like something to me. So I wondered."

"It was nothing," Jack said, ignoring the rush of heat in his blood that made him wonder if it was more than nothing. "Just messing with her."

"That's what I'm saying," Ace said, smiling broadly. "Anyway...why not?"

Anger surged through Jack's veins. "For one because I like my balls where they're at. And if I ever touched Katie, Connor and Eli would remove them. And then Liss would sew them onto the top of a winter hat as a festive decoration. Additionally? She's a kid."

"She's not a kid," Ace said, his eyes fixed across the room. "And I'm not the only one who realizes that."

Jack turned and looked and saw Kate nearly backed up against the wall by some asshole cowboy who had his hat tipped back and his jeans so tight his thighs were probably screaming for mercy. He was leaning in, holding her hostage.

Because he was an asshole. And never mind that

Jack'd had her cornered only a few minutes ago. It was totally different. No matter what Ace thought, he wasn't trying to get into her pants.

But that guy was.

"Excuse me," Jack said, grabbing the sodas and moving away from the bar.

He stalked across the room, his eyes on Kate and the cowboy. And then he stopped, the two frosty glasses sweaty in his hands. He had no clue what the hell he was doing. About to bust in on Kate flirting with some guy... Chad something, if Jack remembered right. Your standard frat bro with spurs.

Not the kind of guy he would recommend she talk to. But she could if she wanted to, and he had no say in it.

She was right. He wasn't her older brother.

A fact he was very aware of right then.

So instead he paused at an empty table for two and set the drinks down, flicking an occasional glance over to Kate. But he didn't sit. Not until he got a read on the situation.

She looked over the guy's shoulder and locked eyes with him, just for a moment, and then her expression turned defiant. She flipped her hair over her shoulder, batting her eyelashes in a near-cartoonish manner.

Then she arched her back, thrusting her breasts outward, and Jack about choked on his Coke. She was... Well, she was being pretty obvious but Jack wasn't sure she knew what the hell game she was playing.

She isn't a kid.

No, she wasn't, but she flirted like a fifteen-year-old who'd only ever seen it done in bad teen movies. Why hadn't anyone ever...talked to her about this shit?

She was over there throwing herself to the wolves. She was playing the game, and she had no idea what the prize was.

He thought back to his rodeo days. To the way he and the other guys had been with women. Love 'em and leave 'em…fast. But those women had known just what they were asking for and Kate so clearly didn't.

Watching her with this guy, who couldn't touch the skill the guys on the circuit had, Jack had a sudden vision of her surrounded by the type of guy he knew waited for her in the pros…

Yeah, lamb to the slaughter was what came to mind.

She was just so damned naive.

She tilted her head to the side, putting her hand on the guy's shoulder, laughing loudly enough for him to hear her.

Then the cowboy leaned in and said something, and Kate's face flushed scarlet, her posture going rigid against the wall. She was saying something back and then the guy leaned in closer.

Jack took a couple of steps closer to the couple—so he could tell Kate her ice was going to melt and make her Coke taste like sadness, not for any other reason— and it put him in earshot of the conversation.

"If you want to get out of here," Chad was saying, "we can get in my truck and I'll take you for a real ride. Especially if you're into giving a little head."

And in a flash Jack saw Kate walking out of the bar. Getting into that truck. Undoing that asshole's belt and lowering her head to…

"Okay. Enough." Jack took two long strides forward, his blood pounding hot and hard. It was time to intervene.

KATE FELT A SHIFT in the air, and it was welcome. Her conversation with Chad had started out well enough, and she could tell it had annoyed Jack. Which was sort of the idea after the shit he had pulled earlier.

Buying her alcohol to make her sweet, pressing her up against the bar, looking at her like she was a fucking sunrise or something. Setting off a burst of heat low in her stomach that made it impossible to pretend anymore that she didn't know what was happening.

Attraction. That was why his presence made her feel itchy. Made her feel restless and hot, like a spark ready to ignite.

It was the worst. It was literally the worst. Worse than knocking over a barrel at a key moment, worse than a fresh cow patty between your toes and even worse than trying to eat a salad without ranch dressing.

Worst. Worst. Worst.

And so she had decided to try to parlay that attraction into an interaction with Chad. Because if she was that hard up for a little male attention, Chad was certainly a better bet. Also, the idea of being into Chad didn't fill her with terror and a whole lot of "dear God no."

But that was before he leaned in and told her just what he'd like to go in the back parking lot and do with her.

And she had no idea if she was supposed to want to, if she was supposed to be flattered, or if she was supposed to punch him in the face. She was just too shocked to process it. Fascinated, really. That somehow a little conversation and back arching had turned into…that.

But she didn't have any time to process it, because

a deep voice broke the interaction between her and Chad and broke into her muddled thoughts. "Is there a problem here?"

It was Jack. And she wondered then if him moving closer was the shift she had felt. Disturbing. On so many levels.

"I don't think there's a problem here," Chad said, tugging his hat down, when only a few minutes earlier he had pushed it back. "Kate?"

"No," Kate said, "no problem." She was feeling completely at sea and in over her head, but she wouldn't admit that, not to Jack. She would fight her own damn battle. If she was even going to fight it. Maybe she would go in the back parking lot with Chad and undo his belt in his truck as he had suggested.

The thought did not fill her with arousal. In fact, it kind of made her feel sick. So she supposed she wouldn't be doing that. But Jack didn't have to know that.

"You look uncomfortable, Kate, and from where I was sitting, it looked like this bonehead was blocking your exit."

Chad turned to face Jack, pushing his hat back again. That was one annoying nervous habit. "How is it your business, Monaghan?"

Jack chuckled and crossed his arms over his broad chest, the muscles in his forearms shifting, and in spite of herself, Kate felt her heart rate pick up a little bit.

"It's my business because anyone who's bothering Kate has to deal with me."

"Oh, really?" Kate all but exploded. "Anyone bothering me has to deal with *me*, Monaghan. End of discussion." And now she was just pissed. She turned her focus back to Chad. "And you. I wouldn't go out back with you and do…that…even if you bought me a whole dinner at The Crab Shanty."

"Oh, come on, Kate. You are obviously asking for it," Chad said, his tone dripping with disdain now. "Shoving your tits in my face like that."

And suddenly, Chad was being pulled backward, then spun around and slammed up against the wall. Jack was gripping the collar of his shirt, his forearm pressed hard against the other man's collarbone. "If you're in the mood to get your jaw broken tonight, then keep talking," Jack said, his voice a growl. "Otherwise I'd walk away."

A hush had fallen over the bar, all eyes turned to Jack and Chad.

And on her, too. She had lost control of the situation, and she didn't like it at all.

"Jack, don't," Kate said.

"Are you actually defending this dickhead?" Jack was incredulous.

"No. But I don't need your help to say no. Let go."

Jack released his hold slowly, but there was still murder glittering in his blue eyes. "Whatever you want, Katie."

And then Chad lunged at Jack. It was a mistake. Before Kate could shout a warning, Jack was in motion. His fist connected with Chad's jaw, the sound rising over the lap steel that was filtering into the room from the jukebox.

"What'd I tell you, asshole?" Jack looked down at Chad, his expression thunderous. "I would've let you off because she asked. But since you made it about you and me… Hopefully, you don't have to get that wired shut. Drinking out of a straw for six weeks would really suck."

Jack stepped over Chad's crumpled form and walked out of the bar. Kate looked around the room. The only people who were still watching were members of the rodeo club. Everyone else had gone back to their darts and their drinks. A punch-up in Ace's wasn't the rarest of events. But seeing as Jack had just punched out one of their own, the club was still interested.

"Well, he was being an ass," Kate said, turning and following the same path Jack had just taken out of the bar.

It was downright chilly out now, the fog rolling in off the ocean leaving a cool dampness in the air. She could hear the waves crashing not too far away but couldn't see them because of the clouds.

The moon was a white blur of light mostly swallowed up by the thick gray mist. She could see only the faint outline of Jack, walking to his truck, thanks to the security light at the far end of the parking lot.

"Are you just gonna leave me here?" she shouted, breaking into a jog and going after him.

"I figured you could get a ride," he ground out.

"I did not need you to come over there and intervene." She stopped in front of him, and he turned around to face her.

She could only just make out the strong lines of his face, could barely see the way his brows were locked together, his expression still enraged. "It looked like you did. Don't be such a stubborn child all the time. If Connor or Eli had been here, they would've done the same thing."

"You aren't Connor and Eli," she bit out.

"No," he said. "But I'm something. And I'm not going to apologize for being mad about a guy talking to you that way."

"Maybe I wanted him to talk to me that way." She hadn't.

"Then raise your standards."

"As high as yours?" she asked.

"At least I know what I'm doing. You're like a... lamb being led to the slaughter."

She laughed, an outright guffaw, in spite of the fact that she found very little about this funny. She was attracted to Jack, she had just caused a major scene in Ace's, and now this. "Does anything about me look adorable and woolly? I didn't think so. I'm like a...a bobcat. I'm not a lamb."

"I thought you were a badger."

"That is beside the point. Maybe I'm a badger-cat. Anyway, the point is I don't need you to take care of me."

"Maybe not. But I'm not going to stand there while he says things like that to you."

"Why not? Why do you care?"

Her words hung in the silence, resting on the mist. And she wished they would just go away, because they felt exposing. And he was looking at her, making her heart beat faster, making her stomach seize up. Now that she knew, it didn't seem so irritating. It seemed like something else entirely.

Her shower the other day, the way her skin had felt so sensitive, the way Jack had flashed through her mind, rose up to the top of her thoughts. She nearly choked on her embarrassment then and there.

But she didn't say anything. She didn't back down.

"Because I could tell he was asking for things you weren't ready for," he said, his voice muted now.

"You don't know what I'm ready for." She forced the words out, her throat scratchy and dry.

He took a deep breath, lifting his head, his expression concealed by shadow. "I guess not. But I'm going to go ahead and assume based on knowing you and the way you were flirting that you don't have a whole lot of experience."

Heat flooded her face. "I don't really want to talk about this with you."

"Why not? As we have established," he said, his voice lowering slightly, "I am not your brother."

A shiver ran down her spine and settled in her stomach, leaving it feeling jittery and uncomfortable. "Right. That's been well established."

He looked pained. "I mean, look, you could maybe...talk to Sadie about this? Or Liss?"

"I'm not looking for advice," she said. "Anyway, Liss feels like crap, Sadie's busy, and they would both rat me out to my brothers, who would... It doesn't bear thinking about."

"Right."

"And I'm good at flirting, Jack."

"You're not."

"Yes, I am. I could have closed the deal with him. All I had to do was shove my boobs in his face and he was good to go. It's not like it's hard. I mean, I didn't really expect for him to say...all that. But it's not like I repelled him."

"That's not how you flirt. That is how you get...not a date. You get something else. And really, what you did had less to do with it than…just the guy you were talking to. You have to understand some guys are just after one thing. You have no idea what you're doing."

The air felt thick between them, and she couldn't blame it on the fog. It was just like earlier, when he dropped her at the bar. When she reached out and grabbed his chin, his stubble rough beneath her skin, so undeniably masculine, so undeniably *something* she'd never felt before.

Damn him, he was right about her experience. Or lack of it.

She'd never even been kissed. Which put Chad's offer firmly in the no column. But…what would it be like to kiss Jack? To feel his lips, warm and firm, and that stubble, all rough and…

"Maybe I'm the one who's wrong," he said. "Did you want to leave with him?"

Jack's question pulled her out of her fantasy. And she was relieved. "No." She was certain about that.

"So obviously, shoving your… Doing the… That isn't what you want to be doing."

Jack tongue-tied was almost funny enough to make the conversation less horrifying. Almost. "And you're an expert?"

"More than you. Look, what is it you want? The way you were acting is definitely going to work for one thing. But if your end goal is a date, you might want to approach it in another way."

"If I want a date?" she asked, blinking slowly, not exactly sure how they wound up in this conversation.

"Yes, a date. And not like…an invitation to go down on a guy in his truck."

Her face burned. "It's not my fault he said that stuff."

"I know," he said. "I'm not blaming you. But you know…if you set a trap for a horny dillweed, that's all you'll catch. And there's a lot of those in the circuit. If you intend to go pro, you're going to be exposed to a lot of it."

She let out an incredulous sound. "Are you…are you actually offering to help me hook up?"

"No. I'm not offering to help with that. But obviously, you could use a little bit of help figuring out how to deal with this kind of thing. Teaching you how to use…different bait."

"Instead of horny-dillweed bait?"

"Yes," he said. "I can help you."

"I'm twenty-three," she said.

"I know. And you're fast and strong and smart. You're the best damn barrel racer around, whatever you think about yourself. You're ready to go pro and take the circuit by storm. You're a hard worker and a good sister."

"So what exactly are you…offering?"

"If you're going to flirt, you should flirt with me."

CHAPTER FIVE

JACK WASN'T QUITE SURE what devil was possessing him at the moment. The same devil that had possessed him when he crossed the room and intervened in Kate's interaction with Chad. Something hot and reckless, which he was used to but not in connection with his best friends' little sister.

You're just looking out for her.

True. It might not be God's work, but it was Eli and Connor's work. He was helping.

Leading her not into temptation, and away from idiots who only wanted to get into her pants.

"Chad didn't hit you, did he, Jack?" Kate asked, her tone suddenly filled with concern.

"No. Why?"

"Because you're talking like someone who has a head injury."

"Lesson one," he said, his tone firm. "Don't insult the guy you want to hook up with."

Kate took a step back, her expression hidden from him by the dim evening light. "I don't want to hook up with you."

"Obviously." He felt like a moron for phrasing it that way. Things had gotten weird in the past hour and this wasn't helping. "I didn't mean that. I only meant that I can teach you how to talk to men."

"I was raised by men," Kate said, holding her hands wide. "I know how to talk to men. I know about horses, sports and even some of the finer points of tractor mechanics. I even like to compare scars."

Jack's throat clamped down hard on itself at the image of Kate shuffling clothing around to show off the various scars she no doubt had on her body.

Want to compare scars, baby?

Yeah, that might actually work as a pickup line. The other stuff, not so much.

"You know how to talk like a man, Kate. That's different than knowing how to talk to men. And it's also different than talking to them the same way you would your brothers but adding the…back arching you were doing."

"How?" she asked, sounding totally mystified.

"It just is. I mean, I don't talk to women the way I talk to Connor and Eli."

"You pretty much talk to me the way you talk to Connor and Eli. Except condescending."

Jack let out a heavy sigh. "Get in the truck."

"See? You're all ordery."

"Kate," he said, through clenched teeth, "get in the truck."

This time something in his tone spurred her to obey and she got in the passenger side of his black F-150. He breathed into his nose and then let a slow breath out through his mouth. He was insane.

He shook his head as he got into the truck, slammed the door behind him and started the engine before Kate could say anything.

He put the vehicle in Reverse and drove out of the

parking lot, gripping the steering wheel tight, tension creeping up his shoulders.

"So," Kate said. He had known his reprieve wouldn't last. "What exactly would this flirting boot camp entail?"

Okay, so she hadn't forgotten. Which meant he was committed. No turning back now. Anyway, there was no reason not to go through with it. Kate was just Kate. End of story. "I figure since we're working together on the rodeo, we might as well work on this, too."

"Why?"

The question of the year. "I don't want to babysit you the whole time we're organizing this. And when you go pro, Kate Garrett, there are going to be cowboys all over you."

"And what? You think I'm so stupid I'm gonna get tricked into bed? Like I don't know my own mind? Or are you trying to help me get some?"

The tension crept higher, climbing up into his neck. "That isn't what I said."

With any luck, him taking control of the situation would keep her from getting taken advantage of. Not that it would be wrong for Kate to get laid.

Even thinking about it threw up a big fat stop sign in his brain, warning his thoughts not to go any further.

Okay, so it wasn't as if he expected she never would. Or even that she hadn't. Because, as she had pointed out a few times, she was twenty-three. And you didn't exactly have to be smooth to get a guy into bed.

But she deserved better than an ass clown like Chad.

"Okay, what you do with my teaching is up to you," he said. "But forewarned is forearmed. If you want to get better at talking to guys, I'll help you. And what will help me is if I know that you'll be more prepared to deal with jerks should any approach you. And that you understand you don't have to do anything with them just because they asked."

"Good grief, Jack. I know that," she muttered.

"Just don't ever sell yourself short."

"Why not? Men do it all the time. I don't understand what all this protecting me from shallow creeps who are only after one thing is about. You *are* that creep. I mean, obviously, with other women, not with me."

He nearly choked on his tongue. "That's different."

"How is it different?"

There was no way for him to say how it was different without sounding like a total jackass. So he kept quiet.

But Kate wasn't content with that. Of course she wasn't. "Come on, Jack. I'm waiting for an explanation."

He let out an exasperated breath. "It's just that there are different kinds of women. There are the kind that you marry. And there are the kind that you..."

A hard crack of laughter filled the cab of the truck. "Are you kidding me? Are you trying to tell me that you marry good girls and sleep with bad girls? And that if I keep pushing my breasts out, the boys will think I'm a bad girl and corrupt me?"

"It's not good and bad." He had no clue how to dig his way out of this. Sure, it sounded wrong when he said it like that. Maybe it was even bad to think it. But the bottom line was there were women who were fair game in his mind, and then there was Kate. And she was an entirely different category.

"All right, then. What kind of girl am I?"

Jack tightened his hold on the steering wheel. "The type that could get taken advantage of by assholes."

"You think I'm stupid?"

"That isn't what I said. Stupid and inexperienced are two different things."

"You think I'm wholesome."

Yes. It suited him just fine to think that Kate Garrett was as wholesome as whole grains. "Comparatively."

"Compared to what? The women you sleep with?"

Heat lashed Jack's face. "You're determined to take this the wrong way."

"Enlighten me. What is the right way to take this? You're sitting here telling me there's a certain type of woman it's acceptable to mess around with and a kind that isn't acceptable to mess around with, and you're putting me in the category that isn't allowed to mess around."

"It's not just women," he said.

"Okay, then. What kind of guy are you, Jack Monaghan? Are you the kind of guy a girl marries? Or are you the kind we're supposed to want to bang?"

Hearing the provocative words on Kate's lips made his stomach wrench up tight. "Kate…"

"Go on. Tell me. It's hardly fair, since you have such a comprehensive assessment of me. I deserve one of you. So tell me, Jack," she said as he turned the truck into the narrow drive that would take them to the Garrett ranch and on to Kate's house, "are you the sort of guy that a girl should dream of getting in a tux? Or are you the kind of guy that a girl should think about getting naked with?"

He slammed on the brakes, without thinking, without meaning to. But he could not drive while she talked like that. "Dammit, Katie."

"For such an experienced man, you're acting very prudish."

"You want to know what kind of guy I am, Kate?" He shouldn't challenge her, and he knew it, but he couldn't help it. Because she was pushing. And when Kate pushed, he had to push back. Now and always. "Let me lay it out for you. I'm not the guy you marry. I'm the guy you stay up all night with. I'm the guy who doesn't call the next day. I'm the guy your mama would've warned you about if she had stayed around."

The last words barely made it out of his mouth before Kate grabbed ahold of his shirt and tugged him toward her. "Now you're being a jerk on purpose," she said, dark eyes glittering in the dim light, clashing fiercely with his.

"You wanted to know what kind of guy I was. I think that should answer your question." He felt like a tool. He'd lost sight of what the end goal was in this weird game they were playing. All he knew was that she was pushing, and he was pushing back. All he knew was that his blood was burning, and his heart was pounding faster than it should have been.

"You did. You're an ass. Question answered."

She raised her hand as if she was going to hit him, and he caught her wrist, holding her steady, their eyes still locked. She was breathing faster than he was, and suddenly, the anger riding over the heat burning in his blood fizzled out. The heat remained, his heart still thundering hard, steady. And he was still holding on to Kate's wrist.

The feeling that had surrounded them back at the

bar had returned. Deeper. Stronger. And there was no pretending he didn't know what it was. He could feel her pulse fluttering beneath his thumb, faster and faster the longer he held her.

Fuck.

He released his hold on her and put both his hands back on the steering wheel. "I am. I'm an ass. I'm sorry. I'm sorry I said that."

"Why did you?" she asked, her voice small now.

"I don't know," he said, lying through his teeth with the truck still idling in the middle of the driveway.

"It was offensive. Not just what you said about my mother."

"I know. I didn't start out meaning to be offensive. Saying it out loud, I realize it's stupid. But definitely in my mind I think of the kind of women that I would pick up in a bar and the kind I wouldn't. Or more specifically, the kind who wouldn't go with me. Of course, saying it out loud forces you to listen to how stupid it is."

"It is stupid."

"I know."

"So," she said, folding her hands in her lap now like a good student. "You're going to teach me to flirt."

He didn't want to. He didn't want her flirting with the guys who were part of her group. He didn't want her flirting with the cowboys who would come in with the rodeo.

And considering what had just happened a few seconds ago, that meant it was exactly what he *needed* to help her learn to do.

As long as he focused on protecting her, as long as he focused on the right angle, the weirdness between them would evaporate. It had to. It was an aberration, something he would have liked to blame on alcohol. But he couldn't, since all he'd had was a Coke.

He could blame it on the full moon or on the way she had grabbed his chin. All things that had passed and would pass.

And since they were going to be working on the rodeo together, he really needed to get a grip.

"Yes. That's exactly what I'm going to do." He eased his foot slowly off the brake, and the truck started rolling forward.

"But chastely."

"I will give you certain tools. What you do with them is up to you. And does not need to be shared. And none of this should be shared with Connor or Eli."

Ultimately, he had Kate's best interest at heart, he really did. But since he wasn't related to her, he was being slightly more realistic than they would be. They would probably lock her in her room and not care about the fact that she was twenty-three.

"Okay. It will be our secret."

He turned his truck onto the little road that led to her cabin. And he tried not to dwell on the way the word *secret* sounded on her lips. Illicit and a little bit naughty. Nothing he and Kate talked about should sound naughty or illicit.

He swallowed hard. "Yeah."

He breathed a prayer of thanks when he rolled up to Kate's house. He needed to get home and get his head on straight. Tonight felt like some kind of weird detour out of his normal life. Suddenly, he'd become aware of some different things about Kate. Some things that he would rather have never been aware of.

And with that had come a thick, heavy tension that just wouldn't clear up.

A new day would fix that. The sun rising over the mountains, bathing everything in golden light, chasing away the shadows that rested on Kate's face now. The shadows that accentuated her high cheekbones and the fullness of her lips. The darkness that blanketed the whole situation and made it seem fuzzy. Made her seem not quite like Kate. Made him feel not quite like a man who had known her since she was a whiny two-year-old.

He put the truck in Park but left the engine running. "Good night, Kate," he said, opting to use the name she preferred. All things considered, it seemed safer.

"Do you want to come in?"

His pulse sped up. "Why would I want to do that?"

"For some tea? For a flirting lesson?"

"Let's hold off on that," he said, his throat constricting. Right now he needed to get away from her.

"Okay. Thank you for coming tonight." She took a deep breath. "And thank you for punching Chad in the face. He's a doofus."

Jack laughed. And for a moment things felt as though they might be back to normal. The kind of normal they had before the past year or two, when everything he'd said and done had been wrong in Kate's eyes. "He really is. I hate that guy."

"I guarantee that he now hates you," Kate said, opening the passenger-side door and sliding out of the truck. "See you later?"

"You know you will. Probably a whole lot sooner then you'd like."

She didn't say anything to that. She simply smiled

and slammed the door. He watched her walk all the way into the house. Because he had to make sure she was safe, after all. Not for any other reason.

Once she was inside, he put the truck in Reverse and backed out of the driveway. The air quality in the vehicle had changed since Kate had left. He could breathe easier.

He wasn't going to overthink it. It would be a non-issue by tomorrow.

The sun would rise, he would be able to put Kate back in the proper place in his mind, and life would go on as it always had.

PERFECT. JUST PERFECT. Now that she'd made the critical mistake of admitting it to herself, it was as if a veil had been torn from her eyes and she could no longer feign ignorance of any kind. She was attracted to Jack.

Heart-pounding, bone-tingling, heavy-breathing, thinking-about-him-in-the-shower kind of attraction. How she'd spent so long pretending it was anything else was a mystery.

Self-preservation. That was clearly the answer. That and deep denial that ran all the way to her bones. Because nothing was ever going to happen with Jack. Never, ever, ever.

On a personal level, she liked Jack okay except when he was being a pain in the ass. Which was always. So often she liked him only minimally.

Apparently, though, liking him or not had nothing to do with sex feelings.

She let out a heavy sigh and dropped her bag on the floor. She had sex feelings for Jack. And it was undeniable. When she imagined getting in Chad's truck and doing all that dirty stuff to him, it made her feel vaguely unsettled and more than a little disgusted.

She allowed herself, just for a moment, to imagine she was back in the truck with Jack, the light low, his blue eyes fixed on her. And she imagined him putting his hand on her cheek. His fingers would be rough, calloused from all the hard work that he did. No matter how much Jack tried to pretend he didn't take things seriously, she knew it wasn't the truth. He was a hard worker, and everything he had was a result of that hard work.

She was sure his touch, his skin, would reflect that. Then she imagined him leaning in, those eyes that were usually all filled with mischief turning serious as his focus narrowed onto her face.

And then she imagined him whispering all those filthy things to her. Except he didn't say the words quite the way Chad had. Not in her fantasy. Of course, what he did say was all very vague and murky because Kate wasn't exactly up on dirty talk.

But she knew Jack would be way smoother than Chad. His voice would go all deep, the way that it did when he talked about something serious, which was so rare it was like finding gold. And it would get a little bit rough, the way it did when he called her Katie.

When she thought of touching Jack, of taking her clothes off for Jack, she didn't feel disgusted. She felt shaky and afraid, and given that this was only a fantasy, she could only imagine how terrified she would be if she found herself in this moment in reality. But she didn't want to run away. She wanted to lean in.

Shit, shit, shit. Undeniable sex feelings.

She turned to her couch, bracing her knees against

the arm and falling forward over the side. Then she buried her face in one of the throw pillows and let out a long, drawn-out moan. What the hell was she supposed to do with this? Attraction to Jack, of all people.

It was the worst thing ever.

In his eyes she was nothing more than a kid. A kid he had to protect from herself. As though her flirting was tantamount to running with scissors. And he was going to teach her how to do it right. Just more reinforcement of the fact that he did not see her as an adult woman. And even if he did, there was no point in going there. He was the baddest bet around and everyone knew it.

He was an unapologetic manwhore who did whatever he wanted with whoever he wanted and never, ever made a commitment.

She tried not to find that assessment of him exciting. She should have found it disgusting. She should have found *him* disgusting. But she didn't. She couldn't. She never had.

From the time she was a little girl, running wild through the fields until she couldn't breathe, until the wind tangled her hair into knots, Jack Monaghan had amassed a whole mountain's worth of admiration in her soul. When the world had been bleak, he'd made her smile. Simple as that.

She wasn't a child now. She was a twenty-three-year-old virgin who had never even been kissed, who still ran like lightning through the grass and let her hair get tangled into a mess. And no matter how hard she tried to fight it, he still held his claim on that turf in her soul. The way Jack walked around doing what

he wanted was more than a little appealing to someone who felt sheltered beyond reason.

Plus, the man was so hot it was entirely possible that
women's clothes incinerated on contact. And if that
happened, what was a guy to do but say yes?

She clicked her teeth together, annoyance at her
own self coursing through her veins. She was making
excuses for him. And for her.

So, two things she knew. She wanted him. And
she shouldn't.

The rest she would have to figure out later.

CHAPTER SIX

THE ONLY PROBLEM with the weekday at the Farm and Garden was that it provided far too much time for thinking. Kate didn't want to think. Not right now. At the moment her thoughts were lecherous and traitorous and she didn't really want to deal with either thing.

But there had been very few customers today and she'd spent the past forty-five minutes dragging a giant hose around and watering the plants in the back. Which meant thinking.

About last night. About her misguided flirting attempt with Chad. About what a jerk he'd been. About the way Jack had looked when he'd strode up looking like an outlaw ready to start a gunfight. And then he'd punched Chad. She had no idea how something like that could be…sexy. Yes, it had been sexy.

Oh yeah, there was also the fact that she was acknowledging that Jack was sexy now.

Thankfully, there were still no customers or they would all have been looking at her blushing right now.

Then there was the flirting thing. He had offered to teach her how to flirt. With other men.

She'd spent the entire night in her bed tossing and turning, trying to figure out what to do with that offer. It was a weird, patronizing offer. One she would normally have been tempted to tell him to shove up his ass. But given her recent revelation, she was looking at it a little bit differently.

She was attracted to Jack. He had punched a guy for her, and it had been sexy. He wanted to teach her to flirt.

Doing the Jack math on that equation was leading her to some interesting places.

If he was giving flirting lessons, they would potentially find themselves in some interesting situations.

Situations that might give her an opportunity to try to seduce him.

She dropped the hose into the planter that was right in front of her, covering her face with both her hands. *Seducing* Jack. She'd never even thought of seducing a man before. Much less this man. The idea filled her with a strange kind of tingly horror and an excitement that mixed together so well she couldn't sort out which one was which.

She supposed at this point it was all the same, really. The fear of the unknown, the fear of a missed opportunity.

But one had far fewer consequences, that was for sure. Because Jack was a person she had to deal with on a fairly regular basis. Of course, the problem with living in a small town was that any guy she chose to get involved with would be someone she had to deal with on a regular basis.

She was not in the market for relationship. She wanted to go pro with her barrel racing and that would mean traveling all over the place, which would not leave any time for a guy. Which, provided things wouldn't get all weird after, actually made Jack the best bet of all. Because he wouldn't want anything more, and neither did she. Because she knew him, knew he wasn't, like, a secret ax murderer or anything. And because she trusted him.

That all had to count for something.

She pointed the hose at a little azalea that was placed in a pot on the ground. She was so focused on that, and on her seduction thoughts, that she didn't realize she had company until said company spoke.

"If you keep making that face, it will get stuck that way."

She jumped and splashed water on her hands with the hose, looking up to see Jack standing there grinning at her. "You scared the piss out of me!"

He made a face. "So that's not all just from the hose?"

She looked down and saw she'd misdirected the stream and that the water was puddling at her feet. She scowled and directed it at the plants again. Her face was hot, embarrassment over her choice of words lashing her. Which was stupid, because she shouldn't be embarrassed to say the normal things she always said in front of Jack. Seduction plans or no.

"What are you doing here?"

"You have two strikes against you already, Katie bear," he said, dodging the question.

"How did I get strikes? I'm not playing baseball. I'm watering azaleas."

"In the flirting game, little missy."

She decided to ignore the fact that he'd called her *little missy*. "Is it three strikes in flirting, too?"

"No idea."

"You're supposed to be the expert."

A slow grin spread over his face, the expression

positively wicked. "I don't know, because I've never struck out before." She felt the heat in her face intensify, spread over her cheeks. "I made you blush. So I'm doing something right."

"You're not supposed to be practicing on me. I'm supposed to be practicing on you," she said, irritated that she was so transparent.

"You might want to turn your hose off."

She scowled and turned around, twisting the faucet handle then discarding the hose. "There. Off."

"Lesson one—don't look at the object of your affection like you want to stretch his scrotum out and wrap it around his neck."

"But what if that's what I want to do?" she asked, keeping her face purposefully blank.

"I didn't realize you were kinky," he said, arching a brow.

She bit the inside of her cheek to keep from reacting. "There's a lot you don't know about me, Jack."

"Oh, really?"

"Yeah, really. I'm a complex woman and shit."

"Of course you are." His blue eyes glittered with humor, and anger twisted her stomach. He still wasn't taking her seriously. Still looking at her as if she was a little girl playing dress-up.

She'd never played dress-up in her damn life. Her mother had left when she was a baby, taking every frill, every pair of high heels, every string of pearls with her. And Kate had seen two things in her household. She had seen her father sit on the couch and waste away, and she had seen Eli and Connor get out every day and bust their butts to make a better life for her, for themselves.

So she'd worked. From the moment she'd been able to. And none of it had been a game.

If Jack thought this would be any different, then he hadn't been paying attention.

"Somehow I don't think you believe me," she said, keeping her eyes locked with his.

"Sure I do." He reached toward her, and her heart stuttered. Then he grabbed ahold of the end of her braid and tugged lightly, in that patronizing, brotherly way that he did.

And that was the end of her rope.

Kate was the kind of girl who rode harder and faster whenever there was a challenge placed in front of her. And this was no different.

So she tilted her head to the side, following the direction he was tugging her braid. And then she reached toward him, but since there was no braid to grab, she reached around behind his neck, sifting her fingers through his hair, ignoring the way a whole shower of sparks skittered from her fingertips to her palm, down to her wrist.

She made a fist, pulling gently on his dark hair. Then something different flared in his eyes. A heat that matched the one burning inside her stomach. The heat she had just identified last night.

Holy crap.

She took in a shaking breath, her heart pounding so loudly she was certain he could hear it.

She leaned in, running her tongue along the edge of her suddenly dry lips as she did. Jack's posture went straight, his body shifting backward slightly, betraying the fact that she had now succeeded in making him uncomfortable.

The realization sent a surge of power through her, one that helped take the edge off the shaking in her knees. She moved her mouth close to his ear, the motion bringing her body in close to his, her breasts brushing against his chest, her pulse an echo like hoofbeats on the dirt.

She took a breath and was momentarily stunned by Jack. By his scent, clean and spicy, soap and skin. Being surrounded, enveloped, by his heat. By him.

A jolt of nerves shook her, and she felt tempted to bolt. And that temptation spurred her on. Because she didn't run.

"If you were telling me a lie," she said, lowering her voice to a whisper, "if you really think you know everything there is to know about me, I hope you consider yourself enlightened now." She moved away from him, her cheek brushing against his, his stubble rasping against her sensitive skin.

The sensation sent a shock of pleasure straight down to her core. She looked up, her eyes clashing with his. They were close enough that if she leaned in just a fraction of an inch, the tips of their noses would touch. And from there, it would be only a breath between their lips.

Jack lifted his hand again, taking ahold of the end of her braid and wrapping his fist around it. But rather than giving it the gentle tug she had become accustomed to, he simply held her

Kate's heart thudded dully, her mouth so dry she felt as though she'd sucked on a piece of cotton. Everything in her was on hold, wondering what he would do next. Would he release his hold on her? Or would he pull harder on her braid, closing the distance between them?

Oh Lord, she could barely breathe.

Then he winked, releasing his grip on her and straightening, as though all of that tension between them had been imaginary. As though he hadn't felt it at all. "Good job," he said, his tone light, dismissive. "You might be a better student than I thought you would be."

She cleared her throat and flipped her braid over her shoulder so he couldn't grab it again. "Maybe I'm not the hopeless little innocent you think I am, Jack. Maybe—" she made direct eye contact with him, doing her best to look unflappable while she was internally quite flappy indeed "—there are a whole lot of things you don't know about me." Then she looked down, very purposefully, to the bulge just below his belt that she usually worked very hard to avoid looking at and back up, meeting his eyes again. Her heart was pounding so hard now she felt dizzy.

But she was going to win this weird game of one-upmanship they found themselves in, because she would be damned if she walked away with him still seeing her as a kid. With him making her feel like a kid.

"Maybe not." His voice was rough now, sort of like she'd fantasized it might be when she'd imagined him propositioning her.

She opened her mouth to say something else, something sassy and sensual and undoubtedly perfect. Undoubtedly perfect before she was interrupted and unable to say it.

"Hi, Kate. Hello, Jack."

Kate turned and saw her sister-in-law, Liss, standing there, her head tilted to the side, arms crossed over her rounded belly.

"Liss," Jack said, nodding his head. "I have to run. See both of you later."

He beat a hasty retreat, leaving her standing there alone with Liss.

"I thought I'd stop by and see if you had time for lunch. I'm in town grocery shopping and things. Generally killing time."

Kate cleared her throat, feeling unaccountably guilty and as if she'd been caught with her hand in the cookie jar. Her hand had been nowhere near Jack's cookie jar. She had no cookies. So that was ridiculous. Still, her face was all hot. "Sorry, I can't take a break yet. No one's here to relieve me for another hour."

Liss wrinkled her nose. "Okay. I'd love to wait for you, but I can't. I need fried fish with more malt vinegar than one person should reasonably consume. And I need it now."

"Yeah, go eat. I'm fine."

Liss did not leave. Instead she stood there, rocking back on her heels, bunching her lips up and pulling them to the side before taking a deep breath. "Kate, I love Jack like a brother. You know that."

Deeply uncomfortable anticipation gathered at the base of Kate's skull and crawled upward, making her scalp prickle. "Yes. I know that."

"He's bad news, Kate. I mean, as far as women are concerned. Nobody's going to reform him. Not even you."

Kate inhaled, preparing to say something. To protest. But instead she ended up choking. She covered her mouth, trying to minimize the coughing fit that followed. When she straightened, tears were running down her cheeks and her throat felt raw. Liss had made no move to help her; rather, she was just standing there looking at her. "Why exactly did you think I needed that warning?" she asked, her voice sounding thin and reedy now, certainly not convincing.

"I see the way you look at him."

"Can you look at someone a certain way? I just thought I was looking at him like I look at any normal human." Lies.

"If you don't need the warning, feel free to ignore me. But if there's any chance you might need it, take it."

Kate was just completely done being treated like everyone's little sister. "Thank you," she said, her voice tight. "I will keep that in mind just in case. Though I'm not sure if you noticed, but I'm not sixteen anymore. Or twelve."

Liss was not cowed. "I did notice. And I bet I'm not the only one. Which is what concerns me. Older, more experienced women than you have suffered a bad case of the Jacks."

"I've known him my entire life. I think it's safe to say I'm immune." Lies. Lies. Lies.

"Forget I said anything. Unless you need to remember that I said this," Liss said, looking extremely skeptical.

"Okay. Should I ever feel like I'm in danger from Jack, I will remember this."

"Great." Liss continued gazing at her for longer than was strictly necessary. "Okay. I'm going to go eat."

"Great. Enjoy your vinegar."

"I will. In fact, I have to go quickly so that I don't die."

"Don't die. Feed my little niece or nephew."

Liss smiled, the weirdness from a moment ago dissipating. "Oh, I definitely will. No worries about the baby skipping meals. Or even going a couple of hours without. See you later, Kate."

And Liss left, leaving Kate there alone to examine both what had just happened between Jack and herself and Liss's observations.

She didn't really care what Liss thought about Jack and whether or not he was good or bad news. Because that had nothing to do with how she felt about Jack. She was attracted to him. She didn't want forever and ever and a picket fence with him.

Still, she was a little bit unnerved that Liss seemed to read her so well. It made her wonder if Connor and Eli could read her just as plainly.

She immediately dismissed that. Unless it was printed on the back of a cereal box, neither of her brothers were going to read too deeply into anything.

Anyway, there was nothing deep to read.

It was just a case of a little harmless desire. And if given the chance, she imagined she could burn it out nicely.

A slow smile crossed her lips. Yes, that was what she wanted.

And with her decision made, Kate went happily back to work.

JACK DID HIS absolute damnedest not to reflect on anything that had passed between Kate and himself in the past twenty-four hours. Because he was sitting in his living room with her two older brothers, his very best friends, men who were like brothers to him. Men who would snap him in half like a matchstick if they had any idea of the thoughts that had run through his mind earlier this morning.

No matter how fleeting said thoughts were.

They had been brief, but they had been way, way outside the boundaries of Safe Kate Thoughts.

For a moment there, when she'd curled her fingers through his hair, those serious dark eyes on his... Yeah, for a moment there he'd thought about cupping the back of her head and closing the distance between them...

And he was going to stop thinking now.

He heard a sudden and violent outburst of profanity and realized he'd missed something on the game.

"Pass interference my ass!" Connor shouted.

"Must be nice to have the refs in your pocket," Eli grumbled, leaning back on the couch.

"Yeah," Jack said, only pretending to have any clue what was happening.

Connor snorted. "I just got a profane text from Liss."

"Is she watching the game in between female bonding moments?" Eli asked.

"You don't think Sadie is watching the game?" Connor asked.

"She pays just enough attention to football to irritate all of us. Though I imagine that if Kate is around, she and Liss will have banded together to commandeer the remote."

"Had we opted to watch the game as a group, I

imagine she would have showed up wearing orange and black and rooting for the Beavers. Even though they aren't playing."

"You chose a real winner there, Eli," Jack said, happy to be on any topic other than the one his brain seemed intent on focusing on.

"Our love transcends football," Eli said, lifting a bottle of beer to his lips.

"And my love for Liss doesn't have to," Connor said.

"And I'm single, assholes," Jack added, grinning broadly.

"I don't envy you," Eli said.

"Because you've forgotten."

"Forgotten celibacy? Feeling lonely, depressed." Connor shook his head. "No, I have not forgotten that."

"Some of us are not celibate," Jack said. Though, come to think of it, it had been a lot longer than usual since he'd picked someone up.

Which could explain some of the weirdness between him and Kate.

And now he was back to Kate.

"So you and Kate are working on a charity thing?" Eli asked.

A sharp sensation twinged in his chest. It was almost as though Eli could read his mind. Which was a dangerous thing right now. "Yeah. Has she mentioned much about it?"

"No, not really. I was curious."

"Well, it isn't just me and Kate," he said, feeling unaccountably guilty. "We've got the whole amateur association involved. And I'm working toward reconnecting with some contacts in the pro association to get them to help, as well. So it's a whole group effort."

"To help Alison?" Connor asked.

His question had a tone to it. A suspicious tone. "Yes. Her and other women in her situation. I'm impressed with what she's doing, improving not only her situation but the situations of others." Which didn't sound defensive at all. Not that he had any reason to feel defensive about Alison. It was the entire situation.

"Is there something going on with her?" This question came from Eli. "You and her, I mean."

Jack was almost grateful they were so far offtrack. "No. I'm sure she's lovely but hooking up with vulnerable women is not exactly my thing." Which was a nice reminder. "They want what I'm not going to give."

"You seem to be giving things," Eli said.

Well, this was the story of his life. He couldn't possibly be doing something nice just to do something nice. He must have ulterior motives. Probably extremely dishonorable ones.

"Because I'm a nice person, jackass."

Eli held his hands up, palms out. "Of course you are."

"I do selfless things."

"Uh-huh," Connor said.

"I have." Maybe not very many.

"Fine. I believe you," Eli said.

Jack snorted and stood up, making his way into the kitchen to grab another beer. Of course, he couldn't be too mad, since Connor and Eli were his oldest friends and they had a lot more context for his behavior than most people did. Still, the citizens of Copper Ridge tended to sell him short. And yeah, some of that he'd earned. But not all of it.

He liked to make people laugh; he liked to provide a good time. He liked to have a good time. And somehow people tended to mistake that to mean he didn't take anything seriously. As though his ranch ran on charm rather than labor. As though he had lucked into his position on the circuit.

Maybe if he did a good job organizing this charity thing, the town would have to realize that he had the ability to see something through. To do something right, to do something noble, even.

Yeah, *noble* wasn't a word typically used to describe him.

Maybe, though…maybe he could get noticed for doing something good. Maybe he could change some things.

Everyone liked him well enough, but no one took him all that seriously. He wondered if that would change if the townspeople had any idea that he carried the same genes as the venerable West family.

No doubt it would, since the oldest of the West children had a fairly large scandal in his past, and yet the town never seemed to talk much about it. As though the influence of Nathan West was mixed into the mist, settling over everything. All-seeing, all-knowing.

But he had no claim to that name; he'd sold it when he was eighteen years old. A little bit of hush money to get his life going, to permanently separate himself from a man who had never given a damn about them anyway. It had seemed like a no-brainer at the time.

Now sometimes he felt a bit as if he'd sold himself. Pretty damn cheap, too.

And the Wests were part of the town—the mortar in half the brick buildings on Main Street. Jack felt somewhat obligated to slide under the radar. Oh, sure, he'd been a pro bull rider; he was a ladies' man; he lived in the same town he was born in. The people paid him no mind, because they thought he was harmless. Thought he was laid-back. Thought he was haphazard, that he came by his successes accidentally.

They underestimated him, and he allowed it.

And he was pretty tired of it.

He jerked open the fridge and pulled out another bottle of beer before slamming the door shut again. Yeah, he was pretty damn tired of it. So he was going to put an end to it.

This charity rodeo was going to be a success. One of the biggest things Copper Ridge had ever been a part of. Maybe it would even be something that caught on. Something that was annual, at least here, if not in other counties.

It would be work. Hard work. And people would have to acknowledge that.

Hell, that was the entire point of his horse breeding operation. No one knew it. No one but him. But he was amassing a reputation for having some of the finer stock around, and he was most definitely gunning for Nathan West. To overthrow him. To diminish the man's empire.

To meet the man at the top of his own game and beat him at it.

Maybe it was petty. To want something just so he could prove to the man who would never lower himself to call himself Jack's father that he wasn't just a little bastard brat who could be swept under the rug. That if he was given money, he wouldn't just go drink himself into a stupor with it because he was poor and unworthy and didn't know what to do with cash. Oh no, he was making himself legitimate competition.

And the old man had provided the seed money that allowed Jack to do it.

It was poetic justice, albeit private poetic justice, that he had been enjoying greatly for the past couple of years.

This would be just a slightly more public showing. The middle finger to his dad, a bid for legitimacy. A way to flaunt himself without violating their agreement. His dad's dirty secret shining in the light, and even if no one else knew it, the old man would.

Yeah, he was all in. No question.

He turned and walked back into the living room, offering Eli and Connor a smile they didn't see, since they were glued to the game.

"Since I've been a pretty awesome friend to you lousy pieces of flotsam and jetsam for the past twenty-some-odd years, I was thinking you could help out with the charity."

"How?" Connor asked. "I feel invested in helping, if for no other reason than Eli and I saw the way that husband of Alison's treated her."

"Time donation, monetary donation, spreading the word. Whatever you feel like you can give."

"You've got it," Eli said.

"It will be good for your reputation anyway, Sheriff," Jack said.

"Well, now you're acting like I need to have ulterior motives to contribute to charity."

"I'm just adding incentive."

"Your pretty face is enough incentive, Jack. It always is," Connor said.

"I'm flattered, Connor but you're a married man, and I'm not a homewrecker."

"That's too bad. Liss is pretty open-minded."

"If I took you up on what you're pretending to offer, you would scamper into the wilderness and never return," Jack said drily.

"Damn straight."

"And I'd run in the opposite direction," Jack added.

"Okay, that call was balls. There is no way this game isn't fixed," Eli groaned.

And after that, they didn't talk about charity, and Jack didn't think much about it. He didn't think about Kate, either. Well, not much.

Sure, there had been some tension between them recently. But ultimately, she would always be the little mud-stained girl he'd helped distract while Connor and Eli had dealt with their drunken mess of a father.

It had given him a place to be, something to focus on besides his unhappy home.

The simple fact was the Garretts were more than friends to him. They were family. Connor and Eli were his brothers, a dream an only child like himself had never imagined could be realized.

Then he'd grown up and found out he had siblings. Half siblings, but other people who shared his DNA. At that point he had another realization about just how little blood mattered.

Colton West was his brother by blood, but he doubted the man would ever cross the street to shake his hand. He doubted the other man had any idea.

Connor and Eli had always been there for him. And they always would be.

Nothing on earth was worth compromising that over. Nothing.

THE LIST OF PARTICIPANTS for each event had grown. And thanks to Jack's hard work it included several people from the pro circuit. Kate felt downright intimidated, she couldn't lie. She was signed up to compete against some of the best barrel racers around, and even though it was just a charity competition, she felt as if it would be some kind of moment of truth.

About her skills. About whether or not she had an excuse to hold back from turning pro. About a whole lot of things.

She looked down and kicked a stone, watched it skim across the top of the fine gray dust in the driveway. She'd come out to get a ride in before the meeting tonight. Before Jack was due to pick her up and take her over to the Grange again. But she sort of felt numb, sluggish, frozen. Not in the best space to do a run around the barrel she had set up in the arena.

But she supposed she had to. She kicked another stone.

She hadn't seen Jack since that day at the Farm and Garden. They had only shared one phone call, where he had rattled off a list of names that had made her stomach heave with anxiety. All the while, her heart had been pounding faster because of the deep timbre of his voice. She didn't need professional psychiatric help at all.

She let out an exasperated breath and shoved her

hands in her jacket pockets as the wind whipped across her path. She upped her pace as she headed toward the barn.

Her fingers were still numb as she tacked Roo up. She pulled the girth tight and checked everything over once. Then she leaned in and kissed Roo right over the star on her forehead. She inhaled her horsey scent, shavings and the sweet smell of the hay. It was like slipping into a hot bath, a moment of instant relaxation.

"Okay," she said. "We can do this."

She led Roo outside before mounting and taking it slow over to the arena. Roo was a soft touch, and it took only a little gentle encouragement to urge her horse to speed up. Then she let out a breath and spurred Roo to go even faster, leaning into her horse's gait, making the turn around the first barrel easily.

She wondered what her time was. She should have grabbed the stopwatch that was hanging on the fence. She leaned back slightly and Roo sensed the change, shaking her head and knocking against the second barrel as they went around.

"Shit." She looked over her shoulder and watched it topple. So that was it. That was her run.

She slowed considerably when she approached the third barrel, then made an easy loop around it before stopping Roo inside the arena. She cursed again, the foul word echoing in the covered space.

She lowered her head, buried her face in her hands and just sat there. Feeling pissed. Feeling miserable.

"It was a pretty crappy run."

She raised her head and looked up, saw Jack standing against the fence, his boot propped up on the bottom rung, forearms rested on the top.

"What are you doing here, Monaghan?"

"I decided to come a little early and see Eli and Connor. Neither of whom are here."

"So you decided to come over and poke me with a stick?"

He lifted his hands and spread them wide. "No stick."

"Verbal sticks, asshat."

"Sure. I have verbal sticks. Why the hell did you suck so bad?"

"What does that mean? Why did I suck so bad? I didn't suck on purpose."

"No, you didn't. But you can do better. So the question is, why did this run suck so bad?"

"I don't think there's an answer to that question," she said, sitting up straighter on the back of her horse and crossing her arms.

"There is always an answer to that question. And if you want to be a lazy-ass rider, then the answer to the question is that your animal acted up. But if you want to get better, then the answer is that you did something stupid. Always put the control with yourself. Then it's your fault when you lose, but then it's up to you to win."

"Are you going to have me wash your truck now?" Wax on, wax off."

"I kind of am your Mr. Miyagi at the moment. Your flirting guru. I might as well teach you how to win rodeo events, too."

"No one asked."

"But I am the only one of the two of us who has competed on a professional level. And if it is something that you really want, maybe you should accept my help instead of being stubborn."

"I'm not being stubborn."

"Babycakes, you eat stubborn-Os for breakfast." He wandered over to the open arena gate and grabbed hold of the stopwatch that was looped over the top rung of the fence. Even while he was here witnessing her failure, annoying her, she couldn't ignore how damn sexy he was. The way his jeans clung to his muscular thighs.

Did women look at thighs? Was that even a thing? Or was it just a bad case of the Jacks?

"I'll reset your barrels." He walked into the arena and made sure everything was lined up, lifted the one she had knocked down. Then he walked back to the fence. "Reset yourself, Katie."

She flipped him the bird while obeying his command. She had some pride, after all.

Then she shut him out. Shut out his voice, shut out his presence and focused. The horse started to move, and she knew that Jack would have started the time at that moment. The start was a little bit slow, and she faltered going around the first barrel. Then she shook her head, spurring Roo on harder into the second. That went better. But she knew she wasn't at top time. Not even her own top time. She was too in her head, and there was nothing she could do about it right now. Not with Jack here. Not with that whole list of professionals she was going to be competing against in front of people.

Not when she was going to be faced with the undeniable proof of whether or not she had the ability to compete professionally and win. And down went the third barrel.

Kate growled, bringing Roo to a halt. She slid off the back of the horse, walked over to the barrel and reset it herself. "I'm gonna call it good now," she shouted.

"Do it again."

"No. I've done it twice—that's enough."

"Your horse can handle more than that. You know that."

"I'm done, Jack," she said, feeling a whole lot angrier than the situation warranted. But she didn't care. Because all of this felt like a little bit too much. Because she wanted Jack, and yesterday, just when she thought he might want her too, he had walked away. He had walked away and acted as though it didn't matter.

And now he was here again, getting in her face, treating her like a kid. He was the worst. He was worse than the run she had just done.

"Do you want things to go well when you compete next month?"

"No," she said, her tone dripping with disdain. "I want to fail miserably in front of a thousand people."

"With those skills, you will." There was an intensity to him that was unusual. And it matched her own.

This was weird. All of this was weird. Sure, she and Jack sniped at each other, but this wasn't normal.

None of this was normal, and she had no freaking clue what to do about it.

She turned away from him and started fiddling with the barrel position again.

"You going again?" he asked.

"Nope," she said. "I already told you that."

"Stop being a baby."

She snorted. "Kiss. My. Ass."

"I don't think I'll kiss it, actually." She didn't see his next action coming. Literally, because she was turned away from him. The sharp crack on her backside with his open palm didn't hurt, but it sure as hell shocked her. "Now, get that pretty ass back on the horse and do it again."

Shock, anger and undeniable lust twisted together in her stomach, forging a reckless heat that fueled her next set of actions.

He had too much control. She let him set the terms in the Farm and Garden, let him mess with her, let him ramp up her attraction and walk away. He thought he was the teacher, in everything, in all things, because he thought she was a kid, easily dealt with. Wasn't that what all of this was? Just him dealing with an obnoxious kid. Teach her how to flirt, keep her out of trouble. No way. No more.

He had too damn much control, and he was too confident in it. She was going to take it. Now.

She reached out, grabbed ahold of the collar of his shirt and pulled him forward, catching him just enough by surprise that she managed to knock him off balance and close the distance between them as she stretched up on her toes to press a kiss to his lips.

She realized her mistake a split second too late.

She'd seen it as a moment to seize power, but what she hadn't realized was that all semblance of control would flee her body like rats off a sinking ship the moment his mouth made contact with hers.

There was no calculation, not now. There was no

next move that she could think of. There were no thoughts at all.

There was only this. There was only Jack. The heat of his body, the sensation of his lips pressed against hers. The fact that this was her first kiss was somehow not at all as important as the fact that she was kissing Jack.

And he wasn't pushing her away.

He didn't move for a moment, simply standing there and receiving what she gave him. But in a flash, that changed.

He wrapped one arm around her waist, holding her hard against him, crushing her breasts to the muscular wall of his chest. So tightly she could feel his heart raging.

Somewhere in her completely lust-addled mind, she was able to process the fact that he was affected by this, too.

She angled her head, trying to deepen the kiss, wanting more, *needing* more. Just as she did, she found herself being propelled backward, released.

Jack turned away from her and walked about four paces before whirling around again.

She felt cold. Shaky. She had kissed Jack. *Actually* kissed him. And for about two glorious seconds he had kissed her back.

And then he had…shoved her.

"Don't do that again," he said, his tone hard

"If you're going to slap my ass, I expect a kiss on the lips first," she said, not quite sure how she was managing to keep her tone steady.

Her insides certainly weren't steady. They were

rocked, completely turned on end. But at least her voice was solid.

"Don't…do that again," was his only response.

"Why not? I thought you were going to teach me how to flirt. Doesn't that fall under the header?"

"That falls under the header of playing with fire, little girl."

Her heart thundered faster, her lips impossibly dry. "Maybe I want to."

"Spoken by a girl who's never been burned," he said, taking another step backward.

"Spoken like a man who's afraid I might be kerosene to his lit match." Apparently, being stubborn and unwilling to back down handily took the place of having experience and confidence.

Good to know.

"We're not going to do this."

"Why?" she asked, not quite as pleased with the tone of her voice this time. She sounded needy. And she hated that.

Her mother had walked out when she was two; her father was a drunk. She'd never had the chance to be needy. Frankly, she didn't like the way it looked on her. She was making a mental note to avoid it in the future.

"You know why."

Because he thought of her as a kid? Because he wasn't attracted to her? Because Connor and Eli would kill him and bury his body in a far-flung field? She didn't know *why*, because there were too many whys. But she wasn't going to go on. She wasn't going to do the needy thing. She was not going to beg.

She had her pride. Sure, she'd never been kissed before today, but she had never really wanted to be kissed by any of the guys she had known. She would go find someone else before she would make a fool of herself in front of Jack Monaghan.

Though it was hard not to beg when her lips still burned from the touch of his. When her body ached in places she hadn't given all that much thought to before.

Yeah, that made it a lot harder.

"Get on your horse. And do the run again," he said, his blue eyes level with hers.

"Still?"

"Are you a quitter?"

"Fuck you."

"Shout that at me all you want when you're doing the run again. Go."

She walked back over to Roo and got on. They walked back to the starting point. Then she looked at Jack, who was standing there holding the stopwatch. She took a breath and started. And her mind was blank. Blank of anything but what had just happened. Blank of anything but the heat and fire burning in her blood from the anger, from her arousal. That moment when her lips had touched his. When he had pushed her away.

She rounded the first barrel and it seemed slow, easy, in comparison to the confusion that was pouring through her. They straightened up and she went to the second, slowing down the moment in her mind so that she could capture the memory of his lips on hers. It had only been a second. A fraction of one, even. But it had felt so important. So altering.

Before she knew it, she was rounding the third barrel, the impression of the heat and firmness of his

mouth still on hers as she let out a breath and finished the run.

It was fast. It was clean.

It was good.

She looked up, saw the stopwatch hanging on the
fence where it had been before Jack had come.

And Jack was gone.

CHAPTER SEVEN

KATE SHOWED UP to the meeting late and pissed. All things considered, Jack didn't really give a fuck about her mental state.

The little wench had kissed him.

Sure, he'd been baiting her to do something. He couldn't deny that. But never, not once, had he imagined she would do that.

Somehow, in the moment, slapping her on the rear had made sense.

He'd shown up at the ranch, and neither Eli nor Connor had been there. Then he'd run across Kate. Riding her horse around the barrels, so obviously holding back it had made him angry for some reason.

Probably for the same reason her putting off turning pro made him angry.

She was selling herself short. Holding herself back. Making herself so much smaller than she should.

He hated that. It was something his mother had done, always. Accepting defeat. Receding into it. A woman who hadn't been wanted by her rich lover, so she'd refused to take anything from him. Refused to fight. Curled so deep into herself she couldn't even love her son, because she couldn't see her value or his.

He didn't want to see Kate doing it, too.

But then she compounded her sins by being…not

the Kate he was used to. When she'd done her second run, he'd been far too aware of how her body moved with the horse's. And it had been far too easy to imagine her riding astride him as he gripped her hips, as she followed his rhythm.

Something in his brain was short-circuiting. And that had been confirmed when she'd started running her mouth, and in his mind it had seemed a perfectly acceptable solution to give her a smack on the ass. Nothing more than a sports pat, something to prove he was in complete control of himself. That she was one of the guys, or just a little sister to him, or something.

It had backfired in a very spectacular way.

Not only because the contact had felt decidedly unbrotherly on his end but because then she had turned around and kissed him.

And it had damn near knocked him on his ass.

More accurately, it had damn near taken them both to the ground, where he would have taken things a lot further than a simple kiss.

He tried to think back to a few weeks ago. When Kate had simply been Kate, the younger sister of his two best friends in the entire world. A woman he'd known for so many years he didn't spare her a second glance when she walked in the room. There had been no need to look at her. He had her memorized already.

No makeup. Long dark hair either hanging down her back or tied back into a braid. And her body... He'd never even bothered to look. Not in a serious way.

He wanted to go back to that time. Sadly, he couldn't. Which meant when Kate stormed into the Grange Hall looking furious, he did look at her.

At the flush of rose in her cheeks that betrayed just

how mad she was, at the dangerous glitter in her dark eyes. The way her hair was disheveled, probably from the ride earlier, but it made him think of the kiss. The possibility that it had been messed up by him.

The kiss had been too brief for that. He hadn't had the chance to sift his fingers through her hair. Hadn't had a chance to do anything much other than brush his lips briefly against hers. Because he had come back to his senses and fast.

He shouldn't be regretting that.

He gritted his teeth and tried to focus on what Eileen was saying about the progress sheet made for their rodeo day. Kate, meanwhile, had taken a seat opposite him in the circle, making such a show of not looking at him that it made her anger all the more apparent.

Okay, so leaving her during her ride and then not taking her to the meeting as they'd agreed had probably been a jerk move. But he didn't really appreciate the kiss, so as far as he was concerned, they were even.

Except for the part where Kate Garrett had made his dick hard and nothing would be right in his life or his head ever again.

So yeah, there was that.

Eileen called on him to speak and he rattled off the list of riders he'd gotten to agree to be a part of the competition.

With the venue confirmed, enough riders on board and enough livestock owners willing to have their bulls and broncs involved in the extra day, everything was ready to move forward.

And he could barely pay attention, because the kiss, the kiss that never should have happened, was still burning his lips.

Shit, he was the one acting like a virgin, not Kate.

The word sent a shock of heat through his body. A virgin.

The odds that Kate was a virgin? Very high. Very, very high and he shouldn't care or ponder that. He shouldn't think of Kate and sex or Kate and no sex at all.

Except he had thought *Kate* and *sex* a lot in the space of the past few minutes, and dammit, he needed a distraction. He needed to chop wood. No, that wasn't good enough. He should go pull a tree down with his bare hands. Anything to expel the extra testosterone currently roaring through his body.

He could sleep with someone else, he supposed. Kate wasn't an option and the best way to deal with being horny was to get some. A simple problem with a simple solution.

He raised his eyes and scanned the room, purposefully avoiding looking anywhere near Sierra or Kate. There were some hot cowgirls in the building. Chicks in rhinestone jeans and pink hats with tight tops and big breasts. Girls who would stay long enough to complete the ride, so to speak, and then get on their way. No hang-ups, no nothing. Just his type.

Except looking at them right now was just like looking at a sunset. Real nice, real pretty, but he didn't want to fuck it.

Not that he wanted to do that with Kate. There was a lot of mileage between a kiss in an arena and full-on…bedroom events.

But the fact that it was on his mind was a bad sign.

By the time the meeting adjourned, Jack wasn't

in the mood to stick around and socialize, even if he should. Especially with the pretty cowgirls.

He didn't feel like it.

He stood and made his way out, looking at Kate one last time. Kate, who was still very definitely ignoring him.

Fine. He walked out the door, and thankfully, no one stopped him. Probably because he looked about as happy as a guy chewing glass.

He crossed the street to where he'd parked his truck. The days were getting shorter, dusk already lowering itself down to the tops of the mountains and blanketing the town in deep blue. There was something peaceful about it like this. The familiar shrouded in darkness. He'd traveled all over the country during his stint in the rodeo, but he'd never found another place he felt as if he could call home.

On the road he'd found what he did or didn't do meant nothing. Because no one who mattered was there to see it.

Copper Ridge, for all the history, good, bad and ugly, was his home. No doubt about it.

Eli was here. Connor was here.

And the Wests are here. And you're still wishing he'd see you.

No. Hell no. The old man could rot, for all he cared. He wanted to be a thorn in his side, sure as hell, but he didn't want attention. Didn't need admiration.

"All right, asshole."

Jack turned and saw Kate storming across the street, her hands clenched into fists at her sides. She painted a sharply contrasting picture to some of the other women in the group. No sequins, no pink.

Oh yeah, and she was looking at him like she wanted to kill him with her bare hands and feed his body to the seagulls.

"What do you want, Kate?"

"Why did you stand me up?" she demanded.

"Why did you kiss me?"

"Because you're sexy and I wanted to. Now, why the hell did you stand me up?" she asked again, her voice cracking. "I waited for you."

"I wasn't in the space to deal with you. And you think I'm sexy?"

"No, dumbass. I think you're a fucking troll—that's why I kissed you." She was mad. And not the normal Kate mad. Not the kind where she wanted to slap his arm and call him a name and call it done. He'd never seen her this mad.

"We can't," he said, because it was the only thing he could think to say.

"You can't say you're going to take me somewhere and then not show up."

"That has nothing to do with the kiss."

"So you didn't leave me stranded because I kissed you?"

It was exactly why he hadn't brought her with him to the meeting. "I didn't strand you," he said. "You have a truck."

"I have waited on too many damn curbs for a man who was at home drunk off his ass to spend ten seconds waiting for you," she said, her voice breaking now.

Kate wasn't just mad. Kate was hurt. And he would have fed his own body to the seagulls about now if he wasn't so attached to it.

"Kate… I didn't… Look, I just thought it was best if we had some distance. I sure as hell don't know what's been…" He trailed off because he couldn't find a way to finish the sentence that didn't force him to confess more than he wanted to.

He looked through the hazy light and saw that her eyes were glittering, filling with tears. The mighty Kate Garrett, whose face he hadn't seen streaked with tears since she was nine years old, sitting on the step outside her house while her dad raged and threw things inside, was about to cry.

Because of him.

She was right. He was an asshole.

He wanted to tug her into his arms and give her a hug. But hugs, touching of any kind, had turned an unexpected direction. Like a mean bull on a bad day. And there was no way he could reach out to her now.

"Katie," he said, his voice rough even to his own ears, "please don't cry."

"I'm not crying," she said, but the catch in her voice told another story.

"Damn it all to hell." He took a step forward and wrapped his arms around her shoulders, tugging her in close. "I'm sorry. I didn't mean to hurt your feelings. I thought we could use some…distance."

She looked up at him and the vulnerability in her eyes caught him off guard, punched him in the gut. "You want distance? From me?"

There was no good way to answer that. "I don't… want…" He released his hold on her and took a step back. "Things are weird right now. You get that, right?"

"You never want distance from me. We're around each other all the time."

"Yeah. And up until today we'd never kissed. So things change."

"It was only a little kiss," she said, sucking her bottom lip between her teeth and chewing it.

"Big enough," he said, his gut burning as the memory flashed through his mind again.

"That you need distance from me."

"Kate…"

"You're supposed to be teaching me to flirt."

"You took it too far."

"Why?"

"For God's sake, Kate, drop it," he ground out, turning toward his truck and starting to open the driver's-side door.

"Is it because you didn't like it?"

He whirled around. "It's because given a few more minutes or a few less thoughts, I would have had you down on the ground and out of your clothes, badger-cat, so unless that's the sort of thing you want to mess around with, I'd suggest giving me the distance I ask for."

Kate's eyes widened, her lips dropping into a rounded O shape. "You liked it, then?"

"This isn't going to end anywhere good." He didn't know if he meant the conversation or what was happening between them. It could be either. Or both.

People were filing out of the Grange Hall now and looking in their direction.

"Can we get inside your truck?" Kate asked, her voice small.

"For a minute." Only because he still felt like such an ass for making her tear up.

She rounded to the passenger side and got in and Jack paused outside the truck, taking in a deep breath of non-Kate-filled air before opening the door and climbing in.

"Okay," he said, slamming the door. "What else do we need to talk about?"

"You said you would give me flirting lessons…"

"And I already told you why that's over."

"And you said you'd coach me with my riding."

He rested his elbow against the place where the window met the doorframe. "You don't need coaching. You need to stop holding yourself back. Get out of your head and just ride. There. I'm all done."

"And I don't want distance."

He let out a long, slow breath, then turned to face her. Speaking of distance, there was less of it between them now than he would have liked. But then, at the moment, a whole arena wasn't distance enough. Hell, a whole small town didn't seem to be enough.

She didn't have tears in her eyes, not anymore. Instead she had that look. That fierce, determined look she got when she was ready to dig her heels in and fight. He'd seen that look many times over the years and he knew her well enough to know there would be no placating her. There would be no gentle words to get her to back down.

When Kate had an idea in her head, she went with it, and he would be a damn fool to do anything but meet it head-on.

"All right, then. You don't want distance. What do you want?" he asked.

"I want… I want more of what happened today."

Shit. "What? You want…you want me to lay you down on the bench seat and screw you senseless, is that what you want? You want me to treat you like you're just any old buckle bunny and not Eli and Connor's sister?"

She wasn't looking at him now. She was looking past him. It was dark in the truck, so it was difficult to tell, but he was pretty sure she was blushing a very deep shade of red. "You're getting ahead of me," she mumbled. "I was thinking maybe we could kiss a couple more times."

Shame lashed him like a whip. He was being a serious dick because he had no clue what to do with everything rolling around inside of him. And pushing her away by shocking her, dealing with his rage at himself by speaking the fantasies he was actually having into reality, as if they were so ridiculous they were only worth mocking, not doing, was the only strategy he had at the moment.

"It's not a good idea," he said.

He looked out the window and noticed that most of the cars were gone, everyone who had been at the meeting dispersed, headed over to Ace's, he imagined.

It was just the two of them now.

And there was no damned distance.

"You were a bull rider for like five years. And at no point in time is it ever a good idea to get onto the back of an angry bull. But you did it a lot. Being smart isn't really a requirement for you."

He wanted to tell her he didn't see her that way, to say it wouldn't work, because she was more kid sister to him than she was a woman.

And a few weeks ago, it would have been true.

But tonight it was a lie.

"I would rather take my chances with a bull than with your brothers."

"Is that the only reason you don't want to…kiss me again, because of Eli and Connor and the likelihood that they would kill you dead?"

He paused, knowing he had no good way to answer this. Sensing he'd started on a bad road long enough ago that there was no turning back now. "It factors in."

"What other factors are there?"

"Dammit, Katie. I do not want to have this conversation with you."

"We don't have to talk. We can kiss."

He clenched his teeth together, so tight he was afraid he might break them. "Do you know why I wanted to teach you to flirt?"

He was going to try a different tactic.

"Because you need a hobby?"

"Because I wanted to protect you. I don't want you getting screwed over by some asshole. Connor and Eli are great. They're my best friends. But I bet they didn't talk to you very much about…dating and things."

"You're acting like I'm sixteen." Kate's frustration was obvious. But too damn bad. He was frustrated, too. And it was her fault.

"No, I'm not. I'm acting like you're someone with a hell of a lot less experience than I have. I'm not wrong, am I, Katie?"

There was a slight pause, and he heard her shift next to him. He resisted the urge to look. "Since I have not slept with half the eligible population of Copper

Ridge, I think it's safe to say I have less experience than you," she said, her tone honed to a razor's edge.

"I'm not going to apologize for my actions. Not to you."

"I didn't ask you to."

"You don't have to be young to be naive. My mother was twenty-five when she had me. She wasn't young. She wasn't stupid. She was blinded by her feelings for a jackass who didn't use a condom. And who sure as hell had no plans of sticking around and helping her raise me. So forgive me if I don't trust my species around you."

"You don't need to trust your species around me. You just need to trust my aim with a .30-06." He didn't say anything, and she continued staring at him. "That means I can take care of myself."

"I don't want you to get hurt."

"Ever?"

His stomach tightened uncomfortably. "Yeah. Ever. Why would I want you to get hurt?"

"Getting hurt is a part of life. I've been hurt plenty." He looked at her then. Because he couldn't stop himself. "I don't really think some guy seeing me naked and never calling is going to hurt me more than my mom abandoning me when I was two. Or my dad dying after spending most of my life as a worthless drunk. Or losing my sister-in-law, who was pretty much the only woman I had around. Yeah, I guarantee you sex will hurt less than that." She blinked rapidly, looking straight ahead. "There are some things I'm inexperienced with, Jack. That's true enough. But I have more experience with all kinds of other shit than any one person should have. And I'm still standing. I'm not all that breakable. So you can stop with the gallant crap. I didn't ask for it. I don't need it."

"So instead you want me to do my damnedest to hurt you?" he asked, his voice rough. "I don't want to add to that."

His head was pounding, the pressure building behind his eyeballs. And his cock was still hard. He was pretty sure it had been since their lips had made contact in the arena. He had just more or less successfully ignored it during the hours since. He was less successfully ignoring it right now. Because the cab of his truck smelled like the no-nonsense soap Kate washed her skin with. It also smelled like hay and grass and sunshine. Stuff Kate had tracked in.

Hell, it *was* Kate.

She was the earth with everything unnecessary stripped away. Leaving behind a kind of beauty a man couldn't make with his hands. As wholesome as a damned apple pie. And for some reason that wholesomeness had worked its way beneath his skin until it had settled in his gut, growing into a dark and twisted need. A need he would have to try to choke out.

He nearly snorted at that. That was potentially a bad way to phrase that. Even internally.

"How could you hurt me?" she asked. She was innocent. So damn innocent.

He could think of a hundred ways. Ways that would be fun for a while but could very well destroy them both in the end. So he didn't say anything.

"I'm serious," she continued. "I know you. I know exactly what I would be getting myself into."

"If you're propositioning me, Kate Garrett, you had

better be sure you know what you want," he said, his patience snapping.

She didn't hesitate. "Kiss me."

That need, the one that was all knotted up inside him, started to bloom like a poisoned flower. Spreading desire through his veins like a sickness. When he had no hope in hell of fighting. Not now. Not anymore. And even though he knew it would lead them straight to hell, he let it grab hold of him.

He reached across the distance, pressed his hand against her back and drew her forward, his lips crashing down on hers with a desperation that would have shocked him if he hadn't been beyond that.

She gasped, the little intake of breath giving him the perfect opportunity to do what he'd held himself back from when she'd grabbed him in the arena. He slid his tongue against hers, the illicit friction sending a shiver of pleasure running down his spine, then settling lower, making his cock hard. Heavy.

He was very aware that these were Kate Garrett's lips beneath his. Because that scent that had been teasing him from the moment they had gotten into the truck wasn't just surrounding him now. It was in him. He inhaled deeply, trying to recapture his earlier thoughts. That she was somehow simple, wholesome.

But that connection was gone now. Her scent was now linked, inextricably, to her kiss.

And her kiss was nothing like apple pie.

She still smelled like grass and sunshine, but now he could only think of pressing her down into the grass, exposing her skin to the golden rays of the sun while he kissed every last inch of her.

His head was still screaming at him that this was

wrong. But his heart was raging, and his body was on fire. And so his brain was outvoted. Two against one, poor bastard.

Kate. It's Kate.

The mantra his mind was pounding through him like a drum didn't do anything to satisfy the hunger that was roaring through him like a hungry animal. The only thing for that was to get more of what he craved. And right now that was Kate.

He lifted his other hand, cupped the back of her head and held her hard against him, deepening the kiss. She whimpered, arching against him, closing some of the distance between them. Then she rested her hand on his thigh, and heat exploded in his gut.

Too much. Too fast.

He couldn't force himself to care about that, either.

Kate had asked for a kiss, and his instincts were racing five steps ahead. To what it would feel like to strip her top off. To what her breasts would look like without the boxy shirt she favored concealing her curves.

She wore the most unflattering clothes. And right now he appreciated it. It left a whole lot to his imagination. He couldn't guess what he might find when he unwrapped the beautiful present that was Kate Garrett.

Would she have a long slender torso that gently curved into hips? Or did she have a more dramatic contour to her waist?

And her breasts... It was impossible to tell just how large they were. Whether they would be tight and perky or whether they would dip softly, perfect for him to cup in his hand.

He wanted to know. He needed to know. And at the same time he wanted to draw out the torture. To leave the questions unanswered for as long as he possibly could so he could revel in the pain, in the deep, intense longing that had sunk its teeth into his throat.

A raw sound escaped Kate's lips, vibrated through her entire body and through his own.

She was wearing denim, dammit. And a big-ass belt with one of those big-ass buckles. It would have been so much easier if she were wearing a skirt, something he could shove up her hips quickly while he pushed her panties to the side.

But she didn't have on a skirt. Because the woman had never worn a skirt in her life.

And he well knew it because he had known her for most of it.

Kate. It's Kate.

Holy shit.

He wrenched his mouth away from hers, his chest heaving, breathing a serious challenge. He straightened, facing forward, his hands on the steering wheel. "Get in your truck."

"Jack..."

"Go get in your truck. Please." He didn't mean the last part to sound quite so much like begging.

"Or what?" Her question was muted.

She was baiting him. And he was tempted to take that bait. To try and shock her. To say something to her he had no right to say to a woman he should think of as a sister. But he didn't take it.

"There is no or, Katie. Get in your truck and go home."

He expected her to argue. She didn't. He listened to the sound of the truck door open, and he didn't watch as she got out.

"We're going to have that distance we talked about earlier," he said, his voice rough. "No more flirting lessons. No more rodeo instruction." He raised his head and looked at her, only for a second. "No more kissing."

Her expression was defiant, flat. Her eyes were glittering again and he knew that she was going to go home and cry. And it would be his fault.

He couldn't stop her. So he looked away from her instead.

She didn't say anything. And he didn't look at her again.

Didn't even look when she slammed the door.

He waited a few minutes, then looked at her truck, watched as the headlights came on, as the engine started and as she drove away. He looked at the truck. He wouldn't allow himself to look at her. But he assumed that as long as the truck was making it away from the Grange safely, so was its driver.

Now all he had to do was put distance between himself and a woman he saw every day. Without rousing the suspicions of her brothers. Who he also saw every day.

He would have to relearn to look at her and not wonder about what she looked like naked. He would have to look at her and forget that he had ever wanted to know about the mysteries of the curve in her waist.

Easy. It would be easy.

He started his truck and let the rumble of the engine drown out everything else. But it didn't quite manage to drown out the voice in his head that was telling him it wouldn't be easy at all.

CHAPTER EIGHT

ONLY FORTY-EIGHT HOURS ago Kate would have said nothing could've possibly made her dread the bridesmaid dress fitting for Sadie's wedding more than she already was. But she had officially found a way to make herself dread it even more.

A dress fitting with only a crappy night's sleep and a few hours between making out with Jack and getting rejected by Jack made the situation seem even worse.

She still couldn't quite believe she'd kissed him twice. That she had gone from kissing virgin to fully initiated since just yesterday. And that it had been him. Jack.

Her face burned and she leaned forward in the driver's seat of her truck, pressing her forehead against the steering wheel. She'd been sitting out in the parking lot of the bridal store for the past ten minutes, avoiding going inside.

Because she was afraid that last night's transgressions would be written across her face in red ink. And if not quite literally, the permanent blush she'd acquired would do so metaphorically.

Sadly, she couldn't avoid facing Liss and Sadie forever. She allowed herself a fantasy where she managed to dodge both of them, and wearing a dress.

Alas, it was only a fantasy.

Still, if recent events with Jack were any indicator, sometimes fantasies came true.

Or at least half-true.

She thought of the way his big hands had moved over her back, the way he'd cupped her head. The way his tongue had felt against hers.

She shivered, restlessness growing between her thighs.

Who knew that having a man's tongue in her mouth could be so damned erotic? It wasn't as if she didn't know she wanted sex. She'd been very aware of men as a species for a while. Quite a while. And had taken great pleasure in tormenting Eli and Connor with her awareness simply because…well, she was their sister and tormenting them was what she did right along with breathing.

But her fantasies on the subject had been hazy, confined mainly to enjoyment derived from looking at men, rather than deep imaginings of what it would be like to be kissed by them. To be touched by them.

And all of that was changing because of Jack Monaghan.

The thought was becoming less and less disturbing. Because kissing him felt so good.

It wasn't like she wanted a relationship with him. She wasn't sure she wanted a serious relationship with anyone, ever. Her parents' marriage hadn't exactly been something to aspire to. Then there was the heartbreak Connor had experienced with his first marriage.

And sure, everything was going great for him now. And Eli was in love, blah blah blah. But they were also in their thirties. She had a long time until she was in her thirties. She didn't know the ins and outs of the love lives of her brothers, and she frankly didn't want to. But she doubted that either of them, Eli especially, had been monks before falling in love.

Frankly, she felt as though she had to have some sex before she ever worried about marriage. And sex with Jack... If he was half as good in bed as he was just kissing in the cab of his truck, it would be electrifying. Altering. Potentially ruining her for other men.

No. She wouldn't let it.

Of course, it was kind of a moot point since he had rejected her. And what was she supposed to do? Beg?

Just get on her knees in front of him, eye level with his...belt buckle. And then she would put her hands on said belt buckle, pull the thick leather of the belt through the loops, undo the fly and button on his jeans...

Holy sock monkeys, she was having a full-on sexual fantasy in the parking lot of the bridal store. And she still had to go face Sadie and Liss.

She pulled her keys out of the ignition and slowly opened the driver's-side door, pressing her foot down slowly onto the blacktop, listening to stray gravel grind against the hard surface. She was in no hurry. Officially in no hurry.

She looked at the store, at the three large windows in front, each with two glittering dresses on mannequins displayed proudly in it. And the building was purple.

The whole thing was Kate repellent.

She'd never seen the point in this kind of thing.

The cowgirls she raced against always complained about rhinestones falling off their jackets and hats. Kate, for her part, didn't have rhinestones on her jacket or hat and therefore never had to worry about them falling off. Really, her take on life seemed a whole lot more practical to her.

But she was a twenty-three-year-old virgin. And she doubted Sierra or the other girls had that same issue.

Maybe men were like magpies and their dicks were attracted to shiny things?

She kept pondering that as she walked through the door and into a ruffle-and-rhinestone wonderland.

Sadie and Liss were standing at the front counter, and both smiled broadly when she entered. For some strange reason Kate had the feeling of walking into a lion's den with two hungry predators staring at her. Only instead of the background being littered with bones, it was littered with silver racks full of gaudy, shimmering dresses. It was not, in her mind, a less grisly prospect than seeing the picked-clean carcasses of previous victims.

Bones or gowns, it spelled doom for her either way.

The pristine dresses were packed in tightly, covered in plastic. Probably to catch falling rhinestones. Maybe her fellow cowgirls should consider wrapping their hats in plastic.

She had a feeling that idea wouldn't go over well.

"There you are," Sadie said, reaching out and grabbing hold of Kate's arm, drawing her in close. As though Sadie knew that Kate was a flight risk. She was not wrong. "Lisa May already pulled a few dresses in your size. They're waiting in the fitting room. Along with my wedding gown. Because I'm going to put it on and you're going to stand next to me. To assess visual compatibility."

"She's gone full Sadie," Liss said, somewhat apologetically. But Kate noticed that Liss was not prying Kate's arm out of Sadie's grasp. No, Liss was interested only in saving herself.

"This is a huge wedding. And since we had to put off fitting and style selection till the last minute because of—" Sadie waved her free hand in front of Liss's baby bump "—that, now we have to get cracking."

They'd already known special order would be futile, since there was no way to know just how Liss would expand. They'd also decided that matching dresses wouldn't work, because the same style wouldn't be flattering on Kate's slender frame and Liss's everrounding one.

And by *they'd decided*, Kate meant that Sadie had decided.

Sadie pulled Kate along to the back of the store with her. There was a row of dressing rooms, each separated from the public by a purple curtain.

Three were open, one with a wedding dress hanging inside and two with an array of dresses in various shades of fall colors.

Eli and Sadie were having a barn-set harvestthemed wedding, which meant absolutely nothing to Kate. Apparently, it meant burnt orange to Sadie.

"Okay, they've been organized by the order you're supposed to try them on in, because some of them pair with each other more nicely than others," Sadie said, releasing her hold on Kate in order to make broad hand gestures. "Of course, there will be some leeway for mixing and matching. I want you both to feel comfortable in the dress."

"You want me to feel comfortable in a dress?" Kate

asked. "Because that isn't going to happen. I say just pick what you like. I'm not going to *like* anything."

"Kate," Sadie said, "I love you. But you're going to have to try to love the dress and make me feel good about it, or I will kill you."

Kate made a mental note to lie about whichever one Sadie looked the most enthused about. As long as it didn't have ruffles.

"I'll try. Because I don't want to be dead," she said, stepping into the dressing room and unhooking the curtain from the pullback before tugging it closed.

She started to undress, her mind blessedly blank until Liss's voice penetrated through the connecting wall of the dressing room. "So how are all the charity plans coming along? Do you all have the venue confirmed?"

Kate pushed her jeans down her hips and turned to face the dresses. "Yes. All that's taken care of."

She picked up the first dress, one with fluttery orange ruffles all down the skirt. She ran her fingertips over the fabric, watching as it caught the lights above. It was shiny.

She pulled the zipper down and lowered the dress to the floor, holding it gingerly by the straps as she stepped into it.

"Has Jack been helpful?"

Being forced to think of Jack while tugging the slippery, soft fabric of the dress up over her mostly bare body made her skin feel hypersensitized. "Yes. He's been very…helpful." Oh yes, Jack had been *very* helpful in a few *very* specific ways. Such as turning her on to a point that was nearly painful.

She felt as though her voice was thick with that unspoken comment.

"Not driving you crazy?" This question came from Sadie.

"Or bothering you?" This one from Liss, and it was spoken a little bit more sharply than necessary, in Kate's opinion.

"Why is my interaction with Jack suddenly so interesting?" She reached behind her back and pulled the zipper up, then stepped out of the dressing room and into the main area of the store. She caught her reflection in the wall of mirrors across from her and stopped, blinking rapidly.

She couldn't remember the last time she'd worn a dress. If she ever had. She'd worn jeans and boots to homecoming. She hadn't gone to prom.

She hadn't had a date for either.

"Kate, that looks beautiful," Sadie said, her face getting all soft.

Kate turned her focus to Sadie. And it was Kate's turn to stare. Sadie was beautiful. Her blond hair tumbled past her bare shoulders, light makeup on her face. Simple. And the wedding dress she had chosen had that same light, simple beauty that her future sister-in-law possessed in spades. A layer of lace sat over a heavier silk layer, which conformed to her curves, while the lace flowed out gently, delicate and sheer, catching the sunlight that was streaming through the window. There were a few scattered beads sewn in, just enough to add a little shimmer. It reminded Kate of webs, heavy with dew in the early morning, strung between wildflowers in the fields on the ranch, catching the light just so and making the ordinary into something that was worth stopping and staring at.

"Oh, Sadie," Kate said, her heart feeling too big for her chest. She was having what might have been the first girly moment of her life. She was about to cry. Over a dress.

But it wasn't that simple. It was more than that. It was everything it represented. "Eli is going to… I don't even know."

Kate looked over at Liss, who was wearing a short cream-colored dress with orange flowers in a style that flowed over her rounded stomach. And she was crying. There was no *almost* about it. "Damn pregnancy hormones," she sniffled.

For some reason Liss's comment twisted the moment. And Kate looked between the woman her brother was about to marry and the woman her other brother *had* married, was having a child with. She was acutely aware of how much things had changed. How much they were changing still.

She'd clung to the ranch, to Eli and Connor, to the safety of sameness for a long time. Because in her life change had rarely been good. So she had held on tightly to the only things that were good. Family. Stability.

Which, more than money, might be the real reason she hadn't gone pro a couple years ago.

She'd been afraid to do any leaving. And now she was afraid of being left behind.

She thought that if she stayed rooted to the spot resolutely enough, she could keep things stable. Keep the world from turning itself over again, leaving everything scattered and out of order. Leaving her to try and rebuild yet again with reduced materials.

But it hadn't worked. Things were changing again. They were just doing it around her, leaving her feeling unsure of her place. Unsure if she even had one.

These thoughts, these concerns, felt treacherous in a way. Because she loved Sadie; she loved Liss. She wanted Connor and Eli to be happy.

But it didn't make all of this any less unknown or scary.

Didn't make her feel any more certain about her place in all of it.

It left her feeling desperate to race forward and try to get ahead of it all. To make a change, to make a move, that would help her feel like she was keeping up.

"Do you hate your dress that much?"

Kate snapped out of her internal crisis long enough to realize that Sadie was talking to her. "I don't hate it."

"You look upset," Sadie said.

"I'm just... I'm really happy for you. I'm happy for you and Eli. And you and Connor," she said, turning to Liss. "I'm emotional about it." The flat tone of her voice undermined the statement.

Sadie laughed and reached out and patted Kate's cheek. "I guess this is the Kate Garrett version of emotion?"

Kate cleared her throat. "Yeah, sort of unrefined. Like the woman herself."

"*Refined* just means that all the dangerous, interesting bits have been sifted out. Never refine, Kate. It would be disappointing," Sadie said, her blue eyes suddenly serious.

Kate felt doubly bad about her moment of fear over

Sadie's upcoming marriage to Eli. Because Sadie was wonderful in every way. Sadie had a way of making Kate see things differently.

Also, Sadie had taught her how to bake quiche.

An invaluable skill if there ever was one.

This wasn't the kind of change she needed to be afraid of. But understanding that didn't make her feel less stagnant. Still didn't make her feel any less of a desire to move.

Maybe that was why this change was so scary. It made her feel so conscious of how far behind she was.

Of the fact that while she stayed in her comfortable little place, the people around her would move forward, with or without her.

"Okay, next dress," Sadie said, all of her authority firmly back in place. "I don't think these are the ones."

Kate was relieved. Because *ruffles*.

She turned and walked back into the dressing room, trying to shake the heaviness of the moment off her chest. She was just trying on dresses. She needed to get a grip.

The next dress had no straps at all. It was a deep cranberry color, the neckline shaped a bit like a heart. She shrugged off what she was wearing and starting getting into the new one.

"What the hell bra are you supposed to wear with this?" she called out.

"Not one," Sadie shouted back.

"That's not going to work," Kate said.

For some reason she could only think about how she would feel wearing this in front of Jack. She would feel naked with just the dress on and nothing underneath it but a pair of panties.

"Just put it on."

Kate unhooked her bra and threw it on the floor, obeying Sadie's command. She held the dress over her breasts and reached behind herself, struggling with the zipper while fighting to keep the fabric in place. Finally, she gave up and turned it sideways, then zipped it up and twisted it so it faced the front.

There was no mirror in the dressing room, so she had no idea how it looked. She gritted her teeth and swept the curtain aside, walking out into the main area. Liss and Sadie assessed her, far too closely for her liking.

"You have to adjust your girls, Kate," Sadie said.

"Excuse me, what?" Kate asked.

"Hoist your boobs up," Liss supplied helpfully.

Kate could see in the mirror that her face now matched the dress. "Why would I do that?"

"So that the dress fits properly," Sadie said, her tone even. "And so men can ogle your cleavage."

Kate nearly choked. "And I want that?"

"Kate Garrett," Sadie scolded, "this is not the time for you to go acting maidenly and modest. We have checked out construction-worker ass together."

"That's different than trying to get them to check *me* out."

Sadie waved a hand. "It is not."

"I'm not sure Eli would appreciate you giving me such advice."

"He isn't here. And I don't ask him permission for everything. I don't ask him *permission* for *anything*. And I certainly hope you don't."

"Of course I don't." But she worried an awful lot about his approval.

"Okay," Liss said, "lean forward."

"Like this?" Kate bent slightly at the waist.

"Yes. You reach down into the top of your dress and pull your boob up and push it in toward the center of the neckline."

"Are you serious?"

"Yes, I am serious. This is a valuable life skill. Now do it."

Kate turned away from Sadie and Liss and reached down beneath the fabric of her dress, following Liss's instructions.

"Okay, do your other boob."

Kate cringed but did as she was told. "Done."

"Now straighten up and admire your work."

Kate did, then turned to face the mirror. She watched her eyes widen, watched her mouth drop open in shock, because she scarcely recognized the woman she was looking at.

First of all, she was a woman and not a girl.

Kate knew she was a woman, but there were a whole lot of days when she didn't exactly feel like one. There was no denying it now.

The color was rich and brought out a lick of brandy color in her brown eyes, reflecting a similar shade in her hair. The dress left her shoulders bare and exposed a healthy amount of pale, slender leg that she had never before given a whole lot of thought to. But the bit that really shocked her was her cleavage. And the fact that she had achieved it. Now that she had done as Sadie and Liss had told her, the dress no longer sat over her curves. The dress was now shaping itself to her body, the dark berry color shocking against the pale white of her breasts, which looked rounder and fuller than she had ever imagined they could.

There was nothing ambiguous about this. It screamed out to anyone who saw that she was a woman. A woman who wanted to be looked at. A woman who was worthy of being looked at.

A woman Jack would have to look at.

Her breath caught.

"That's the one," Sadie murmured.

"Oh yeah," Liss agreed.

"You can wear cowgirl boots with it," Sadie said. "They would look cute."

"Uh-huh." But Kate wasn't really listening anymore, because her mind was stuck on what Jack's face might look like when he saw her in this dress. On what he would think of her. On how he would react.

On whether or not he would be able to tell her no again.

She needed to change. And this was a change. But it wasn't enough.

She was ready to do something, something crazy, something reckless.

She was tired of sitting still. She was tired of being where she was.

She wanted Jack. And she was going to have him. The Kate standing in front of her right now could have him.

"Yes," she said, finding her voice again. "This is definitely the one."

CHAPTER NINE

JACK MONAGHAN'S DAY had been terrible from moment one. It started when he opened his eyes. He didn't feel rested, and he was hard. That wasn't unusual, not at all. Just your standard-issue morning erection easily solved in a routine morning shower.

But this was no generic morning erection. At almost the exact moment he became aware of it, the events from the night before flashed back through his mind. Kate. Her mouth, her lips, her tongue. Her hands. Her body.

And no matter how hard he tried, he couldn't banish those images from his mind. And he could not make his erection a generic one. He grabbed ahold of himself in the shower with the mind to get some relief. But then Kate joined him.

He couldn't even picture her naked. Because he still had no idea what her body looked like.

And what kind of idiocy was that? Fantasizing about a woman when he didn't even have a handle on what her figure would be like. Literally or metaphorically.

Kate was slim and strong, capable. She had a bit of light muscle tone in her arms from all of the hard work she did. A stubborn set to her jaw, brown eyes that were shot through with golden flame, and hair that hung lank and straight no matter how much humidity blanketed the air.

Oh yeah, and she was the virginal younger sister of his two best friends, and she kissed like a wicked little goddess.

There were a lot of things he didn't know, but apparently, he knew enough to fantasize.

To imagine what it would be like if it wasn't his hand wrapped around his cock but hers.

Yeah, he'd given up at that point. He'd gotten out of the shower, unsatisfied and in a foul temper. He'd gone on about his ranch chores in the same manner. Hard and pissed off about it.

He'd figured if he couldn't work his sexual frustration out in the preferred method, he would do it with actual physical labor. Too bad it hadn't worked.

It was a gray day, the air cool and wet. Even so, by the time he headed back from the barn to his house, sweat was rolling down his chest and back.

He let out a long sigh when his boot hit the bottom step that led up to the deck. For some reason as he walked up the heavy wooden steps, he remembered the feel of the hollow metal steps that had led to the front door of the single-wide trailer he'd grown up in on the outskirts of Copper Ridge.

He paused when he reached the top, moving his fingertips over the railing. It was hard to believe how far he'd come. From the place he'd been too ashamed to invite his friends to, to a custom-built home on a successful ranch.

He took a lot of things for granted. That he could talk his way out of trouble. That he could get laid if he wanted to. He didn't take this for granted. Never. Not one day of his life.

The front door of the house opened and his housekeeper, Nancy, stepped out, practically wringing her hands. "There's someone here to see you, Jack."

Jack frowned. "Inside?"

She nodded. "I told him you were busy, but he said he would wait."

Nancy was friendly, and the presence of a visitor wouldn't normally have her acting nervous. That was enough to make Jack's stomach tense. He wasn't sure why. Unless he was about to get served or something, but he couldn't think of a reason.

There were no outstanding debts or bills to be paid, not anymore. So it wasn't that, either. Though a holdover from a childhood spent in poverty was a lingering anxiety about bills and bill collectors that was hard to shake.

His mail sometimes made him nervous. Because a stack of envelopes had never meant anything good when he was a kid. It had meant stress. It had meant his mother closing the bedroom door and crying. She didn't think he knew, but he did.

For some reason this moment reminded him a lot of that.

"Did you get his name?" Jack said, striding across the deck and following Nancy into the house.

If Nancy answered, Jack didn't hear, because the moment he saw the tall lean figure of a man in a white Stetson, facing away from him, Jack knew exactly who it was.

"What the hell do you want?" He had never spoken to this man in his life. Had never seen him any closer than across a crowded bar or the street. But he knew who he was. And he knew he didn't like him.

The stranger turned and Jack felt a strange release of tension in his muscles. It was both a relief and an utter horror that the man in front of him was just an aging gray-haired human with lines around his eyes and mouth, rather than the imposing monster his mind often chose to play stand-in.

A relief because who wanted to face a monster? And a horror because it meant dealing with the fact that a very average man held so much control over what Jack did and why.

"I came to talk to you."

Jack looked around the room and noticed Nancy had made herself scarce. "Well, you don't want to engage in father-son bonding. I know that much. Because I took a fuck-ton of money from you to keep quiet about our relationship. Such as it is."

"You got that damn straight. I'm not here to talk to you about that. We're never going to talk about that."

The moment felt surreal. Jack was, for the first time in thirty-three years, face-to-face with his father. There had been no warning and no fanfare. Just the specter that hovered over Jack's every action and decision made manifest in his living room.

"Then what are you here to talk about?"

"I came to talk to you about a horse."

The hair on the back of Jack's neck prickled. "None of mine are for sale."

"I don't want your horses. I just wanted to tell you in person that Damion Matthews isn't choosing your stallion to sire Jazzy Lady's foal."

"What the hell are you talking about?"

"I know the two of you had been in talks. Just about to sign an agreement."

"Yes," Jack bit out.

"Then you punched his son in the face, and he's not real happy with you. I'd rather not take a win just because your low-class bastard genes took over your better instincts in a bar fight, but make no mistake, I *will* take it."

Fire burned through Jack's blood. "I'm only a bastard because you don't know how to keep it in your pants."

"You're a bastard because you were born one. That kind of blood outs itself eventually. Genetics are important. You don't breed a Thoroughbred to an overused plow horse. The same is true for people. You're the end result of that."

Jack had a sudden flash of what would happen if he lost his temper. If he hauled off and punched Nathan West in his smug face. He would probably get arrested. Probably by Eli. And whatever reputation he wanted to cultivate would be completely destroyed.

Yeah, none of that made him feel less inclined to do it.

But his feet stayed rooted to the spot, and his hands stay down at his sides, clenched into fists.

"I didn't think we were going to talk about me," Jack said, a hint of the violence pounding through his body evident in his tone.

"Don't think I don't know what you're doing, boy. I'm well aware. You starting this ranch, stepping on my turf. There was a day when there would've been no question as to which breeder people would come to, and now there is. But it won't last. It can't last. You're not wired to be better than you are."

"I would punch that jackass one hundred times even if I knew I would lose the deal. And I'm happy not to work with him. Because I have ethics. We both know you don't."

"According to your reputation, you and I have some similar ethics. You are my son, after all. But your mother's half is the one that will hold you back. Don't forget. You're out of your league. You're only here because of me, because of the money I gave you. If you had one bit of shame, you would have taken the money and got out of town. But you don't have any. So you stayed here and set up a ranch designed to compete with me. A ranch I bought for you."

Rage flared up in Jack's stomach, molten heat that spread through him, testing his control. "I entered rodeo events with your money. I made smart investments with your money. At this point, it's difficult to tell what you paid for and what I paid for."

"Don't pretend you earned it. Without me you would be nothing."

"Without you deciding you wanted to ensure that no other living soul ever found out that I was your son? That's more accurate. Don't act like you did me a favor."

"Oh, I won't. I'll go back to not thinking of you at all soon enough. This little venture of yours is doomed to fail."

"Are you going to sabotage it for me?"

He laughed, walking past Jack, bumping into him on purpose with his shoulder. "I believe you'll do that for yourself, son. You already have."

"Get out of my house. Don't come back here."

"Which part did you buy with my money?" his father asked, deep blue eyes making contact with his own.

They were Jack's eyes. Staring back at him without even a glimmer of warmth.

His mother's eyes were a light grayish blue, different from his own. This was where the color had come from.

The realization made him feel unclean somehow.

"I think I used part of your money to dig out the septic. You're welcome to come back and stand in that, if you have half a mind. Otherwise, keep off."

"You do remind me of your mother." And Jack knew he wasn't being complimented.

"And you remind me of a piece of shit I stepped in once."

The old man shook his head, chuckled and walked out the door.

It wasn't until the front door slammed shut that Jack realized he was shaking. Shaking with the effort of preventing himself from punching his father in the face. Shaking because for the first time he had been within punching distance of the old man.

Shaking with pure disgust, directed at himself, because in spite of the fact that his dad was nothing more than a prick with money, a part of him had hoped he'd been here to tell him he hadn't ignored him after all.

But no. Instead he'd been here to remind him of something Jack had been doing his best to forget. That he was a bastard. A bastard who would never earn this town's approval. Who would never permanently rise above the circumstances of his birth.

"Bullshit," he said, into the emptiness of his living room.

His custom-built living room, which was part of his near-million-dollar home on a massive parcel of land. Because he had transcended his birth.

That kind of blood outs itself eventually.

Yeah, like when you grabbed hold of your best friends' little sister and kissed her the way you kissed a woman you intended to take to bed.

Oh yeah, that was bleeding every bit of bad out for all to see. Staining his hands. Hands that had been all over Katie. No doubt he'd gotten it on her, too.

He was ready to put a fist through the wall of his custom home.

The phone in his pocket vibrated and he reached his hand inside and pulled it out, opting to deal with that rather than punching a hole in his house.

It was Kate. He took a deep breath and answered the call. "I thought I told you I needed distance."

"I'm distant."

"You're on my phone."

"It's not like I'm physically pressed against your ear, Monaghan. I'm at home."

"Calling me is not distance."

"What happened to you? You sit on your spurs?"

"I got a visit from my dad," he said, his voice hard. He had not intended to tell her that. He hadn't intended to tell anyone that. Because he could never tell anyone that Nathan West was his father. So what was the point in bringing it up at all? There was no point. There was no point to any of this. To wanting his approval, to believing anything that he said. And yet he couldn't erase the words the old man had spoken into the room.

Bastard. Bad blood. Bastard. Bad blood.

"I'm coming over," she said, no hesitation at all.

"That would be doing a pretty piss-poor job of distance."

"You shouldn't be alone."

"It's a great time to be alone with a bottle of alcohol."

"Connor and Eli would be lousy at helping you deal with this."

"I don't need help dealing with anything."

"Clearly not. You sound extremely well adjusted at the moment."

"I don't need to talk right now," he said, his bad blood boiling over now. That was what was driving him. No question. "I could use your mouth for one thing right about now, and it isn't talking."

He hated himself more than ever. For proving his father's point, for believing him. But he didn't know what else to do. Didn't know how else to be.

And hell, his dad was right. He was doing a good job building his business, and he'd punched that asshole Chad in the face and lost himself a lot of money. He couldn't even blame it on the fact that he'd simply forgotten the connection between Chad and his father. Even if he had remembered that Chad was Damion Matthews's son, he would have punched the ever-loving hell out of him because of the way he'd talked about Kate.

Because that was who he was.

The silence on the other end of the phone spoke volumes about the fact that he'd finally gone over the line. Good. Maybe she would stop messing with him now. Maybe she would understand just who it was she was dealing with.

As long as she'd been a little sister to him, she'd been safe. But she was determined to play with fire, and he needed her to understand the fire burned.

"I'm coming over, Jack," she said finally, her tone even.

"I'm telling you right now, Katie," he said, his voice rough as he searched for just the right words to make sure she would stay away, "if you come over tonight, you're not leaving my house a virgin."

Silence settled heavy between them, no sound but her breathing coming over the other end of the phone. And then the line went dead.

He'd finally done it. He'd succeeded in scaring her away. Well, it was about damn time.

He looked up and saw Nancy standing in the doorway, looking pale.

"You have a comment?" he asked.

Now he was being an ass to Nancy. Fantastic.

She shook her head slowly. "No. Your dinner will be out of the oven in half an hour. I'm going home."

"Whatever you heard…none of it's repeatable."

"I figured as much. I'm sort of insulted you felt you had to tell me that."

"I have some trust issues," he said, his tone hard.

Nancy arched her brows and took her purse off the hook by the door. "I can see why." Then she paused for a moment, her hand on the doorknob. "Don't do anything stupid."

"Like drink myself under the table?"

"As long as you do that at home, it's probably your

safest bet. Get drunk, pass out, don't do anything you'll regret."

And with that, Nancy left, taking her judgment with her.

He imagined she had heard him talking to Kate, and while she wouldn't know who it was, it didn't really matter, seeing as everything he'd said was offensive no matter the context.

Fortunately, he wouldn't be given the chance to do anything he regretted, because Kate had hung up on him. Because Kate clearly wasn't coming to comfort him, since he'd likely succeeded in putting her off him for life.

It was for the best. Definitely for the best.

He went into the kitchen and opened up the oven door. There were enchiladas. That wasn't terrible. It was the one part of his day that wasn't terrible.

He put his hands flat on the kitchen counter and lowered his head, replaying the conversation he'd just had with Kate.

He had no right to talk to her that way. But he had even less of a right to touch her, and with him in the state he was in, if she came over now, begging for him to kiss her...

Yeah, it was better to warn her off.

Because that's how low you are. You would screw Kate if she asked for a kiss because you can't control your damned dick.

Yeah, that was where his dad had things wrong. It wasn't his mother's genes he worried about. It was the West genes. The ones that made you walk around like you were an invincible, bulletproof paragon capable of doing whatever the hell you wanted without having to pay for the consequences.

He raised his head when he heard a sharp pounding on the front door. He wondered if Nancy had forgotten something.

"Come in," he called.

He heard footsteps on the hardwood floor, and they stopped right around the kitchen doorway. "I don't... I don't have sexy underwear or anything."

"Oh, fuck."

Kate was standing there looking like she was out of breath. The color high in her cheeks, and her braid in disarray, stray tendrils escaping, hanging loose around her face. She was wearing a T-shirt that was shaped like a rectangle, not doing anything to accentuate her figure, and a pair of jeans that had most certainly seen better days.

And she was the most terrifying, unwelcome, enticing sight he could have imagined.

"I got here as quickly as I could," she said, her dark eyes trained on him.

"You weren't supposed to come." It was all he could think to say. Well, he could swear again. But other than that, he had nothing else to say.

"I was never very good at doing what I was supposed to."

"Katie." He just said her name, because he was out of words. His mind wasn't forming sentences anymore; he was just feeling. Angry, desperate, turned on beyond what he felt capable of handling.

She took a step into the kitchen, a step toward him. "I have to keep telling you not to call me that."

"Yeah, well, I'm a bastard. In every sense of the word."

"You can be. But you aren't always."

He blinked hard, trying to superimpose the image of Kate as a girl over the image of the woman walking toward him. It seemed like not that long ago that when he thought of her, he still thought of that skinny long-limbed girl with freckles and scrapes on her elbows. But not now.

And as hard as he tried, he couldn't recapture that vision now.

The past wasn't in the room with them, and he wished like hell it was.

Her dark eyes met his, concern evident in the crease between her brows. She reached out, pressed her hand on his face, her smooth skin scraping across the stubble on his jaw. "Are you okay?"

For just a moment he thought of the past. Thought of driving up to the front of the Garretts' house, seeing Kate sitting on the porch, a blank look on her face.

Kate rarely cried. She was too tough for that. Too tough for her own good.

Eli and Connor had been nowhere to be seen and he'd heard a crash coming from inside the house that told him they were probably dealing with one of their father's drunken benders.

So he'd sat down beside her, put his hand on her shoulder, "Are you okay?"

And now she was asking him.

It made his chest feel tight, made it hard for him to breathe.

"I've never met him before." Just like the admission he'd made on the phone, this one just spilled out.

"Why today?"

He forced out a laugh. "It wasn't for a reunion."

"Tell me."

"I can't."

She put her other hand on his face, holding him steady, her eyes never leaving his. "He's an asshole." Her voice was fierce, shaking.

"I didn't even tell you anything about him."

"I don't need to know anything about him. If he knew where you were and he never met you until today, then he's useless. The worst piece of garbage in the world. Almost as bad as a mom who walks away from her two-year-old daughter and her two boys. She knew where we were and she never came back. It was her address for sixteen freaking years. She knew how to get back to it. She just never did. She's bad. Not us. He's bad. Not you."

"Do you believe that?" About himself, about herself.

"Sometimes," she said, the shaking in her voice becoming even more pronounced. "And sometimes I'm sure it was my fault even though I can't remember her face. I'm sure I must've done something."

"He never even met me. I guess he just knew that I wasn't worth it," Jack said.

"You are, though, you know."

He reached up and grabbed her wrist, tugging her hand down from his face to his chest. "Do you think so, Katie?" His heart was raging, the promise he'd issued to her over the phone looming large over them.

"Yes."

"You don't even like me. Everything I do makes you mad."

"I do like you. Maybe that's why everything you do makes me mad."

He knew exactly what she meant. Because the more he started to like her, the more tense he felt. His body's attempt at convincing itself he didn't want to be anywhere near her, when in fact he wanted to be as close to her as humanly possible.

For what purpose? To have those questions about her body answered?

It didn't get much more selfish than that.

But maybe that's just who you are.

Yeah, selfish was the only thing it could be. Because he couldn't give her anything else. The realization of how wrong it was to touch Kate made him feel slightly sick about his entire adult sex life. Because if it felt wrong to use Kate for sex, with nothing else on offer, it had been quite possibly wrong to use other women that way, too. Though they had most definitely been into it.

Still, he had made his excuses based on a sorting system in his brain that said some women were okay to have a good time with, while women like her were off-limits. He'd never thought it explicitly, not until that conversation with Kate about flirting. But once he outlined it then, he'd realized what a dick he was. And this was all underscoring it.

But no matter which way he twisted the reasoning, there was no justification for following through with the attraction that had popped up between Kate and him.

None at all.

But still, he had his hand wrapped around her wrist. Still, he was holding her palm to his chest.

"I never told you I was a virgin," she said, her voice thin, almost a whisper.

"But you are."

She looked down, swallowing hard. His heart rate increased as he waited for her to respond. That was one of those things that shouldn't matter, either. Even if she had slept with someone before, she was still off-limits to him.

But if she hadn't…

It would make their encounter more significant. Hell, he remembered his first time and there had been a lot of times after. Still remembered the woman. Two years older than him, more experienced. It had been fast and disappointing. For her. He had enjoyed the hell out of it.

But he had learned quickly that if he didn't figure out what he was doing, women wouldn't come after him for a repeat performance. So he'd gotten good. And he'd gotten good fast.

But in a long line of sexual experiences that had been hotter, better, that first one still stood out.

Being that first one for Kate would mean something. And he wasn't good with meaningful sex. Meaningless was the name of his game.

"Yes," she said. "I am."

He swore, but he didn't move away, keeping his hold on her. "Why do you want this?"

"Because I know you. I trust you. I know you'll make it good." Her words were a balm he didn't deserve on his scarred, mangled-up soul. No one trusted him. Kate seemed to trust him. "But you have to want it, too. I don't want my first time to happen because I talked you into it."

"You don't need to talk me into it," he said, his voice almost unrecognizable to his own ears. "I've spent the past week trying to talk myself out of it. Because I can't offer you anything. Nothing more than sex." He raised his hand, trace the outline of her upper lip with the edge of his thumb. "Make no mistake, badger-cat, it'll be good sex. I'll go slow. Taste every inch of you, not just because it'll make you mindless, not just because it will make you beg, but because I want to. Because I crave you. It will be more than good—it will be amazing. But it will still stop at sex. Nothing else."

"A good first time isn't nothing." Her cheeks were bright red, her words a thready whisper.

More evidence that he should back off now. She was too sweet. Too innocent.

"It's less than you deserve."

"What did you want from your first time?"

"To get off. Simple as that."

She closed her eyes, the blush remaining on her cheeks, a smile curving her lips. "I want that. I really want that." Her lashes fluttered, her lids opening again. "I realized today that I've been standing still for a long time. Everyone is moving forward and I'm just the same. I'm tired of being the same."

"This will change things," he said.

"I know. I want things to change. More than that, I want you."

He looked into her eyes, let his gaze drop to those soft, sweet lips. Kate Garrett contained the promise of hell wrapped up in a pretty little bit of heaven.

It would feel so good, but once it was all over, there would be nothing but regret and purgatory to deal with.

He knew it. It was wrong. It was bad. It was a betrayal of the two men who had stuck by him all of his life.

He'd protected Kate from some of the pain that came from living with a drunk. Had done his damnedest to make her laugh at impossible situations. Had punched Chad for daring to overstep with her.

He'd locked the door on so many of life's evils, shielded her from them. Only to discover he'd locked her in with an even bigger threat. Himself.

He was the fox in the henhouse. But even knowing that didn't stop him from wanting to eat her.

"Kiss me, Katie."

CHAPTER TEN

THE ROUGH COMMAND on Jack's lips was enough to send Kate over the edge then and there. She was trembling. Had been ever since she'd hung up on him during their phone call earlier.

She'd been certain of two things during that call. He needed her, and he was trying to push her away. She'd decided she wasn't going to let him get away with that.

Someone had to be there for him. She wasn't going to leave him to go through this alone, not when he'd been there for her countless times over the years.

Anyway, his "threat" just wasn't all that scary.

He'd promised her that she wouldn't leave his house a virgin. And she was very much hoping he followed through with that promise.

But she wouldn't worry about that just yet. For now, she would just follow that deep, throaty command, enjoy the way it made her feel. Enjoy the way he said her name.

Katie.

That lush sensation of having velvet rubbed across her skin. The one she had resisted for so long because it had frightened her. Because it had confused her.

She wasn't confused now.

Though she was a little scared. The virginal nerves were to be expected, probably. She had never actually talked to anybody about virginity loss before. Because she'd had a tough time bonding with girls when she was in high school. And by the time she was out of high school, it was weird that she hadn't lost it—at least, she assumed. So she didn't really want to ask anyone anything, because that would mean admitting her status.

She liked her friends well enough, but she didn't really trust them with information like that. The commonality between herself and her friends was horses, not boys.

But her nerves were going to have to take a backseat, because Jack wanted her to kiss him. So she was going to.

She trailed her fingertips along the edge of his jaw, relishing the feel of his stubble beneath her fingertips. It was such a masculine thing.

She was used to men. She'd grown up in a house full of them. She was used to whiskers, used to heavy exposure to the top half of men's bodies as her brothers traipsed through the house in towels or just sweatpants. Accustomed to the way they talked, the way they swore, the way they kept house—or, in Connor's case, didn't.

But this was different. Different from all those easy, domestic male things she had been exposed to all of her life. Different from watching shirtless men sweat and build decks and barns, which she'd spent a fair amount of her time enjoying.

That kind of distant observation left her a degree removed. Allowed her to feel a little bit of excitement while holding herself back. Without ever risking anything.

Sort of like barrel racing on the amateur circuit when she could probably go pro.

She shook off that thought. She didn't need to have any serious non-Jack thoughts right now. And so she let her world shrink down, reduced to nothing more than the feel of his whiskers beneath her hand. Nothing more than the beat of her heart and the echoing beat at the apex of her thighs.

Her heart beat out a rusty, unfamiliar rhythm against her breastbone, one hand still rested on his chest, held there by his iron grip.

She leaned forward, hoping he couldn't tell that she was shaking. She slid her thumb along the outline of his lower lip, mimicking what he'd done to her earlier. A short, deep sound rumbled in his throat and she took it as confirmation she'd done something right.

"You're sure taking a long time to kiss me," he said.

"I'm thinking."

"Second thoughts?"

"No. Just thinking about how sexy you are," she said, deciding she wasn't going to turn into a shrinking violet just because the prospect of getting naked with him loomed. He was still Jack. And she'd never been very good at watching what she said around Jack. "I've never seen a naked man before."

A gust of air escaped his lips. "Dammit, Katie."

"I'm looking forward to it," she said.

"What if you don't like it?" he asked, leaning forward slightly, his breath fanning across her cheek.

"I'd say the odds are pretty low. I mean, I like the way you look with clothes on. But I really like your skin. Your throat."

"My throat?"

She swallowed hard, ignoring the little rash of embarrassment that broke out across her skin. "Yes. It's hot. Your Adam's apple. Because it's very much a man thing."

"That's the strangest compliment I've ever gotten."

"Well, I'm not finished yet."

He chuckled, but it wasn't an easy sound. "Sorry, I didn't mean to interrupt you."

"Your forearms."

"Those are good, too?" he asked, a smile curving his wicked mouth.

"Really good," she said, her throat dry now. "Your muscles, the dark hair. Your wrists. Your hands."

He moved in just a little closer, his lips so close now all she would have to do was tip her chin up just slightly and she would close the distance between their mouths. "What about my hands?"

"They look strong. And when I imagine having them on me…all over me…"

"What do you imagine me doing to you with my hands, Katie?" he asked, his voice almost a whisper now.

"Touching me."

He made a sound that was somewhere between a groan and a growl, one that resonated deep inside her. "Not good enough. Tell me more. Tell me what you want."

"T-touching my breasts." She closed her eyes to try and get the rest of the words out without melting into a puddle of embarrassment. "Sliding down my back, holding on to my hips."

"What about touching you between your thighs,

baby?" he asked, his voice so rough now it was like a stranger's.

She opened her eyes and they clashed with his intense blue gaze. "Yes. I want that."

"Good. Now, are you going to stop talking and kiss me?"

She figured that was a rhetorical question. So her answer was to press her mouth against his. There was no anger between them this time, no challenge, no dare. But it didn't defuse the heat, the passion that burned between them.

His lips were hot and firm, commanding. He directed the kiss with unerring skill, delving deep, sweeping his tongue across hers, the slick friction sending a sweet honeyed sensation down through her veins, all the way down, leaving her wet with wanting him.

He released his hold on her wrist, wrapping his arms around her and tugging her body tightly against his. He was all strength and warmth, comforting and terrifying at the same time. She could feel his arousal hardening against her stomach.

Jack Monaghan was hard. For her.

She couldn't help but smile at that. And then a little giggle bubbled up in her throat and managed to escape.

Jack broke the kiss, his mouth still hovering near hers. "Something funny, badger-cat?"

"No," she said, unable to suppress the smile.

"Good." Then he leaned forward and bit her bottom lip before kissing her again, harder than before.

The sharp pain from the bite shocked her, especially followed closely by the deep, unending pleasure that came from his wicked, skillful tongue. And then she couldn't remember if the bite had hurt at all or if it had just felt good. It all felt good. Jack felt good.

He moved his hands down her back, just as she'd told him she wanted him to. All the way down to her hips, holding her steady, held tight against his body, against his hardened erection.

This time she was the one who pulled back. She studied his face and was struck by how familiar and different he was all at the same time. This was Jack. Her Jack. The one who would always try to make her smile even while the world felt as if it was crumbling around her. The one who always gave her a hard time and tugged her braid and called her Katie.

He was that, but it was like she'd always been looking at him through a fog and suddenly it had lifted, revealing details, facets of him she'd never been able to see before. She'd caught glimpses of them, little moments of intensity, a look, a smile, but this was different. More. Like looking full on into the sun.

And she didn't want to look away.

"What?"

"Just looking at you," she said.

"And?"

"You're the most handsome man I've ever seen," she said, immediately feeling out of her league as the strange old-fashioned compliment hung in the air between them.

Something sharp and hot passed through his eyes. "Is that so?"

"Yes."

He moved his hand to her shoulder, then down the length of her arm, and curled his fingers around her wrist and drew it close to his mouth, pressing his lips firmly against her palm, his eyes never leaving hers. "You're beautiful, Kate Garrett."

She shifted, leaning in and kissing him again. Because she was afraid that if she didn't, she was going to cry. And she'd already cried in front of him one too many times. Crying was stupid. It was passive. It didn't accomplish anything.

It most especially wouldn't accomplish her number one goal of the night, which was to get in bed with Jack.

The thought sent a shock wave down through her body. It was really happening. She was going to bed with Jack. Which was also a terribly old-fashioned way of thinking about things. But her thoughts had suddenly gone a little bit coy now that actual sex was imminent.

"I'm going to pick you up now," he said, his lips moving against hers as he spoke.

"What?" But even as she asked the question, she found herself being swept up off the ground, cradled close to his chest.

"We're going upstairs."

She looped her arms around his neck and held on while he carried her from the kitchen, through the living area and up the wooden stairs that led to the second floor of his home. She'd never been upstairs at Jack's house. There were only bedrooms up there. And she'd never been in his bedroom.

She shivered.

Jack paused midstride. "You okay?"

"Yes," she said, her teeth chattering.

"I'm only going to ask you this once. From this point forward I'm going to assume this is what you want. That even if you're nervous, you want this. You tell me right now if you aren't completely certain."

She didn't hesitate. "I'm certain."

"You are certain about what?" he asked, his voice uncompromising.

"I want to make love." She could have bitten off her tongue. Why couldn't she have said something dirty like *screw*? Or at least straightforward like *have sex*? Why was she suddenly shy?

"You understand what this is, don't you? Nothing outside the space, outside the house, outside tonight, changes."

Her heart twisted. "I understand."

He nodded once, then continued on his journey up the stairs, down the hall. His bedroom door was partly cracked and he shoved it open the rest of the way with his knee, then kicked it closed behind him.

It was a big bedroom, with wood floors and a braided rug in the center. Beyond that was a large bed with a rustic wood headboard and footboard and a quilt spread over the mattress.

If there were more details to take in, she didn't grasp them. She was focused simply on the way Jack was holding her, on the purpose with which he was walking through the room, toward that bed.

He set her down on the edge of it and took a step back, looking at her.

Then he gripped the hem of his T-shirt and tugged it up over his head, exposing his body.

Her mouth went completely dry, her heart thundering so hard she was afraid it would sprout hooves and gallop straight through her chest.

She'd seen Jack without a shirt before, but she'd always done her best not to look. Always done her best not to feed the wicked little monster that lived inside of her, harboring a Jack obsession she'd always tried to pretend wasn't there.

So now she indulged herself. Taking in every detail, every inch of exposed skin. More than that, she let herself feel. Let the full impact of him hit her square in the chest and spread out, all the way to her toes, and hitting some very interesting places in between.

His chest was broad and muscular, tapering down to a narrow waist with well-defined abs. He had just the right amount of dark hair on his chest, thinning out as it spread downward, then becoming more pronounced again in a line that disappeared beneath the waistband of his pants. A line she most definitely wanted to follow.

Happy trails to her indeed.

He took a step closer to her, and her eyes were drawn lower, to the front of his jeans and the aggressive bulge that was now at eye level. The fantasy she'd had earlier today in the truck outside the bridal store flashed through her mind.

She reached out, grabbing hold of his belt buckle, but he took firm hold of her and lowered her hands. "No. Not that. Not yet."

"Why not?" she asked.

"Because we're not starting with something that's about me."

She cleared her throat, feeling nervous, embarrassed. She'd been confident a moment ago, but maybe that wasn't something a woman was supposed to want. "I… I mean… I want…"

"Me, too. But I don't think I can handle it right now."

"We're going to have to stop talking in euphemism, because I'm kind of worried we are talking about the same things, and I'm worried that I don't understand you," she said, the words flowing out in a nervous rush.

He laughed, his chest pitching, his abs rippling with the motion. It wasn't an easy laugh; it was forced, strange. "I don't want you to suck me off right now, because I'll come in about ten seconds. Was that straightforward enough for you?"

Her face felt like it was on fire. "Yes."

"Were we talking about the same thing?" She nodded, swallowing hard. "Good. I'm glad you want to."

She felt relieved by that statement. Relieved that it was okay for her to want to taste him. Relieved that they were tracking.

He looked at her for a moment, then moved forward, putting his knee down on the mattress right next to her thigh. Then he leaned in, kissing her, propelling them both backward so they were lying on the mattress. He was holding himself up, palms flat on either side of her shoulders, his body not making any contact with hers.

She arched upward, desperate for something, desperate for more.

"Be patient," he said, angling his head to kiss her neck.

Desire ignited in her, a spark meeting a pool of gasoline. And it was just a kiss on her neck. But it was unexpected, and it was new. And it was so much more powerful than she'd imagined simple contact could be.

His lips embarked on a journey down to her collarbone, half his kiss landing on her T-shirt and the other on her bare skin. He raised his hand, curled his fingers around the fabric and pulled it down low, making a V that peaked between her breasts.

He looked up at her, hungry blue eyes meeting hers, and a sharp stab of anticipation hit her low and deep.

He kissed her then, on the curve of her breast, and she let her head fall back, let her eyes close again.

Abruptly, he abandoned her, straightening up, sitting on his knees. She looked at him on the bed, so close to her, and she knew she was staring with an expression of dumbfounded wonder on her face, but she couldn't bother to care.

Yes, she had seen plenty of shirtless men, but not like this. She'd never realized before that there were different kinds of nakedness. There was the kind where men stripped their shirts off while they were working, wiping sweat from their skin before going about their business. The kind you saw at the beach, when shirts off was the casual dress code for every male in the vicinity.

And then there was this. An intimate, raw kind of nakedness. Where the knowledge that they would touch each other, taste each other, all over their bare skin hung between them.

A kind that promised more secrets would be revealed, along with more skin. A kind that made her whole body feel electrified.

His eyes were unreadable, watchful. As though he was assessing her, deciding what to do next. She wished he would hurry and make up his mind, because she was afraid she would burn up and incinerate into a little pile of Kate-shaped ashes before he did.

His next move was fast, fluid. Suddenly he was over her again, taking hold of the bottom of her T-shirt and wrenching it over her head. He looked at her, his gaze dark, intent on her. He swore, harsh, hard.

She watched his face as the intensity in his eyes sharpened, as his lips parted slightly, his jaw slackening. He looked like... He looked an awful lot like she imagined she had only a few moments ago when she'd been examining his body.

"Why are you looking at me like that?"

He dipped his head, kissing her neck. "Because you're so damn sexy I can hardly stand it."

"But you've seen a lot of naked women." She didn't feel jealous about it. She was about to benefit from the fact that he'd seen and touched a lot of naked women, so she was hardly going to be shrewish about it now.

"But I've never seen you." His words moved over her like warm oil, soothing and arousing all at once. "And believe me, I've put quite a lot of thought into this over the past few days."

"You have?"

A wicked smile curved his lips and he reached down, unfastening the button on her jeans, the sound stark and loud in the bedroom. "Hell yeah."

She didn't really know what to say to that. So she didn't say anything. Instead she relished the slow torture of him lowering the zipper on her pants, tugging them down her legs and throwing them down onto the floor.

She wasn't wearing anything now but her underwhelming white seamless bra and matching cotton panties. There was nothing exceptional about the cut of said panties. They provided full coverage, both in the front and the back, and while she was somewhat grateful for that considering there were some scary things involved in being naked in front of someone for the first time, she was also aware that men didn't exactly get hot and bothered over demure underwear that covered more than your average bikini.

But judging by the blue flame burning in Jack's eyes, he wasn't really bothered by the style of her underwear.

"Told you I didn't have any sexy underwear," she said, her tone apologetic.

"But you've got a hell of a sexy body," he said, resting his hand on her rib cage, then slowly letting his fingertips drift down her torso, tracing the line of her slight curves down to her hips, down to those nondescript panties. "I've been torturing myself wondering about your shape. Wondering what your breasts look like. Damn, baby, you hide yourself well."

She sucked in a sharp breath. "Nothing special."

"I'm going to be the judge of that. And one thing I need you to be really sure of is that I'm not comparing you to anyone else. I can't even remember anyone else right now."

His words quieted some of her nerves, identifying the source in a way she hadn't been able to and cutting them off at the root. There was no room for doubt. Not when the way he looked at her proved the truth of every word he'd just spoken.

He pressed his forefinger to where bra cup met skin and traced a slow line upward until he reached the strap. He curved his finger around the fabric, drawing it down her shoulder. Then he repeated the motion on the other side.

He looked at her, lowered his head, his tongue following the path his finger had just taken. Instinctively, she reached for him, threading her fingers through his hair, holding him tightly to her as he teased her with his mouth.

He reached behind her, unhooking her bra and sending it the way of her jeans and T-shirt.

Raising his head, he looked at her, a ragged breath shaking his frame. "Katie," he said, his tone reverent as he lifted his hand to cup her breast, slowly sliding his thumb over her nipple.

Pleasure so sharp it cut like a knife sliced down through her. She wanted to close her eyes, to block out some of the sensory input battering like a ship against the rocks, but she was desperate to watch his face. Desperate to hold on to every moment.

Because this was her moving forward. Running forward full tilt.

And she didn't want to let one moment blur, let one escape without turning it over, fully experiencing it.

"Beautiful." He cupped her with his other hand, teasing both tightened buds with slow precision. Then he bent, drawing her deeply into his mouth, pulling a harsh, hoarse cry from somewhere deep inside her.

She worked her hips in time with the expert rhythm of his tongue, trying to ease the cavernous ache that was building, building, building between her legs.

He shifted his denim-clad thigh and she rocked against him, a white-metal burn scorching through her, internal muscles tightening.

She reached out toward his belt buckle again, and this time he didn't stop her. This time he let her get it undone, let it hang loose while she went after the button on his jeans.

But from her position it was awkward, and after

watching her struggle for a few moments, he relieved her of her burden. He stood and shucked his jeans, keeping his eyes trained on her as he straightened and pushed his underwear down along with them.

She was in entirely new territory now. She'd never before seen a naked, aroused man.

But she had been right in her theory. Jack had nothing to worry about, because she liked it. She liked it a hell of a lot.

Although along with the liking came the return of her nerves. Because big. He was very big. Not that she had any basis of comparison, but at the moment she felt she didn't need one.

He leaned forward, grabbing hold of her hips and dragging her down toward the edge of the bed, then hooked his fingers into the waistband of her panties, tearing them from her body.

"I'm all out of patience." He adjusted her position, drawing her even nearer to the edge of the mattress, then lowered himself to his knees, turned his head and pressed a kiss to the inside of her thigh.

Her stomach tightened, every muscle in her body tensing as she waited for him to make his next move. He cupped the most feminine part of her with his large, warm hand, parting her slick flesh, his breath fanning over sensitive skin as he moved closer.

She curled her fingers around the quilt, bracing herself. But her feeble attempt at preparing had been for naught. Because there was no preparing for the extreme altering sensation of Jack's tongue over the part of her that had been screaming for his touch.

He tasted her, slow and deep, thorough. It was so strange and alien, something she had never even fantasized about and yet something he had known she had wanted. In spite of the fact she hadn't known she'd wanted it.

He continued to lavish attention on her with his tongue as he shifted his position slightly, his finger teasing the entrance to her body. She swore and arched her hips, pressing herself more firmly against him, demanding more.

He pushed his finger deep inside of her, testing her, working it in and out of her slowly, the sensation new, joining a whole host of other new sensations that she hadn't even begun to grow accustomed to before he added another.

A second finger joined the first, slowly stretching her, uncomfortable where the first had been easy. But she realized what he was doing. What he was getting her ready for. And she was thankful, yet again, for his experience.

Slowly, the discomfort faded and pleasure built inside of her. He increased the pressure of his tongue over that sensitive bundle of nerves and pushed her over the edge with effortless precision, her muscles tightening around his fingers as wave after wave of sensation pounded over her.

He withdrew from her, stood and walked over to the nightstand. He opened the top drawer and pulled out a strip of condoms. He tore one packet off the rest, then made quick work of getting the protection on.

She was fascinated watching him, his strong, masculine hand rolling the latex over his thick erection. It was strange, incongruous and perfect seeing Jack in this context. She couldn't look away.

"Scoot up," he said, his voice strained.

She complied, her legs feeling a lot like wilted asparagus stems as she tried to will her trembling, useless muscles into doing her bidding.

She lay back, her head rested on the pillow, her thighs parted slightly. She forgot to be embarrassed about the fact that she was naked in front of him. Really, how could she be embarrassed about anything now that he had put his mouth there. Now that he had tasted her in the most intimate way possible.

Well, she supposed she *could* be. But it would be a little silly.

She still hadn't touched him in the way she wanted to. Still, she hadn't put her mouth on him. She wanted to slow things down, ask for more. Because she was afraid this was all he would give her. And it wasn't enough. Not nearly enough.

But before she could say anything, his body was covering hers, and he was kissing her deep, a reminder of her own pleasure flavoring his lips and tongue.

He flexed his hips, the head of his arousal testing her, teasing her. The hollow ache was back, a new orgasm building inside of her already. Impossible, she would have said. But Jack seemed fully capable of accomplishing the impossible where her body was concerned.

Abruptly, he ended the kiss, lowered his head, buried it in the curve of her neck as he moved, wrapping one hand around both of her wrists and pushing them up over her head while he thrust deep inside of her.

She couldn't hold back the sharp, shocked sound that was forced from her in time with that deep thrust. She'd heard years of horse riding made this kind of thing easier, but if this was easier, she was going to thank God for her horse habit every day for the next five years.

Because easier or not, it still hurt like hell.

She screwed her eyes shut tight and waited. She couldn't hear anything but his ragged breathing in her ear and her thundering heartbeat echoing in her head.

Slowly, she became less aware of the pain between her legs, more aware of the viselike grip he had on her wrists, the pain there slowly intensifying as the pain at the place they were joined lessened. As though it was simply draining from one part of her body to another.

She opened her eyes and met his fierce gaze. She nodded slowly, answering the unspoken question she saw there.

It was all he needed. He withdrew slightly, then thrust back home. She gasped, but this time not because of pain. He went slowly at first, allowing her to get used to the sensation of being filled by him. Until she went way past being used to it and crossed over into needing it, craving it.

She arched toward him, resenting the fact that he was holding her hands captive, but he didn't respond to the clear physical request that he release his hold. Instead he bent his head to her breast, tracing the outline of her nipple with his tongue before scraping it lightly with his teeth.

Jack was in her. Deep inside her. And it wasn't just pleasure overtaking her but the unending sense of being part of another person. Of him being part of her.

Not just anyone. Jack.

Always Jack.

She'd had no idea. She'd really had no idea.

He kept full and total control of the movements,

keeping her pinned, trapped by his strong hold and the weight of his body. It was maddening, drawing out the building pleasure to almost unbearable intensity. With his other hand he traced the outline of her lips, her jaw, sliding his hand down, curving it around her throat, the subtle show of his strength and power sending another electric surge of pleasure through her.

Then he moved on to her breasts, her waist, her hip, where he gripped her tight, pulling her hard against him in time with his thrusts. He was going to kill her. He was honest-to-God going to kill her with a promise of release not delivered, keep her poised on the edge forever.

She wiggled, managing to break free of his hold. She cupped his face, pulling his head down to hers, kissing him deep before moving her hands down to his muscular shoulders, over his back, down to his ass. She hadn't gotten a good look at it, not yet. Later. She would look later. For now, she would just feel and enjoy.

Something about her exploration tipped him over the edge, and she could feel the moment his tenuous control snapped. His movements were no longer measured, his thrusts no longer even. It became wild and desperate, the ride of a cowboy hanging on for dear life.

She moved in time with him, pushing them both closer to the brink. He pressed his forehead against hers, a long, low growl rumbling through his body, the clear sign of his desperation ramping up hers.

If there had ever been any doubt that he wanted this, if there had ever been any fear that he was only doing this to keep her out of trouble, because he felt sorry for her, that growl effectively frightened it off into the very far distance. It was raw; it was real. And it was all for her.

Then he froze above her. She could feel him pulsing deep inside of her. And it was as if the heavens had broken open inside of her, pouring forth torrential downpours of pleasure. She had a thunderstorm raging beneath her skin. Heavy and electric, loud. Roaring through her with the force of a tornado. Powerful, devastating and no less destructive.

All she could do was cling to him. All they could do was cling to each other until it passed. All she could do was hope they both survived the aftermath.

Jack was pretty sure he was dying. At the very least, he had set a foot on the road that would lead to death the moment he had touched Kate. Because if Connor and Eli ever found out, they would kill him. Spectacularly. Slowly.

A damn harsh truth to have to consider with the flavor of Kate still on his tongue. But it was a factor in this whole thing.

"Just a second," he said, pushing up from the bed, trying to ignore the chill on his skin caused by separating from her beautiful body.

His questions had been answered. Her breasts were just the right size to fit in his palm, her nipples a pale pink. Perky. That was his official description. Her waist ran more straight up and down than hourglass, her skin paler, softer than he had imagined it would be. Her hips were perfect. Perfect for holding on to while he slid into her hot, tight body.

He was getting hard again. He was such a bastard.

He turned away from her, walking into the bathroom that was connected to his bedroom. He discarded the condom and caught sight of his reflection in the mirror. Yeah, he was still himself. And he'd just taken a good long look at Kate, so he was certain she was still herself.

And he had just taken her virginity. He felt a little bit sick.

He walked back out into the bedroom, and Kate was still lying there at the center of the bed, completely naked. She sat up when he returned, dark hair sliding over her shoulders, only part of it remaining in a now nearly wrecked braid. She looked up at him, questions in her dark eyes. Questions he knew damn well he didn't have answers to.

Because he didn't know much of anything right now. He really knew only one thing for certain. He was one hell of a son of a bitch. She was so young. An entire decade younger than he was. So much more in terms of experience.

"Well," he started.

At the same time she said, "So…"

He stopped talking and decided to wait for her. Because hell if he knew what to say.

"Should I go?" she asked.

She looked so vulnerable. So young.

"Don't go," he said. But he knew even as he said the words that he couldn't allow himself to touch her again. Shame was crawling over his skin like ants, unfamiliar and unpleasant.

Bad blood. Dirty.

Oh yeah, he'd more than proven that.

He bent down and retrieved his T-shirt from the

floor and tossed it over to Kate. "Why don't you put this on?"

She obeyed, even though she looked confused while complying. Though the sight of his white T-shirt settled over her bare curves didn't do much to quiet the arousal that was roaring through his veins like a beast. He could see the outline of her nipples through the thin fabric. And now he knew what they looked like. Now he knew what she looked like all over. And he would never be able to forget.

He wasn't about to compound his sins by sending her out into the cold or by touching her again. Those two things were kind of at odds, since he had proven he did a lousy job of keeping his hands off Kate when she was anywhere near him.

"I have some things to do. Before I come to bed."

Her eyes got larger. "Oh." She scrambled to the edge of the bed, swung her legs over the side of the mattress and stood. "I thought we might...talk, maybe?"

His chest got tighter, breathing almost impossible now. "Later," he said. He had no intention of talking to her later. He had every intention of avoiding his bedroom until she was asleep.

She frowned. "If you have something to say, you should just say it."

"Sometimes, Katie, things need to be left unsaid."

She looked hurt. Confused. Shit, he was a bastard. "We never leave things unsaid."

"Yeah, well, until tonight we never had sex before, either."

"I would have thought we would talk more now that we've seen each other naked."

He tried to force the corners of his mouth to lift

into a smile. He imagined it was closer to a grimace. "That's not how it works."

One side of her mouth pulled sideways, straight across. He imagined that was her attempt at a smile. Then she lifted her shoulder, as if shrugging off his words of more experienced wisdom. She reached up, sliding her hand around to the back of his head while she stretched up on tiptoe and kissed him.

And he was weak. Just a man. So he let her. More than let her—he wrapped his arm around her waist, held her to him for a moment, relishing the feel, the softness of her breasts pressed against his chest.

"I'll be here," she said, getting back into bed, slipping beneath the covers.

And he would be anywhere but there, because his resistance was low. "Get some sleep."

He walked out of the bedroom and down the hall, down the stairs. He didn't have anything to do. It was almost 10:00 p.m. and all he wanted to do was climb into bed with the soft, beautiful woman upstairs.

But the soft, beautiful woman upstairs was someone he never should have touched in the first place.

Dammit. Why had his conscience shown up now? He'd been more than willing to let it all burn earlier. It should have arrived before he'd taken Kate to bed or not at all.

Unfortunately, his ability to justify had run out.

Mainly, it was because of the way she'd looked when he'd come out of the bathroom. That gut punch of reality that had hit him square and hard.

No matter what she said, he was going to hurt her. He probably already had, probably would even leaving it at this once. But continuing on wouldn't make it any better.

He'd made it his mission to protect Kate from some of the uglier things in life when she had been younger and surrounded by ugly things. Surrounded by empty booze bottles, the smell of alcohol and her father's disconnected, slurring speech.

He'd been there when her father had died. And had comforted her when Connor's first wife, Jessie, had been killed. And after all that, knowing everything she'd been through, knowing how battered her heart was, he'd done this. But he was going to fix it.

He was going to protect her, as he always had.

He'd let himself lose sight of that, mired in his own shit. But he wouldn't forget again.

CHAPTER ELEVEN

IT WAS POKER NIGHT. Somehow Kate had forgotten last night when she'd decided it would be a good idea to go to Jack's to comfort him and see if he would make good on that dirty promise he'd issued over the phone. Somehow she'd forgotten that he and her entire family would be getting together to play cards only twenty-four hours later.

She'd been dreading it for most of the day. At least, once she'd stopped turning over and over the events of the night before. And once she'd stopped dealing with the very real desire to curl up into a ball and lick her wounds. Wounds left behind by what had followed the most incredible sex anyone had ever had.

Not that she knew about all the sex that had been had, but there was no way in hell it could top what had happened between Jack and her.

The sex had been perfect. It had been the unspoken weirdness that had occurred after. In many ways, she wished he had freaked out. Wished he had yelled and said he was never touching her again. Wished he had thrown things and shouted and said it was a terrible idea and they should never touch each other again. But he hadn't. He had left, saying nothing. Promising he would be back. He hadn't come back. She had lain in bed awake for hours after he had gone downstairs, waiting for him. She hadn't been able to move. Glued to the mattress as though he'd stuck her there. She didn't wait. Never. Not for anything.

But last night she had.

Had lain there with her eyes open, gritty, until the sky outside had started to lighten. Finally, she had drifted off, only to wake up two hours later. The bed was still empty of anyone but her, cold except for where she was nestled beneath the quilt.

When she had finally gotten up, she had dressed. Except she had kept his T-shirt on in protest of his abandonment. And then she had gone downstairs looking for him, but he hadn't been there.

She'd thought about calling him. Thought about looking around the property.

Then she'd realized that this was probably what he did with every woman he slept with. And they probably all felt needy and desperate after, searching high and low to see if they could find him, to see if they could talk him into touching them one more time.

She had a case of the Jacks. She'd promised herself she wouldn't get those.

She had promised she would be cool and sophisticated. Because she didn't want a relationship anyway, so there was no reason to let him hurt her feelings. Though she did want more of what they'd done. There was so much left for her to experience. And right now she couldn't fathom being with anyone else. Not when he was still her primary obsession.

It wasn't just that, though. He'd hurt her feelings. She didn't want him to have that kind of power, but he did.

Still, she was balanced. So she had spent only half

the day fetal over all of that. She'd spent the rest of it panicking about the poker game. About whether or not he would be there. If he was there, it would be incredibly awkward. If he wasn't there...

Knowing he was avoiding the house because of her would hurt. Seeing him for the first time since they had been naked together, with Connor, Eli, Sadie and Liss looking on, would be terrible.

Of course, she could always skip the game. But it would be suspicious because she never had other plans. Which was why she was tromping over to Connor's house, her hands stuffed in her pockets, her boots crunching on the gravel.

Jack's F-150 wasn't in the driveway. Her heart slammed against her breastbone, then slid all the way down into her stomach. She gritted her teeth and stomped up the stairs, the noise created by her feet hitting the solid wood doing a little bit to satisfy the irritation that was rioting through her.

She opened the door to her brother's house without knocking and shut it firmly behind her. Not even the smell of pizza in the air offered her any comfort.

She walked into the dining area and saw that everything was all set and ready to go, the green-and-yellow Oregon Ducks bucket sitting in the center of the table filled with beer and soda. She was not messing around with soda tonight. "Beer," she said.

"Did you get kicked by Roo?" Eli asked.

"No," she said, sitting down at the table and scowling at her older brother. "Why?"

"Because that was a strange little one-word greeting. I thought maybe you were having trouble stringing thoughts and sentences together."

"Just had a bad day," she said without thinking. She shouldn't have said anything, because now they would ask for an explanation. Well, Connor and Eli probably wouldn't. But Sadie and Liss...

"Oh," Sadie said, the sympathetic sound grating across Kate's nerves, "what happened?"

"Work stuff," Kate lied. Because it had been her day off. But sometimes her schedule got shuffled around, so it was feasible that they might not realize.

"Drama with a flat of pansies?" Connor asked, his mouth curving upward into a crooked smile.

Kate nodded, her expression mock serious. "Yes, pansies are the most dramatic of all flowers."

"Azaleas are the most apologetic," Sadie said, laughing at her own joke. A wide grin spread over Eli's face, too. Kate remembered the apology azalea that Sadie had purchased from her more than a year ago in an effort to engender some of Eli's goodwill.

Obviously, it had worked. Or if not the azalea, maybe something else.

Maybe she should buy Jack an azalea.

"What about petunias?" Liss asked. "What are their dominant emotional characteristics?"

"I hear petunias are the hardened criminals of the plant world," Eli said.

"I'm sure you would know," Sadie said, kissing Eli on the cheek.

Kate heard the sound of the front door opening and her heart scampered up to her throat, resting there, fluttering madly like a nervous animal. Because there was only one person it could be. Only one person who would show up on poker night and not knock.

She looked down at the center of the table, determined not to watch the doorway.

Her pulse was pounding in her ears, and if there was conversation going on around her, she couldn't distinguish it from the roar of blood that had taken over all the space in her head.

She heard shoes on the hard floor and knew that she couldn't keep not looking, because not looking would eventually appear a lot more suspicious than looking. She lifted her head slowly, trying to prepare herself to face Jack for the first time.

Preparation had been futile.

It was Jack, Jack, whom she had known for almost her entire life. He was familiar, from his dark hair, nearly black, to his blue eyes, always glittering with humor. Broad shoulders, muscular frame. The very same Jack she had always known. But more. So much more.

There was an intimacy to having been with someone that she'd never realized existed. The source of the special looks that passed between her brothers and their respective lovers.

Like different kinds of nakedness, this was another new discovery. She had known Jack before, but now she *knew* Jack. Had learned things about him she could never unlearn. Knew what his skin tasted like, felt like, looked like all over.

Knew how he shook when she traced her tongue along the line of his jaw. Knew how his whole body shuddered as he found his release. Had heard that feral growl as he thrust deep inside of her.

She hadn't just been skin to skin with him; he had

been inside of her, as close as two people could possibly be.

Wow, so much for trying to act casual about all of this. She was not feeling casual.

And now she had passed from normal looking at Jack in greeting to staring.

But…she realized that Jack was staring, too. He was frozen in the doorway, his lips parted slightly, his eyes trained on her.

"Hi," she said, knowing she sounded subdued. But she felt subdued, so all things considered, it was fair enough.

"Hi, Katie," he said.

She didn't correct him.

He walked into the dining area and sat down in the only available chair, which was—thank God—between Eli and Liss and not next to her.

"So are you all ready to lose your money?" he asked.

There, that was slightly normal. She was struggling with normal. She was struggling with anything beyond guppy dry-drowning on land.

"I don't know," Eli said. "I'm feeling lucky tonight. I'm getting married in two weeks to the most beautiful woman in the world. Frankly, I'm untouchable."

"Your wallet is very touchable. And I'll prove it," Jack retorted.

"I think you're all forgetting that last time I cleaned up," Kate said.

Jack turned his electric-blue gaze to her. "I suppose you did."

"No suppose about it. If we had kept going, you

would have left wearing a barrel, because I would've stolen the pants right off you."

She regretted her words, but not until it was too late to do anything about it. Not until she had spoken them, not until they were hanging awkwardly in the air like dazed fruit bats.

"I bet you would have, Katie bear," he said, his jaw tensing.

The group seemed oblivious to the tension between them. Which was insane, as far as Kate was concerned, because it felt so thick, so real. A physical presence in the room rather than a simple feeling. She felt as if the tension was sitting there drinking a beer, holding a sign that said They Totally Had Sex Last Night.

"Deal. Somebody deal," she said, hoping that no one took note of the edge of desperation in her tone.

"Kate's in a hurry to lose," Connor said, grabbing the deck and setting them up for a little bit of five-card draw.

"More like your face is in a hurry to lose," she said. Admittedly, it was not her finest comeback. But she was not on top of her game. Since most of her brain-power was devoted to not looking at Jack to see if he was looking at her.

"His face lost at birth," Eli said.

"Nice." Liss smiled with approval.

"Can you believe that? My own wife." Connor shook his head, but he didn't look irritated in the least. Instead he just looked pleased to be able to say the word *wife*.

"Wives are the worst," Sadie said. "I can't wait until I'm one."

"Soon." Eli looked at Sadie and smiled. That secret smile that Kate suddenly understood. They looked as though they had secrets because they did. Because there was a wealth of knowledge they each held about the other that no one else would ever have.

And she'd gone and given herself all that knowledge about Jack. She hadn't realized. Hadn't realized how much it would change. It was as if she'd spent her entire life thinking that *Old Yeller* had ended before the final chapter and had been suddenly introduced to the actual ending years later.

Because then a heartwarming story about a boy and his dog became something else entirely. All of the previous story was there, but that last bit changed everything. Changed all of what it was.

That was what sex with Jack had done.

He wasn't a hideous dead-dog book. In fairness, the sex they'd had was hardly a tragic final chapter. It was just…different. He was different.

Everything that came before this new chapter had taken on an extra facet. Given her new understanding. It was so much more than she'd expected. So much more than she'd wanted.

Unsurprisingly, she lost miserably. Her poker face was off because she was putting all her energy toward applying it to keeping Jack feelings off her face.

Jack didn't win any rounds, either. It was Eli, in keeping with his bold prediction, who won the night.

"You suck, Eli," Liss said, eyeballing her diminished pile of change. "Stealing money from a pregnant lady."

"Unless pregnancy hormones interfered with your

bluffing abilities, I don't see what it has to do with anything," Eli responded.

"If you make her mad, it's on you," Connor said.

The banter continued for a few more moments, but Kate and Jack sat it out. She stole a glance across the table at him, the first time all night that she'd chanced anything more than looking in his direction but looking through him.

The corner of his mouth lifted slightly, and she felt the impact of that small gesture down deep. She couldn't think of anything to say, couldn't think of anything to do, so she just stared at him.

Thankfully, no one else noticed. She took a sharp breath, noticed his eyes lowering to look at her breasts. She felt a flush creep up her neck and over her face.

It reminded her of the expression on his face last night. Reminded her of that sharp need in his eyes as he'd thrust inside of her.

She felt like she'd stuck her head in a barrel of bees.

"You look tired, Kate." This comment came from Connor. "Were you out late last night?"

"What? No."

"I saw you pull out around eight. You got back after I was in bed."

Horrified heat punctuated by pinpricks of ice flooded her face. "I just… I mean, it wasn't late to me. I guess to an old guy like you, maybe ten or eleven or whatever is kind of late."

"An old guy," Connor said drily. "Do you hear that?" He addressed the group. "We are old."

"Maybe you all are," Sadie said, "but I'm not."

"Where were you?" And the interrogation started with Eli.

"Am I supposed to give you an accounting of my whereabouts now?" She knew that she was sounding guilty now, which was stupid. She should have just played it off. The defensiveness was making it worse. But she hadn't been able to hold it back. Because she wasn't good with subterfuge. She had never engaged in it.

If only she had realized that being a straight arrow for so many years would come back to bite her in the butt one day.

She might have worked harder at cultivating a little rebellion earlier.

"I just went over to Ace's for a drink." She couldn't look at him, because she was lying, and she was a terrible liar. She'd been told by more than one customer at the Farm and Garden that she had an honest face. Honest faces tended to do strange things when dishonest words were being spoken.

Sadie and Liss exchanged glances, and Kate knew that more questions were imminent. "I met *girl*-friends," she said, heading them off at the pass. "Sierra West and some of the other women who barrel race." Neither of them would probably ever talk to Sierra about it. Her alibi was most likely never going to get checked.

"Hope you had fun," Sadie said.

Kate had a feeling Sadie didn't believe her. Which hurt her feelings, really. Silly, since she was lying. But she wasn't exactly rational at the moment.

"I did. But now that you mention it, I am tired. I think I'll head to bed. I have to be at work early." She stood, the chair sliding inelegantly behind her, causing her to stumble. "See? Tired."

She waved halfheartedly and walked out of the dining room. Once she put some distance between herself and the dining room, her breath left her body in a gust, and she realized she had been taking in only shallow bits of air and releasing it very slowly ever since Jack had walked into the room.

She heard another chair scrape against the floor, and instinctively, she knew it was Jack's. She wanted it to be Jack. She wanted to talk to him. She also wanted to avoid him.

Her feelings made exactly zero sense at the moment.

She couldn't hear what he was saying, but she could feel the rumble of his deep voice, feel it moving through her, making her all soft again. Wet again.

The man was made entirely of wicked magic.

She heard his heavy footsteps and froze, waiting for him. Of course she was waiting for him. She was predictable. She would love to walk out and scurry back to her house as quickly as possible. But she wouldn't. Because no matter how upset she was for the way things had gone earlier, she wanted to be near him again. She wanted to hear what he had to say.

Anyway, she saw him all the time. They had to work it out. She couldn't avoid him forever, so she might as well not ever start.

He appeared in the doorway of the dining room, and their eyes clashed. She nodded once and turned, heading out the front door and into the chilly, wet night air. There was a breeze blowing in off the sea, the sharp, briny smell mixing with the smell of earth and pine.

Kate folded her arms, shivering but not from the cold.

A moment later Jack appeared on the porch, casting a quick glance back at the house before walking toward her.

"Did you drive?" he asked.

"No."

"I'll walk you back."

"You sure I won't try to jump you again?" she asked, knowing that she sounded pissy and not really caring.

"As long as you aren't worried about me jumping you," he said, his tone dry.

"*Worried* isn't the word I would use."

"Come on, let's walk and talk." He took two strides, evening his position with hers. Then they both started back down the road that led to her cabin.

She shoved her hands in her pockets, keeping a healthy distance between them. Jack seemed content to do the same.

"So—" she kicked a pinecone that was in the middle of the driveway and sent it flying "—why did you leave me in bed alone, asshole?"

"Because I'm an asshole," he said, surprising her with the frank admission.

"Okay, that's honest, but it doesn't really help me."

"Because I didn't want to be tempted to do that again."

"Why? Just…once? How is that even…reasonable?" She snorted out a breath. "Wait, never mind. You probably have sex with a random woman one time with great frequency."

"I can't dispute that," he said, his tone somewhat rueful.

"I know you can't. Your reputation is pretty well established. And I know it, Jack, I do. It isn't like

I want anything serious. I just thought maybe more than one time."

"Sure. I mean, it would be great. I can't deny that. There's no sense in denying it. What we have… It was explosive. I'm not going to pretend differently. I had to leave because if I had stayed, I would have pinned you down to the bed and had you again. There is no question. I had to leave because my good intentions are about as easy to strip off as that T-shirt of mine you were wearing last night."

"I stole that T-shirt," she said, her voice raspy then because his words had affected her so deeply.

"You can keep it."

"If you want me, why won't you let yourself have me? I mean, you aren't exactly known for your restraint."

"Because you are Connor and Eli's younger sister. Because they are two of the most important people in my life and if they found out that I… I kind of joked about them killing me, but I actually think they might."

"They wouldn't kill you."

"Maybe not. What little respect of theirs I have, I would lose. I would lose their friendship."

She knew he was right. No matter how angry it made her, no matter how unfair it seemed that his actions, her actions, be dictated by the potential reaction of her brothers, she couldn't pretend that there would be no reaction. Couldn't pretend that it wouldn't upset their lives. She never talked about sex with Connor and Eli, but she had a feeling her brothers would take a dim view on whomever she decided to sleep with. If they found that Jack was having sex with her just for the sake of sex…

Yeah, that would go down about as easy as swallowing a hedgehog.

But it didn't erase her longing for him. Just because she understood, didn't mean she was opposed to changing his mind.

She opened her mouth to say something. Something like "They don't have to know." Or "We can keep it a secret." But she realized she was verging on begging. She was inexperienced, sure, but even she knew that wasn't ideal.

They walked on in relative silence, the only sound their feet crunching on the rocks and pinecones as they made their way down the dark tree-lined road that led to her little cabin.

Too soon they rounded the slight curve and her little outdoor light came into view, shining a welcome, representing tonight's finish line. The end of this new development in her relationship with Jack.

An end she wasn't ready for.

She half expected him to turn and leave then, but he kept going with her until they reached the steps.

"Really quick," she said, sensing he was about to leave, not ready for him to go, "I just wanted to tell you that it was good. And I'm glad you were my first." She bit the inside of her cheek, battling stupid, unwanted tears that were starting to fight for escape. "It was good."

It wasn't exactly the eloquent speech she had felt building in her chest. Not exactly the sophisticated and magnificent parting words she might have hoped for. But they were true. And she needed him to know.

I've wanted you forever.

She left that part unspoken, because it was too revealing. Not just for him but for her. She didn't want to say the words out loud, because she didn't want to ignore all of them or what else they might mean.

He nodded slowly. "It was."

She took a timid step toward him, half expecting him to move away, but he didn't. He stood rooted to the spot, watching her. The glare from the porch light cast deep shadows on his beautiful face. Highlighted the sharp cheekbones, the straight line of his nose, the squareness in his jaw. The perfect curve to his lips.

And now she knew for sure why his lips had always been so fascinating. Knew why staring at them for too long had always made her stomach feel fluttery and tight.

Because her body had been reading the promises there, and now that she'd seen them fulfilled, she felt it all even more vividly.

Just one more time. One more kiss.

She put her hand on his face, stretching up on her toes, pausing just for a second before she leaned in. He raised his hand and curved it over hers, holding her to him, looking intently at her in the dim light. It was all the consent she needed. She angled her head, kissing him deep, and he returned it.

It occurred to her then that she'd never kissed Jack goodbye before. And that that was what she was doing now. She screwed her eyes shut tight, softening her lips, opening for him, submitting to the sensual assault that originated where their mouths met and carried through her entire body.

She was going to have to try to unlearn all the

things she knew, going to have to try to forget the new chapter she'd read. This was goodbye to Jack as she had come to know him.

There would be no secret looks for them to exchange, no little touches that served as brief and electric reminders of what they shared behind closed doors.

There would be none of that. Because it was over. Because this was it.

Too soon the kiss ended. When they parted, they were both breathing hard.

She curled her hands into fists, digging her short fingernails into her palms, biting the inside of her cheek to keep herself from asking him if he wanted to come in.

He had already given his answer, he had given his reason, and it wasn't wrong. She'd told him he wouldn't hurt her. Told him she knew what to expect. So now, even though it hurt, even though she had expected more, she had to pretend none of it was happening.

"Good night," he said, his voice low, rough. "See you tomorrow, Kate."

Don't call me that.

Those words were on the tip of her tongue. In that moment she hated the sound of her preferred name on his lips. Because it wasn't what he called her. It wasn't teasing. It wasn't designed to get a rise out of her. He was treating her the way everyone else treated her.

And he used to treat her like she was special. She realized that now, an epiphany that had come at the very worst time.

"Good night," she said, turning away from him and

walking up the stairs to her front door, ignoring the gnawing feeling of incompletion that grew with each bit of distance she put between them.

CHAPTER TWELVE

IT WAS A CLEAR, crisp afternoon and Kate hoped that was a good omen for tomorrow. Because tomorrow was Eli and Sadie's wedding and she wanted very much for it to be perfect for them. Eli deserved perfect.

He had given up so much to ensure that she didn't feel the neglect of her father, who'd wandered around the house like a drunken ghost who couldn't interact in the mortal realm.

Connor had spent his days working on the ranch, keeping it running, keeping them fed, making sure they had a roof over their heads. Eli had done everything he could to keep the house clean, to keep her taken care of. He had brushed her hair, braided it, picked her clothes out for her. He had ridden his bike with her on the back in a special seat down to a day care every morning so that he could be sure she was being taken care of while he continued going to school.

He had done everything in his power to make sure the residents of Copper Ridge thought their household was running as normally as a home could after the woman of the house had up and left her family.

Eli had made their house a sanctuary even while a good portion of the storm raged inside the walls.

In many ways, Connor and Eli had been her parents. She'd been raised by two teenage boys, and she couldn't begin to thank them enough if she started now and kept going for the rest of her life.

"It's sunny," Liss said, a smile on her face as she looked out the kitchen window of the Catalog House, one of the oldest structures on the property, ordered by her great-great-grandpa from the Sears catalog. Eli and Sadie would be spending the night separately, with all of the girls bunking in Sadie's B and B.

"Yes, but the weather here is a fickle mistress," Sadie said. "So hopefully, the fog won't roll in before tomorrow."

"I guarantee you it will roll in at least three times before tomorrow," Kate said. "We just have to hope it rolls back out again at the right time."

"True enough," Sadie responded.

"But the sun will shine on you," Kate said, with a certainty she felt all the way down to her toes. Because God, the universe, whatever, owed her brother a sunny wedding day.

"I will take your certainty as prophecy." Sadie patted Kate on the cheek.

"I don't really mind a little bit of cold," Liss said, her hand on her stomach. "It does not take much to make me sweat. I would rather not sweat all over my bridesmaid dress."

"You can sweat on your bridesmaid dress. I don't mind," Sadie said.

"Alternately, you can reschedule your wedding for after I give birth."

"Nope. I have roughly three hundred dinners—fifty salmon, two hundred and fifty filet mignons—scheduled to be brought tomorrow to feed very hungry people. There is no rescheduling this wedding. Oh, and I love Eli and cannot spend one more minute without being joined in the bonds of holy matrimony."

"You've been abstaining for your wedding night, haven't you?" Liss asked.

"Yes. Yes, we have. There will be no rescheduling," Sadie said.

Kate blinked, trying not to think about any of this information too deeply. Liss, on the other hand, seemed highly amused. "Why are you doing that? It was his idea, wasn't it?"

"He thinks it's romantic and traditional. I told him not exactly since we have been sleeping together since before we were actually in a relationship. He did not take my point."

"This is hilarious," Liss said, her smile wide.

"Don't be smug," Sadie said, eyeballing Liss. "It isn't like you can get up to anything at the moment."

Liss's smile turned naughty. "That isn't true. We're very creative."

Kate was suddenly applying all of this personally rather than feeling indignant or disgusted, as she normally would have. Because this wasn't forcing her to think of her brothers as sexual beings; it was forcing her to think of herself as one. Of what long periods of abstinence would mean for her now that she knew just how good it could be. And a long period of abstinence was most definitely what she had stretching in front of her.

Also, there was the small matter of her wondering what all being "creative" might entail.

She imagined that Jack could be very creative.

"I think Kate is getting ready to stuff her socks in our mouths," Sadie said.

Kate felt her ears get hot, because that had not been what she was thinking at all. "Yeah. I don't need to hear any of the sordid details about your personal lives. I like you, no offense, but you know."

"Sure," Liss said.

"It's time to head out for the wedding rehearsal anyway," Sadie said. "Okay—" she took a deep breath "—this is going to be fine, and I'm not going to trip on my way down the aisle."

Kate had never seen Sadie trip. "You aren't really known for your clumsiness," Kate pointed out.

"But if I was ever going to contract a case of the clumsies, it would very likely be on my way down the aisle."

"Probably," Kate said. "But if you fell, Eli would just come and help you up. That's what he does."

Sadie's blue eyes misted over and she grabbed hold of Kate, pulling her into a tight hug. "You're right. You're so very right." She released her quickly and slid her forefinger beneath her lashes, wiping the moisture away. "Okay, let's do this."

ELI, CONNOR AND JACK were standing around in the field, having just set up six rows of chairs in front of an arbor that was heavily laden with flowers.

"You ready?" Connor asked, the question directed at Eli.

"It doesn't seem like a strong enough word." Eli's voice rang with certainty. For a moment Jack envied that certainty. Eli knew who he was; the community knew who he was; he knew what he wanted. Jack didn't know shit.

Holly, the wedding coordinator, walked up the aisle,

a clipboard in her hand. "The ladies are ready. We have the music cued up. Connor and Jack, I need you. Eli, you're going to go wait over by the sound booth. Tomorrow you will have the pastor with you." She looked at them expectantly. "Okay, move."

Connor and Jack exchanged a look and followed Holly back down the aisle and around behind the barn. Sadie was there, her blond hair piled high in an exaggerated bun, a bouquet made of wrapping paper and ribbons in her hand, Liss by her side.

But it was Kate who made him feel as if he'd been hit in the chest with a ton of bricks. He had pretty successfully avoided her for the past couple of weeks. Bachelor-party stuff had taken the place of the poker game, and he'd made vague noises about work commitments when he would normally have come by the ranch to visit or help with an extra project.

He had been avoiding things because of her. Because no matter what he had said about their need to be finished with the kissing, and the sex, and the completely inappropriate attraction, his body wasn't on the same page. His body saw her and growled, starving for her in spite of the fact that she was wearing another of her ill-fitting T-shirts and shapeless jeans.

"Okay," Holly said, interrupting his thoughts, "I will be back here during the ceremony to cue you when it's time to go. The music will start—" and just then the music did start "—and then we'll give it a few seconds. Eli will walk out with the pastor. Liss, you and Connor walk out together, followed by Jack and Kate. Then Sadie."

The music changed and she pointed at Connor, who took Liss by the arm and began to walk back with her down the aisle. Kate looked at Jack, catching his eyes. He tried to smile as he extended his arm to her.

"Okay, badass badger-cat," he said, trying to sound brotherly, "no chewing on the ankles of the guests on your way down the aisle."

She squinted one eye, the left side of her mouth pulling down. "What?"

"You have to be a lady. This is a wedding." Somewhere in the murky depths of his brain, he thought maybe this would be the key to getting things back on track. If he treated her like he had before he'd started noticing her breasts and things, before he had kissed her, they would revert back to the way they'd been.

So he would just ignore the feeling of being scorched currently assaulting his forearm where she had her hand placed on him and move forward.

She didn't get a chance to respond to his comment, because a few seconds later they got their cue, and they were making their way toward the arbor. He could feel her tense up. He leaned in and whispered in her ear. "Easy there, Katie." Because that was what he would have done before. So that was what he was going to do now.

It didn't work. She only grew more rigid with each step.

They parted at the head of the aisle, Kate going to the left, while he went to the right. He looked across the way and saw that she was glaring at him, her dark eyes blazing with anger. He gritted his teeth and turned his focus to the aisle again, to Sadie, who was practically skipping toward them.

Holly was hot on her heels. "Okay, then Sadie says her piece when prompted by the pastor—" Jack noticed

that Eli looked slightly confused by this but said nothing "—and comes up to join Eli. Vows, kiss, the song
will start, you will be presented to the guests. Then
we walk out. Reverse order, Eli and Sadie first." She
made a sweeping gesture indicating they should walk
back now. They complied. "Jack and Kate."

Jack shot Kate a look and they both started walking, meeting in the middle, where he took hold of her
arm again. The contact sent a shot of sexual hunger
down to his cock that rivaled some of the better blow
jobs he'd had.

Which got him looking at her mouth and wondering what it would be like to have it on him. She had
a pretty mouth. He had never put much thought into
it before.

He was now.

Get a grip, idiot.

He needed a distraction. Possibly to meet another
woman. A woman at the wedding tomorrow. A little
bit of casual sex to burn the feel of Kate from his skin.

He ignored the violent twisting in his stomach, the
instinctive and emphatic *no* that screamed through his
body. This was, in his estimation, a lot like getting bitten by a snake. You had to inject yourself with more
venom to fix what was wrong. Which meant having
more sex. With someone else.

That had made more sense before he had actually
thought it through with actual words.

Still, it was the only solution he had.

That and to treat Kate like he really wanted to want
to treat her. Which was the golden rule or some shit,
he was pretty sure.

Soon they reached the other side of the barn, and

she released her hold on him a little bit too quickly. "Afraid you're going to get cooties?" he asked.

The glare she shot his way could be described only as evil. "I'd say I probably already have them," she said, her tone deadpan but dangerous.

Eli and Sadie seemed oblivious to the exchange. They were too busy talking to each other in hushed tones and gazing deeply into each other's eyes.

It was on the tip of his tongue to say something about how she couldn't have caught anything from him, seeing as he'd used a condom. But that would have been crossing the line. Even if her older brother hadn't been standing right behind him, it would have been over the line.

Screwing her in the first place was over the line.

Yeah, no argument. Which was why he was fixing this.

Or at least, was trying to fix it.

Judging by the stormy look on Kate's face, he was failing.

Connor and Liss joined them in the back of the barn then, and Holly clapped her hands, her red curls bouncing. "Okay. That went great. So now all you have to do is the exact same thing tomorrow, but also you'll be married at the end of it."

"So are we done?" Kate asked.

"Yes," Holly said. "Really looking forward to this wedding. It's going to be beautiful."

"I just need to go back to the house and get some clothes," Kate said, directing her comment at Liss and Sadie. "I'll be by the B and B later."

She turned and walked away from the group. He knew he was risking looking suspicious, but he felt like he needed to go after her. Because they needed to get something settled between them tomorrow before the wedding.

"I just need to go ask her something about the rodeo thing," he said, realizing when he spoke the words that the excuse seemed more suspicious than a simple *I'll be right back* ever would have. But it was too late now.

He broke into a partial jog, headed after Kate. "Katie," he said.

She stopped, her shoulders straight, her back stiff. "What?" She started walking again, not turning around to face him.

"Hey." He reached out and tugged lightly on her braid. "Are we okay?"

She whipped around, her expression angry. "Don't do that. And you know what? Just…do what you did that night after the game. Call me Kate. Don't call me Katie."

"I don't want things to be different. I would hate to think that what happened messed things up permanently. Avoiding you like I have been doesn't work."

"If you don't want to…be more than friends, or whatever we are, that's fine. That's fine." She reiterated the last bit. "But things won't be the same as they were before. It's impossible." She turned and started walking away again.

"That's bullshit."

"This whole thing is bullshit," she said, spreading her hands, still not stopping, still not looking at him.

He reached out and grabbed her arm, forcing her to stop. But she refused to look at him. "I don't want things to be different," he said, his voice rough, his hand burning from the intensity of touching her. Mocking everything he was saying.

"They are. Honestly, Jack, I thought I was the stupid virgin." She pulled out of his hold and this time he didn't go after her.

If he hadn't already known it, this proved it. He was the King Midas of fuckups. Everything he touched turned to shit.

This was why he liked it easy. This was why he liked things surface. Charm could fix everything when no one was overly invested. A smile, a joke, a round of beer… It solved whatever problem he had.

But he couldn't fix this thing with Kate no matter how hard he tried. Feelings. Too many of them.

Guys like him had to stick with simple for this very reason.

Bad blood.

Yeah. But if no one saw you bleed, they never knew.

Too bad Kate Garrett had seen him bleed. Too bad he'd bled all over her.

Yeah. Too damn bad.

It made him wonder if the charity event would prove anything at all. Or if it was just another thing he was destined to destroy.

THE DRESS DIDN'T seem as special as it had when she bought it for the purpose of seducing Jack. Now it just seemed pointless. She'd seduced Jack already. In a T-shirt, jeans and cotton undies. And it was over without him ever having seen this.

She looked at herself in the mirror. Her hair was down and straight, since as far as she knew, curling was not in the listed skills on her hair's résumé. Liss had promised she would weave some flowers into it so that it matched hers. And while that was going on, Sadie was going to do her makeup.

Kate had never worn makeup before. She wasn't sure how she felt about it.

Well, she might have been excited about it if she'd had a seduction to look forward to. As it was, she had an awkward postseduction walk down the aisle to look forward to. Which was not the same thing.

She didn't have time to worry about Jack. Didn't have time to allow herself to be derailed. Once the wedding was over, she was going to redouble her focus on the barrel racing. Getting ready for the event at the charity day. Getting ready to kick some serious butt.

Her stomach tightened with anxiety when she thought of that. If she really did this, if she really did well, it was just one more change. One more step forward. She was starting to realize how difficult that was for her. How much it scared her.

But even though it sucks, you survived Jack.

Yes, she had. Maybe that was it. She needed to look at it as a step forward where her foot had landed in a cow pie, and she had slipped and fallen on her ass. But it was still a step forward. Still a change. And now she'd been with a man. One of life's great mysteries was now known to her.

Progress. Progress towing a boatload of awkwardness and hurt feelings, but progress nonetheless.

Liss walked into the light, airy bedroom Kate was currently standing in. "You look beautiful, Kate." Her tone was a little bit too kind.

"Thank you?"

"Was that a question?"

"The tone of your voice is strange."

Liss lifted her hand, showing a little bunch of baby's breath with little dried roses mixed in. "Not intentionally. I'm just here to fix your hair. Sit on the bed."

Kate obeyed, and Liss started fiddling with her hairstyle immediately.

"So," Liss started. And here it was. Kate had instinctively known something was coming. "Are you okay?"

"Why?"

"You're acting weird. And so is Jack. And I am not stupid."

Kate's throat tightened and her stomach along with it. "It's fine," she said, knowing she was completely unconvincing.

"If he did anything to you, I will kill him. Cheerfully." She sounded cheerful but lethal.

For some reason that made Kate mad. Which was strange, because she was mad at Jack. Or more accurately, she was hurt because of him. But she didn't like the implication that what had passed between them was him "doing something to her." She had wanted it. She had asked for it. He hadn't done anything she hadn't wanted except stop. And she couldn't imagine why Liss, who had known Jack almost as long as Kate had known him, would act like he was someone or something Kate needed to be protected from.

"You know, Jack is a good guy," Kate said, her tone defensive. "He would never do anything to hurt me. He would never do anything to hurt anyone."

"But that's the thing about Jack," Liss said, her tone more firm. "He doesn't mean a lot of things. He can be… He's very charming, but he can be selfish."

Kate thought about the evening she'd spent in Jack's bed. Selfish was the last thing she would call him. Even now, even while she was upset with him, she couldn't say that anything he'd done was selfish. In fact, he was thinking of Connor and Eli and their relationship. Was considering her feelings, even if it was in a way she didn't want them considered.

"Jack isn't selfish," she said. She knew she sounded upset, and she didn't really care. She was comfortable being mad at Jack. She was not comfortable listening to Liss talk about him this way. "Who do you suppose helped take care of me when my dad was miserably drunk and Connor and Eli had their hands full? Jack did. And he's helping with this charity thing, and he's offered to help coach me on my riding so I can win this event. Because it's important to me, and he cares about that. And yeah, he pisses me off. Because he can be obnoxious. But he's a good man. You're supposed to be his friend. I wouldn't think you'd have a hard time seeing that."

Liss continued calmly weaving flowers to Kate's hair. "I am his friend, Kate. Which means I have a realistic viewpoint on his shortcomings. It's difficult to have a realistic viewpoint when you have feelings that go somewhere beyond friendship."

"And if I did, maybe it would be a problem," Kate said, her teeth clenched.

"There are easier men to set your sights on. Jack likes a good time, but he won't stay around for a long time."

"Easier men? Is that the goal? Because if so, I don't think you ever would've married my brother."

Connor had been the grumpiest, most closed-down

man in town until Liss had managed to get him to fall
in love with her and, along with that, drag him up out
of his grief.

"I'm not telling you what to do. Or what not to do.
I'm just telling you I've observed that there is something different between you and Jack. And if you need
to talk to me, you can."

She swallowed hard. "Don't say anything to Connor?"

"I don't keep secrets from my husband. But right
now I don't know any secrets," she said, her tone full
of meaning.

"There aren't any to tell," Kate lied.

"Okay. If you say so. Anyway, your hair is done.
Sadie will be up in a second. She's just getting the
finishing touches done on her makeup. Then she'll do
your face before she gets into her dress."

Kate nodded mutely. Liss turned to go. "Wait," Kate
said. "Thank you for looking out for me. I've lost every
woman who has ever come into my life. But now I
have you. And Sadie is here to stay... I'm glad you're
my sister, Liss. And I appreciate you offering advice."

"Anytime," she said, smiling slightly before leaving the room.

A few moments later Sadie came in, a bag of
makeup in her hand. "Ready?"

Kate took a look at her reflection, which was still
barefaced. Her hair was partially pulled back, some
of the strands twisted around blossoms. There was
something satisfying about how different she looked.
As if her outside finally matched her insides. Ever
since that night in Jack's bed, something had felt off.

Now at least she looked a little bit more like a

woman. Sure, she'd always been a woman—the loss of her virginity didn't change that. But Jack had made her aware of just how much of a woman she was.

"Yes," Kate said. "I'm ready."

JACK HADN'T WORN a suit since Connor's first wedding. His wedding to Liss had been casual, jeans and button-up shirts, no ties, down by the swimming hole they'd frequented as kids. The casual dress had been due in large part to the cold weather of the winter wedding, but it had also been a reminder of their past. Of the good things in the past, while they walked into the future.

Eli and Sadie's wedding, on the other hand, was not casual at all. Sure, it was all wrapped up in the rustic flavor of the Garrett ranch, but everything was elegant and styled, down to the most minute detail. Much like the bride. Sadie had that way about her. That effortless, free-spirit vibe. But beneath all of that she was much more thoughtful, much more purposeful.

All in all, someone he was glad to see marrying his best friend. Even if he did have to wear a suit.

The wedding was due to start soon, the seats placed out in the field filling up with guests.

He'd been assisting in the seating arrangements, but soon it would be time for him to take his position behind the barn with Sadie, Liss, Connor and Kate.

Kate, who he was no closer to fixing things with.

So much for his attempt at bringing things back to normal. He'd spent a good portion of last night pissed at himself about that and mad that he couldn't even get drunk, because he couldn't afford a hangover on the day of his friend's wedding. He scanned the crowd, spotting a host of familiar faces.

Instinctively, he homed in on the single, attractive female faces. Lydia was here, Holly the wedding co-ordinator and Alison. Alison was still a no-go, as far as he was concerned. But Lydia and Holly didn't have any relationship baggage that he knew of. Neither of them had a reputation, but that didn't mean they were opposed to a good time. It just meant they were discreet.

And that was fine with him. He wasn't looking to flaunt, wasn't looking to hurt Kate in any way.

It was just his snakebite theory. Kate Garrett made him feel snakebit. He needed antivenom.

Still, neither of those possibilities created even a kick of excitement in his gut. Which was dumb. Lydia was beautiful. Dark hair, dark eyes, petite, feminine frame. Holly was tall, willowy and pale with curly red hair and freckles across her nose. They represented some fine variety. Either one of them should do something for him. But no. Nothing.

His gut clenched tight, his whole body freezing, when an unexpected set of guests walked in. Nathan West, his beautiful wife, Cynthia, and three of the adult West children. Sierra, Madison and Gage. Colton, predictably, wasn't anywhere to be seen. But he very rarely was.

Of course the Wests would be here. All of them. Eli was a prominent figure in the community, and so were they. They had deep pockets and donated large sums to the sheriff's department. So obviously, they would be here for the wedding of the sheriff. For some reason Jack simply hadn't been prepared.

He started walking toward them, his stomach

churning, anger firing through him. Nathan caught his eye, a warning look in the icy depths of his own, and Jack stopped. What the hell was he doing? He was going to make a scene at his best friend's wedding? For what purpose? There was none.

Jack stopped, but Nathan kept walking. He didn't look away from Jack, his eyes fixed on his.

"Mr. Monaghan," Nathan said, extending his hand, a smile on his face.

Jack felt sick. But he wasn't about to be outdone. He took his father's offered hand and returned volley with a smile of his own. A smile that was far too similar to the older man's for his taste. "Mr. West."

"I had to come shake the hand of my most worthy competition. Enjoy the wedding. Tell the bride and groom congratulations on my behalf."

Jack squeezed West's hand. "Absolutely." He released his hold, continuing away from the seating area and toward the back of the barn, rage now a living thing inside of him.

Nathan West got to walk around without ever having his reputation questioned, while Jack had to work his ass off to get any respect. There was something wrong with that.

There was also something deeply wrong with the fact that Jack had now made eye contact with his father twice. And there was no satisfaction in it.

Attention. Acknowledgment. It was a cold and bitter thing.

Big surprise—life wasn't fair. He'd known that from moment one. He just wished he didn't have to be reminded so damn frequently.

And then he felt a little bit like a prick for complaining, because at least he'd gotten a payout to keep his identity a secret. A lot of bastards just had to deal with the stigma and never got the reward.

It was all the child support his mother had never accepted. And then some. She had been furious when she found out he'd taken the money. When she found out he'd lowered himself, his pride, to that level. She'd sworn she'd never speak to him again. And she hadn't.

He still couldn't regret it. His mother'd had the power to give them something else and hadn't. Realizing that, he'd been angry, too.

They were both still angry.

Though now some of his anger was at himself.

He'd sold himself, but he hadn't sold himself on the cheap.

The first thing he saw when he rounded to the back of the barn was Sadie. Jack had never harbored any fantasies about getting married, but he could well imagine that any man who had would immediately want to snatch her up and carry her to the nearest church. She looked perfect, like an angel, like everything Eli deserved.

Then he turned and saw Kate. After that there was just nothing else.

She was wearing a dress the color of cranberries, little flowers in her dark hair, which hung loose around her shoulders. She so rarely left her hair down. Even the night they'd been together, it had been back in a braid. And he wanted desperately to sift his fingers through it, to feel the softness, the weight of it, to spread it out over his pillow.

Her eyes were highlighted with gold makeup, picking up all the subtle color she had naturally and making it even brighter. And her lips…painted the same color as the dress. He'd become increasingly aware of those lips in recent weeks and seeing them highlighted like this was torture.

They were vivid in his mind's eye now, softening for a kiss, parting so that they could wrap around his hardening—

He wasn't sure he would survive this wedding.

Sadie let out a long, slow breath. "Okay. Nothing to be nervous about," she said.

"Nothing at all," Connor said, putting his hand on her shoulder. "Welcome to the family, Sadie Miller. I had to call you that since you're going to be a Garrett in a few minutes."

She smiled. "Oh, come on. I've been one. This just makes it official."

"True," Connor responded.

The music changed, and the sounds of the crowd noise dissipated as everyone took their seats.

Silence fell between the five of them, too. Waiting.

Instinctively, he went to stand next to Kate, seeing as it was his position for the wedding. Also, his body wanted to be close to hers. Simple as that.

She looked up at him, her expression shaded by her lashes, which looked longer, thicker and darker than usual. She didn't say anything, and neither did he.

Holly cued Liss and Connor. Connor took hold of his wife's arm, his smile broad, and the two of them began their journey to the aisle.

He extended his arm to Kate, who slowly accepted it, her eyes never leaving his. Because he couldn't resist, he leaned in slowly, his lips next to her ear. "You look beautiful."

She shivered. "Thank you," she said softly.

Holly pointed at them and mouthed the silent "go" and then he started to lead Kate around the barn. They walked through the field and to the aisle, now flanked with full chairs. He refused to look at any of the guests. He wasn't taking a chance on making eye contact with West. Not now.

Instead he kept his focus on walking that straight line up to the arbor. And then narrowed his focus still. To the feel of Kate by his side. Her fingertips digging into his forearm as she held on to him. Her shoulder brushing against him with each step.

He stole a glance at her out of the corner of his eye. Red lips. Her beautiful red lips.

In that moment, he let them become his whole world.

Because the real world wasn't something he needed to deal with just now.

They reached the head of the aisle, and he reluctantly released his hold on her, going to stand beside Connor.

The music changed and so did the atmosphere out there in the field. It was as if suddenly everyone in attendance had taken an indrawn breath at once. As if they were all holding it. Waiting.

And then Sadie appeared, backlit by the sun, making it look as if she had a halo around her face. She was most definitely glowing. Jack glanced at Eli, and he was pretty sure he was glowing, too. Without the benefit of the sun. It was just Sadie.

Sadie stopped at the head of the aisle and Pastor Dave, a man Jack knew only by reputation rather than by any time spent in church, smiled at her.

"Traditionally, this would be the moment when the bride is given away. But Sadie has something she would like to say instead," the pastor said.

Sadie smiled, her focus on Eli, as though he were the only person there. "I left here when I was seventeen. And I spent most of those years after that alone. Wandering around, never settling. Not belonging to anyone. Then I came back here. And I found you. Right where I left you. Now I give myself away. To you, Eli Garrett. Because I trust very much that you will honor my gift. Now and forever."

Eli broke away from his position and went down to stand with Sadie, taking her hand and leaning in to kiss her. "I give myself to you, too," he said.

For some reason the declaration made Jack search for Kate. It must have had the same effect on her, because when he looked in her direction, their eyes locked. Heat streaked through him as the words echoed inside of him.

I give myself to you.

A trade. A choice.

"Wonderful," Pastor Dave said. "Now let's begin."

THE CEREMONY WAS OVER and Eli and Sadie were officially Mr. and Mrs. Garrett. Kate was seated at the bridal party table, picking at a piece of cake, watching them dance beneath the hanging lanterns in the barn.

She felt Jack's presence before she saw him. "What do you want, Monaghan? Come to harass me more like yesterday?"

She still felt jittery and unsettled from his compliment earlier.

You look beautiful.

He'd said the same to her when she was in a T-shirt and jeans. He was probably just being nice. And it shouldn't have mattered. But it did.

"Why aren't you eating your cake?"

"Because. It's a carrot cake. Which is a horribly named food. Maybe, *maybe*, you could call it a muffin. And then I wouldn't find it so offensive. But it isn't cake. It certainly isn't wedding cake. Sadie has good taste most of the time, but I question this."

"That was probably Eli's decision. You might not know this but we used to go to Rona's for his birthday. Back when we were thirteen, fourteen and maybe a little older. No one at home made a cake. She used to give him a piece of carrot cake on his birthday."

Kate's heart twisted, her breath stalling out. "Really?" She looked back down at the previously offensive cake. "He always made my birthday cake."

"I remember. They were ugly-ass cakes. He used a mix so they tasted okay but he couldn't frost worth a damn."

"He always made sure I didn't go without. Him and Connor." She cleared her throat. "And you."

"Well—" he sat down in the empty chair next to her and she squished her legs together, making herself smaller, in an effort not to touch him "—it's nice to know I wasn't always a source of bad feelings for you."

"You aren't a source of bad feelings. Don't be dramatic. Again, you're the one that's kind of acting like a virgin," she said, careful not to look at him as she spoke the offending words.

"I don't want you to be upset."

"Sorry, not sorry. I have the right to be upset. I thought… First of all, I thought there would be a little more to it than that. Second of all, whatever I said about how I would react isn't really valid. I didn't know. I had never done that before. My inexperience absolves me."

"It does not," he said.

"It sure as hell does. No jury in the world would side with you on this. You're the town stallion."

"Everyone has had a ride, ha ha ha."

"So you've heard that one before?"

"It's just maybe not as clever as you think." He leaned in and her breath caught. "And anyway, it isn't true."

"It isn't?" she asked, her tone a tiny bit too hopeful for her taste.

"Yeah, come on. That's ambitious, even for me. There are quite a few women I haven't slept with in Copper Ridge. Though you have to take into account the fact that I spent a lot of years traveling on the circuit."

"Right," she said.

"Jealous, Katie?" And if she wasn't mistaken, his tone sounded a bit hopeful, too.

"Why should I be jealous? I had you, didn't I?"

"Once."

She looked down, taking a deep, furious breath. "That was your decision, not mine. I wanted more."

"What do you think I can give you? It's an important question, and I need to know the answer."

She stared down more determinedly at her cake, catching sight of his thigh in her peripheral vision. He was wearing a suit, which wasn't normally her thing, but he made it look sexy. And now, with the ceremony hours behind them, he had ditched his tie, the top two buttons on the white shirt undone, his jacket discarded, his sleeves rolled up to his elbows. He looked disheveled and dashing, and there was no point pretending she thought otherwise.

But there was a point in doing her best not to look at him so that he couldn't tell she felt that way.

"I'm tired of being afraid," she whispered, surprised at the words that tumbled out of her mouth. But as soon as she said them, she knew they were true.

"What are you afraid of?"

"Change. It's why… It's why I haven't gone pro. Because if I do, I'm going to have to leave. Because if I do, I'm going to put distance between myself and Connor and Eli and the ranch. Everything that matters to me. I've lost enough. I want to keep it all close. I like things to stay the same. So…I work at the Farm and Garden and live on the same property I was born on, and I had never even gone on a date. Never kissed anyone. Because doing different things and being different is so scary. But with you…it wasn't scary, Jack. Because it's you. It couldn't have been anyone but you."

She chose that moment to look at him and the expression in his eyes made her heart flutter around her chest like a terrified bird. Lust, need, naked, raw and completely undisguised, burned from those familiar blue eyes. Rendering a man she knew as well as her own flesh and blood a total stranger yet again.

She knew without a doubt there were more chapters of Jack to read. And she wanted to read them. To devour them.

The craving for that knowledge was so strong she ached with it.

"It has to be me?"

She nodded slowly. "Yes."

CHAPTER THIRTEEN

KATE'S WORDS WERE BALM for a wound he hadn't known he had. Or maybe he'd known he had a wound, but he'd just imagined it was a different one. But he'd been searching for something—approval, accolades, from the town, from his father—for as long as he could remember.

Had been seeking out just one person who might realize he was more than easy smiles, pure dumb luck and shallow affairs.

Right now he saw it in Kate's eyes. That simple gift he'd spent so many years chasing. With wild behavior. Bull riding. Ranching.

She *knew* him. She understood him. More than that, she needed something from him and believed that he had the ability to give it.

And he wanted her, dammit. Wanted those perfect red lips on his mouth, on his neck and everywhere else.

"It's already weird," he said slowly.

"What is?" She blinked rapidly.

"You and me. We did it once, and not doing it again didn't make it normal again. Like you said, it can't be normal. It changed."

"Jack. Please, please don't tease me."

"I'm not."

Her face turned pink and she directed her gaze

down to the uneaten cake on her plate. "And I don't want you to sleep with me again because you feel sorry for me. Or because you're trying to fix something you already broke."

The simple fact was he had come to the wedding with the aim to fix something broken. He'd thought he would pick up another woman, that he would have some easy, fun sex that would have no emotional implications. Sex that wouldn't be hard and wouldn't threaten the most important relationships in his life.

But it wouldn't work. He'd ignored the most essential part of the antivenom principle. It had to come from the same sort of snake.

That meant either he had to keep sleeping with Kate until he was cured of his desire for Kate, or he had taken the metaphor too far. But he was going with option one since it meant he got to sleep with her again.

Yeah, he would have loved to believe he was being altruistic. That he was simply trying to restore order, that he was trying to give her what she wanted. The simple fact was it was just a side effect, albeit a pleasant one. He wanted her. Beginning and end of it. And somehow over the course of the wedding, over the course of the day, he'd begun to lose sight of the other things.

The fact that she was Connor and Eli's sister. The fact that she was ten years younger. The fact that he was a lot more experienced and should know better than to fool around with her.

All those things were somewhere way off in the distance now. And Kate was so close he could smell the clean, simple scent of her soap, of her skin.

"I don't feel sorry for you. And I'm not trying to

fix the damn thing." His voice sounded like gravel, his words strained, but there was nothing he could do about it. He was beyond control. Beyond himself. "I want you." He lowered his voice, conscious of the fact that they were still in a room full of people, though most everyone was out on the dance floor, music playing heavily over top of their conversation. "I can't tell you how it changed. When exactly it began. I *realized* it changed that day you kissed me. But it was different long before that." He looked around to make sure they hadn't caught anyone's attention. They hadn't. "It would only be physical. I don't have anything more for you than that."

"Good thing. I don't have anything more for you or anyone beyond that. I told you, I'm tired of being afraid. I'm making changes. I'm going to go pro, and that means I'm going to be traveling, pursuing my dream. I'm not going to be hanging around here mooning over a boyfriend." She cleared her throat and raised her eyes to meet his. "Or a lover."

Hearing the word *lover* on Kate Garrett's painted lips was one of the most erotic experiences of his life, and he couldn't possibly begin to break down why.

"Sounds like we're on the same page, then."

"I'm going to go for a walk," she said slowly. "Down to the old barn."

Heat pricked the back of his neck, and guilt pricked his conscience. He knew exactly which barn she was talking about. Mainly because he had taken a woman there nearly a year ago with the express intent of getting it on with her during Eli's election party. He had been thwarted since he'd encountered Connor and Liss making out, before anyone had known they were more than friends.

That memory should have been enough to get him to tell her no. Should have been enough to highlight the differences between them.

At least, it would have been if he were a decent human being. He wasn't.

"And I'm going to get a phone call a couple minutes after you leave. And I'm going to have to go check something back at the ranch." He chose his words carefully, and Kate clearly understood.

"Okay." She stood, taking the napkin that was in her lap and setting it on the table, her eyes never leaving his. "See you later."

He watched as she slipped through the crowd, kept an eye on any and every hint of crimson he could catch through the thick knot of people. This part, the waiting, would be torture.

So he wasn't going to wait. No one was paying attention to them anyway. Eli was dancing with Sadie. Connor and Liss were across the room, Liss's feet propped in Connor's lap while he rubbed her ankles.

He opted to go out a different door, following a different path from the one Kate had just taken. He cut across the driveway that led back to the Catalog House to a different road that went back to the old barn.

Kate deserved better than a quick, rough screw in a barn during her brother's wedding. But then, she deserved better than him. So he supposed it was all in keeping with the theme.

He broke into a jog, not caring anymore that he wasn't acting casual, fully committed now to his need. How different this was from the last time he had come out here with a woman. That had been…normal. He had wanted the person he'd been with, but not like this. He hadn't felt desperate, hadn't felt desire and guilt clawing at his insides in equal measure, each one agitating the other, making it fight harder for pride of place.

He hadn't been shaking with need, ready to tear his clothes off during the walk over so that things would go faster once he was inside.

No, this wasn't like that last time at all. It was unlike anything.

He pushed open the barn door and saw Kate crouched down in the corner by a lantern, turning the switch, the artificial flame lighting up.

"Well, that's handy."

Kate straightened and turned to face him. "I thought so."

"Come here."

Crimson lips turned upward. A small, wicked smile. Just for him. "If I don't?"

"Then I'm going to have to go get you."

Her eyes sparked with humor and a streak of defiance so uniquely Kate it hit him in the gut like a sucker punch. And the realization, the reminder, that this was Kate only made him want her more.

Amazing to see another facet of a woman he'd known for so long. To know for sure and certain beneath her makeup was the person he'd always known. Who could keep up with the boys, who was full of strength and sass. But that she was also this woman. This siren who was seducing him with such little effort.

With no resistance on his part.

"Why don't you come get me, then?"

He began to walk toward her, slowly undoing the buttons on his shirt, her lips going slack, her eyes widening slowly. Watching Kate watch him was an immensely gratifying experience. One he never could have predicted. When it came to sex, he considered himself jaded. But he'd never been with a virgin before. Much less a woman who had never kissed anyone else. The novelty of being her first, her only, was more intoxicating than he could've imagined.

The way she looked at him, awe mixed with admiration, was like a shot of Jack Daniel's that went straight to his head. He shrugged his shirt off and let it fall to the floor before putting his hands on his belt. She licked her lips and he felt the impact resonate in his groin.

"That lipstick should be illegal."

She blinked, her expression one of genuine surprise. That was another thing about Kate. She possessed no guile. None of this was an act, a show or a game. She was experiencing it for the first time, sharing it with him, making him feel as if it was a first all over again for him, too. "Why?"

He reached out and slid his thumb along the line of those lips. "Because it makes me want to do damned dirty things to you. Do you know what I've been thinking about ever since I saw you this afternoon?"

"No," she said, taking a step backward, her voice a whisper.

"Of course you don't." Because she was innocent. And he was a bastard. By the end of tonight, she would know. And the next time he, or another man, told her her lipstick was giving him dirty ideas, she would know exactly what it meant. That made him feel guilty. It made him feel angry, because he was thinking about her with another man. And she would be with another man someday.

But right now she was his.

"When I came around the back of the barn and saw you," he continued, "my heart about exploded. All I could think about was you kissing me. Leaving your lipstick behind on my skin. I'd already been thinking impure things about your pretty mouth. But that lipstick made it that much worse. Made me want to see your lips on my cock."

Her face turned the same shade of scarlet as her mouth from her perfect, beautiful cleavage up to her hairline. He'd gone too far, and he knew it. But he felt compelled to push. Maybe because he thought if he did, she would back out. Except when he really thought about it, that made no sense. Kate Garrett had never backed out of anything. And presenting a challenge would only make her push back harder.

Maybe that was the real reason he was doing it.

"If you want it, come over here and get it. It seems like I kiss you an awful lot, Monaghan. A girl doesn't like to feel like she's the one doing all the chasing."

"She says with her two weeks of experience."

She tilted her head, a familiar stubborn set to her jaw. "I know what I like. I know what I want."

He felt his lips curve upward into a smile as he continued to slowly work his belt, tug it through the loops on his dress pants before undoing the ridiculous hooks that held them closed, drawing the zipper down and pushing them onto the barn floor, kicking off shoes and socks along with them. They would be dirty. Very obviously so. But he didn't care.

He pressed his hand over his hard, heavy erection. "You want this?"

"Yes." There was no hesitation, none at all.

"Good." He quickened his pace, closing the distance between them and wrapping his arm around her waist, cupping her chin with his thumb and forefinger, looking deep into her dark eyes, searching for any sign of fear, of potential regret. There was none of that. There was nothing but need, a desire that burned as bright as his own.

It didn't surprise him. In some ways Kate's insides matched his own. Wild, fierce.

A bit too bold. A bit too reckless.

Just one of the many reasons that the moment attraction had begun to spark between them, there was only one place it could end. Neither of them knew how to back down. He should have seen that from the beginning. Should have seen that this was the only place it would ever end.

"If I had known a dress would make a man look at me like this, I would've started wearing them a long time ago," she said.

"When was the last time you wore a dress besides today?"

"Never. At least, not that I can remember. They've always seemed pretty useless to me."

Arousal burst through him like an electric jolt. "They have their uses. They have their conveniences."

"Is that so?"

"Let me show you." He bent his head and kissed

her neck, embraced the roar of satisfaction that rocked him as she shivered beneath his lips.

"I didn't expect that."

"This will be the only time I surprise you tonight." He kissed a line along her jaw to her chin and from there to her lips. He thought his heart was going to burst, thought he might come on the spot, just from the taste of her, from the feel of her slick tongue sliding against his own.

He could feel her perfect little breasts pressed up against his chest. He was going to taste her again. And suddenly, he couldn't wait. He broke their kiss, lowering his head and tracing the deep V of her cleavage with the tip of his tongue. She'd worked some kind of voodoo magic with this dress, and he wasn't complaining at all.

A rough, hoarse cry escaped Kate's lips and satisfaction rolled over him in a wave.

"Do you know what I like about dresses?" he asked, his voice almost unrecognizable to his own ears. It was broken, rough. Not the voice of a man who was used to casual hookups, not the voice of a man who treated sex like something easy and fun. It was the voice of a man who was desperate, close to shattering.

"They let your man parts breathe?" Kate asked, each word punctuated by a heavy breath.

He let out a laugh. "Try again." He moved his hand down between her thighs, reaching beneath the soft, flowing skirt, tracing the edge of her panties where they met her inner thigh, slowly, teasing them both.

"Oh. Oh!" She gasped sharply as he delved deeper, encountering sweet, slick wetness that let him know just how much she wanted him.

"Easy access," he said, pushing deeper, sliding a finger into her tight passage.

She raised her hands and gripped his shoulders, clinging to him tightly, her fingernails digging into his skin. "Yes, Katie." She clung harder, pain burning through him at the point where she held him. "Leave a mark, baby."

He brushed his thumb over her clit and she leaned forward, pressing her lips to his collarbone before parting them and biting down. The intensity of the sensation sent a white-hot flame burning a trail from his shoulder down to his dick. He'd never been into this kind of thing before, but for some reason, with Kate, everything felt good. More was only better.

"You're so wet for me, Katie," he said, pushing a second finger deep inside of her. "I love that you want me so much."

"I do. Only you." Her words were broken, a sweet sob that soothed wounds deep inside of him.

"I'm the only one that's ever touched you like this," he said, not a question, because he knew. Still, she answered with a nod, her bottom lip clenched tight between her teeth. "The only one who's kissed you. The only one who's been inside of you."

"Yes," she said, breathless.

"You have no idea how fucking hot that is. And it shouldn't be. I should be disgusted with myself for taking advantage of you. But I'm not. Because that first kiss was mine. This is mine," he said, pushing his fingers deeper, sliding his thumb in a circle over her clit.

"I'm glad it was you," she panted.

He withdrew from her body, slid to his knees, shoved her dress up over her hips and wrenched her panties down her thighs. "Spread your legs for me," he said. She complied without argument. "You're much nicer to me when you're naked."

"Well, you're nicer to me when I'm naked, too," she said.

He chuckled, leaning in, inhaling her sweet, musky feminine scent. "Very true. So beautiful." He took a long leisurely taste of her, enjoying everything. Her flavor, the way her body shuddered beneath him, her fingernails going back to his shoulders, digging into his skin.

He tasted her as deeply as he could, relishing the evidence of her arousal, taking each and every cry of pleasure on her lips as his due. His reward. He continued on until she froze, until he felt her climax wash over her, sending his own arousal up another notch until he was so hard it hurt.

He stayed down there on his knees, one hand cupping her ass. "What do you think about dresses now?"

"They are a lot more practical than I imagined," she said, her voice thin, breathy.

Never in all his life had he thought he would say things like this to Kate Garrett. Never once had he imagined he would hear her familiar voice sounding out her climax, hear her speak to him in the aftermath of her pleasure.

He'd never imagined it, but now he wondered how he'd ever lived without it.

"Stand up," she said, her voice stronger now.

"You think you're giving orders now?"

"Stand up. And show me your—" she swallowed "—cock."

He wasn't about to say no to an order like that. He

rose to his feet, carefully removed his underwear and kicked them to the side. They would be full of hay and dirt just like his pants and he honestly didn't care.

"It's my turn," she said, her eyes locked with his.

She reached out, wrapping her hand around his dick. His breath hissed through his teeth, fire lashing over him, so hot, so destructive he was sure it would consume him.

"I didn't get to touch you last time. Not like this." She squeezed him, her expression full of wonder. Wonder he sure as hell didn't deserve. But wonder he was most definitely going to take. "You're so hard. Big."

That kind of thing shouldn't turn him on. But it did. Normally, that was just a line. Thrown out to boost a guy's ego. But Kate meant it. That did things to him, touched things that went a whole lot deeper than ego.

She lowered herself slowly down in front of him and he had the suspicion that somewhere along the way, between when he had stood up and she had begun to kneel down, they had traded experience. Because he was the one shaking now; he was the one left in wonder of what might happen next.

Then right in front of him, his darkest, dirtiest fantasy, the one he had indulged in at his best friend's wedding, began to play out in front of him. He raised his hand, cupped her face, slid his fingers back through her hair. He didn't want to guide her actions, didn't want to direct her. Kate was the fantasy. It wasn't about a woman going down on him and giving him pleasure. That was generic. Nice under some circumstances, certainly, but generic. He wanted to know how Kate would do it.

She parted her lips slowly, then flicked out the tip

of her tongue and tasted him. Instinctively, he tightened his fist in her hair, pulling up as she went down. She looked up at him, a smile curving her lips. And he knew right then and there he would never be able to pull on Kate Garrett's hair in that playful way he'd done for years without remembering this moment.

It didn't seem fair that a few stolen moments could obliterate years' worth of history, but he had a feeling it could. Could and had. Or maybe *obliterate* was the wrong word. Maybe it was more like mixing two handfuls of sand. One that represented their past and one for this.

Put them both together in a jar, and you would never be able to separate the two again. They would be mixed forever.

Though right at this moment, with Kate's tongue sliding over his length, he couldn't imagine why he would want to. He closed his eyes, trying to shut out everything but the way she felt. His knees nearly buckled when she opened her mouth and took him in as deep as she could. It wasn't all that deep, her movements hesitant. He could tell this was her first time doing this.

Why did that make it hotter? Why the hell did that make it sexier than anything else he'd ever experienced?

It was Kate. And she was doing it all for him. Well, for her, too.

And that was the answer to his question.

She reached up, taking hold of the base of his shaft, squeezing him tight while she kept working her own strange kind of magic with her lips and tongue.

His thigh muscles were shaking, the joints in his

knees turned to liquid. He was having trouble standing. Having trouble hanging on to his control.

He opened his eyes and looked down, his eyes meeting Kate's. It was as if all the air had been pulled from his body, and along with it every bit of restraint.

"Stop," he rasped, the word weak and ragged.

She moved away from him, the color high in her cheeks, her expression full of confusion.

"I have you again," he said. "We're not finishing like this."

"Do you have a...condom?"

Shame lashed him with the force of a whip. Because he did and he was far too aware of why.

"Yes."

Thankfully, she didn't question it. He abandoned her for a moment, going after his pants, his wallet and the condom he'd placed inside just this morning.

He looked back at the barn door, which he had closed behind them, a bit of unease gripping his throat. Guilt. *Because you should feel guilty, you prick.*

He did feel guilty. About a few things. But not guilty enough to stop.

He strode back across the empty space to Kate. He grabbed hold of her waist and propelled them both deeper into the back of the barn, beneath the hayloft, behind the ladder. "Give us a little warning in case we get interrupted," he said, then kissed her deeply.

Her eyes widened. "We won't, will we?"

"We don't have to do this."

She grabbed hold of his shoulders and tucked him toward her, moving them both backward until she was up against the barn wall. "Yes. Yes, we do."

She kissed him again and he just let himself get lost in it.

He tore the condom open without breaking the kiss and used one hand to roll it over his cock before shifting their positions. He put one hand on her side, pulling her leg up over his hip, opening her to him, while he held tightly to her with the other arm, bracing her against him, trying to shield her from the rough wood as best he could while he pushed in deep.

White spots exploded behind his eyelids, pleasure so acute it was almost pain as her tight, wet heat surrounded him. His mind was blank. Of any previous experience, any other women, anything else but what it was like to be inside her.

He forced himself to open his eyes, to meet her gaze, to watch her face so that he could be certain he was doing it right. He had no other way of knowing. He was lost at sea right now, any and all skill he might have claimed to possess completely forgotten in the moment.

He flexed his hips and coaxed a small sound of pleasure from her. He repeated the motion, his movements growing more frantic with each and every thrust. He did his best to keep his focus on her, on her responses, on her pleasure. Because if he didn't, if he let go, he was going to lose it before she did.

He couldn't remember the last time he'd done that. But experience didn't matter. Whoever had come before didn't matter. They weren't Kate. This was Kate.

So he had to hold on. Had to hold on until she let go.

He moved one hand to her breast, sliding his thumb over her nipple as he bent his head to kiss her neck. Both actions made her moan with pleasure, sending a kick of satisfied desire through him. "Is that good, Kate?"

He felt her nod, her hold on him tightening as he moved deeper, harder inside of her, pinching her nipple lightly between his thumb and forefinger as he did. "Good?" he asked again.

Again, he got a silent nod.

"Say it. Tell me it's good," he said, repeating the action.

"Yes. Yes, it's good." The words sounded torn from her.

And before he could stop them, stereotypical, asinine words he'd never uttered in his life spilled out of his mouth. "Say my name when you tell me it's good," he said, an edge of desperation there that he couldn't fathom.

And she complied without hesitation. "Jack. It's good, Jack."

He lost it then, pressing her firmly against the barn wall, any rhythm, any finesse to his movements, gone completely. "Kate," he ground out, "come for me."

He was begging now, because he didn't have it in him to hold back. Not anymore.

And with her name on his lips, she gave it all up to her release, her internal muscles tightening around his cock. His mind went blank, his world reduced to the slick hot feel of her, the sensation of her pleasure around him. Her soft skin beneath his fingertips, her breath in his ear. If there was anything else in the entire world, he didn't know about it, and he didn't care about it.

His climax seized him like a wild animal, tearing at him, threatening to consume him. And he let it.

CHAPTER FOURTEEN

As THE FOG of pleasure receded, Kate couldn't help but wonder if she would be wearing the evidence of this encounter on her skin for the next few months. It had all been fine and dandy during the main event, but now she was afraid she had splinters the size of tenpenny nails driven deep into her back. And she was feeling it.

Of course, she supposed that could be a metaphor for every sexual encounter she'd had with Jack.

It seemed like a good idea at the time…

She winced as she pushed away from the wall, watching Jack dress slowly, the contraception discarded somewhat haphazardly in a little hole he'd made in the dirt floor. She felt as if she'd been scrubbed down with poison oak, the burning and itching on her skin getting worse with each passing moment. And along with that was a growing sense of dread. Because she knew that any moment now Jack was going to turn to her and tell her what a giant mistake they had made.

Though that was probably a bit confrontational for him. Maybe he would just take off again. Flee into the night and leave her naked in the barn by herself.

He pulled his shirt over his head and straightened, looking at her and frowning.

Here it came…

"Why are you looking at me like you want to stab me clean through with a pitchfork?" he asked.

"I'm not," she sniffed, turning to the side to see if she could find her panties, doing her best to right her dress.

"Holy shit," he said.

"What?"

"Your back."

She reached around and touched her shoulder blade, wincing when she came into contact with a splinter. "Yeah."

"You should have said something."

She let out an exasperated breath. No real surprise—he was trying to tell her what to do. "I was too focused on getting what I wanted. I wasn't really bothered by it."

"But you are now."

"If you try and use this as a teachable moment regarding the heat of the moment and certain consequences, I'm going to knee you in the balls."

His dark brows shot upward. "I need those. If you want to keep enjoying what we just did."

"What do you mean, keep enjoying?"

"We tried ignoring it. We tried going back to normal. It didn't work. From where I'm standing, that wasn't enough to take care of it."

She squinted. "By *take care of it* you mean…"

"It wasn't enough."

Her throat ached. "You really want me, Jack? I mean, you *want* me?"

He let out a long, slow breath. "Do you have to ask? After all of that, you have to ask? I can't control myself around you."

"What changed?"

He just stared at her like he'd been hit in the back of the head with a two-by-four. "I think you did."

The words made her stomach flip, a strange, uncomfortable tightening working its way from there up her throat. "I haven't changed." It was a reflexive response, a funny one considering this had been about moving forward. About making sure she wasn't left behind. Really, it was about changing. But she'd been thinking more of changing her position in life, not herself.

"It's not a bad thing."

"I think maybe you changed. Because it used to be that I looked at you and saw a guy who was basically another brother. Who was great and funny and made me mad and made me laugh. But then…then my skin started feeling too tight when you were around. And you made my scalp prickle and my heart beat too fast."

"You have a crush on me," he said, his lips curving into a wicked smile.

"I don't… That's not… You make it sound juvenile."

"You were mean to me because you liked me. That's juvenile."

She shoved his shoulder. "Making fun of me for it isn't any better."

"I never said I wasn't juvenile. Completely childish. Like I said, I'm not the one who changed."

"How did I change?"

He looked down at her cleavage pointedly. "Well, other than the obvious."

She put her hand over her uncharacteristically exposed bosom. "Yes. Besides that. You aren't that simple. You can have whatever boobs you want—you don't need mine. Particularly since mine are aggressively average."

"I'm going to have to stop you so that I can correct you. There is nothing average about your rack."

"It's not that big."

"Quality, honey. Not quantity."

Humor tugged at the corners of her mouth. "You are naughty."

"And you like it."

"I do. And it surprises me a little."

"It surprises you, Kate Garrett? I've seen you leer at passing men with all the subtlety of a construction worker."

"Looking and touching are two very different things," she said.

What struck her most about this exchange between Jack and herself was that it was easy. Easier than quite a few of the interactions they'd had since attraction had combusted between them. At least, it was easy now that she didn't feel so much like he was trying to protect her without actually listening to her.

"They definitely are," he said, looking his fill.

"Okay, calm down."

"You know what else changed?"

She blinked. "No. You have to tell me."

"You have been Connor and Eli's younger sister since the moment I met you."

She snorted. "Of course I have been."

"No. That's not what I meant. That's the number one thing you've been to me. They cared about you, so I cared about you. Because they are like family to me. And because of that, so were you. But I don't know…

Every year, you seem to become more you to me. Not Connor and Eli's sister. Kate. And what I want, and what we do, doesn't have anything to do with them."

"You don't care what they think?"

"I wouldn't go that far. But I'm not going to make decisions based on that. I know that if they found out, there would be hell to pay, and that's one bill collector I'd like to dodge for as long as possible. And seeing as this isn't ever going to turn into anything beyond the physical, I don't see why they have to know."

"No. I wouldn't tell them no matter who it was. I'm not looking for marriage or even a long-term relationship. My brothers don't need to know about my sex life. Also, I don't want you to die."

"Yeah, they would kill me." His eyes held a glimmer of humor.

"So we should keep doing this."

"Until we don't want to."

"Simple," she said.

It was difficult to fight the feeling of smugness that built up inside of her. She was a late bloomer, there was no disputing that, but here she was handling a physical-only relationship like a pro.

"We can keep working on the charity event. I can help you with your riding. And when we feel like it, we can take some very rewarding breaks."

"I like the sound of that."

"Right now we better go back."

She cleared her throat, nodding. There really was no excuse for missing more of her brother's wedding reception. But she didn't really want to go back to reality. Didn't want to stand in a crowd of people and pretend that things were as they'd always been with

Jack and herself. Not when things had changed on such a deep level.

She wanted to go into the woods alone, spend some time in the quiet turning over her newest treasure, studying it, holding it close to her chest.

Too bad that wasn't an option.

She started to walk toward the door and Jack swore harshly. "Your back."

She added a matching swear word to his. "What are we going to do about that? I must look like I got into a fight with a porcupine."

"Yes. If that porcupine was a barn wall you got banged against. It looks like exactly what it is."

"Okay. We walk back. I'm going to hang around outside the edges of the reception. You give me your jacket. You left it back at the reception, right?"

"Yes."

"Okay. I'll pretend to be cold. You pretend to be a gentleman."

Jack laughed, smiling, his whole face lighting up. And Kate's heart lit up right along with it. "I'll try."

JACK SLIPPED HIS JACKET from the back of the chair sitting at the table that was designated for the bridal party and walked back out of the new barn to where Kate was standing on the outskirts of the celebration. "Here you go, badger-cat. So you don't get chilly."

She began to reach for the jacket but he stepped to the side, sliding the sleeve over her arm, drawing it around behind her and doing the same on the other side. "So." She gave him a sweet, shy look that burned straight down to his gut. Now that the guilt had been washed away by that last encounter, it was just lust.

Simple, not pure at all. "You're just going to call me badger-cat now because I'm not on your ass about calling me Katie?"

"I miss being yelled at," he said.

"I can yell at you."

He looked over his shoulder and saw that no one was nearby. He leaned in, his lips touching her ear. "I could make you scream again."

Kate looked at him, a self-satisfied smile on her lips. It made him feel warm all over. "Probably not tonight."

"I could."

"It wasn't doubt about your ability. It's just… It's Eli's wedding. And I need to stay. And you need to never have your truck parked out in front of my place overnight. And I won't be able to leave inconspicuously."

"Why don't you come to my place after work tomorrow. Hitch up your trailer and bring Roo. You can do a run on some barrels there. We'll do a little planning for the charity day. And I'm sure we'll find some free time in there." He listened to himself constructing a careful alibi for the express purpose of getting her naked again and keeping it secret. And he felt more than a little bit like a dick. But he wanted it. She wanted it. So he wasn't going to waste too much time worrying about it.

"Sounds good."

"We'd better get back," he said, stepping away from her, putting a careful distance between them.

She nodded and started to walk ahead of him, the sleeves on his coat hanging down to the tips of her fingers, the bottom hitting just above the hem of her dress. His gaze was linked to her, almost as if it was chained there. And the sight of her, petite but strong, covered by something of his, tightened that chain around his throat until he could barely breathe.

They walked back into the barn, the heated barn, which made it a little silly for Kate to be wearing the jacket, but it was a whole lot less silly than her displaying her war wounds to the roomful of people. He felt bad about that. Bad but also perversely satisfied that he'd marked her somehow.

Because dammit, she'd done something to him.

Sex for him was easy. A quick road to satisfaction. And it had never much mattered to him who it was with. He liked his partners, but he didn't need them. He needed Kate. Had woken up every night since she'd kissed him aching, with a hard-on that wouldn't quit. And fantasies that would only take the shape of her.

He would have been pissed about it if it didn't feel so good. He had no clue how the hell this woman had taken on this new form. To slip beneath his bedcovers, to slip beneath his skin.

It was the slow shift. Because he'd never put distance between himself and Kate, had never believed he might need to. So he'd had no defenses in place when she moved in for that kiss.

When she'd been all covered up in dirt and clothes and a scowl, she'd been Connor and Eli's little sister. But now that she'd smiled at him, kissed him, stripped for him, he'd seen the whole woman. And then it hadn't mattered anymore. Who she was related to, what they might think. She mattered. On her own. She was every inch herself. All strength, dreams and meanness when she got poked too many times. In bed she was fire. Unschooled, uncontained.

Now in his mind she stood alone, not attached to anyone else. She wasn't just a woman; she was a whole storm. Too much to be simply someone's sister.

It was a damn shame that he couldn't reach out and uncover all that again. That he had to stand here and pretend she was just Eli and Connor's sister when the secret was out and he knew different.

Kate stepped deeper into the barn, getting caught up in a group that contained some of the people from the amateur association. He held back, in part because he wanted to be near Sierra West like he wanted a screwdriver to the scrotum, and in part because he didn't want to stand near Kate and pretend.

Not right now.

Not while it was all still raw. Not while his blood was still hot and he could still feel her on his skin.

"Now it's just you." Jack jumped and turned as Connor clapped a hand on his shoulder. "Well, and Kate."

Discomfort wound its way through him. "Uh... what?"

"You're still single. You're the last holdout. Kate isn't really a holdout yet. She's just a kid."

Jack bristled. "She's not really a kid."

"She damn well is. And that's good, as far as I'm concerned. Better to be young when you're young and...whatever."

"Are you drunk?" Besides the occasional beer, Connor had given up drinking a little over a year ago.

"No. Just thinking. I want you to find someone."

Jack nearly choked. "Uh. Thanks. I'm fine. With-out."

"You think you are, but come on, all the whoring around has to get old."

A sweet, illicit memory of recent "whoring" flashed through his mind. Made instantly ten times more awkward by the fact that he was standing in front of his partner's brother. "No. It really doesn't. I know that was never what you were into. I respect that. But... I don't want marriage and babies and domesticity. It's not me."

"Yeah." Connor's gaze drifted off and Jack followed his friend's line of sight. To Kate.

"She was cold," Jack said, knowing he sounded defensive. But she was standing there in a jacket, and he was without one, so he felt as though he had to throw in an explanation.

"You've always helped take care of her," Connor said. "I appreciate that. I was always busy on the ranch, and Eli had to pick up all the house and Kate slack. Sometimes I think I should have done more."

"Oh, hell, Connor. When? You were a kid and you were running a ranching operation while your dad soaked his liver in booze." Jack looked away from Kate and back to his friend.

"Still. I worry about her. A hell of a lot more than I worry about you."

"She's tough," Jack said, his throat getting tight, his heart suddenly too large for his chest.

"She is. But she reminds me of a spooked horse. They're scary. Tough. Could mess you the hell up. But they're afraid. Afraid to let you touch them."

"Because not every horse needs to be broken," he

said, feeling as if the analogy, which was bad to start with, had broken down completely.

"She's pretty amazing when she's wild."

Another image. Kate with her head thrown back while he thrust deep inside her tight little body…

"She sure is," Jack said, knowing that if he hadn't been hell bound before, he was now.

"But I don't want her to be alone. I don't want to think we messed up so bad she couldn't…have this," he said, indicating the decorations, the event around them.

"Maybe she doesn't need this. Maybe she just needs barrels and some dirt. That's happiness, too."

Connor let out a long sigh. "I suppose. I think sometimes you see her a little bit more clearly than any of us. You were always able to cheer her up when she was a kid."

Jack waited for the guilt, but he didn't feel any. Yeah. His conscience was seared like flesh stuck in a fire. To the point where he didn't feel a damned thing.

Hell. He was going to hell.

"But you gave her stability," Jack said, making a belated and weak attempt at atonement. "And she should believe in love and commitment, because you and Eli gave her that. You gave it all up for her. I just came by and made jokes when shit was tough. There's a difference. You both stayed. And you're still here. If she doesn't end up with anyone, it'll be because she chose it, not because you did anything wrong."

As far as inspiring speeches went, it wasn't bad. It also wasn't his to make. Because he had a feeling if things went south with Kate at any point after this, it would be his fault. That if she didn't end up with a guy, it would be his fault.

Ten-gallon ego you got there, Monaghan.

Yeah. But it was because she'd been a virgin. Because he was the first. If he fucked up, then he would pave a bad road for the bastard who came after him.

A small evil part of him was satisfied by that thought. He wanted things to be hard for the bastard who came after him. He wanted to kill the bastard who came after him and he didn't care whether that was fair or whether or not it made sense.

If he didn't want forever, he couldn't fault everyone who would come once they were over.

But he did.

Because her kisses were for him. Her body was for him.

If she could get a look at his thoughts right now, she would tie him to the train tracks, but he didn't care.

Connor was looking at him funny. "Why are you single?"

"What the hell, man?"

"I mean, that was a good speech. If I was half that good at making speeches, Liss would want me dead a lot less often."

"I'm single because I'm good in small doses. Like I just said. I'm not the guy who stays." He let out a long breath and his gaze drifted over to where Eli and Sadie were just leaving the dance floor. "Speaking of, I think the couple is about to leave."

"Well, then, let's go send them off."

CHAPTER FIFTEEN

KATE DIDN'T WASTE any time getting Roo into the trailer after work. She'd hooked it up to the truck before leaving, and now she was ready to spend the afternoon with Jack.

Practicing her barrel racing, specifically. And also planning the charity event.

Okay, and the sex.

She had spent only a little bit of extra time laboring over her underwear selection. Black. Black cotton was the sexiest she had. She needed to remedy that. Practical underwear took on a whole new meaning when their primary objective wasn't simply not riding up your ass crack. Seduction added a new dimension to panty requirements.

And since seduction panties looked as if they would do just that, she was thinking she'd need seduction panties and everyday panties.

Being a woman was exhausting. She bet Jack was just going to stick with the one kind of underwear.

Her internal muscles clenched unexpectedly as she thought of just how he filled out said underwear.

She blinked and revved the engine on the truck, pulling forward to the long driveway. Her old truck bounced and groaned over the potholes until she turned out onto the two-lane highway. It still groaned as it rolled over the asphalt, but it bounced less.

Sex was a whole thing, she was discovering. She hadn't given it a whole lot of thought before she'd had it, and now she seemed to ponder it a lot. Along with underwear.

She'd known sex would change things between herself and Jack—she wasn't an idiot, even if she was innocent—but she hadn't realized sex would change so much of what she thought about.

That it would change the context of simple things like underwear.

She turned left off the highway and onto Jack's property. A wooden frame arched up over the road, an iron sign hanging down that read Monaghan Ranch.

Every time she came here, she was in awe all over again. About what he'd accomplished with his life. About how far he'd come.

So far from his days in a single-wide buried in the brush by the sea. She'd been to his house only once, and she'd waited in the car on Eli's orders.

She'd been little, but she remembered. She'd rolled down the windows and taken a good look at the little yellow mobile. Stained by salt, moss climbing the side, a product of the eternal dampness.

The smell of cigarettes had soaked through the walls, pushing on to the driveway, combatting the brine-and-seaweed scent that lay heavy in the air.

Bleak, washed out, so unlike the young man she knew. It had made her wonder where Jack got all his humor. Because he certainly hadn't collected it on the dirty, bramble-covered beach near his house.

This ranch, the place he had built for himself, was

much more in keeping with who he was. A little bit over the top, a little bit showy, but functional, and pure country. She drove past the house, headed toward the arena. Jack was already there, facing away from her, his arms spread wide, hands rested on the top rail of the fence. She took a moment to admire that broad chest, narrow waist and very, very fine ass.

An ass she had touched.

She couldn't hold back the smug smile that pulled at the edges of her mouth.

She put the truck in Park, killed the engine and took the keys out of the ignition, hesitating for a second before opening the door and climbing out. "Hey," she said, walking over to where he stood.

He turned, a blue flame flickering in his eyes for a moment. "Hey."

For a moment she wasn't sure what to do. Her instinct was to launch herself at him and kiss him, but she wasn't sure if that would be okay. She wasn't really sure what the protocol was for a temporary sexual arrangement with your brothers' best friend. And then she figured she didn't really care. Because this was only temporary. And anyway, she and Jack had already waded through a whole swamp of awkward. If emphatic greetings weren't acceptable they would talk about it. And it couldn't possibly be more of a minefield than previous discussions.

She picked up her pace and closed the distance between them, wrapping her arms around his neck and stretching up on her tiptoes, kissing him as deep and long as she wanted. Jack put his hands on her hips and held her steady while she explored his mouth. The slow glide of his tongue against hers, the warm firmness of his lips. She slipped her hand from around his neck, sliding her fingertips across his jaw, his stubble rough beneath her fingertips.

She pulled away, rubbing her nose against his, following some instinct she hadn't known she'd possessed. "You remind me of a sexy outlaw," she said, then kissed him quickly again.

He arched a dark brow. "An outlaw?"

That question knocked a bit of the shine off that perfect moment of clarity and confidence she'd just experienced. For a while she had been convinced that there was nothing she could do wrong. Now she was questioning that. She was a novice, after all. A novice who still possessed nothing more than cotton panties of the most demure variety.

"Yeah," she said, her tone less certain now. "Because…kind of…dark and dangerous. And…"

He cupped the back of her head and pulled her in for a hard kiss. "Dangerous?"

"Stop making me feel silly."

"You shouldn't feel silly. I like hearing what you think about me. It's a lot better than having you snipe at me."

She pulled away from him, snorting. "I do not snipe."

That earned her a smack on the butt. She yelped and rubbed the spot he'd just made contact with. It didn't hurt. If anything, she liked it. "You snipe."

"If I do, you deserve it."

"Honestly, I like talking to you rather than just circling you. I feel like that's what we've been doing for a while."

Kate took hold of her own hand and started picking at the dirt beneath her thumbnail. "Maybe. But it was pretty off-putting to realize I wanted to kiss you more than I wanted to punch you."

"Out of curiosity, when did you realize that?"

She dug deeper beneath her nail, putting most of her focus and energy onto that task. "I don't know if I fully realized it until after."

"After we kissed?"

"After we had sex." She cleared her throat. "Before that, I was still on the fence about whether or not kissing would be more satisfying than punching."

A strange smile turned up the corners of his mouth. "But sex officially tipped you over."

She dug harder at her thumbnail, then realized she was standing there picking dirt out from under her nails in front of her lover. Reflexively, she grimaced and put her hands down at her sides. Her lover. Jack was her lover. Having a lover was weird enough; having it be Jack was weirder still. Or maybe not. She couldn't actually imagine assigning that label to anyone else.

"Well, you presented a convincing argument."

"Did I?"

"Yeah. Your um…body made a very convincing argument."

"Stands to reason. My dick did very well on the debate team in high school."

"Debate? I would have thought that PE was more your dick's forte."

"Possibly. Though my member is very convincing. Even without words."

This was weird, talking about more intimate things in a tone they would have used prior to actually having experienced anything intimate together. A strange mixture of old and new.

"Well, as difficult as it is to believe, Monaghan, I did not come here to discuss your penis, or the virtues thereof. I came here to ride."

"That begs the question if we're still on the subject of my manhood, or you actually brought a horse in the trailer."

"I brought a horse. And if you don't behave yourself when I'm done riding Roo, I might not *ride* you."

"I don't believe that, baby."

Kate's heart fluttered and she rolled her eyes, mainly at herself, but she was content to let Jack believe that the expression was directed at him.

"Your ego is stunning."

"It is, isn't it? I'm glad you notice, because I just got it resized."

"Did you?"

"Yes, it's gone up about three sizes ever since Ms. Kate Garrett decided it was better to kiss me than punch me."

How did he do that? It was a stupid thing to say. Arrogant and obnoxious. And yet somehow it made her feel all warm inside.

"Well, Kate Garrett giveth, and Kate Garrett taketh away. I'm expecting you to coach me through a few runs on the course first. Otherwise, I will have to leave you with nothing but a shrunken ego."

"Shrinkage is never good. Get your pony out, and let's do this."

She shot him a deadly look before turning, heading back toward the trailer and opening it up. She readied Roo and led her out, the horse's hooves clopping on the ramp that went down to the gravel, where the sound changed to a muted crunch. Kate brought her to the arena and looped the lead rope over the fence before opening up the side of the trailer and setting out to get her tack ready.

"Roo is not a pony, just so you know."

"Thoroughbred. I know. I was being an ass."

"You *should* know, Mr. Rodeo. I'm counting on the fact that you have actual expertise to help me through all of this."

"I do, I promise you. Not just from the rodeo." He hesitated and she looked at him. He reached back and rubbed his hand over the back of his neck. "You know, the breeding operation is going really well."

She was tempted to say something in the same smart-ass vein as he just had. To banter back. But somehow she sensed it wasn't the time. He was looking for something.

Approval. Her approval.

Which was strange, because she had never thought of Jack as needing approval from anyone, least of all her. And yet it was there in his voice. She couldn't deny it. And she wouldn't deny him.

She offered him a smile, continuing her work on Roo. "This whole place is amazing." She turned her focus back to Roo's tack. "And I've never liked all this talk about luck where you're concerned. I've never seen anyone work as hard as you and change their position in life so drastically."

He shrugged, a halfhearted laugh on his lips. "I only moved about five miles down the road. Not sure that counts as changing position."

"You did," she said, thinking about that washed-out trailer again.

"I think you're the only one who sees it that way."

"Well, everyone else is an idiot. I'm pretty confident in that assessment."

"One of the many things I like about you."

Kate tightened the girth on Roo's saddle and straightened. "Okay, I'm riding right now. So I guess you just stand there and yell at me if I do a bad job?"

"Yeah, I can handle that."

Kate mounted Roo and rode her over to the open gate, staring down the course with determination. She remembered the last ride. The one that Jack had walked away from. The one she'd never seen the time for, because her timekeeper had taken off after the angry kiss.

She had been thinking of *him* during that ride. Not about success, not about failure, but about Jack.

Of course, thinking about Jack was as natural as breathing.

She took a deep breath, made her mind a blank space until she saw nothing but the barrels in front of her.

And then she went.

Her movements blended with Roo's body, adjusting to the rhythm. It felt easy to slide into it, to follow the leads of Roo's movements. And she felt that in turn Roo followed hers.

Kind of like kissing. She hadn't known what she was doing, but paying attention to the subtle way Jack moved his lips, flicked his tongue, had made following along intuitive.

This was similar in a way. Required an awareness

of her whole body so that she could sense subtle shifts and respond with perfect control.

Memory blended with the present, memory of what it had been like to be pressed up against Jack only a few moments ago, her muscles languid as she let arousal roll over her. Every touch, every taste, every shift of his hands working together.

And before she knew it, she had rounded the last barrel. Nothing was knocked over, and nothing felt slow.

"Holy shit!" She didn't bother to hold back the exclamation. "It was good."

"Yeah, it was," Jack said, smiling. He was holding a stopwatch that he hadn't shown her before, and he looked at the time. "Damn good, Katie."

"One more?"

He nodded. "Do one more, and then we'll get on with this charity stuff."

And get on with the rest of their afternoon together.

He left the rest of it unspoken, but she heard it all the same.

The second run was as successful as the first, and Kate was on a high by the time they sat down in Jack's living room with the details of the charity rodeo day spread out in front of them.

Kate picked up one of the spreadsheets, reading the extensive list of business names. "I can't believe you got all these vendors confirmed."

Jack leaned back on the couch, his hands behind his head, displaying his extremely tantalizing biceps, thanks to his very tight black T-shirt. Another thing about sex. It made her think of words like *tantalizing*. Usually words like that were reserved only for pie.

"Lydia had a hand in it—I can't take all the credit. Plus, Eileen has been on top of things. And Ace is overly generous. When Ace gets involved with something, the other business owners tend to follow. Plus, the guy is always willing to donate beer, and that is about the most valuable thing I can think of."

They were both sitting on the couch, with about a foot of space between them, trying to keep focus on the task at hand. Kate wanted to close the space and press her body against his. Just so she could touch him. Though like the "kiss or not to kiss?" dilemma from earlier, that wasn't strictly sex, either.

The spreadsheets for the charity event were working so well she was considering suggesting making a spreadsheet of the particulars of their arrangement. An arrangement was all it was, really. It wasn't a relationship, that much was certain.

Which meant she was going to go ahead and speak the words that were rolling around in her head, making her tongue restless. Because before they'd started doing *stuff* together, she would have spoken them.

She looked up at him. "If you didn't minimize your contributions to everything, maybe people wouldn't think all of your achievements were dumb luck." As soon as she spoke the words, she realized how accurately they described Jack.

He was quick to extol the virtues of Connor and Eli, to remind her of everything they had done for her, and yet he never brought up all the ways he'd been there. In fact, when she tried, he often changed the subject.

And now he wouldn't even accept a compliment for the event that he had inspired.

He shrugged, leaning forward, the casual gesture

exposed for the lie it was by the tension in his jaw. "I'm being honest. I'm not the kind of guy who has to trumpet his own achievements. I know a lot of people assume I am, but I'm not."

It hit her then what a funny mix of things Jack was. He had an easy kind of cockiness, and only moments ago she had accused him of having a massive ego. But when it came to important things, he was quick to shift the credit.

In contrast, he never shifted blame.

He was quick to call himself a bastard or a jackass or any other derogatory name, all while laughing it off. She wasn't quite sure why.

"Jack, it's more than that," she said, her tone grave.

He raised his brows. "Listen to you, missy. Pulling rank now like you gained a decade on me instead of being one down. Why? Just because we've…"

"Shut up," she said. "I'm serious. If you're going to be an ass just because I stepped into some thorny business, then shut the hell up right now. I'm not in the mood to listen and separate out what you said just because I scared you and decide what should offend me."

"Scared?" he asked, his tone incredulous.

"Yes. Scared. You know how I know it's scared?" She didn't wait for him to answer. "Every time I took a shot at you, it was because I was scared. Of what you made me want. Of what you made me feel. I was so scared I shoved it down deep enough that I couldn't recognize what it was. So scared I never let myself think the word *want*. But it didn't change the fact that I felt it. And you know what? It's better this way. Brought up to the top and dealt with. Naked and…

and...and raw and real. It's better than pretending it isn't there."

He was silent for a moment. Then he leaned back, his gaze assessing. Dark. "But in your scenario you got sex instead of sexual frustration. What will I get?"

She gnawed on the inside of her lip. "Release? From...issues?"

He snorted and shook his head. "Right. Because you're so into talking about your feelings?"

She frowned. "What do I need to talk about my feelings for? I'm fine."

"So am I," he said.

She rolled her eyes. "We just had a discussion about the not fine."

"You had a discussion. You drew conclusions. All on your own. I think it's bullshit."

She stared him down, that familiar feeling of uncontrollable determination gripping her, anchoring itself deep in her gut. When she had that feeling, backing down wasn't an option. Ever. Sometimes it got her in trouble.

It had earned her a scar on her shoulder blade when John Norton had dared her to walk the top of a fence like a tightrope back in second grade. And right now who knew what it would get her. But in the moment the consequences never mattered. Only the win.

"Jack..."

He looked back down at the papers in front of him, pen in hand, discussion clearly closed.

Her anger reached its peak, and there was no one left to help Jack Monaghan now except for God. And she doubted Jack would ever even ask *him* for help.

Jack would never ask. And he was apparently done listening.

Fuck. That.

She gripped the hem of her T-shirt and stripped it up over her head, that bullheaded determination steering the ship now. And now that it was, there would be hell to pay.

It just remained to be seen whether hell would bill Jack or her.

She reached back and unhooked her bra, then let it fall to the floor with a soft thump. That garnered Jack's focus.

His blue eyes connected with hers, then lowered, heat flaring bright and hot in their depths. For a moment she lost the thread of her intentions completely. She could only stand there and bask in her newfound power.

She'd always been strong. Hell, she'd been able to beat up every boy in her class before they started growing body hair. She was tough, and no one had ever questioned that. She hadn't, either.

But this power? This was new. This was different.

Her body had the power to turn some kind of tide inside the infamous Jack Monaghan. To take him from anger, to take him from purposefully ignoring her to looking at her with the kind of keen focus she'd never seen him train on anything.

She'd known there was power in strength. In a closed fist and a quick tongue. In the ability to ride faster than the boys, fix the fence with better skill. But she hadn't realized how much power there was in her body. In its softness, its innate being. No walls up, no clothes on. No front of bravado or show of toughness.

She'd already realized that she'd discovered a hidden layer of Jack, a deeper level of who he was. In this moment she realized she'd found the same in herself.

She took a step toward him and pressed her knee down beside his thigh on the couch before following suit with the other, sitting on his lap, facing him. "Is that paper still more interesting than what I have to say?"

His eyes flickered downward. "No. But now you have the issue of what you have to say not being quite as interesting as how you look."

Completely against her will, a smile tugged at the corners of her lips. "I've heard women complain about that, but I don't think I've ever had that problem. It's certainly an interesting one."

"I'm being offensive. At least have the decency to get mad at me." He reached up and cupped one of her breasts as he spoke, teasing her nipple with his thumb.

"Can't," she said, her voice thin now, breathless. "It's impossible to be mad at you when you do that."

"That's interesting," he said, flashing a wicked smile at her. "Makes a man want to try."

He wrapped his arm around her, planting his palm between her shoulder blades, holding her steady as he let his other hand drift down to her stomach, all the way down to the waistband of her jeans.

"Somehow I don't think you're trying to make me mad."

"No. But I might be trying to change the subject." He flicked the button on her jeans open and drew the zipper down slowly.

"And I might allow it. For now." She had achieved one portion of the victory she'd been aiming for. She hadn't allowed him to push her away. So she would stick a little flag in that and claim it as a triumph for Kate Garrett.

It was either that or she was weak.

She didn't really care which it was at the moment.

He slipped his hand down between the fabric and her skin, his fingertips teasing the edge of her underwear. His expression changed, the mischief, the wickedness gone, replaced by that intense focus he'd treated her to earlier. As all-consuming as the things he made her feel were, as intense and wonderful as it was when he dipped his fingers beneath the fabric of her panties, gliding through her slick folds. Watching the intensity on his face as he set about the task was almost more compelling. Almost.

His touch set her on fire, created a deep, restless ache, the impression of a spark that was about to burst into flame.

She touched his stomach, hot and unbelievably hard, pushing the hem of his shirt up before pulling it resolutely over his head. It forced his hands away from her body, but it was a small price to pay to earn the pleasure of seeing him.

Of giving herself another chance to look at him and really feel what it did to her. Rather than trying to push it down, rather than getting angry, rather than acting disgusted. She had spent so long pretending because she hadn't been able to deal with what it meant. That gnawing, beastly ache in her stomach that seemed to appear whenever Jack was around. It grew more intense when he lifted something heavy or stripped down to nothing more than his jeans.

She remembered, vividly, when he'd done that during the rebuilding of Connor's barn. The show she'd put on about being irritated that he was showing off.

No wonder Liss had figured it out. With hindsight, with less innocence, Kate could see her own excuses for the paper-thin constructs they were.

"You've gone very still," Jack said. "Either there's a rabid wolverine behind my head about to attack, or you're thinking."

"Wolverine. Stay perfectly still if you value all of your body parts." He went still beneath her hands, his muscles tensing. She leaned in, kissing his neck, angling her head and biting his ear.

"I'd say I have to worry more about the badger-cat than the wolverine," he said, his voice rough.

"It's true. I am fearsome." She pressed her mouth to his, then nipped his lower lip.

She reached between them, making quick work of his belt, opening his jeans, then pulling his underwear down to reveal the package beneath. He shifted, raising his hips and reaching behind him, digging in his back pocket until he produced his wallet. "Very important," he said as he opened it and fished out a condom.

"Very."

He took care of the necessities, his jeans only partway down his hips still since she hadn't ceded her position on his lap. "Katie. I'm desperate." He sounded it. And she would have been lying if she said she didn't like that.

She stood, getting rid of the rest of her clothes before moving back to him, over him. She waited for nerves, for uncertainty. She'd never done this before, and it was putting a lot of the control into her hands when their other two times Jack had firmly led the way. But her nerves didn't show. The confidence she had found in a fleeting moment during their kiss outside, and more permanently when he'd demonstrated just how much she affected him, held fast.

She put her hands on his shoulders and rose up on her knees, adjusting her position carefully, reaching down and taking hold of his thick arousal and guiding it slowly inside of her body as she lowered herself onto him. He wrapped one arm around her waist, anchoring her, and reached up, gripping her chin between his thumb and forefinger, tilting her face down, forcing her to meet his eyes.

Jack was big on eye contact, and that was another thing that sent a wave of satisfaction through her. He wasn't tuning her out, concentrating only on the physical feeling. He was forging a connection between them. Far from denying that she was the woman he was with, the way he looked at her, with such focus, proved that he was embracing this. That he wanted her, not just the way sex made him feel.

She moved above him, trying to recall the way he did things when he set the pace. The speed and pressure at which he seemed to lose control. She rocked forward and he released his hold on her chin, moving his hands to grip her hips, holding her steady without taking the control.

"Is that okay?" she asked, breathless, barely able to force the words out.

He didn't say anything. His only response was to kiss her, deep and savage, none of his skill or carefully learned moves on display. But it was okay. She liked it. Jack was all around her, in her. And she was more than happy to be consumed, by him, by this. By the firm grip of his hands on her hips, his lips, his teeth, his tongue. And those blue eyes that looked into hers, unflinching, uncompromising.

Emotion expanded in her chest, blending with the pleasure unfurling in her stomach, both of them bleeding out and meeting the other, mixing together until they were one and the same. It was so all-consuming, so very much, that she could barely breathe.

And all the feelings down deep beneath that layer she had uncovered today rushed up inside her. It was too much, too much for a woman who had only just discovered that all of this existed within her. And now she was being pelted with it, like raindrops, hard and sharp, threatening to break through her skin in the downpour.

And the only thing keeping her from succumbing, from being completely destroyed, was those blue eyes. Familiar where everything else was so foreign.

"Jack." She hadn't meant to say his name out loud, but she was beyond thought, beyond control.

His grip tightened as he began to meet her thrust for thrust. And then she lost the thread of who was in control and who wasn't. It was equal, a joint pursuit. Him following her, her following him, each of them recognizing what the other needed, what the other wanted.

His movements became erratic, rough, pulling her body down on his as he thrust up to meet her. He moved one hand from her hip and placed it on her cheek, drawing her down nearer to him and kissing her throat, his teeth scraping over her delicate skin. She tightened her hold on his shoulders, bracing herself as he flexed his hips one last time, pushing her from the outskirts of the storm into the center of the tornado.

It roared over her, in her, through her, but Jack held her steady. Even while his own release shook his frame, he held her.

When it was over, she raised her head, half expecting to look around the room and find furniture upended, papers scattered everywhere. But everything was the same. Even the spreadsheets they'd been looking at before were in their place, completely undisturbed by what had just passed between them. It didn't seem possible. The disconnect between what had happened inside of her and the state of the room was too sharp for her to process.

He patted her thigh and somehow she recognized it as a signal he needed her to move. She complied. He disappeared from the living room and returned a few moments later with his jeans done back up and the protection taken care of. She hadn't bothered to get dressed again. Instead she took the blanket that was draped over the back of the couch and pulled it over her body.

He returned to the couch, sitting next to her, his denim-clad thigh pressed against her blanket-covered knee. She wanted to say something, to use words to connect them now that their bodies were separated. She poked at the woven elk on the blanket, considering, flashing back to the conversation they'd been having right before they'd stopped talking altogether.

"I don't remember our mother at all." The words slipped out before she'd fully committed to speaking them. Jack had that effect on her. Always had. "Sometimes I think maybe that's a good thing. How can you miss something you don't even remember?" She swallowed hard, her throat getting tight. She resented the emotion that was creeping over her. It was messing with all of the good things Jack had just made her feel. And she didn't like feeling anything on the subject at all. "But…at least if I had a memory, it would be clear. The pain, I mean. Instead it's just this weird ugly black hole that opens up inside of me sometimes. At the strangest moments. Not on Mother's Day or anything like that. Just sometimes when I see a woman taking care of a child. I remember one time I saw a little girl pestering her mother in the store, and the woman looked so tired. And she was frustrated, it was obvious. Obvious that parenting wasn't easy or fun all the time. But she was there, Jack. She stayed. And I… I just stood there staring. Wondering why my mom couldn't stay for me. I don't have an image of her in my mind, nothing specific to even be angry at. But sometimes I am." She cleared her throat. "I don't even feel like I have the right to be. Eli and Connor gave up everything to take care of me. They are the ones that should be angry. I didn't lack for much, because of the way they handled things. Why should I feel sad at all?"

She searched his face, because part of her really wanted an answer to that question.

Jack was staring straight ahead, his jaw clenched tight, his gaze distant. "The way I figure, if people have a right to leave, if they have the right to never show up at all, we have the right to be as angry as we want to be. Appreciating what Connor and Eli did for you doesn't mean you can't be hurt by why they had to do it."

"Are you angry?" she asked, the question almost a whisper.

"All the time."

She studied his profile. Strong, visually perfect. Straight nose, square jaw, dark brows and a fringe of lash that somehow never, ever made him look feminine. He appeared to have it all together. He seemed happy, carefree. Her brothers had often commented that Jack never had to try, that good things fell in his lap, that luck followed him around like a slobbering puppy.

But he was angry. And in that moment she saw it. In the hard lines of his face, the tension in his muscles.

All the time.

He was angry all the time.

"You don't show it," she said, her words strangled.

"You don't show yours, either."

"I don't feel like I deserve it." She sucked her lower lip between her teeth. "How would it make Eli and Connor feel if they knew…?"

"Screw them, Kate." He turned to her, his eyes blazing. "This isn't about them. Your feelings aren't about them."

"But they—"

"Right. They're wonderful. And they love you and they cared for you, but shit, that doesn't mean that everything was fine. It doesn't mean that being raised by your teenage brothers was as good as two functional parents would have been. Of course you're angry. Of course you are."

He spoke with such strength, such conviction, and she knew that beneath those words, that vein of anger running through them, was rage for himself.

She had a feeling she would have to show hers first.

That he needed permission to let his out. Well, hell, so did she. So maybe they could give that to each other.

"I am angry," she ground out, "because…because my mom left and what the hell was I supposed to do when I needed a bra? Or…or pads or tampons or whatever? Ask my brother's wife. Ask a school nurse." She should have been embarrassed, but she was too upset to feel embarrassed. She had never talked to anyone about this before, had barely let herself feel it. "I sure as hell wasn't going to talk to my drunk dad. Sometimes Eli and Connor would need him to pick me up from something. And he would…get drunk and forget. I remember being in junior high and sitting there waiting. Teachers just look at you all sad and kids wonder who gets forgotten. What must be wrong with you."

"He was a drunk, Katie. That's why he forgot."

Her throat became impossibly tight, an ache spreading down from her chin to her chest, blooming outward. "I don't think he really forgot."

"Of course he did."

She shook her head. "No. I think he hated me. I think he was punishing me." She felt as though she'd just ripped back the skin on her chest and exposed a dark, ugly secret that lurked beneath. Exposed all her blood and organs and a darkness she'd never wanted anyone else to see.

"Why would you think that?" Jack asked. And she was glad he hadn't tried to tell her she was wrong.

"I reminded him of her. Not because I looked like her, but because I was… I was the reason she left. I was an accident. The kid they weren't supposed to have. The one that tipped it over into being unmanageable. The one that made her leave." Her voice broke and she forgot to be horrified by the show of emotion. "I'm the one who made her leave."

Jack leaned in, folding her up into his strong arms, holding her against his bare chest. "You didn't make her leave. Best argument she could make in her defense is that her demons chased her away. Though in my experience, demons like you where you're at. The better to torment you. She walked with her own two feet, and nobody made her. Certainly not a two-year-old girl who deserved her mother. There was nothing for you to earn, Kate. That's the kind of thing we're supposed to be given from the moment we come into the world. The love of our parents. I've earned a lot of bad things in life based on my own actions. But I didn't earn my father's abandonment. Not right at first."

"Are you talking about when you met him? A few weeks ago."

She hadn't asked him about that. Not since that night. Because he hadn't brought it up, and she wanted to respect his silence. But they had gone somewhere past careful respect in the past few minutes. She was open; she was exposed. And she craved something similar from him. So that she didn't feel like she was alone, sitting here on his couch with her heart out in the open.

"I didn't know my father. I still don't. But I've known who he was since I was eighteen."

"You…you have? Do Connor and Eli know that? Does anyone know that?"

"No. Because I found out who my father was the day his attorney offered me a payoff to never tell anyone. They thought I knew. I didn't. But I took the money. And I signed their nondisclosure or whatever

the hell it was. I paid to make myself disappear. I sold
myself." She wished that she could see his face, but he
was still holding her close. She wondered if the look in
his eyes matched the bleak tone in his voice. "It wasn't
luck that made me rich. It was my father."

CHAPTER SIXTEEN

JACK DIDN'T KNOW why he was sitting here opening a vein and bleeding all over Kate. Maybe because she had gone first. Because he wanted her to know she wasn't alone. Because for the first time he didn't feel alone.

A strange shift had happened in his life, and he could hardly figure out how or why. Eli and Connor had been his best friends for as long as he could remember having friends. And he'd never even been tempted to talk to them about this. In turn, they'd never spoken about the way they felt. With their mom leaving, their dad a drunk, their entire life focused on the responsibility of caring for Kate and the ranch. Of course they hadn't. They were men and men didn't talk about their feelings.

And he'd never had a long-term relationship with a woman. Never been in a situation where he wanted to talk to women about anything but which position they liked best.

Kate was different. She was different from those women, and she was different from a friend.

She was Kate. That was the beginning and end of it.

"Your dad gave you money in exchange for you... keeping yourself a secret?" Kate's tone was incredulous, and he couldn't blame her.

"Yes. And I took it. It was all the child support money my mother had refused all of our lives. And then some. I was so angry, Kate. So angry when I found out, because we had lived in that trailer that was falling down around us for all of my life. Because she wouldn't take his money. Because she had too much pride. She was disappointed to discover that I didn't suffer from the same problem."

"Is that why she…?"

"Why we don't speak? Why she moved into a different trailer about fifty miles away? Yeah, I think so." He laughed, leaning his head back, tightening his hold on Kate, suddenly very aware of the warmth of her body pressed against his. "I traded a lot of things for that money. My relationship with her. My fantasy of ever having a relationship with my old man. My fantasy that he was somehow decent, just unable to be with us for some reason. My self-respect. It's tough to feel proud about that kind of decision. So I felt like I better make damn sure I used that money well."

"That's why you ended up in the rodeo."

"Something I never would have been able to afford to get into otherwise. Without it, I don't know. I would probably be working at the gas station store or working as a hired hand for Eli and Connor. Sometimes I think that might've been better. There's a lot of honor in something like that. Working for every bit of what you have instead of getting ahead of the game by taking a handout."

"That isn't what you did. What your father had was yours."

He shrugged. "Is it? I mean, I get that legally he owed us a certain amount. I get that morally you could make the argument that what a parent has also belongs to their children. But I'm not sure that in reality it made his money mine."

"You were eighteen. Of course you took it. And you should have. Look what you got because of it!" She waved her hand around, indicating the large living room around them. The high ceilings with natural log beams running across them, the expansive windows that provided a view of the mountains, of the spread that Jack owned. His land. "You can't regret it. You achieved your goal. You made what you needed to."

"It doesn't always feel like it. I mean, I have all of this, and I'm happy to have it. I love my house. I'm proud of it. I'm not going to pretend that I'm somehow above the money, not when it's created the kind of life I always wanted. But I do wonder what would've happened if I had just told him to go screw himself. I think that's what my ranch is, honestly."

He was treading a dangerous line, one that risked violating legal papers he'd signed. He wasn't sure he cared. He prized this moment over any of that. This moment of honesty like he'd never had before.

"I'm still listening," Kate said, her way of asking for more.

"Nathan West is my father." He knew he didn't have to impress upon her how important it was she kept it a secret. Knew he didn't have to demand her silence, because she would give it. He believed that down to the core of his being.

She said nothing. She simply went perfectly still in his arms. He listened to the silence for a while. To the sound of her breathing, the tick of the clock that he never looked at on his wall. That the interior designer had insisted go there because that was the kind of thing that went in houses like this. He'd had to hire someone to put furniture, and the blanket Kate was currently wrapped in, in his house. Because he'd lived in a glorified cracker box and he hadn't known where to begin in terms of filling a house this size with things. In part because there were things for houses he hadn't even realized existed.

"Sierra flirts with you," Kate said, breaking the silence. "That is seriously messed up."

He laughed—he couldn't help it. Of all the things he'd expected her to say, that wasn't it.

"Oh my gosh," she continued, "what if you didn't know? This is a really small town. Sierra likes you. She would… If you didn't know…"

"Stop. Stop right there. You're turning this into an after-school special."

"I'm just saying."

"I'm sure he never thought it would be an issue. Seeing as I'm sure he never thought one of his daughters would ever want to slum it with me."

"How can he think that when he wanted your mother? And I don't mean that your mother is slumming it. I just mean that it's awfully hypocritical."

"Yeah, well. He's a hypocrite. A very comfortable hypocrite, by all appearances."

"You have brothers and sisters," she said, her tone muted.

He nodded slowly. "I traded them for this place, too."

"Well, I suppose, especially when you're eighteen, money means a whole lot more than half siblings who might be as terrible as your dad."

"That's about the size of it."

"What happens if you tell?"

"I have to give the money back."

"Can you?"

He stared straight ahead at a knot on the wooden wall. "Yes. I can. But I've been so focused on building a competing empire and messing with them I haven't really wanted to yet."

"You got his attention."

"I guess I did. I think maybe I even scare him." He swallowed. "It's less satisfying than I imagined it would be."

"Why?"

He laughed. "Good question. Maybe because it means my dad is a dick. And there's no alternate scenario, no outcome other than that. It just is what it is. And now I can't pretend different."

"If it helps, my dad is dead. And I lost the chance to yell at him."

"What's that supposed to help?"

She snuggled deeper against him. "I don't know. Misery loves company?"

"You're pretty good company."

"Good miserable company." She yawned and he wished that she could stay the night. He never wished women would stay the night. They never did. But he wanted her to. Because she was different. So he wanted to keep feeling different.

He took hold of a lock of hair, tugging it gently. "You're a pretty fantastic little misery, it has to be said."

She reached up and covered his hand with hers, slowly locking their fingers together before lowering them so their clasped hands rested on his knee. He wasn't one to sit still. He worked, and when he was with a woman, they went about their business, and then she left. Jack was only still when he was sleeping.

Except now. And he found he didn't want to do anything but sit here. It was the most productive bout of stillness he'd ever been a part of. Whether because of the words that had just been spoken or because of the calmness that came from sitting next to her, he didn't know. But it felt more substantial than a whole day of hard work.

"I suppose you should go," he said after the minutes had turned the hand on his largely ignored clock halfway around.

"Probably." She angled her head and he responded to the invitation, bending down and kissing her. They didn't have time for the kiss to be anything else, and there was something deeply sensual and desperate that he couldn't quantify in that. Kissing for the sake of kissing had gone extinct in his life once he'd lost his virginity. He was starting to think that had been some shortsighted stupidity on his part.

He let himself get lost in the softness of Kate's lips, the slow slide of her tongue, the little sighs that rested on the back of her indrawn breaths.

"I have to go. We're all having dinner tonight."

"I was invited, actually," he said, feeling a kick of guilt that he hadn't mentioned it before.

She looked at him, her expression hopeful. She wanted him around. It shocked him how much that assurance meant to him. "Are you going to come?"

"I don't have to. If it's weird."

"It's weird. But I would rather see you again than avoid the awkwardness."

"I think that's the best compliment I've ever gotten."

"Good." She kissed him again, then stood, holding the blanket around her body. "You better come." She started to collect her clothes and he grabbed hold of the edge of the blanket, tugging hard until he seized possession of it. She squeaked, holding her clothes to her chest as she scurried across the room toward the bathroom.

A smile tugged at the corners of his mouth. He wasn't quite sure how Kate managed to take him from one of the hardest subjects he'd ever talked about to smiling in the space of a few minutes. His smile broadened. Because he would see her again tonight, and that was about the best thing he could think of.

CHAPTER SEVENTEEN

IT WAS A fine day for a rodeo. She could only hope tomorrow was, too. The weeks had passed quickly, much more so than Kate had anticipated. The leaves had changed, dramatic red, orange and gold replacing the vibrant green. Though the mountains remained that particular shade of pine that earned the name *evergreen* with ease.

The day was crisp and clear, and vendors were setting up around the outside of the expo's indoor arena without fear of rain.

As she walked down to the gates where the competitors would assemble, her stomach flipped. A twitching feeling in her stomach like a horde of spiders skittering around overtook her for a second. She had to stop, pressing her palm flat against her midsection. She took a breath, in slow, out slow.

A few of them had volunteered to spend the night at the fairgrounds over the next four days, keeping an eye on the booths. Kate was one of the volunteers, and she had brought a small tent to put up near her horse trailer and the stall Roo would be in.

Tomorrow. Tomorrow was the competition. And even though it didn't count toward overall scores or earnings of any kind, it felt like a big deal to her. She was competing against Jessica Schulz, Sierra West,

Maggie Markham and basically anyone else who was considered a contender in barrel racing, professional or otherwise.

But as she stood there, nerves immobilizing her, she realized that she wasn't afraid to win anymore. She had been. She'd been afraid that wanting this was somehow disloyal, that wanting to leave was wrong. She'd been afraid to go off and create a life apart from Connor and Eli because they had invested so much of their lives in her.

But they were happy now. They had Sadie and Liss.

And Jack... Well, Jack had told her it was okay to be angry. She had been turning that over ever since. Thinking about all the implications. About the fact that maybe, just maybe, her life, her emotions were separate from theirs.

Such a small sentence, and yet it had echoed through her like a pebble tossed into a canyon.

"There you are. Sierra told me you were around." She turned around and saw Jack walking toward her. In a tight black T-shirt, a cowboy hat and jeans, the man was lethal.

A part of her had imagined that after such frequent exposure, particularly to his naked body, he would have less impact upon sight. That part of her had been very, very wrong. The T-shirt enhanced his muscles, reminded her of how strong he was, how it felt to be held in his arms. The jeans, hugging very relevant parts of him, reminded her of secrets about him that she knew intimately. His hat and the dark stubble on his jaw added to the outlaw fantasy. That was just for fun.

"Yes, I am standing here and processing nervous excitement."

"Oh yeah?" He rubbed his hand along his chin, the sound of his whiskers scraping against his skin resonating inside of her. "What are you nervous about?"

"I've never competed in a venue quite this spectacular. This is reserved for the pros."

"Reserved for you."

"Not quite."

"After this. You're going to turn pro after this."

She lifted her shoulder. "Maybe."

"If it's money, Katie, let me help." His blue gaze was so earnest she couldn't be offended by the offer. Especially since she knew he would make it whether they were sleeping together or not. Because Jack took care of her. He always had.

Whatever his track record with past relationships, Jack Monaghan had been faithful to her for about twenty years.

"I have the money."

"Then we won't argue about it. I did find something out you might be happy to hear."

She hopped in place, stirring up some of the fine gray dust that surrounded the gravel on the ground. "Tell me."

"Today's event is sold out to capacity. With the rental fee waived for the day, that means we've raised well above what we projected we might. Enough to make a sizable donation to local battered women's shelters and Alison's bakery, specifically to establish a training program for work experience."

Kate close the distance between Jack and herself and wrapped her arms around him, pressing her body close to his. He hesitated for a moment, then pressed his hand to her lower back, squeezing her gently. She was tempted to kiss him, but she knew that with so many people hanging around, it was a chance she couldn't take.

The realization made her chest ache, which was strange, because keeping it a secret hadn't felt like a problem before. She'd been fine with the fact that it was just between them. Perfectly happy to keep it a secret because it was never going to progress beyond where it was now.

So why did it feel as though it already had? Something had changed. Something in her, something in him. She didn't know what it meant. She didn't want to.

She pulled away from him. "I volunteered to spend the night tonight. Here, I mean. We won't have much time to be together this weekend."

They were still stealing moments in the afternoon when they could. Once, she had left much earlier than necessary for work and ambushed him on his way out the door to do chores. But in the interest of maintaining secrecy, neither of them had thought it would be a great idea to park at each other's places overnight. Sure, they could have circumvented that, but a lot of cloak-and-dagger would've had to be involved. And that was a lot of work to go to simply to spend the night together, when that was obviously taking a step deeper into the relationship than either of them were supposed to want.

"That's handy, because I volunteered to spend the night, too. But I didn't bring a tent," he said, his blue eyes intense.

"Well, if somebody asks where your tent is pitched, what are you going to tell them?"

"That when you're around, my tent is pitched in my pants?"

She snorted out a laugh, reluctantly amused. "Except no, you can't say that ever."

"Right. Because romantic declarations are off the table."

"That was not a romantic declaration."

"It's the best I've got."

She shoved him, a thrill rushing through her because she got to touch him again. He caught hold of her wrists, holding her steady. Another moment that was reminiscent of things they'd shared prior to their relationship becoming more. But now the playfulness was wired with electricity. She liked it.

Though on the heels of the electric shock came the concern that this would always be there. That going back to normal was the real fantasy.

She pushed that thought away, because she didn't have time to deal with it right now.

"In all seriousness, if anyone asks, I'll say I'm sleeping in my truck. But what I would like to do is sleep with you. Really."

"It's a tent."

"Then you will have to be quiet."

"Okay, Monaghan, but that means you're going to have to lower your game."

"On second thought, if anyone asks, in the morning we'll just say it was coyotes."

She narrowed her eyes. "I do not sound like a coyote."

"No. You sound like a badger-cat. But in fairness,

most people won't be familiar with the call of the badger-cat." He reached toward her and pulled on her braid, the gesture entirely welcome now rather than irritating. She wondered if it had never really been irritating. "Don't be nervous. You're going to be amazing."

"Thank you."

"Just 'thank you'? Not 'thank you, asshole'? Or 'thanks, I couldn't have done it' without me?"

"No. Just thank you." She looked down below his belt buckle pointedly. "Now, are you just going to stand there pitching a tent, or are you going to help me with mine?"

"OKAY, I HAVE made the rounds. Thanks to no help from you," Kate said, climbing inside the tent and zipping it up tight before kneeling down next to where Jack was reclining.

"I'm being discreet."

"Oh, is that what you call it?" She pushed at his shoulder. "You sort of planned this thing. You might want to make a show of helping out."

He grinned at her, and her heart turned over. "I'm letting others have the glory now. And I'm protecting your reputation, Ms. Garrett. You should be thankful."

"I can protect my own reputation, thank you."

He frowned slightly. "All right, then, maybe I'm protecting me. Because people would want to run me out of town on a rail. Whatever the hell that means. Probably with pitchforks and torches."

She adjusted her position, lying down, resting her head on her hands. "You think so?" Of course, thinking of how Liss had reacted when she had imagined there was something going on between her and Jack, she had a feeling he was closer to the truth than either of them would have liked to believe.

"I have a certain reputation. And it's not unearned. I won't pretend that I was chaste before we got together." The way he said that, *got together*, made her stomach turn over. "I've fooled around with a lot of women. And people know that. Like I told you before, there are some things that happened to me that aren't earned. But I went out of my way to raise hell and now that I would rather be known for something other than that, the town hasn't exactly changed their perception of me on a dime. Can't say that I blame them."

"Maybe not. But if I don't hold your past against you, I wouldn't think it was anyone else's business."

He reached out and wrapped his arms around her, pulling her up against his body. "One of the many things I like about you. You see through my bullshit. No one else does. No one else even tries."

"I've always seen through your bullshit." She smiled and leaned in, kissing him.

They just looked at each other for a moment, and then the light in his eyes changed, sharpened. "Are you feeling brave?" he asked, his voice wicked.

"Is that a trick question, Monaghan? I always feel brave." Such a lie, because her insides were quaking. Had been for some time now. But in spite of her fear, she wouldn't back down. She never did. Whether that was a handicap or an asset, she wasn't certain.

"Brave enough to let me have you out here? All those people who know us are just a canvas wall away. Seems a little bit naughty."

His words sent a shiver through her body. She was a lot of things. But naughty had never been one of them.

"I'm not...opposed to naughty."

"Good. I like that. But you're gonna have to try not to scream my name when you come." His blue eyes were electric, intense. "You're going to have to be very quiet. Do you think you can do that?"

She should have been appalled by his ego. Instead his words were pure heat, setting fire to her blood, making her insides melt like honey.

"You might have to give me something to bite on to," she said, not certain where the words came from. She was a different person when she was with Jack. Or maybe she was the same person. But she'd changed. Had found whole new parts of herself, things that she wanted that she'd never known before, things she could say, things she could do that she had never imagined she could.

She'd grown up without much female influence in her life. No one much to talk to about love and sex and flirting. She'd just imagined she wouldn't be much good at it.

The fact was, she was damn good at it. And she was extremely pleased with herself.

"I can give you something to bite," he said, a feral light in his blue eyes. "If you behave. Or don't." He assessed her slowly, sending a shiver through her. "This tent is a pretty cramped space. You're going to have to get naked for me. I can't wrestle around with your clothes without making a scene."

She snorted. "You've got to get naked for me. Tit for tat and all that shit."

"I love it when you talk dirty." Without hesitation,

he stripped his T-shirt up over his head and set to work on his belt buckle.

Never one to be left behind, Kate undressed as quickly as possible, freezing when she looked up and saw Jack. Naked and so hot she was surprised he wasn't burning a hole through the tent wall. She still marveled at the sight of Jack's body, every damn time, but it was amazing how that awe combined with comfort. There was a familiarity to those acres of bare skin, the satisfaction of secrets known. Only to her, only to him.

She wasn't embarrassed to show him her body. She knew that he liked it. From every angle, no matter what. He had never given her a moment to be insecure about the fact that she wasn't soft or particularly chesty, because he was so quick to speak his appreciation. He had never once made her feel like he was comparing her to other women. Had never made her feel like she should compare *herself* to other women.

And even if she'd had men in her past to compare him to, she knew there would be no comparison. Not really.

"Damn," he said, the reverence in his tone reinforcing the confidence planted there and grown by him. "I have woven whole fantasies around what your body might look like, and I'm honored and a little bit surprised every time I get to see it. Every time I realize that you've let me know it so well."

Her face heated. "Same goes."

"You feeling adventurous?"

She frowned. "Depends on what you mean by *adventurous*. I'm not exactly in the mood to go climb a mountain. I'd rather fuck."

He laughed. "Well, that is what I had in mind. Not the mountain climbing. I just thought you might want to try something we hadn't."

Her scalp prickled. "Well, that depends, too."

He leaned in, his voice low, husky. "Trust me, Katie."

"I do." She realized how very true that was the moment the words left her lips. Jack had never given her a reason to doubt his word. He was reliable, dependable, another person in her life who had stayed.

If the town of Copper Ridge couldn't see that, if Nathan West couldn't see what a wonderful man his son was, then they were blind-ass idiots.

"Not sure I deserve your trust," he said, "but I'll take it. Which maybe says some bad things about me."

"You're only bad in a fun way."

"We'll see if you still think that in a few minutes. Get on your hands and knees. Show me your pretty ass."

Those words, those surprising, dirty words, sent an arrow of heat straight through her midsection that hit its target, fear rippling through the tailwind. But still, she didn't hesitate, stopping now never occurring to her.

She liked Jack like this, all rough and commanding, because she knew he got that way when she pushed him to the limit, pushed him straight to the edge of his control. She'd learned that she was never more in power than when Jack was making demands, and she knew that she could push that power, push his control, further by obeying him.

Strange, maybe. But she was discovering that the politics of sex were different from anything else.

She held her breath, waiting for his next move. A firm, warm hand slid across her backside, the friction over her skin hot, perfect. He moved his hand lower, teasing the entrance to her body with strong, blunt fingertips before pushing his finger deep inside of her.

She'd been with Jack countless times over the past weeks, and she'd started to think they'd done all there was. This was different. She couldn't see him, couldn't guess what might be coming next.

She heard him tearing a condom packet, knew that now he was rolling it over his thick length. She knew this routine well, knew just how long it took to go from grabbing the pack to protected to inside of her.

She held her breath and she waited, but he didn't do anything yet. He simply waited, one hand firm on her hip, the other moving between her legs, drawing the moisture from inside her body and sliding it over her clit.

That was one of the new sexy words in her vocabulary, added thanks to Jack and his very dirty mouth.

"You're ready for me, Katie," he said, his voice rough. "So wet. So hot."

"Yes," she whispered, "I'm ready."

He replaced his fingers with his cock, pushing inside slowly. This new angle of penetration was a revelation. She felt fuller, and he went deeper. And she saw stars. But she couldn't see his eyes. This was a departure from the way they typically made love, his gaze trained on hers as he thrust hard and deep.

She couldn't see him now; she could only feel him. The intense fullness of him being inside of her, the strength in his hold, the sound of his breath. There was familiarity in his rhythm, because she knew exactly the way that Jack moved to bring them both to orgasm.

This position should have felt more distant, but it didn't. If anything, it felt more intense, more intimate somehow, because it was up to her to know him by touch, by sound, rather than by sight. She did. She knew his body; she knew his strength. It was Jack. Only Jack.

It could only ever be Jack.

He shifted, bringing his hand forward to tease her clit, intense, deep need riding through her as he did, bringing her closer and closer to climax.

Her arms were shaking from the exertion of holding herself up, because while she had strength from lifting bales of hay, demanding her muscles work properly while being subjected to this assault of pleasure was a bit much.

Unable to hold herself up any longer, she relaxed, lowering her upper body down to the sleeping bag, while Jack thrust hard into her from behind.

She pressed her face into the pillow and let it capture all of the sound she couldn't control as Jack propelled them both over the edge. Release roared through her, stars bursting behind her eyelids. Little pops of white light that burned bright before fading, leaving behind impressions of flashbulbs and fireflies.

His fingers dug deep into her hips and he froze behind her. Made a low, harsh sound, no concession being given to the fact that they were not in a soundproof environment.

Maybe, just maybe, the people around them wouldn't guess what that sound was. But she knew. She knew it intimately.

Jack. It's Jack.

He withdrew from her body, releasing his hold on her for a moment before tugging her up against him, his chest pressed against her back, his breathing hard and uneven. He held her like that until they had both settled a bit, the aftereffects of their climaxes fading slowly. Their muscles relaxing, sleep edging closer. It was an amazing thing to be so in tune with another person. To reach the heights at almost the same time and to come down together.

"Just a sec, baby."

Jack moved away from her, rustling around in his things for a moment before coming back to her. "I came prepared for contraceptive disposal," he whispered, his voice husky.

"You make it sound so classy," she whispered.

"You know me better than that." He kissed the back of her neck and pulled her more tightly against him, nestling her bottom up against him.

"Hell, Jack, you know *me* better than that."

He traced his fingertip down her arm. "Yes, I do."

"I'm glad that you don't have to leave."

"I'm glad I don't have to leave."

This felt right. Staying together, holding each other after they'd made love. Rather than both of them getting dressed hurriedly and her scurrying home. She had told herself that this would be awkward. But spending the night was unnecessary, because she hadn't known what to do with the steadily growing feeling that separating from him afterward was wrong. That growing sense of wrongness was... Well, it was *scary.* Because it proved what she wanted to deny. That whatever was happening between herself and

Jack wasn't stagnant. It was growing; it was changing; it was moving forward.

Which was balls, because the sex was supposed to be a vehicle to help her move forward. They weren't suddenly supposed to be moving forward together.

She shivered and he moved his hand down to her stomach, so warm and perfect, strong. Firm. And she figured she would just let this moment be. It was hard to worry about the future when the present felt so nice.

She had been short on luxury in her life. She was a hard worker, and to the same degree she tended to ignore sore muscles and fatigue, she ignored all too often the velvet feel of grass under her feet and the perfect warmth of the sun on her skin. She didn't get caught up in the details.

But she was letting herself get caught up in this. In the luxury of being held against Jack. The strength in his arms, the warmth in his body, the sound of his heart beating steadily behind her. That was better than grass between her toes any day.

And it was a better way to earn sore muscles than doing ranch work.

She rested her hand over Jack's and forgot to worry about what any of this meant. For a while she was just going to let herself have the luxury.

CHAPTER EIGHTEEN

JACK HAD WOKEN up early the next morning, before anyone else, because it had been important that he get dressed and get his ass out of Kate's tent before anyone saw. Fortunately, he'd managed. He was starting to think she didn't much mind anybody finding out about them, but that wasn't the way to go about it. And there would be an order to things.

Which was a shame, because he really liked his balls where they were, and he wasn't entirely certain that Connor and Eli would let him keep them when the truth came out. But it would have to. The only other option would be ending things, and soon, because sneaking around wasn't doing it for him anymore. And he wasn't doing that. Ending it. No way in hell.

He hadn't wanted to get up. He'd wanted to lie there with her forever. Still. Calm. Tranquil.

The first time in his life he'd ever found peace in stillness. A revelation.

It was tempting to think, as he often did, that the feeling was an illusion of darkness. That with the sunrise, things would change. But the sun hadn't changed a damn thing. It'd just shone a light on them. Made it that much clearer.

He had something with her...something he'd never

had with anyone else. Something he'd never even imagined he wanted.

How had he ever thought she would leave things inside him the same as they'd always been? Kate Garrett was a gale-force wind, and he'd believed he could tangle with her and come out unchanged.

That was some kind of dumb arrogance.

He took a deep breath, trying to dispel the weight that was settling on his chest, and looked around. People were already filing into the fairgrounds, the first event starting soon. Thankfully for both his nerves and Kate, barrel racing was event number one. He had told her not to get worried and not to be nervous, but he couldn't follow his own advice. He wanted her to win. He wanted her to see what he saw. That she was good enough. More than good enough, she was brilliant.

She had the potential to be whatever she wanted. And sure, the idea of her going on the road with the rodeo was kind of a tough one. It would mean being separated. But that was just one more reason they needed to go ahead and figure out how they were going to navigate this relationship.

He felt like he'd been sucker punched. Relationship. Well, that was what it was. He had never before made a habit of spending the night with a woman. Had never spent multiple nights with the same woman. Maybe a few here and there, but not more than a month. He had never wanted to. But he wanted to hold Kate forever, and he supposed that meant it was a relationship.

He took a sip of his coffee and sighed as the hot, strong liquid slid down his throat. It was a fairly clear day for autumn but the air was still cool. A nice day for the events since neither horse nor rider would get as sweaty as usual.

Kate had already gone off to get ready and to get Roo warmed up, and he was trying to be inconspicuous and not hover over her. Since he had a feeling if he got anywhere near her, no one would confuse his attachment to her. He was most definitely more lover than older brother, and that much would be clear if anyone so much as saw him look at her.

He was loitering back by where the riders would come in, rather than going to the stands, because he figured however this shook out, Kate would need a big hug afterward. And he would be the one to give it to her.

His pocket buzzed and he reached into it, pulling out his phone. It was Eli. "Hello?"

"Are you at the fairgrounds?"

"Of course I am. Just ready to watch her ride." He didn't bother to specify who. And he realized that it was awfully familiar of him, but then, they were awfully familiar. Right now he couldn't bother with trying to act like it was different.

"Are you in the stands?"

"Nope. Hanging out by where they come in."

"Are you going to come and sit down?"

He cleared his throat, turning in the direction of the stalls. And he saw Kate walking toward the arena. She was wearing a pair of tight black jeans and a button-up shirt, also black, with little silver stars up by the collar. She had on her black cowgirl hat with the silver buckle on the band, her long dark hair in its usual braid.

Some of the other women had their hair loose, in bountiful curls, bright pink lipstick, turquoise and gold. But Kate was the one who stood out to him. Kate shone the brightest. Because she was Kate. It was that simple.

"No," he said, his chest tight. "I'm going to stand back here. Just in case. I mean, I've been coaching her and stuff." It was a lame finish, he knew.

"Okay," Eli said, no concern in his tone at all. Which made him feel like kind of an ass. Because no matter how obvious he felt the relationship change with Kate was, Eli clearly suspected nothing. Because, of course, as far as Eli was concerned, there was just no chance of Jack ever touching Kate. Because she was too young, because she was Connor and Eli's sister.

But those things were so small to him now. Minimal parts of the complex beauty that made up Kate Garrett. And he couldn't bring himself to care.

"Talk to you after." He hung up, walking toward the temporary fences, keeping his distance. He didn't want to distract her. But then he noticed she was looking around, searching. Probably for Connor and Eli, Liss and Sadie. Her family. Probably not for him. But just in case, he took a few long strides down toward where she was, keeping himself across the arena from her. She turned and saw him. And the smile that lit up her face felt like the best, most undeserved gift he could've ever received.

He smiled back, gratified by the blush that colored her cheeks.

Then she turned her focus back to the task at hand. She wasn't searching anymore. Which meant she had been looking for him. That did something to him. Made it almost impossible to breathe.

The first rider went, then the next. But he didn't pay

attention. His eyes were locked on Kate, who was staring straight ahead at the arena. When she was next up, she mounted Roo and took her position in the chute.

The ride ended to thunderous applause, and Kate was motionless, waiting for her gate to open. He let his eyes flutter closed just for a moment, and for the first time in his memory, he uttered a prayer.

He took a breath, and the gate opened. And Kate flew.

Her braid bounced against her back, dirt flying up behind the horse's hooves. She went around the first barrel clean, picking up the momentum she had lost on the turn and burning flawlessly into the next. When she finished, he cheered the loudest.

The next three riders went. Then it was all reset for the second round. More waiting.

Her turn came around again too fast and not fast enough. She turned back and looked at him, the first time she had looked at him since before her run. He wished that he could touch her. Tug her braid. Give her a kiss. Judging by the flush of color in her cheeks, she understood what he wanted.

"Go, badger-cat," he whispered.

She nodded once, then turned her attention back to her ride, taking her position in the chute. For a moment everything inside of him went still. His heart, his breath. All of it frozen.

This was it. There were good times on the board, and she would have to do better this time than last time to pull ahead.

Her gate opened and she was quick off the mark. He didn't watch the timer on the board; he watched her, willing her to go fast, to go clean. And she did.

When she finished, her time had blown away everyone that had gone before her. And he knew without a doubt no one would ever catch her.

Because no one could catch Kate Garrett. Not in the arena, not in life. She was too far out ahead of the crowd. And for some reason she saw something in him. That strong-willed, determined woman who had survived and thrived even with the abandonment by her parents, both physically and emotionally. Who had lost more than any one person should, who'd had burdens placed on her slim shoulders that men twice her size could never have carried.

She saw good in him.

If the whole town never saw it, if his father never saw it, he didn't give a damn. Somehow, over the course of the past month and a half, he'd lost that drive to prove himself by organizing this charity. Had started caring about only one person seeing him at all. Because it didn't matter. It didn't matter what anyone thought. Not when Kate saw who he was.

She came around to the back of the arena just as the next rider was breaking out of the gate. And he didn't care if people saw, didn't care what they thought. He jogged toward her, slowing as he approached her horse.

He reached up, and she looked down at him, arching a brow.

"Come here," he said, no room for argument in his tone.

She began to dismount and he caught her, holding on to her waist and lifting her down to the ground. She smiled, a small one that curved the edges of her lips up just so. He wanted to kiss them. Right at the curve, then again at the lush center.

Too bad he couldn't. Not here. Not now. But he didn't want to release her, either. Not yet.

"Kate! That was amazing."

He stepped away from Kate slowly, not responding to the jump and wiggle on her end. He turned and saw Connor, with Eli, Liss and Sadie trailing behind, a broad grin on his face. Again, the intense trust his friends had for him was evident in the way neither brother raised a brow over his physical contact with Kate.

"It isn't over yet," she said, scuffing her boot through the dust, her eyes fixed on the trail she left behind.

"No one is going to beat you," Connor said.

She lifted her shoulder. "Sure. Probably not. But you paid for your tickets. You should probably watch the end of the event."

Eli grinned broadly. "Who cares about all that. We were here to see you."

"You guys suck. You're going to make me cry," Kate said.

"I didn't think you had tear ducts," Connor said.

"Turns out I do. Please don't make me use them."

"I'll do it for you," Liss said, "since I'm an emotional mess."

"I'm not even pregnant," Sadie said, "and I might."

"I haven't won yet."

"Just one more ride. She didn't even have a better score than you in the first round." It was Jack who pointed this out.

"Stop with your logic," she said, waving a hand. "I'm not going to watch. I'm going to go put Roo away. You come get me if I win."

"You should go after her," Eli said, when Kate was out of earshot.

"Me?" Jack asked.

"Yeah, you were her coach. Go say something encouraging. We'll keep watch."

He'd wanted to go after Kate; he just hadn't figured he would do it in front of her family. But he would now. "Text us as soon as the results are in," he said. Strange how easy *us* had come out of his mouth. Or not strange at all considering the things he'd been turning over lately.

"I'll text you," Liss said. "That brick Kate calls a phone probably can't get text reliably."

Jack nodded and turned away, headed toward the stalls. He went ahead and walked behind Kate, enjoying the view. She paused midstride and turned to look over her shoulder, one brow arched. He was caught.

"What are you doing?" she asked.

He jogged up to her. "They sent me after you to act coach-like."

"They wouldn't have done that if they had any idea."

"Oh, sure as hell not."

"Thank you for coming," she said.

He wasn't sure if she meant now or to the whole event. "Of course." That answer worked either way. "You're going pro now, Kate Garrett."

"We don't know if I won."

"You don't need to win. That was a winning ride, whether it wins this particular time or not. You're going to do this."

She laughed nervously, brushing a strand of hair out of her face. "You want to get rid of me that badly?"

"I don't want to get rid of you at all. I want you with me, in my bed, every night. You have to understand that my telling you that you need to do this is just because I believe in you that much."

She looked up, startled. "Why?"

"A man has to believe in something. I'm going to go ahead and believe in you."

"You sure that's smart?" she asked, a forced laugh laced through her words.

"I'm known for my luck, not my smarts."

"But it's there all the same."

He smiled. "Then how dare you question me?"

"Sorry, Monaghan. It will never happen again. I promise to preserve your ego at all costs."

It occurred to him just then that it wasn't his ego he cared about. "I want to take you on a date."

Her blue eyes widened, and she blinked rapidly. "You...what?"

"You. Me. A restaurant, a walk along the harbor. A date."

"In public?"

"In public. Out of bed. With clothes on."

"That...doesn't sound like as much fun as the way we normally do it."

A strange sharp sensation lanced his chest. "Maybe not. But it is what normal people do."

She looked over his shoulder, likely squinting to see her family in the distance. "But they'll find out."

"I know. I'm starting to think they should."

"But this..."

"Can't be anything if we don't move forward."

Kate hesitated, moving her hand over Roo's neck. "I thought... I thought we said..."

"We did. But things change. Dinner. Tomorrow night. We'll have it in Old Town."

She thrust her chin into the air, wrinkling her nose. "And what will I be wearing, Mr. Monaghan?"

"Provocative. We're going to have to deal with that later."

Her cheeks turned pink. "Well, you're being all demanding."

"And you like it. Wear whatever you like, but I'm picking you up at six."

The phone buzzed in his pocket and he took it out. There was a text with one word: yes!!!

He couldn't hold back the smile. The flood of pure joy that burst in his chest like a firework and crackled outward.

"You won, Katie," he said.

She looked at him, shocked. "I did?"

Just then Eli and Sadie appeared, out of breath. "Connor stayed back with Liss. They're on their way. She can only waddle," Sadie said. "You won! Kate, you're amazing!"

"I… It was because of Jack." Her brown eyes met his and he felt everything in him tighten. "I couldn't have done it without him."

Liss and Connor found them, and immediately their excitement took over the conversation. He looked past everyone, at Kate, and mouthed, "Six."

She looked at him, her face serious, and nodded slowly.

It wasn't emphatic, but he would take it.

CHAPTER NINETEEN

In Kate's opinion, she was just acting stupid. She had seen Jack a million times, at restaurants, at her brother's houses, at the rodeo only last night. He had seen her dressed in her Sunday worst for when she worked at the Farm and Garden and he'd seen her in her rodeo clothes. He'd seen her naked, for goodness' sake. There were no surprises left.

So there was no reason on earth to start getting worked up now over what she might wear to go out to dinner with him. It wasn't as if she owned a dress, other than the bridesmaid dress, or makeup. It wasn't as if she was going to do anything with her hair but put it back in a braid.

She looked at her reflection in the mirror, at her heavy straight hair, hanging free. Okay, maybe she would leave it down. Just for something slightly different. She was regretting the fact that she hadn't made it over to the mall in Tolowa to pick up some under wear. Maybe she would have gotten a pair of jeans she hadn't bought folded on a shelf at a sporting goods store. Probably not, though.

She sighed heavily. It was what it was. Jack would be by to get her in fifteen minutes, so she supposed she needed to make a decision.

She thought back to that night he'd stood her up before the meeting at the Grange. She knew without a doubt he wouldn't stand her up tonight—that wasn't why she was reflecting on that night. She was just reflecting on her nerves. On that feeling of excitement, as if he was coming to get her for a date. And now he really was. Strange how a couple months changed things.

She decided on a pair of black jeans and a white button-up top that had a faint floral pattern etched in tan all over it, along with some fancy pearl buttons. It was more of a competition outfit, but nowhere near as flashy as what a lot of her contemporaries considered a competition outfit. Really, she was probably still underdressed for a date.

A date. They really were going on a date. He didn't mind if people found out about them.

The strangest sensation gripped her, one of fear, exhilaration. Like riding her horse full speed through a fog bank. No clue what was ahead. Unable to slow down. She had no idea what was on the other side of tonight, what it would mean for each and every one of her relationships. For her future.

Then there was the small matter of making the decision to compete professionally next year. And that would change things, too.

Suddenly, she wanted to strip all her clothes off and scamper back to her room, crawl under her covers and hide her face. Will herself back in time to the simple ranch girl she had been before she'd tasted Jack Monaghan's lips. It was all his damn fault. He was the one who had changed things. Who had reached inside of her and rearranged all of the familiar scenery into something she couldn't sort through.

Damn Jack Monaghan.

Damn him to... Well, not to hell. But maybe to a city. That was close enough.

She didn't strip her clothes off. And she didn't hide. Instead she took one last look at herself in the mirror, at her dark hair tumbled down loose, at the way her outfit hugged her curves, showing off a bit of her figure in a way that was honestly not that unpleasant.

She took a deep breath. She was a lot of things. She was tough, and lately, she was even naughty. She was also brave. Which meant she was going on this date. Her nerves didn't get to tell her what to do.

KATE WAS TWITCHY and borderline sullen the entire ride from the ranch down into Old Town, and her twitching only increased when she saw the restaurant they would be dining in.

"Beaches?" she asked, wrinkling her nose at the white facade of the historic building. It was right on the harbor, overlooking the bay on one side and the ocean on the other. It was one of the nicer places Old Town Copper Ridge had to offer. Unassuming for all its fanciness, bleached and weathered from the salt water and wind, but it was the freshest seafood around and they made their own beer batter for the fish and chips, which in Jack's mind meant it was a damn respectable date restaurant. At least, if one was going out with Kate Garrett. He wasn't all that experienced in terms of going out on dates. Generally, he met women at Ace's or at one of the bars in a surrounding town. He met them out; he didn't take them out. There was a difference.

Which only underscored the difference with Kate.

And why he had to do this. She was different in every way, so he was damned if he was going to treat her like some dirty little secret. Like it was just another physical affair.

Like his father had treated his mother.

She wasn't a dirty secret. She was the most beautiful secret a man could ever have, and he was too damned proud to hide it anymore.

"Yeah. First of all…I don't want to keep this a secret."

Kate shifted, tucking her hair behind her ear. "Right."

"But this isn't the way I want Connor and Eli to find out, either. So I figured we would go somewhere off the beaten path. Then we can talk about what to do from here but I thought we should…test the waters first."

She cleared her throat. "Right. Because you want to tell them."

"I don't want to keep sneaking around, Kate."

She nodded mutely. "Still. Beaches is fancy."

"I'm a classy bastard. If you hadn't noticed." Likely, she hadn't. Because, really, he wasn't. But he was trying to do right by her. Trying to prove to her that he was sincere. That he could do this. Screw the town. Screw his dad.

All that mattered was Kate.

"Well, obviously. I just figured we'd go to The Crab Shanty and sit on the dock and I would pretend to pinch you with a dismembered crab claw."

He had to smile, because that did sound like her. "It's not too late for that. Sounds fun."

She hesitated, the war in her eyes so very transparent. She wanted this, but for some reason she was nervous about accepting it.

"No," she said slowly, "you planned this. So we need to do it."

"But I did it for you. So if this isn't something you want, you need to let me know."

"No, we'll do the unsophisticated crab thing when I take you out," she said, her tone firm. "But I'm very messy."

"I'll lick the butter off your fingers."

"Ew."

"You like me," he said, unable to suppress the smile that was tugging at his lips.

She shrugged. "You're okay," she said, swinging her head in the motion that normally sent her braid slapping against her back. But she'd left her hair down, and instead it rippled, a shimmering wave that he itched to touch. It was a tease. Because usually, Kate's hair was only down like this when they were in bed. "I'm hungry," she said, arching her brow and walking toward the restaurant.

He caught up to her, grabbed hold of her hand and placed his fingers through hers. "We'll get you food."

She froze, her expression nervous. "Pretty bold," she said, but she didn't let go of his hand.

"Yeah, well, I am."

They walked toward the restaurant and he paused at the door, pulling it open for her, releasing his hold on her hand and waiting for her to go inside first.

"Fancy."

"Kate, stop looking at me like I'm going to bite you on the neck and suck your blood."

She winced. "Okay," she said, walking past him and into the restaurant.

The hostess wasn't anyone he recognized, someone young, probably someone from the high school. Which was good. Since Kate was twitchy as a bull facing the prospect of becoming a steer.

The young woman led them to a table that was right up against the windows, providing a view of the rolling waves. There was, in fact, a candle in the middle of the table. It was romantic. He and Kate Garrett were engaging in romance, which individually would've been strange enough but with the two of them combined would be a damned spectacle if anyone in the restaurant recognized them.

"Are you getting a hamburger or fish and chips, Katie?" he asked, skimming his menu quickly, finding he didn't actually care what he got.

She raised her brows. "Maybe I want the tuna tartare, asshole. You don't know."

"Do you?"

"No. Fish and chips. And a beer."

"Me, too. What beer?"

"A Caldera."

"Sounds good."

The conversation was a little bit inane, but he couldn't think of anything better to talk about. If he did, he might start speaking in poetic verse about the way the candlelight flickered across her hair, the way it highlighted the hollows of her cheeks, making her look like a classic painting.

He had a feeling she would excuse herself and run off to the bathroom if he did something like that.

He didn't know what the hell was wrong with him.

He was almost sick over her. Sick over Kate Garrett. Ten years younger, practically a virgin. And he was losing his shit for her.

After their waitress, also blessedly a stranger, came and took their order, they made small talk about how well the rodeo had gone, Kate being careful not to compliment him too profusely, likely so that he didn't have to shift credit. Since she had already identified that he did that. She saw him so clearly. Much more so than anyone else. Much more so than he did.

He said something funny—he didn't even really pay attention to what—and Kate laughed, putting her head down, her hair sliding over her shoulder, full lips curving into the most beautiful smile he'd ever seen. She was out of his reach. Being the man he'd always been wouldn't be enough with her. He would have to change. He would have to want more. He would have to be more.

It hit him then just why he wasn't comfortable accepting accolades. Why, no matter what he said about wanting to improve his reputation, he never really took steps to do it. When he got positive attention, he was quick to shift the focus. Because striving for more was hard. It demanded all the time. Living down to a bad reputation was a lot easier than living up to a great one.

He'd watched Eli live beyond reproach from adolescence. He knew how hard it was. Knew what it cost. He'd never had that kind of confidence in himself. But then, he'd never really had incentive. Kate was that incentive.

He was going to be good enough for her, because he had to be. Because she deserved the best, and even if he could never be the best, he would be everything he could.

Because his other revelation in that moment was that he simply couldn't live without her. And he wouldn't. He wanted more than to just take this public; he wanted to take it legal. Permanent. He wanted her forever.

He loved her. He motherfucking *loved* her.

Their food appeared a moment later, and Kate grabbed the bottle of Portland ketchup from the center of the table and popped the lid off, then smacked the bottom with gusto, trying to get some on her fries.

She looked up, her expression sheepish, her hand poised presmack. "Sorry. Fanciness isn't my strong suit."

"You have to get your ketchup somehow."

She set the bottle down and placed a knife inside the narrow neck, drawing out as much as she could. And even completing this silly, clumsy task, she was the most captivating creature he'd ever seen.

Yeah, it was love. What else could it be? Love, he was pretty sure, was watching someone smack a ketchup bottle while wanting to drag them into the bathroom and have them against a wall.

Well, it was more than that. But that was part of it.

She dipped her fry in her hard-won ketchup, crunching loudly.

"I need to tell you something."

She paused midcrunch, her eyes widening. "What?" she asked around a mouthful of potato.

"Something I should have realized sooner."

"If you brought me here to tell me things are done..."

"Why would I do that? Why the hell would I do that?" He was defensive now, and he knew it. Because she was supposed to know him better than that.

"I knew this felt like a bad idea."

"Is that right, Katie?" he asked, anger firing through his veins. "Then you don't actually know anything. I brought you here because I'm tired of sneaking around. Because I'm tired of hiding the fact that we are together. I don't care what anybody thinks about it. No, I don't deserve you. Everyone here knows that. But I have you, and I'm so damn proud of that fact. And I'm going to do everything I can to be a man who's worthy of you."

She was still holding her French fry up by her mouth, her lips parted slightly. "What exactly are you saying?"

She didn't look happy. She didn't look hopeful. She looked… She looked scared, and when a man was making confessions, shaking down to his core, that wasn't what he wanted to see.

But it was too late to turn back now. The burning that had been growing, spreading in his chest for a while now, had taken hold completely, and there would be no stopping it until he said this, until he admitted it.

"I'm trying to say that I love you." He waited for a smile. For something that looked even a little bit like happiness. But Kate just sat there, her eyes glittering, darting back and forth as if she was looking for an exit. Looking anywhere but at him. But he'd never been accused of being a fast learner. So he kept talking. "I love you, Kate. I want more. I want everything."

Kate braced her hands on the edge of the table, like a passenger grabbing hold of the dash when she saw an accident coming that she couldn't do anything to stop. "Jack… You can't… That's not what this is." She looked wild, panicked. Like he'd told her he was dying of a terrible disease, not like he'd confessed to having feelings for her. "You said. You told me this would be sex only. Only sex."

"Yes. I said that. And in the beginning, I meant it. I've never had anything more with anyone else. It changed. I changed. That's what it is now." He took a deep breath and looked at her, at the woman he'd known for so many years. The woman who had been part of his life for so long he couldn't imagine living without her. The woman who had recently become his entire world. Whether her hair was braided or free, her lips naked or painted red, she made his heart beat. "I love everything about you, Katie. Probably always have. You see me. You're the only one who sees me."

She blinked hard, her brows locked together. "But that doesn't mean…that doesn't mean that I love you. That doesn't mean that I can love you. Or that I want… Jack, I'm going to go professional next year. I'm going to travel all around the country."

"Yes. I know. And I'll… I'll go to some of it. I'll travel with you sometimes. Or I'll just stay here and wait for you if that's what you want."

"You… You told me… You were the one who said this was only physical. You were the one who was worried about me getting hurt. You can't just change the rules," she said, her eyes glittering, her voice fierce.

And it hit him then what an arrogant asshole he was. Because in his momentary revelation he hadn't imagined she might tell him no. He'd been so focused on his own journey, on his revelations about himself, that he hadn't stopped to think she might not be on the same page. That she might not love him.

Looking at her now, at the anger, at the terror in her eyes, he knew he had miscalculated, and badly.

She was rejecting him. She was honest-to-God rejecting him. He'd never been rejected by a woman in his life.

Because you never asked for more.

And now that you have...

He gritted his teeth against the searing pain, the burning anguish in his chest.

"I have to go." She stood up, pushing her food back to the center of the table and turning away from him, then walking quickly out of the restaurant.

He would have bled less if she'd shot him. As it was, he was just sitting there feeling like he'd sustained a mortal wound with nothing to staunch the flow.

He reached for his wallet and dropped sixty dollars on the table, knowing he was overpaying and not caring. He stood and followed the path Kate had just forged with all of her righteous indignation, well aware that everyone in the restaurant was looking at him. Well aware that everyone had just seen him get rejected by a woman he didn't deserve.

If there were people in there who knew them, and there very likely were, they had just seen Jack get put in his place. They had just seen his unworthiness confirmed on a grand stage.

He walked outside, his breath visible in the cold air. People were dining out on the front deck, outdoor heaters lit, the warmth warping the air around them. And Kate was standing there, wringing her hands and looking both ways. Probably pissed because she'd just realized she'd stormed out on her ride.

"Kate," he called down to her. He realized that he'd captured the attention of the outdoor diners, but he didn't care. "Come back. Let's talk." He started down the steps toward the street and she turned partly away from him. As if she didn't want people to know he was talking to her.

And it hit him then. She wasn't the dirty secret. She never had been.

It was him.

Of course it was. He was no good. The town bike, bike that everyone had ridden once. The bastard son of no one.

She was Kate Garrett, sister to Connor and Eli Garrett, the best men in town. She deserved better and everyone knew it. Apparently, so did she.

He took a deep breath, the salt air burning his lungs, his heart pounding heavily in his head, and asked himself how the hell he'd gotten here. Breaking into pieces over a woman he would have called a girl only a few months earlier.

She had been honest when she'd said she didn't want more and when he'd decided he'd believed he was being honest. But he was a liar. Apparently.

He just stood there, his hands clenched at his sides. He was holding back a flood of heartbreak and poetry, and neither were anything he had experience with. And behind the poetry were small mean things that he wanted to say to hurt her, to get a reaction out of her. To make her understand what he was feeling.

All of it was better left unsaid. He might not have

any experience with this kind of thing, but he knew enough to know that.

Too bad he was past the point of giving a damn. There was no point in pride, no point in preserving any damn thing when his heart was already broken. She was ashamed? She wanted it to be a secret?

Too bad. He didn't.

Because he was proud of her. Proud of what he felt. He didn't deserve her shame. He deserved for her to at least listen to him. To say it to his face if she didn't want him.

His father had sent a damned legal team and payment to get him out of his life. He needed at least a conversation from Kate.

"Fuck it." He strode toward her, and she turned away, starting to walk in the other direction. "Kate! Wait. Listen to me."

"No."

"You don't have to commit to anything. Not right now, but we need to talk. You are not running from me."

He closed the distance between them and she looked up at the audience they'd gained. "I'm not having this fight with you in front of half the town."

He looked up at the diners. "That's not even close to half the town. And you're trying your best to not have this fight with me at all, and I'm not going to have it."

"I didn't ask your permission to not have it. I'm not having it." She turned away from him again and he caught her arm.

"You're gonna run away with your tail between your legs like a scared little animal?"

She whirled around, jerked her arm from his hold

and planted her hands on his chest, shoving him back. "I am not afraid."

"Could've fooled me. You look like you're running scared."

She took another step toward him and he wrapped his arm around her waist and pulled her up against his body. "Don't," she said, her tone warning.

But he had never been very good at taking warnings.

He dipped his head and kissed her.

It wasn't a kiss to try and seduce her around to his way of thinking. It wasn't even a show for the crowd. He just wanted her to taste his anger. So that she could feel the desperation he did. So she could feel how wrong it was for them to be anything but together.

She didn't push against him. Instead she kissed him back, giving him a taste of her own rage.

Fine. He would take that. It was better than her walking away. Better than her refusing to fight. He would rather fight. Would rather go down in a blaze of bloody glory than offer her his heart and watch her walk away in a huff as though they'd done nothing more than disagree about politics.

He would drag it all out right here so everyone would know it had existed. That it had been real. She wanted it to be a secret? She wanted it to stay hidden? Too damn bad.

It was too big for him to hide, too big for him to walk away from unchanged. And he was tired of being invisible. He would be damned if she tried to make him invisible to her, too.

All those stunts he'd pulled, all the things he'd done

to get his father's attention… They were a boy's rebellion. A boy's bid for what he'd been denied.

This…this was a man's desperation. From deep within his soul.

He wanted her to cry for them, for this. Because he would cry. He wanted her to break, because he was shattering inside like glass.

If she was going to walk away, he wasn't going to make it easy.

She was holding tight to him now, clinging to his shirt, but in spite of that, he found himself being propelled backward.

"What the fuck, Monaghan?"

Jack found himself off balance and staring at the hulking silhouette of his best friend Connor, standing there backlit by the streetlight, his hands clenched into fists. Jack was having a hard time figuring out what the hell Connor was doing in town, and in the middle of that confusion was the instinctive fear he felt for his safety.

Even with the darkness keeping his expression vague, Jack knew that Connor had murder on his mind.

Jack was having trouble making his mouth work. So it wasn't a huge surprise when the words that came out of his mouth were both asinine and self-destructive. "It's exactly what it looks like."

That had been a mistake, and he knew it. When it came to physical strength, if it were Eli, Jack was pretty sure he would have a fighting chance. They were about the same height, with lean muscle. Connor, on the other hand, was roughly the size of a rodeo bull and, much like a rodeo bull, had no qualms about stepping on your head.

"Connor," Kate said, "just... Don't..."

"Stay out of this," Connor said, his voice hard.

"No. I will not stay out of it. I'm in it. What are you doing here?" Kate asked.

"I was out having dinner with my wife and I got a text from our friend Jeanette saying you two were out here making asses of yourselves on Main Street. That's what I'm doing here. I don't know what I expected but that," Connor said, pointing to Jack, "that was not it."

"Connor," Jack started, but his words were cut short when Connor's fist connected with his face. Jack went down, the sharp, hard crack of the sidewalk on his knee enough to offset the throbbing in his head.

"Connor?" Another voice was added to the chorus calling out Connor's name. Liss had just appeared behind Connor, holding on to the edges of her coat, the yellow streetlights igniting her hair like a red flame.

"He was kissing her," he said, pointing down at Jack. Then he turned his focus back to Jack. "I saw you two yelling at each other. Heard you yell at her. And I saw you grab her and make her kiss you."

Yeah, as things went, that was probably the worst way ever for Connor to discover his relationship with Kate wasn't entirely platonic. The yelling. The kiss, which could be viewed as somewhat of a rough kiss.

"I care about her," Jack said. "And you know me. Think about those things right now."

"You care about her?" Connor asked, his tone incredulous. "Like you care about all the women you pick up at bars and fuck?"

"Don't," Jack growled. "Don't say that shit when you don't know what you're talking about."

"You," Connor said, rounding on Kate now. "How

could you be that stupid? You know him. You know what a damned ass he is. Tell me you're not sleeping with him."

Kate had her arms wrapped around her midsection, as if she was trying desperately to fold into herself and disappear. "Connor... I..."

"Shit," Connor bit out. Then he turned his focus back to Jack. "Give me one good reason not to kill you here and now."

"Two. There are witnesses and your brother is the sheriff. I'd hate for Eli to have to arrest you." It was a bad time to make a joke. Though it wasn't entirely a joke. He half believed Connor would kill him where he stood if he didn't give him a good reason not to.

"I swear to God, Monaghan..."

"I love her," Jack said. His pride was dead and buried anyway. Might as well make it roll over in its grave. He directed his gaze to Kate. "I do. I love you. I'm proud to love you. I want more. I want more than just sneaking around. I don't care if he knows it. I don't care if they know it," he said, gesturing up to the people who were now avidly watching the scene unfold. "Maybe I'm not good enough for you. No, hell, I know I'm not. But I thought you at least knew me well enough... I thought you trusted me. You know my past—everyone here does. I thought you knew I was more than that."

Kate was shivering now, her eyes resolutely dry, her teeth chattering. "I do know you. That's the problem."

The last bit of hope he carried died a slow, howling death inside of him, begging for mercy as Kate's words pushed it to a place beyond healing.

Connor was just standing there looking grim. Liss

was a few paces back, her skin waxen. And Kate was in the center, determination in her face even while she shook so hard he thought she might rattle apart.

All of them standing away from him.

A clear line.

He stood alone. As always. He'd been a fool to think it could ever be different.

"Perfect." He turned away from them, the feeling of isolation growing inside of him. Pain bleeding outward, pain no one else saw or cared about.

Because they saw only what they wanted to when they looked at him. Maybe in the end, they were right. Could everyone be wrong about him? It didn't make much sense.

Maybe, all this time, he'd been the one who was wrong.

He'd been such an idiot. He had imagined that if he tried, he could be good enough for Kate. But he should've known. Bad blood. He would never be good enough for her; he would never be right for her. Even the people who were supposed to love him most felt that way.

He'd told Kate that he was wrong for her. But somewhere along the line he had stopped believing it. But she still did.

Damn himself for being so convincing.

KATE WATCHED AS JACK walked back to his truck, started it up and drove away. Then she turned and looked at her brother and at Liss, who were both staring at her awaiting an explanation she wasn't sure she could give. She wasn't giving any sort of explanation right now, because her throat was too tight, and her head was throbbing.

He loved her. Jack loved her. He had said the words and everything had frozen inside of her.

And now everyone around her seemed frozen, too. She couldn't face it.

"I need a ride home," she said, the words sounding far away and fuzzy. Not just like someone else was saying them—but like someone in another time and space was saying them.

Liss moved to her, wrapping her arm firmly around Kate's waist. "Of course."

Kate didn't want to be touched. She felt so damn fragile. As if a touch might break her. But she also wasn't about to push her pregnant sister-in-law away from her.

They walked down the street, Liss holding her tight, holding her together, Kate imagined now, since she felt as if her body was made entirely of cracks and splintering glass. Connor was behind them, acting like a shield against everyone rubbernecking to get a look at the situation.

Liss opened the door to Connor's truck and stood waiting for her to climb in.

"I... Can you sit in the middle?" Kate asked.

Kate needed an easy escape. She didn't know if she would survive the ride home. She needed to let part of the splintered bits of herself break open entirely. To let some of this pressure escape so it didn't dissolve her entirely.

"Sure." Liss climbed in ahead of her, surprisingly agile given her advanced stage of pregnancy.

For the first time ever in her whole life, Kate really wondered what it would be like to have a baby. A whole new wave of longing broke over her. Dreams, desires she'd never once let herself have, clawing up from deep inside her, threatening to overtake her.

Her stomach cramped and she got in quickly, slamming the truck door behind her just as Connor got in and closed the driver's side.

She wasn't going to think about shit like having babies. She'd never thought about it before.

She thought of Jack. Jack's hands on her skin. Jack looking at her, his blue eyes so deep and earnest.

I love you.

That meant...that meant this stuff. Getting married. Having babies.

The pang hit harder, echoing through her, a metallic taste lingering on her tongue.

No. She couldn't do that. He would depend on her then. A child would be depending on her...

Shit. No. Shit. No.

That mantra echoed in her head the entire ride back to the ranch, Connor and Liss, blissfully, letting silence fill the cab of the truck, letting it surround her like a fuzzy blanket, cushioning her from reality.

From the pain of the moment.

They pulled into the driveway and Kate felt her body start to tense. They would want to talk tonight. And she would have to explain.

And she couldn't explain. Not without the dam bursting and her becoming a whole flood that washed away everything she knew. Everything she was.

They pulled up in front of the main house. Of course Connor wasn't taking her home. Of course he was bringing her here. And Liss would make cocoa and they would want to talk and she couldn't. She couldn't.

She felt for the handle and flung the passenger door wide, undid her buckle and stumbled out of the truck.

She had told him she wasn't running. But she was. And she was going to do it again. She turned away from Connor and Liss and she ran. Not toward her house, toward the barn. If there was any clarity to be had, she would find it there.

There was no sound around her, only the desperate gasp for breath and the sound of her feet on the ground. She closed everything out and listened closely to that rhythm, counting footsteps, counting breaths. That at least did something to stem the pain.

She wrenched open the side door of the barn and walked inside, waiting for the immediate peace and calm that always came when she breathed that air in deep.

Instead it broke loose that frozen block that had lodged itself in her heart. All the cracks that had formed on the drive over breaking apart, bit by bit. And once that happened, the sob that had been building in her chest all this time released.

Tears flooded down her cheeks and she didn't make any move to stop them. She walked over to Roo's stall and pushed the door open. Stepping inside, she put her hand on her horse's rump, sliding her fingertips along up to her neck before wrapping her arms around the animal and burying her face against her. And then she cried like she didn't remember crying in her whole life. Not when her dad died, not when Jessie died.

She had cried—of course she had. She had grieved. Because she had lost. But something in her, a wall of some kind that she'd built up strong around herself, had held the flow in check.

That wall was gone now. And she was certain it had something to do with Jack. Stupid Jack. Stupid Jack who probably had Connor's knuckle prints in his cheek. She should have felt bad about that. Later she would feel bad about that. But right now she was glad that someone who was stronger than she was had knocked him flat. She wanted him to hurt the way she did, to feel afraid, to feel as if the rules had been changed.

Because she was small and petty. And she wasn't brave.

She had spent so long pretending to be brave. Convincing herself she was brave. Because she ran into everything with guns blazing. Because she didn't cry—she gritted her teeth and got to work. But the truth was, she did that only because she was afraid of all the other emotions she might accidentally feel. Bravery wasn't just being tough. And she was only just now realizing that fact.

Fine, then. She was a coward.

But things were changing too fast. She had changed; what she wanted had changed. And she was afraid she would keep on changing until she got to a place where she didn't recognize herself anymore.

This is what happened to Mom.

Fear gripped her throat and shook her hard, a sob racking her shoulders.

"Kate?"

The sound of her brother's voice penetrated her weeping.

She looked up, dragging her arm over her cheeks,

wiping the tears away. "Shouldn't you be out rallying the townsfolk with pitchforks and torches?"

"Did you want me to? Because I would happily go torch Monaghan's ass. He would deserve it."

She sniffed loudly. "Why are you so convinced of that? You haven't even asked me what my part in all this was."

"He deserves it, because you're my sister. And you're upset. There's only one side for me to take."

"You probably shouldn't hate him."

"I don't know. I was sort of thinking I should call up Eli and make sure he hates him, too."

She shuddered, another sob working its way through her. "Don't."

"I do have to tell him. Otherwise the gossip chain is going to wrap itself around him when he goes to get that foofy coffee of his tomorrow morning before his shift. I imagine you would rather have me controlling the conversation instead of some old busybody."

"I guess we did make gossip. But it was his fault."

"Then I'll ready the pitchforks," Connor said, his tone casual.

She wiped at a tear that was running down her cheek. "No, you dumb asshole. I meant the spectacle was his fault. Because he wouldn't just…"

"Kate Garrett, this is the first time I've seen you cry outside a funeral since you were a little girl with two skinned knees, two scraped elbows and a split lip from a very ill-advised stunt you pulled climbing around in the hayloft. Which in my mind means Jack Monaghan might need killing. But I would rather know for sure before I go risking jail time over the demise of my oldest friend."

She paused for a moment. "Well, on the one hand, if you did kill him, Eli might help you cover it up."

"Kate. He said… He said that he loved you. The only thing I have ever heard Jack say he loved is a hamburger and a piece of pie. He doesn't do things like that. He doesn't get attached to people. Well, people other than me and Eli. He doesn't get attached to women."

Another tear trailed down her cheek. "I know."

"Maybe tell me what's been going on with few enough details that I don't end up emotionally scarred."

She blinked rapidly, trying to stem the flow of moisture that was running endlessly from her eyes. "We've been…together. You know. Together."

"Yes. I know exactly what you mean. Picnics in the field with a good foot of space between your bodies. The begrudging allowance of hand-holding after several dates. That is what you mean."

"Well…"

"No. For the purposes of this conversation. That is what you mean. Continue."

A reluctant laugh pushed through her tears. "Right. Picnics. And it was supposed to just be picnics. That's what he said. That's what I wanted. It's what I agreed to. But then…then tonight happened. He told me that he loved me. And I just…" Tears and misery struggled to the forefront again, choking off her words. "I can't. Connor, I can't. How can I? With everything… With Mom…"

Suddenly, she found herself being tugged away from her horse and pulled into Connor's embrace. "Whatever Mom's issues were, they were hers. Only hers. You're not why she left, Kate. I'm sure there were a million reasons, but you weren't one of them. You weren't the reason she left. But you are damn sure the reason we stayed. You were our glue, Katie. You're the reason Eli and I didn't just give up and go off and do Lord knows what while everything here fell apart. We didn't stay for Dad. It was all for you. So don't for one moment think that you somehow can't have love."

She took a shuddering breath. "At the risk of sounding a little bit egotistical, I actually do know that, Connor." She took a deep, shuddering breath. "You and Eli did such a good job of letting me know that you never resented me. And letting me know just how special I was. All of the baggage and crap that I have because of Mom and Dad… That's all on them. And it's so much smaller than it probably should be. Because of you."

"So what's the matter, then, Katie? If you don't love him, you don't love him. And that's fine. But you're in here crying like someone reached in and pulled your heart out. You look like someone who just lost love. I'm the last person on earth to push anyone toward Jack. I know him well enough to know what he's done, and that when it comes to love he's unproven. But I don't want to see you like this." He released his hold on her. "Do you love him?"

"It isn't that simple."

"Bullshit it's not. It's completely that simple."

"No, it's not. I'm not afraid of not being lovable. You've proved to me that I am. Eli has proved it. I'm afraid of… I'm afraid of me. I've changed so much just in the past couple of months. I tried so hard not to. For a long time. But then I saw myself being left behind. You're married. You're having a baby. Eli is married. I was still just me. I got afraid. And I thought maybe

I needed to do something. So I started aiming harder for the rodeo stuff. And…and then there was Jack. I know you worried about being Dad. That's not what I worry about. I worry that I'm Mom. So I spent a hell of a long time just working hard, trying to be everything good that you and Eli were. And then I allowed just a little bit of change, and everything feels outside my control. Where will it end? I'm afraid of what I'll change into. I'm afraid that someday I'll be the one who walks out the door. On my husband. On my kids. Dad always… I swore when Dad looked at me, he was seeing her. I'm better off just doing the rodeo thing. I'm better off if nobody needs me."

"Katie," he said, his voice rough. "I love you. That's a load of shit. You have to get out of your own way."

"Easy for you—"

"Think real hard before you finish that sentence," Connor said, his voice hard. "I know all about life kicking you in the balls. I know better than most. I would venture to say I know better than you. I also know that there's a point where you can't blame other people or even fate for the crap in your life. If you hold on to her too long, it's all you get." He sighed heavily. "I almost lost Liss. And it wouldn't have been anyone's fault but mine."

"But what if I—?"

"Who controls your life, Kate? Sure, none of us chose the parents we had. I didn't choose to lose Jessie. But you? You control you. If you don't want to leave, don't leave. If you want to be faithful to your husband, be faithful to your husband. If you want to have children, and you want to be a good mother, choose to do that. Don't you let people who abandoned us determine how happy you'll be. Don't you let them stop you from having love. And don't you ever let fear decide what you'll become." He grabbed hold of her arms and looked her in the eye. "I don't care what you do. If you ride on the circuit and only come home off-season. If you marry that asshole Jack and have ten babies. As long as it makes you happy. Be happy."

She swallowed, her throat so dry it felt as if she'd swallowed a handful of dust. "I'm scared." It was a hard thing to admit, a hard thing to say. She'd lived so long thinking she was brave.

"That's okay. Me, too. I'm about to be a father. I don't know how to do that. But it isn't the fear that's the problem. It's what you do with it. It's whether or not you let it win." He patted her shoulder and looked at her hard.

"Connor," she said.

"Yes?"

"You do know how to do that. How to be a father. Listen to all the things I just told you. About how I never felt unloved. You're going to be great."

The corner of his mouth lifted. "Thanks. I needed to hear that. But if I'm going to listen to you, you need to listen to me. You aren't anyone but you, Kate. Remember that."

She nodded slowly and watched him walk out of the barn.

She didn't feel relieved at all. In fact, she was starting to feel angry. He wasn't listening to her excuses. They were good excuses. They would keep her safe. They would keep her from getting hurt.

Like you aren't already hurt? You're in here crying like an orphaned calf.

Yes. She was. But pretending to be tough, shutting out every emotion, every deep desire, meant that she couldn't get her heart broken. If she didn't pay attention to her heart, what would she care if it was, anyway?

But she did care. Right now she did, because she felt like she was dying. Maybe it was just too late for all this self-protection. Maybe this was as bad as it got.

This misery of her own making was possibly the most painful thing she'd ever experienced.

Did she love him? She was afraid to answer that question. Connor was right—she could control herself. She could control what she did. And for the majority of her life that had meant protecting herself. As life had raged on around her without asking what it should or shouldn't do, as people had been torn from her life in various different ways, she had built up walls around herself, stronger, higher. Had honed herself down to the basics. Tough. Hardworking. Loyal. Those things were simple; those things were sure.

But the rodeo had been the start of it. The start of wanting more. And once she had opened up that desire inside of herself, more had followed.

But no matter how well she protected herself, no matter how tightly she controlled her desires, she couldn't control life. She wouldn't be able to build a wall around Jack that contained them both, that kept them safe from everything.

It was easier to forget him. To curl up into a ball and find the bricks that had been destroyed by the shattering weeks with him and start to rebuild.

She had been blindsided by life too many times. Had felt like nothing more than a helpless little girl

who was at the mercy of stronger forces. She had found
ways to shield herself from that, and she had been stupid to forget them.

She could control herself. So she would.

CHAPTER TWENTY

THE WEST RANCH was one flipping fancy place. From the gated entry to the sprawling Spanish-style mansion and the top-notch boarding and riding facilities.

For one moment, one brief moment, Jack allowed himself to imagine what it might have been like to grow up here. To spend his days wandering across the manicured lawns before meandering idly down one of the paths that led to the stables.

But it was a very brief moment.

He hadn't grown up here. He'd grown up in a dirty, moldy trailer that had made his skin break out into a rash. Because even his mother had felt as though she had to pay homage to the mighty Wests by not even asking for the child support she was due. Well, he was done.

He was done being anyone's dirty secret. And if that meant becoming the dirty laundry spread out all over the yard, so be it. But he wasn't hiding. Not for anyone.

He made his way up the manicured walk and rapped the brass knocker against the door. Apparently, the place was too damned fancy for something as practical as a doorbell. And God forbid any of the invited guests tax their knuckles requesting entry.

He waited. And he realized that he had no guarantee of who might be behind the door when someone answered. If someone answered. It could be Sierra. Could be the older West daughter, Madison. Or one of the sons. The other sons. The ones who weren't him.

It could also be Nathan West's wife.

And he could be standing on the doorstep holding the final nail in the coffin of their marriage. It was hard to say.

Even if you are, it isn't because of anything you did. It's because she's married to a bastard.

A bastard who produced more bastards.

He heard footsteps on the other side of the door and his muscles tensed. Momentarily, nerves took over, and they were almost strong enough to blot out the pain that had been radiating around his heart since the moment Kate had rejected him. Almost.

The door opened. It was Madison, one of the Wests he'd had very little contact with. She was younger than he was by quite a bit, older than Kate or Sierra. She always looked like she was irritated to be wherever she was, her expression tight and restless. As though she was in far too much of a hurry to deal with whatever was in front of her.

She was looking at him like that right now.

"Is your father home?" he asked, just barely restraining himself from asking if *their* father was home.

She blinked slowly. Even her blink was bored of him. "He is. May I tell him who's here to—?"

The door opened wider behind Madison to reveal Nathan West. "Whatever you want to discuss, Mr. Monaghan, we can do so outside privately."

"Fine with me," Jack said, taking a step away from the threshold.

Nathan moved past his daughter, closed the door

and led them a few paces away from the house. "Am I going to have to call the police on you?"

"I doubt it. You should know that the sheriff is one of my best friends. So." At least, the sheriff had been one of his best friends. As it stood, Eli might arrest him cheerfully.

"What is it you want? We have an agreement."

"That's actually what I'm here about. I'm here to release myself from that agreement." He reached into his pocket and pulled out an envelope. "There's cash in here. You can count it. It's the exact amount you gave me. It's my hush money. And I'm paying it back because I'm not going to be quiet anymore. And now you can't make me." But it was different now. This was about freedom. He wouldn't be making more bids for attention, wouldn't ever care if Nathan West looked his way again.

Nathan's eyes blazed. "You can't do this. You're just going to walk around ruining my reputation? Ruining my family?"

"This may come as a shock to you but I have no desire to ruin you—" as he spoke the words, he realized they were true "—but I'm not going to pretend. I'm not going to hide. And I'm not going to owe you a debt. Now, I know I needed your money to get the start I got. Because frankly, growing up like I did, with nothing, it would have made getting to my position a whole lot harder, if not impossible. But I'll take the loan as my due, since you were able to dodge child support for the first eighteen years of my life. I'll consider it payment for keeping the secret all that time, for allowing you to stay married to a woman who probably has no idea what a jackass you are. For letting you keep your family intact while your kids grew up. You know, the kids you acknowledge. And now I owe you nothing. That's the most important thing I can think of."

"Did you expect I would respect you for this? Because I don't," Nathan said, sticking the envelope in his pocket. "I don't think much of anything about you."

Jack waited for pain, for a sense of rejection. There was none of it. Nathan was just a man. An old man. And he might have been responsible for some of Jack's genetic material, but not for anything else. And now there was no debt between them. Whatever Jack wanted to do about their relationship, if he wanted to do anything at all, he wasn't bound by any sort of agreement.

"Did you expect me to cry when you said that, Dad?" Jack asked drily. "Because I promise you I won't. I'm going to go home, to my nice house. I'm going to figure out a way to win the woman I love, and when I do, I will treat her like a queen. I will stay faithful to her all my life. That's a lesson you taught me, whether you meant to or not. Because I've seen the other side of it. I will never be you. And I am glad of that. I know you think I should be proud that you're my dad, that you should be ashamed I'm your son. But nothing could be further from the truth. I may go on hiding the fact we're related because I'm ashamed of you."

Jack turned away from the old man, not waiting for a response. And with every step he took, he felt as if he was shedding years of weight from his shoulders. And as he reached his truck, he felt as though a tether snapped between himself and his father. Whatever he owed him was settled. It was done.

And now he was going to make good on the promise he had just made to his father.

He was going to win Kate's heart. And when he did, he was going to do everything in his power to keep it.

THE WAITING ROOM at the birthing center was filling up with friends. Where the Garretts were short on family, they didn't lack for support.

Kate was sitting next to Eli and Sadie, her fingertips biting into the pink patterned fabric that covered the arms of the waiting room chairs. She had underestimated just how terrifying Liss giving birth would be. Everyone around her seemed calm, firmly accepting that this was the normal order of things. That women had babies, and everything was fine. But Kate was terrified.

Because life wasn't always fine. And she knew it.

She couldn't fix it. She couldn't control it. Here in the waiting room, she was just a little girl, sitting on the step at the school, waiting for a father who would never show. At the mercy of the wind or life or whatever it was that saw fit to play so dangerously with her.

She hated this. She hated everything about it. Why was life so fucking scary?

It was so much easier when you didn't have all these people to love, all these opportunities to bleed.

Jack was just one more. And she just couldn't. She couldn't.

"Are you okay?" Eli asked, his tones hushed.

"Fine," she lied.

"Connor told me a little bit about what happened with Jack," Eli said, his voice measured.

She was almost relieved that he was asking about

Jack instead of dredging up the deep brokenness that
was in her. The screaming, knowing little fear beast
that exposed her for the coward she was.

"He told you?"

"Yes. I had to talk him out of killing Monaghan, so
you should be grateful he came to speak to me." Eli
paused for a moment. "Unless you want him dead."

"I don't want him dead," she said, her heart fluttering. "I don't even like to joke about that. We are kind
of a lightning rod for crap, if you hadn't noticed." The
entire situation had set her on edge.

"Of course we're not going to kill him," Eli said.
"But I do have questions."

Sadie's head appeared around her husband's shoulder as she leaned in, her expression keen.

"Obviously, Sadie has questions," Kate said, her
voice monotone.

"About a thousand," Sadie said.

"There isn't anything to say. It happened. It's not
happening now."

"But how did it happen? Why did it happen? How
long did it happen?" This was from Sadie, and Eli just
sat there looking visibly uncomfortable.

"I don't think Eli wants the same level of detail you
do," Kate said.

"That is a fact." This came from Eli.

"What happened?" Sadie asked, deciding to be
more selective in her questioning, clearly.

"Things. Stuff and things," Kate said. "I'm over
it," she lied.

Just then the thing she was most definitely not over
walked into the waiting area, a fluorescent green visitor tag on his shirt.

Eli simply stared at him, not offering a greeting. Sadie looked from him to Kate, then did a noncommittal half wave.

Then Eli stood. "What are you doing here?"

"I was looking for everyone. Stopped by the Farm and Garden to see if Kate was there and was told you were all here. So now I'm here, too."

"Nobody called you," Eli said.

Guilt twisted Kate's internal organs. Because if not for her, him and all of the fallout, there would have been no question about him coming today. He had been friends with Connor and Liss for years, so of course he would have been here for this. She had ruined it. They had ruined it.

"I'm well aware nobody called me, Eli. But I'm here all the same. Because I'm not about to let something that happened between myself and your sister, who is an adult, by the way, keep me from supporting Connor through this. Liss is a friend, too. Why would I miss this? Just because you're pissed right now? Anyway, I'm pretty sure I would be mad in your situation, too, but I'm not sure you have the right to be. Kate makes her own decisions. She always has. There is no pushing her when she doesn't want to be pushed—you know that. I've recently had a reminder of that. She does what she wants. She knows her own mind. I didn't talk her into anything."

Kate could barely tear her eyes off the ground to look at him, but even though it was hard, she did. "You should also know that Kate doesn't like being discussed like she's not here."

"I didn't figure you were speaking to me," he said.

"Well, I didn't figure you were speaking to me."

"I went looking for you, didn't I?"

"Not sure why you would."

"The little matter of being in love with you."

Eli straightened a little bit at that. "What?"

"So you didn't hear about that part," Jack said.

"No," Eli responded.

"It doesn't matter. That shouldn't matter. And let's not discuss this now," Kate said. "Better yet, let's not discuss this ever. Jack and I have said everything that needs to be said to each other, and the rest isn't your business."

She wrapped her arms around herself, holding herself tight. Protecting herself. She would be tough.

But you aren't being brave.

Yeah, well, screw bravery. She didn't want to be brave.

She wanted to be safe.

Of course, Liss was in there giving birth, and Connor was in there trying to cope with that. The people around her seemed to refuse to climb into her little bubble and insulate themselves. And what could she do about that?

Then there was Jack, who was trying to tear it all open, expose her to the elements.

In this moment, she hated them all.

"I'll just go sit over there." Jack turned away and went to a row of chairs that was unoccupied, then sat there resolutely, his arms crossed over his chest.

Her heart felt as though it was cracking open all over again. How did other people not see the faithfulness of Jack Monaghan? He was here. Even when he wasn't wanted. Here because it was right. That was how deeply he cared, how true his loyalty ran.

How could anyone think he was fickle? How could anyone think he was nothing more than bad blood? Even Liss had doubted him, and he was still here for her.

She would have been proud of him if she wasn't so irritated with the bastard.

Minutes stretched into hours. Kate got up from where she was sitting and walked down the hall toward the water and ice machine that was there for their use.

She heard heavy footsteps behind her and she didn't have to turn to figure out whose they were.

"What?"

"I want to talk to you," Jack said.

"Not now," she said.

"Fine. After."

"Assuming everything is okay."

"Of course everything is okay." In spite of herself, she looked at him. "Everything is going to be fine."

He could see straight through her; more to the point, she let him. She showed him her fear. She didn't know what it was about him that compelled her to do it.

"You don't know that," she choked.

"I guess I don't," he responded. "I guess we can never really know for sure. But without hope, what do you have, Katie?"

"Protection? Protection from disappointment."

"Do you really think expecting bad things to happen makes bad things hurt less?"

She shook her head slowly. "I don't know. But all we can do is survive the best we can, right?"

He looked at her for a long moment, his blue eyes assessing. "I would have agreed with you not too long ago. But now I think maybe we should try for better than surviving. I think maybe we should try living."

Living. It was an entirely different image than survival. Survival conjured up a picture of her huddled in a cave, knees drawn up to her chest, arms wrapped around herself while the storm raged outside.

Living made her think more of dancing in the rain, daring the lightning to strike.

She wasn't sure she could do that. The cave wasn't all that appealing, but it was safe.

"I can't talk about this right now." She turned away from the machine and headed back to her seat, only realizing once she was in view of Sadie and Eli again that she had forgotten to get the water she had gone to fetch in the first place. Great.

Just then the door to the delivery room cracked open, and the nurse came out. "She's here. Healthy. A beautiful baby girl."

All of the breath in her lungs escaped on a rush, her ears buzzing. "Everything is okay?" she asked, unable to disguise the fear in her voice.

"Everything is okay."

The nurse disappeared for a moment, then reappeared. "Kate? Your brother wants you to come in and see the baby."

Kate stood, her legs wobbly. "He wants *me* to come in?"

The nurse nodded. "We'll start with you."

Kate walked forward, and any pretense of being fine and together was out the window. They walked into the room, the sounds of bustling and a baby crying hitting her hard. The nurse swept the curtain aside. Liss was lying in the bed, her feet still up in stirrups. Kate chose to look away from that. It wasn't hard anyway.

Because Connor was standing there, big and strong and as infallible as he'd always been in her mind, with the smallest baby she'd ever seen nestled in the crook of his arm and a tear on his cheek.

He looked up from the baby, only for a moment, meeting her eyes. "She's just perfect, Katie. Isn't she?"

Kate felt like she'd been punched in the chest. "Yes."

"A girl," he said, smiling now. "My daughter. Ruby. I have a daughter."

She looked at the baby, at Connor, at his wife. At a whole second chance playing out right in front of her that would never have happened if Connor had chosen to simply survive.

Something felt as though it was swelling inside her. Growing too large for her to breathe around. She couldn't breathe.

"I'm so happy for you," she said, her voice barely a whisper. "I'll let… I'll let Eli and Sadie come in now."

She turned and walked out of the room, and then she walked out of the waiting room, out of the hospital. She got in her truck, and by the time she started the engine, tears were streaming down her face, matching the rain that was starting to fall from the sky.

WHEN KATE GOT back to the ranch, she parked her truck in front of the barn, killed the engine and got out, her boot pressing down deep into the muddy ground.

The rain was falling hard and fast now, and a smart person would take shelter. That was how you survived, after all. She should go back to her house and light a fire in the woodstove, put on her sweats and hunker down. That was surviving.

She was tired of surviving.

She was tired of being stripped down to the essentials. She kicked her boots off, and the mud was slick between her toes, the gravel that was mixed in painful as it dug into her tender skin. But she could feel it.

She moved toward the stretch of green field in front of her. She walked through a gap in the fence, the mud deeper now, velvety blades of grass creating a barrier between her and the squishy ground. She just stood there for a while and looked up at the sky, letting the rain roll down her face, mixing with the tears she was certain were falling now.

Standing here, stretched out like this, facing the broad expanse of sky, she could feel the stiffness inside of her, the strain from having been curled up, stagnant for so long. She was never one to sit still physically, perhaps in part because it gave too much voice to the internal.

So she stood still now, and she let herself feel. The cold, the rain, the grass, the mud. And her heart. Beating steadily, painfully.

Beating for Jack.

Emotion rose up inside of her, grew, expanded. Love. She loved him.

And it was worth every risk, every possible outcome. Because she would so much rather stand out in the storm than keep hiding.

She thought of Jack's face, of the pain in his blue eyes when she had rejected him. She had hurt him. She had been so focused on her own fear, on her own trauma, that she hadn't paused to consider what he had risked. She hadn't thought of his pain, because she hadn't imagined she could possibly hurt him.

She had. She had made him feel as if she thought he was a secret, as if she was ashamed of him.

Protecting herself had hurt the man she loved most. And if she had needed any other bit of confirmation that she had to change, that was it.

She heard the slam of a car door and turned to see Jack standing by his truck. The sound of the rain must have obscured the sound of the motor.

She stood there frozen as the rain washed down her cheeks, watching as he approached. He was wearing his hat, that hat that never failed to make her heart squeeze tight, the tight black T-shirt that outlined his perfect body and the jeans that knew him almost as intimately as she did. It was like watching her soul walk toward her. And the closer he got, the more complete she felt, the more right everything felt.

"Did you follow me, Monaghan?" she shouted over the rain.

"Yes, I did. I wanted to make sure you were okay." He moved through the same gap in the fence that she had and stopped when he was about a foot in front of her. "And I wanted to make sure you didn't weasel out of our talk."

"Nothing quite that calculated. I just needed… I just needed some time."

He swallowed, his Adam's apple bobbing up and down. "And have you had it?"

"Yes," she said. "You were right. I was being scared. I've spent my whole life being scared."

"You, Kate Garrett? Scared?"

"Yes. Me. My mom left when I was two. My dad died when I was in high school. My sister-in-law... Life has always been kind of a scary, unpredictable thing for me. But the one thing I could do was make myself tough. Make it so I didn't feel it quite so deep. I told myself I was fine because I had Connor and Eli to take care of me. Because I had you. Except then things changed between us. It wasn't just you taking care of me, making me smile. You broke me open and made me feel. That was scarier than anything. Scarier than going pro, scarier than facing down an angry mama bear. Scary. I told myself I was upset because of the changes. Because I might turn into something I didn't want to be. But the simple truth was, I was just afraid to feel. When you feel, when you want, loss can hurt you. Not just hurt, devastate. It changes things inside you that you can never put back. It's a terrifying thing to sign on for, Jack."

He cleared his throat. "I can't even pretend to know loss the same way you do, Kate. I know in some ways I have more experience, but in other ways I feel like you've lived more life than I have. And not life I envy."

"Connor tried to talk to me, but I wasn't ready. Then today... I saw him with Liss. Their baby. Jack, he has all of that because he refused to give in to fear. He has life—he made life. I want that. More. Everything."

"Everything?" He took a step toward her, gripped her chin with his thumb and forefinger. "Really, everything?" His expression was fierce, his voice hoarse. "Does that mean you love me, badger-cat?"

She didn't even bother to hold back the tears that welled up in her eyes. "Yes, Monaghan. I do. I love you. I did even when I said I didn't. I didn't mean to lie, but I was too afraid to even think it."

His blue eyes, normally so wicked, glittered with moisture, too. "Well, I'm glad to hear that. Damn glad."

She expelled a breath on a broken sob. "I have so many sorries to say to you. For hurting you. For making you think I was ashamed, rather than admitting that I was just a coward. Jack, I don't deserve your forgiveness. I don't deserve for you to love me."

He leaned down, kissing her lips lightly. "That's where you're wrong. You deserve for me to love you always. No matter what. Kate, don't you understand that you are the reason I'm not ashamed of myself anymore? I spent a lot of years sabotaging myself. Telling myself I wanted approval while going out of my way to make sure I didn't get it. Because I was ashamed of what I had done. Ashamed of who I was. Wanting recognition I couldn't have, because I'd signed that away. But I'm free of that now. You saw me more clearly than I ever saw myself, and it took that for me to finally change." He swallowed hard. "I gave the money back to Nathan West. And I don't know if I'll ever tell anyone that he's my father. But I could. I'm not hiding anymore. Not where I come from, not who I am. That's all you, baby."

"I guess we both helped each other."

"I hear that's what love is for. To make you better. To make the person you love better."

"I believe it."

"I still want you to do the rodeo. Because you want to."

She smiled up at him.

"Really?"

The rain slowed, the clouds parting slightly, pale yellow light breaking through.

"Yes. And I will support you however you want me to. By going with you. By staying away… Bribing judges. Holding a bake sale."

She laughed. "You would do all that for me?"

"Happily." He tightened his hold on her and bent down, sweeping his other arm behind her knees and lifting her up, cradling her against his chest. "Do you know why?"

"Because I let you do me in a barn?"

"That doesn't hurt. But that's not why."

"Because I am a badass badger-cat and you fear me?"

He laughed and kissed her nose. "No. Because you're mine. And I love you. Which means nothing on earth will ever separate us. Even distance. I'm in this. For real. Forever."

Kate put her hand on his cheek, angling her head up so that she could kiss him. "Same goes, Jack Monaghan. Same goes."

"Well, I am awfully glad to hear that."

Kate Garrett had never much belonged to anyone. And that was the way she had liked it. But as Jack carried her through the field, down the driveway and back to her house, she couldn't help but think that belonging to someone, having someone belong to you, was a whole lot better than being alone.

And when he laid her down on the bed, the bed that she'd thought was big enough for only one, and pulled her into his arms, she knew for a fact that spending the rest of her life living with him would be a much better adventure than simply surviving on her own.

EPILOGUE

IT HAD TAKEN a little bit longer than usual to get the game started. But Ruby Kate Garrett ran the show these days, even though she was only two months old. Named for her hair and for her fearless aunt, she had taken over the Garrett ranch with ease.

She was the cutest thing any of them had ever seen. Also, a grumpy little pink cuss. In that way, she took after her father. Though Connor didn't seem to mind putting up with his daughter's crankiness. Far from it—it was the happiest Jack had ever seen his friend.

Right now she was asleep in the crook of Connor's arm, while he balanced both her and his poker hand, which Jack had caught glimpses of. Enough to know that Connor was definitely not the one who was going to win tonight.

Not that Jack cared either way. As far as he was concerned, he had a winning hand no matter the cards that were dealt to him.

He had Kate. He didn't need much more than that.

"So how are the new digs, Katie?" Connor asked.

"Jack has a housekeeper," Kate said, putting her hand on his thigh beneath the table. He fought the wicked impulse that told him to move it up a little bit higher. "It's pretty awesome."

"That's the only reason she moved in with me. She sleeps in the guest room," Jack lied cheerfully.

"I don't mind that," Eli said, grinning.

The moment Jack and Kate had told her family that they were in love, the issues they'd all had with the two of them as a couple had vanished.

"You act like such a prude," Sadie said, digging her elbow into Eli's side. "Sheriff in the streets, freak in the sheets."

"I like that," Liss said. "I would come up with one for Connor but he's pretty much only one way."

"I'm genuine," Connor said. "And honest."

"And less grumpy than you used to be," Liss said. "Which I appreciate. And I assume everyone else does, too."

They all raised their various beverages in salute.

"Nice. Thank you," Connor said, touching the edge of a little pink blanket around his daughter's sleeping form.

It was an amazing thing, this new normal they were creating. With couples and a baby and love. And for the first time in a lot of years, Jack truly felt like part of a family. Oh, sure, the Garretts had always made him feel like one of their own. But with any luck, soon he actually would be.

They played a few more rounds until the new parents started getting droopy from lack of sleep. Then they divvied up the food, Kate snagging all of the dessert, and headed out. It was a strange and wonderful thing to be leaving together. Going back to the same house.

A house that was a home now, because she was in it.

It was dark outside, the air holding a sharp chill that

stabbed deep into his lungs like an ice pick. Or maybe that was just nerves.

Once they were on the bottom porch step, Jack pulled Kate up against him. She clutched the boxes of pie closer to her chest. "Don't make me drop this. It's a s'mores pie. I don't know if you understand how much that means to me."

"Of course I do. I would never do anything to compromise your pie."

"Sure." She wiggled her hip against his. "Is that a rock in your pocket or are you just happy to see me? Fun fact, I totally didn't get what that meant until after you and I... Well, you get the idea."

"That's adorable. And while I am always happy to see you, I actually do have something in my pocket. Incidentally, as with the other option, it is also for you."

She blinked, her eyes wide. "What is it?"

"It might be a ring box," he said, his throat getting tight.

"Oh, really?"

"I know you're not big into sparkly things, but I thought you might like this one a little bit. To wear while you compete this summer."

"Jack Monaghan, I have never worn a piece of jewelry in my life." She stretched up on her tiptoes and kissed him. "But I know for a fact that I'll wear this one for the rest of it."

* * * * *

Shoulda Been a Cowboy

CHAPTER ONE

JAKE CALDWELL HAD most definitely improved with age. It really didn't seem fair. Rather than gaining five pounds around his hips like she had, his chest and shoulders had grown broader, his waist trim, his stomach washboard flat. It almost, *almost*, made her rue her addiction to the loganberry tarts she stocked in the pastry display at The Grind. Almost.

Cassie Ventimiglia slowly sank down behind the counter, putting Jake, who was outside dismounting his motorcycle, out of her sight. She didn't need to spend any more time looking at him. She needed to take inventory of her soy milk. She opened the mini fridge that was built into the counter and began to dutifully do just that.

Her soy milk supply was sufficient. Which was good to know. Important. Much more important than taking in the view outside.

Cassie rose again slowly, eyeing the small dining room. Most of the women in it were casting subtle glances outside. And Cassie figured they weren't checking out Copper Ridge's main street.

Jake had that effect. But he always had. Even back when he'd been that dark scowling boy with perfect hair and wicked blue eyes wandering the halls of the high school, tattooed and bad news, and everything that kept mothers of good girls awake at night. And ensured that the fathers of good girls kept their shotguns close by.

Actually, that was probably why he had been so fascinating. As far as Copper Ridge, Oregon, went, he had been universally disapproved of. And what was more attractive than that, when you were seventeen and just starting to figure out that there was more to life than what your parents had told you? Nothing. At least not as far as she'd been concerned.

Of course, she had actually gotten to know him. Had seen beneath some of his tough exterior. Had bothered to see him as a human being. For all the good that had done her. She'd just ended up with a crush wider than the Columbia River Gorge. And before she'd been able to confess that, before she'd been able to tell him just what she wanted from him, he'd left.

She seemed to have that effect on men. But she wasn't going to think about that right now. She was going to think about muffins. She could inventory those next. So hooray for that.

Anyway, she had no reason to be…staring at him, thinking about him, drooling after him. He'd given no indication at all that he was interested in her as anything other than a tenant he happened to live near. He was aloof to the point of being cool. That was something that had changed.

When he'd been a teenager he'd had an air of intensity, anger and restlessness about him. Now he just seemed… Well, he seemed almost bored to be here. Like he was looking through things.

Like he was looking through her.

The little bell above the door chirped and she

looked up just in time to see Jake walk in. He had been here for more than a week. Back in town, staying in the apartment next to hers. It was a complicated situation, really.

Jake's father had owned the building that housed her coffee shop and the apartments above it, in addition to a couple of other properties in town and a ranch just outside of it. That meant Jake was the owner now. And effectively her landlord.

At least he hadn't changed much since he'd arrived, with the exception of inhabiting the neighboring apartment. She only hoped he continued to not change things.

He came into the coffee shop every day and ordered an Americano and a muffin. Which meant that she should be used to him by now. It meant that her stomach should not go into a free fall, her heart should not skip several beats, and her palms should most certainly not get sweaty.

In addition to the fact that his presence was old news by now, she was thirty-two. She was, in the immortal words of *Lethal Weapon*'s Roger Murtaugh, too old for this shit.

And yet the second he'd walked in each morning, her heart rate had indeed increased, her stomach had plummeted, and her palms were definitely starting to get a little bit damp.

She forced her breathing to slow as he approached. He was holding his bike helmet beneath his arm, propping it against his hip. There was something epically badass about him when he stood that way. It was as appealing now as it had been fifteen years ago. And she had no idea why that was. He'd never been a good idea for her, never been a logical match. Her hormones had never registered that fact.

He laid his helmet on the counter and pushed his hand through his dark hair, drawing her eyes to the tattoo of dark evergreen trees that wrapped around his arm. They started at his wrist and extended up to his elbow. His tattoos fascinated her, now and always, because she'd never been able to imagine voluntarily undergoing something so presumptively painful.

That he'd been willing to do it only added to his mystique.

Oh, shoot. She had a feeling her internal monologue had been running for quite some time, and it was very possible Jake had been standing there for a little longer than she realized.

"The usual?" The question came out a croak, and she was none too impressed with herself.

Jake lifted one broad shoulder, not sparing her a smile. Smiling did not seem to be a part of his emotional vocabulary. That much she had learned over the past week. "Sounds good."

"The only kind of muffin I have left is blueberry."

"That's fine." He shifted his weight from one foot to another and for some reason she found it fascinating. "Every muffin you've ever served me has been delicious."

Cassie nearly choked. "I'm glad you like my…muffins." For some reason it all sounded dirty. Maybe her mind was in the gutter by default because he was here.

Maybe it didn't even have anything to do with him. Maybe it was her. After all, it had been three years since her divorce and even longer since she'd made skin-to-skin contact with a man.

That was a long time. She hadn't been conscious of just how long until Jake had blown back into town.

"There's nothing to dislike about your muffins."

She sucked in a sharp breath and choked on it, coughing violently. She turned her head to the crook of her elbow, trying to suppress it. "Sorry." She patted her chest as she grabbed the portafilter from the espresso machine. "Swallowed wrong."

She went over to the grinder, ignoring the heat in her cheeks as she turned it on, putting the portafilter beneath it and releasing enough grounds to produce a double shot. She tamped them down and went back to the machine, fitting the portafilter back in and pressing the button, counting the seconds on the shot as it filled the little tin cup she had placed beneath it.

It was a nice distraction, and once again she felt justified in her selection of a manual machine versus an automatic one. She emptied the completed shot into a paper cup and then poured hot water over it, putting the lid on and setting it on the counter. Then she reached into the basket and pulled out the last remaining muffin.

She extended her arm to hand it to him, only realizing her mistake when the tips of his fingers brushed hers and the shock of pure electricity ran through her body, immobilizing her for a moment.

She looked up and compounded her mistake as their eyes clashed and she was hit by a second bolt of lightning. And for just one nanosecond, she saw something flash through his eyes, too. Something not entirely cool and neutral.

She took her hand off the muffin and it went flying over the edge of the counter and onto the floor somewhere around his feet. She wasn't sure exactly where, because she was too horrified to look. "I thought you had it. I'm sorry. I'm sorry. No charge. Nobody wants a floor muffin."

He arched a dark brow, bending down and retrieving the muffin before standing back up and holding it out. "It's still wrapped. I'm sure it's fine."

"No, really. I insist. Everything is on me." Because, if she charged him, she would have to take his cash and if that happened they might touch again.

"All right, I'm not going to argue with that." He took his helmet, the muffin and the coffee and turned away, giving her a half wave with the hand that was clutching the coffee cup.

He walked outside again and rounded the back of the shop toward the exterior stairs that led up to his apartment. Cassie let out a breath she hadn't been aware she was holding.

She really needed to get it together. Yes, Jake Caldwell was back. But now, just like back in high school, there was no point in lusting after him. Nothing had happened then, and nothing was going to happen now. End of story.

And she had more inventory to take.

JAKE SET THE muffin and the coffee down on his counter and jerked the fridge open. It was early, but he was going to go ahead and grab a beer rather than that afternoon caffeine hit he'd been looking forward to.

Because he didn't need to be any more amped up than he already was. Something about this damn town screwed with him. Always had. Foolishly, he'd imagined that after so many years away the place might have less power.

Nope. Between the afternoon he'd spent at his dad's place clearing junk out and that little interaction with Cassie down in the coffee shop, he needed to cool down, not rev up.

He wasn't the same man he'd been when he left town. So what was it about this place that made him feel like he hadn't changed all that much? Still not quite able to handle all the shit at home. Still finding himself drawn to the kind of women he shouldn't be allowed to touch.

Cassie Ventimiglia was one of those nice girls. Caring, way too sweet for her own good. She'd been one of the few people who'd spoken to him back in high school. They'd been thrown together, part of a tutoring program to help his delinquent self get it together and get his grades up.

She'd been tempting, inexplicably. Because she was not the kind of girl he would normally look twice at. But she'd looked at him like she'd seen him, and he'd…

Well, it was just a damn good thing for her he'd left when he had.

But even now, when he'd come back to deal with selling his family's properties, she'd been first in line to welcome him back, even if it had been unintentional.

By default, he owned the building her business was in, and the place she lived. Going over his dad's paperwork he could see that before Cassie the building had been out of use for years, and bringing no income in. And while Cassie was getting a better deal than was reasonable, her being in the place was preferable to it sitting there bringing in no revenue at all.

Yeah, Cassie was definitely not the kind of woman for him to go messing around with. Probably he was looking at celibacy for the duration of his sentence in Copper Ridge. He had a history with too many of the women here. Either they'd already been with him in high school, or they hadn't wanted to be for very specific reasons.

Plus, a one-night stand would be almost impossible here. The odds of you running into each other the next day on the street were way too high. Just another reason Seattle suited him a whole lot better than this place.

A little anonymity was much better for a guy like him.

And possibly right now a cold shower would be the thing for a guy like him. Dammit. How long had it been since he'd gotten hard over brushing fingers with a woman? Answer: fifteen years.

He thought again of his last night in Copper Ridge. Sitting in an empty library with Cassie, all of his focus zeroing in on her lips. He'd been saying something about his family and she'd reached out and put her hand over his.

A caring gesture. One that had sent a rush of heat straight through his body and he'd wanted... He'd wanted to close the distance between them then. To kiss her. Deep and hard. To make that connection he felt with her real, physical.

He shook his head. What was it about her? What was it about *here*?

He grabbed the bottle opener off the fridge and

popped the top on his beer. Taking a sip, he turned to look out the window. His view was of Old Town's main street. Painted clapboard buildings, with red brick interspersed. An American flag rising up above City Hall. And beyond that was the ocean. Without seeing it he could still picture the coastline. Evergreen trees, yellow bursts of Scotch Broom, and weedy blades of grass with edges sharp enough to cut into your skin.

Across the street, behind the apartment building he was currently residing in, was a long stretch of winding highway, forest and ranches. Yeah, he knew all of that, could picture it all without having to look.

Copper Ridge hadn't changed, but he had. He wasn't the same Jake Caldwell he'd been.

He wasn't a juvenile delinquent who couldn't do a damn thing right to save his life. Hell no. He managed a successful business in a very competitive environment. His boss trusted him, and he had done everything he could to earn that trust.

Unlike his old man, his boss actually believed he could do things right.

Which made him wonder yet again why he was here and not back in Seattle in the mechanic shop.

He sighed heavily. That was all because of John, too. The older man, who was, unquestionably, a mentor to Jake, had told him he had to come back and handle his family affairs himself. He'd said that was what a man did.

So he was here, handling his family affairs like a man.

And there would be no handling of pretty female

tenants while he was at it. So his body was just gonna have to calm down.

He had a feeling this was going to be a long couple of months.

CHAPTER TWO

WHEN CASSIE FINALLY made her way back up to her apartment she was exhausted. She also had no fewer than three missed calls from her mother. She kept her phone on vibrate during the workday, which probably gave her mom fits. But then, her mom was the main reason she kept it on vibrate.

Work hours seemed to mean nothing to the woman.

Cassie was about to call her mother back when the phone started to shiver in her hand, the screen lighting up and her mother's picture appearing on it.

Cassie groaned and hit "accept."

"Hello?"

"Cassie, I've been trying to get a hold of you all day."

"Yeah, Mom, I've been working all day."

"Did you just get home?" The note of worry in her mother's voice did not inspire any warm fuzzy feelings in Cassie. Not at this point. Not considering Cassie lived directly above her workplace. Her commute was a staircase. "It's late, Cassie."

"I know, Mom. But such is the hazard of running your own business. Anyway, I walked back up to the apartment using the interior stairs. Nothing is going to happen to me between work and home."

"But you work too much. How in the world are

you supposed to meet anyone when you're working all the time?"

Ahhh, and here we came to the bottom of Mama Ventimiglia's worry. Not so much for Cassie's safety, but for her singledom.

The guilts would come next. They were her mother's specialty. A single mom, she'd always been hyper-invested in keeping her daughter from making the same mistakes she had.

The biggest mistake being getting pregnant with-out securing a man. Cassie was always thrilled to be numbered as one of her mother's mistakes, even if the other woman didn't really mean it that way.

"You know, Mom, I serve people coffee all day. I talk to people all day. I meet new people every day."

"But I bet you're going to tell me you can't date a customer."

Cassie sighed heavily. "You never know. Never say never. Never assume windows are locked when doors are closed, or something like that." What she really wanted to say was absolutely *no*, never, no. But she knew that would only keep her mother on the phone longer. And it wasn't like she didn't enjoy talking to her, sometimes. Her mom was nothing if not well-meaning, but when it came to the topic of Cassie's love life, or lack thereof, Cassie would rather she left well enough alone.

"I worry about you. I don't want you to end up like I did."

Alone. With nothing but a daughter and no man. "I know. But I'm fine. I really am. I'm happy."

"I don't see how you can be happy, losing Allen like you did."

Cassie fought the urge to scream and hurl the phone across the room. "I don't feel like I lost much of anything divorcing him. He was a dud. Better to have no potato chips than broken potato chips, or something."

"It's still a potato chip, Cassie."

Cassie sighed. Hoisted by her own bad analogy. "Right. Well, I'm on a diet."

"Do you still have the meals I sent for you in the freezer?"

"Yes, I do. I'll have one of those, thank you."

"I only say these things because I worry. Because I love you."

"I know." Cassie sighed again, heavily. "I love you, too. I'll talk to you later."

"Talk to you tomorrow."

Cassie disconnected the call and flipped it from her hand onto the couch, walking through the open-floor-plan living room and into the kitchen to rummage around for dinner. There was meatloaf in the freezer. Along with frozen mashed potatoes all portioned up for her already, and cooked with love by her mother. So yeah, she could be a bit overbearing, but there were some things Cassie really couldn't complain about.

She put the plastic container in the microwave and started it, then wandered over to the couch and flopped down. The couch butted up against the connecting wall to Jake's apartment. She heard a squeaking noise, then the sound of running water and realized it was the shower. She and Jake must typically run on different schedules, because she hadn't heard his shower noises before.

She'd never lived in this place while someone else

lived in the adjacent one. It had originally been open space, and at one point in time, both units had been rented out. Then it had sat empty for ages before Cassie had rented it from Dan Caldwell, and until now, she'd never realized how thin the walls were.

And now she was terminally distracted wondering if Jake had taken his clothes off yet. Realizing that he was naked just on the other side of the wall. She jumped up off the couch and scurried back to the microwave, tugging open the door and closing it as loudly as possible in a vain attempt to drown out the sound of running water.

She pulled the lid off the Tupperware and grabbed a spoon, stirring the potatoes with much more vigor than was necessary.

Taking a bottle of wine and a glass out of her cabinet, she poured herself a generous amount. The wine would help. It would dull her senses. Hopefully make her slightly less edgy, and slightly less aware of what was happening in the apartment next door.

She took a sip of wine, and eyeballed the couch. That was usually where she ate but she wondered if she was inviting disaster by moving back over there.

But then the alternative was huddling in a corner of her kitchen just because she couldn't get a handle on her hormones. That was ridiculous.

She sniffed and collected her dinner, walking back over to the couch and setting the plate on her coffee table. She startled when she heard what sounded like his shoulder bumping up against the shower wall. It sounded very slippery. And solid.

She took another gulp of wine.

She found herself thinking back to the last conversation they'd had before he'd left town. The one that had made her realize she had to tell him how she felt. She'd been tutoring him. Meeting with him twice a week after school in the library to go over math.

She'd been the only one to volunteer for the job—at least, the only one who'd been qualified to do the job who had volunteered for it. It had been intoxicating to be near him finally. And something else entirely to actually spend time talking with him. She'd been certain that there hadn't been more to the guy than everyone thought he was.

Yes, he'd been into some trouble. There was no denying that, and he didn't try to. But there was more to him than that, and she'd seen it clearly.

It had been an unseasonably warm day in Copper Ridge. The sun taunting them as they sat inside, beneath stale fluorescent lights. But Cassie hadn't been sad to miss it. Because looking at Jake for an hour or two during their study sessions had quickly become the highlight of her week. They had been the only two students left in the library, and she'd been able to see his stress written in every muscle, every tendon in his body.

He'd actually been picking up on all the math really well, but that day he hadn't been able to concentrate.

She'd asked him what was wrong.

Just family shit.

He hadn't said anything else, but she hadn't been able to stop thinking about it. About him. And for a moment she'd been overcome by a sense of longing that was much stronger than fear. She put her pencil down, and her hand over his.

That had been the first time they'd touched. The

second time had been today, when she'd brushed his fingertips handing him a muffin.

Fifteen years between those touches and both had affected her much the same. Electricity that shot straight down to her bones.

She'd jerked her hand away then, too. But she had decided that night that when she saw him again she wouldn't pull away. Because they had a connection, she had felt it.

She'd been an idiot, which was basically her track record with men, as she knew now. But she'd been so innocent then that she hadn't realized she could be so wrong about another person.

Jake had been her introduction to that. Jake should've served as a warning. Because the next day, Jake had been gone. And the day after that Jake had still been gone. And the day after that.

He had never come back. Hadn't graduated. At least not at their school. His father was still in town, but Jake was gone. The older man had never reported him missing, so she'd assumed he knew where he was.

But she hadn't.

She hadn't seen him after that day in the library until last week when he'd come riding back into town, but that didn't mean she hadn't thought about him in the years between.

She'd thought about Jake Caldwell far more often than was reasonable.

And she was still thinking of him, though it was sort of hard not to when the man was showering just on the other side of her living room wall.

She heard another thump, followed by a very male

sound, something that verged on a grunt. She froze, her wineglass touching the edge of her lip.

She shouldn't be listening to him. It was a violation of his privacy, and there was no excuse for her to be sitting there trying to work out exactly what was going on.

But then, in her defense, this was sort of an invasion of her privacy, too. She was a hostage to the noise. Yes, she could move farther away from the wall. And yes, she did not have to lean in closer to it, or hold her breath so that she didn't miss anything, but this was her home and if she wanted to sit at an awkward angle and listen intently to the activity happening next door, she had every right.

She heard another sound, similar to the first and heat flooded her face as realization crept over her. She suddenly had a guess as to what exactly was happening in the shower. That realization should have sent her searching for a pair of earplugs. Instead, she set her glass of wine down on the coffee table and, biting her lip, leaned even closer to the wall.

Unbidden, her eyes fluttered closed, images filtering through her mind. His muscular body, water sluicing over his bare skin, and his hand wrapped around his—

She swallowed hard.

Her heart was beating in her ears, and she willed it to slow down so that it didn't block out any of her auditory entertainment. Guilt played companion to the tightening ball of adrenaline in her stomach. But it wasn't enough to stop her.

It had been a long time since she'd felt like this. A long time since she felt that sweet anticipation, that low-level hum of excitement that ran along every nerve ending, shooting sparks through every vein.

She was unwilling to let it go. Unwilling to do anything that might break the spell she was under.

She heard one more sound, a short, harsh groan and a curse, then the water shut off and she was left feeling unsatisfied, hollow and unsteady.

She picked the wineglass back up and gulped the rest of the contents down. She was going to need another glass to forget the sound of Jake's self-administered pleasure. Another glass to soften the need that was currently cutting into her like a knife.

The temptation to take her own shower and indulge in exactly the same activity was almost overpowering. But she was going to see him tomorrow. She was going to have to look him in the eye and make his coffee, and it was already going to be nearly impossible. If she thought of him while doing…that…it would be the most terminally uncomfortable moment in the history of mankind.

She was going to drink another glass of wine, watch reruns of *Gilmore Girls* and forget that this ever happened. It shouldn't be too hard.

She ignored the fact that the moment when she'd put her hand over his fifteen years ago remained one of her most vivid memories. Ignored the fact that that probably meant tonight would be burned into her brain forever.

Because there was no point in dwelling on Jake Caldwell. None at all.

CHAPTER THREE

JAKE WAS SO caught up in the hell that had been his day that it wasn't until he was inside the coffee shop and in front of the counter, that he remembered.

Then, as his eyes connected with Cassie's, it all came flooding back.

His shower, and exactly what had gone through his mind when he'd jerked off in what had proven to be a futile effort to get sex off his brain. All he'd wanted was a little relief, but inescapably that moment when her fingers had brushed his hand kept playing through his mind, and then he would picture her face. But not looking uneasy, or blank and carefully professional as she usually did. No, he'd imagined her brown eyes clouded with desire, her full lips pink and swollen. Her dark hair out of its usual ponytail, and spread out over his pillow.

Yeah, he'd pictured that. And now he was standing in front of her in The Grind, those images intermingling with reality. It was official, this place regressed him. He needed to get out. If hours up to his elbows in mud and sheep shit hadn't proven that, his reaction to her certainly did.

He turned his head at the sound of the bell above the door. A man in a uniform, whom he recognized from high school as Eli Garrett, walked in. Eli was as clean-cut as ever, tall, dark-haired and smiling. Also fully able to beat the ever-loving shit out of someone should the need arise, Jake had no doubt.

Anyone in a law-enforcement field tended to make Jake nervous. Even though he hadn't been arrested since high school. And even then, no charges had ever been formally filed.

He deserved it, at least in one case. Stealing money out of the register of the Farm and Garden where he worked had been pretty low. Especially considering how nice the owners had been. But while he'd been cuffed and taken down to the station, in the end the owners had said there must've been some mistake. A little scaring him straight combined with some mercy he knew he hadn't deserved.

Cassie looked past Jake and smiled. That was not a smile he'd ever seen directed at him and he found himself feeling annoyed that the other man was on the receiving end of it. "Hi, Deputy Garrett. The usual?"

"Yes, Cassie, thank you."

"Of course. Deputy Garrett, do you remember Jake from high school?"

Great. Now he had to be friendly. He took a breath and turned so that he was facing Eli, then held out his hand. "Jake Caldwell. Back in town for a bit." He didn't need to be intimidated. And he didn't need to stand there feeling ashamed of who he'd been.

"Yeah," Eli said before accepting Jake's offered hand and shaking it firmly. "I remember you."

"That might not be a good thing."

"Do any of us really want to be remembered for who we were in high school?"

That was a bit more kindness then Jake expected. "I don't guess."

"So, what brings you back into town? Moving home?"

Jake bristled at the description of Copper Ridge as home. "My dad died. He left me his estate. I'm just back to get the ranch and things into shape before I put it on the market."

"Sorry about that."

"It wasn't unexpected." Which was sort of an odd response, but he wasn't going to stand around and pretend to be grieving. Not considering that he hadn't even seen his father once in the fifteen years since he left. No one was more surprised than he was that the old man had left him the place.

He nearly snorted. The place and all the shit in it. Junk on the front lawn, stacks of paperwork he would need six months to get through.

"Even so," Eli said, "sorry to hear it." Cassie handed a cup of coffee back to him and Eli handed her a five dollar bill before nodding once. "See you around." He turned and walked away.

"You make a practice of serving customers in front of the line last?" Jake asked, directing the question a Cassie.

"No, it's just that Deputy Garrett is a busy man."

"You don't think I'm a busy man?"

Color flooded her cheeks, and he couldn't deny that he took a small amount of pleasure in having rattled her. "I'm sure you are. Speaking of busy, you must want your muffin."

"I would. I would like my muffin." He didn't really care about the muffin.

"And your coffee?"

"You can't eat a muffin without a coffee. I'm not a barbarian."

"No, I daresay you aren't. In fact, a lot of people would say muffins are quite civilized. Not really a manly food."

"Muffins aren't manly?"

"Well, I don't get a lot of men in here ordering them."

"Well, screw that. Muffins are delicious."

She lifted a shoulder. "Fair point. Delicious blueberry or delicious chocolate?"

"Do you even have to ask? If there's chocolate, the answer is always chocolate." Other than securing the rental of the apartment this was the most talking they'd done since he'd come back.

"On that we can agree." This time, she put both the muffin and the coffee on the counter, rather than handing either directly to him. He was weirdly disappointed by that.

"Since you didn't drop the muffin, I insist on paying for it today."

"I suppose I won't argue with you on that, either."

"Still cash only?" he asked, tugging his wallet out of his pocket. She was not the only business in Copper Ridge that didn't take debit or credit yet.

"Yeah, for now. I'm getting one of those things for your phone that lets you take credit payment, but I haven't done it yet."

"How long have you had this place open?"

"Two years."

Which explained what seemed to be a bare-bones staff and the very late nights she put in. All the hallmarks of a business that was still trying to get on its feet. "Well, good for you. It's a lot of work running a business."

"Do you run one?"

"Not really. I manage one. But I don't own it. The owner is a friend of mine, and he's semiretired." He'd be all retired soon, and Jake was poised to take over. If he could shake off the bonds that held him here. "The friendship part is just one reason I was able to come here and settle my father's estate." Calling that dilapidated piece of property—and the vacant building downtown and this place—an estate was almost laughable, but he wasn't sure how else to phrase it.

"When you say settle it, what exactly do you mean?"

"What it sounds like. I don't have anything keeping me here. I'll be going back to Seattle as soon as I can."

Cassie drew back as though she'd been slapped. "Oh. Will you have a property manager, or...?"

"No. I won't need one. Because I won't have property here anymore."

Her dark eyes widened and she shot a quick look out to the dining room, before looking back at him. "You mean you're going to sell?"

"Yeah."

"All of it, though? Not just the ranch?"

"Yeah, did you think I was planning anything else? I'm not going to stay here and play cowboy. It's not my thing."

"Well, I thought you might make your intentions explicit considering you own the building I live and work in."

"I'm a little ways off from listing it, and I had intended to offer the place to you."

"I can't get a loan for it."

"Then you can continue to lease it from the person who buys it for me."

"You're assuming that the person who buys it from you will allow me to continue leasing it. And that they won't raise the rate."

Jake rubbed the back of his neck. This was not the kind of complication he needed. If he had a hope in hell of buying John out eventually like he was planning, he needed to offload these properties. He was in a decent financial situation, but buying a very successful business wasn't cheap. And sure, he could keep the properties and lease them, but that would rob him of money he could use as a down payment, and land him with a bigger mortgage than he was comfortable with. In addition to that, he would have to get someone to manage things in Copper Ridge for him, and all of it would just keep him tied to a place he had no desire to be tied to.

And he felt sorry for Cassie, he did. But warm fuzzy feelings weren't going to get him where he needed to go.

"Well, we have some time to figure it out." Even though he knew he would arrive at the same conclusion regardless of how much time passed.

"I'm not sure I like that."

"What?"

"That non-answer. It might be easy for you to just leave things up in the air, because you have all the control. I'm the one whose livelihood and home hang in the balance."

"Look, I really hate to be a jackass about this, but

it isn't my problem. My problem right now is getting all of the shit off my dad's property. Because if I don't do it myself it's going to cost me a crapload of money that I don't want to spend. And trust me, coordinating the removal of rusty cars, old toilets and fucking chickens is not as much fun as it sounds."

"It doesn't sound fun at all."

"I know, that was kind of the point."

"You're removing chickens and helpless coffee shop owners. Big week for you."

"I'm re-homing them. And I'm not doing anything with you. Yet."

"As you make your decision, remember, you owe me for yesterday's muffin."

He frowned. "It was on you. Because you dropped it on the floor."

"That was before I knew you were intent on throwing me out onto the streets."

"I am not throwing you out onto the streets."

She lifted her hands and then slapped them down against her thighs. "You might be. You don't know. You're going to wash your hands of me. And leave me to be devoured by the winds of fate."

"That is…just a little dramatic, don't you think?"

"It's not dramatic at all! You are talking about selling my building out from under me. I don't think there is an overdramatic where that's concerned."

"If that were the case. But nothing has been decided, there is no specific buyer threatening to take anything from you, and I am not paying you for the muffin."

"You know what? That's just petty, is what that is.

You were going to pay me for the muffin, and then I told you not to, but now I want you to, and you won't."

"That's because you're being retaliatory. And I think it's small." He was more amused by all this than he should be. More amused by her than he should be. But she was quick, and she was a lot more fiery than he remembered her being in high school.

"Oh, so now I'm small? Yeah, I'm small. That's what I am. A small-business owner. And I'm being crushed by The Man."

Jake had never been accused of being The Man before in his life. He didn't exactly have the look for it. "I am not crushing you. And I'm going upstairs now. Where I can eat my muffin without being abused."

"Abused? I would've thought you were a bit sturdier than this, Caldwell."

"I'm very sturdy. I promise you that. I just also happen to have an aversion to histrionics."

He turned and headed back toward the door. He didn't have the luxury of worrying about Cassie Ventimiglia and her coffee shop. Yeah, it would suck if whoever bought the place took it out from under her. But he was sure there were terms that could be worked out. And yeah, maybe her rent would go up, but she was underpaying. He also knew she didn't have a predetermined amount of time on her lease. So she didn't have any protection in that manner, either.

And sure, it made him feel bad. But not enough to willingly submit to holding on to a piece of Copper Ridge. Not enough to submit to holding on to a piece of the Caldwell family.

There was a reason he had left all those years ago. And the reason was as valid today as it had been then.

Cassie didn't know. Nobody did. And that meant the way he handled things was nobody's damn business but his.

CHAPTER FOUR

CASSIE HAD SPENT the rest of last night feeling incredibly annoyed, and stirred up, and like her entire life was being upended yet again. She felt like she'd already had enough upheaval for one lifetime. Yes, it had only happened once. But once was enough. She did not want to start over again. How many times was a woman supposed to reinvent herself?

She, of course, had not found that answer while pacing around her apartment growling. And today, the answer continued to elude her as she sat in the driver's seat of her car, unable to get it to start. The hits just kept on coming.

She cursed and got out of the car, fighting the urge to kick her tires. She had errands to run, and this was one of her only days off. So, of course, the car that she rarely used refused to perform its function.

She released another growl into the universe and slammed the door shut, stomping around toward the front of the coffee shop. She was going to have to call her accountant and let her know she was going to be late. Liss would do her best to reschedule her, but Cassie hated to put the other woman out.

Just as she was about to go inside The Grind, Jake appeared from around the back of the building. She froze, feeling slightly sheepish about the way she had behaved toward him yesterday. She was justified, but she'd been childish. And she really could've been a little bit more mature. If only because she imagined having him feel positively toward her was better than having him angry with her. All things considered.

And she wasn't usually one to make waves, but then, Jake had always brought out feelings in her that were less than typical.

"Good morning." There, she had greeted him. And she hadn't even spewed any fire and brimstone in his direction.

"Good morning." He raised his brows, clearly just as surprised as she was that she'd managed to be civil.

"I hope you slept well." She hadn't heard him showering last night, so thank heaven for small favors.

And that was not what she wanted to think about right now. Not when she was annoyed. Not when she was looking at him, and would probably start blushing.

"Yeah, I slept fine."

She bit back a rude comment. "Well, that's good."

"You sound thrilled. You don't work this morning?"

"No, I have the day off. Which means I have to do the business things I can't do while I'm in the shop."

"Exciting times in Copper Ridge."

"You aren't lying."

"So where you headed?"

"My accountant's. To drop off financial stuff."

"Ahh, I see. As opposed to dropping off badger-related things at your accountant's."

"Charming. Now, while you do a very good impression of the sarcastic jerkface, I am in a bit of a rush, and having car trouble so…"

She couldn't really figure out why Jake made her

feel so damned obstinate, only that he did. And that she didn't really mind. To the contrary, she sort of liked it.

He gave her something to kick against when she generally felt like she was simply drifting downstream.

"I'm going to ignore the fact that you called me a name I haven't heard since I was in elementary school. What kind of car trouble are you having?"

"I don't know." She hated that feeling of not knowing. Or more accurately, of knowing she was in over her head, and that she needed help, but didn't have it.

Frankly she couldn't afford to get the car repaired, and she had no idea how to replace anything herself. Her husband had done that stuff, and these were about the only times when she felt his absence. Most of the time she felt like she was better off without him—enriched even. But when the drain was clogged, a car needed repairing, something heavy needed lifting, or a jar lid was being particularly stubborn, she really missed the bastard.

"Well, if you show me your problem I'm sure I can tell you what it is."

"The thing is, I'm late to meet Liss."

"Where is her office?"

"It's up the road about five miles, not something I can sprint. Even if I started walking now, I would still be late."

"If you wait down here for a second I can come back with a solution to your problem."

She blinked rapidly. "Well, that sounds…almost too good to be true."

"I promise you it's not." He turned and walked back around the building and she just stood there gaping.

And staring after him. Because even though she was officially annoyed with him, he was still nice to look at.

Something about being exposed to Jake was a whole lot like jumping from a sun-soaked rock into a freezing river. For the past five years she'd been comfortable. Comfortable right where she was, finding her feet again, letting go of a marriage that had lasted eight years instead of a lifetime. Once she'd done that she'd settled in and found purpose in her new life. She hadn't wanted what she'd lost again.

Jake made her want things. Not love and commitment-type things, other things. Naked things. Sweaty things.

It made her feel a little bit flushed just thinking about it.

And right on cue, just as her face was overheating from her libidinous thoughts, Jake reappeared, holding a motorcycle helmet.

"I'm not sure what you think you're doing with that." She eyed him suspiciously.

"I'm offering you a ride." He extended the helmet, her face reflecting in the shiny black surface.

She looked up from her own wide-eyed stare, and presented it to him. "I don't ride on motorcycles."

"Well, you can start today."

"I think you misunderstood. It's not that I've never had the opportunity." But she hadn't. "I don't ride on them because the idea is about as appealing as inhaling dandelion fluff and then licking a pig's foot to get the taste out of your mouth."

"Evocative."

"I'm trying to get my point across that I don't find the idea very appealing at all."

"Yeah, I actually got that out of your simile," he said.

"Wow, you even knew it was a simile."

"I had a good tutor back in high school."

SOMETHING ABOUT BRINGING the past into the present made Jake's chest tighten. He didn't like to think about the past and he had good reason. But Copper Ridge made it impossible not to.

"I tutored you in math, not English. I was not the one to teach you about similes."

"Maybe I just absorbed some of your intelligence."

"See, you think I'm intelligent. Therefore, my concerns about riding on a motorcycle are probably valid."

"Probably. But then, I've been riding on one for about seventeen years and I seem okay."

"Okay, I don't have time to stand here quibbling with you about this." She snatched the helmet from his grip and put it down over her head, so that only her nose and eyes were visible, a strand of dark hair hanging down the middle of her forehead and disappearing beneath the face mask.

"That's a good look for you, Cassie."

She blinked, and he was suddenly very aware of just how long her eyelashes were, and how very attractive that was to him. Seriously, the brush of her fingers against his and her eyelashes. He needed to get a grip. And not the type he'd gotten in the shower a couple of days earlier.

"It doesn't surprise me that badass biker chick is kind of my thing."

"Speaking of," he shrugged off his leather jacket and held it out toward her, "You need to complete the look."

"What about you?"

"We'll be driving through town, so I'll go slow. But I would still feel better if you wore the jacket."

She took the jacket and shrugged it on, the sleeves hanging over her hands and the bottom extending to midthigh. There was something sexy about that, too. And he was just done questioning his sanity, because it was clear the question was answered. It was gone, and he needed some kind of sexual release.

But not with her. Maybe he would drive up to Tolowa and look for someone to hook up with. One-night stands weren't really his thing these days, but exceptions could be made.

At least with someone he would never see again.

"Okay." The word was jittery, and so was she, her fingers trembling. At least what he could see of them peeking out from the jacket sleeves. "Let's do this, I've got an appointment."

"And you have all your paperwork?"

"Yep." She tapped the large purse that she had slung over her shoulder.

"All right then." He walked over to his motorcycle and put on his helmet then got on, waiting for her to do the same.

"So I...just get on behind you."

Oh, shit. He'd sort of overlooked this part. "Yes," he said, conscious of the roughness in his own voice.

She took a tentative step to the bike, then disappeared from his field of vision as she moved behind him. He felt a light touch on his shoulder, which was quickly taken away.

"It's fine, you're going to have to hold on to me anyway." Sexual tension was making him testy.

Two hands gripped his shoulders, and he felt her settle in behind him. Her thighs rested on either side of his.

"You need to put your arms around my waist." Yeah, this was going to kill him.

She complied, her grip so tight around him it was like she was attempting the Heimlich. "This feels slightly unstable," she said, her voice in his ear, muffled by the helmets between them.

"It's not, I promise. As long as you're not going to let go of me suddenly."

"Yeah, it's safe to say I'm not going to be doing that."

He started the motor. "Good. Are you ready?"

"No."

"We're going anyway, okay?"

He felt her nod against his back and he smiled, putting the bike in gear and moving forward, careful to take off gradually so that he wouldn't terrify his virgin passenger.

He gritted his teeth. All things considered that wasn't a very good descriptor. It stuck his mind straight back in the gutter.

He did his best to keep all of his focus on the road, on the passing scenery. Belatedly, he realized he hadn't exactly gotten directions from her. But he figured he would keep going straight until she gestured wildly.

In his defense, he had been distracted. By trying not to be distracted by his attraction to her.

Maybe that was the real issue. Maybe his attraction to her was an attempt at distracting himself from other problems. From the ranch, and all of the ghosts that it held. It was strange seeing it now, fallen into such dilapidation. In order for the excuse to wash, he had to ignore the attraction he'd felt to her back in high school, but for the sake of his sanity he was willing to do that.

The ranch had never been a mansion by any stretch but it hadn't been run down like this. But his mother had been gone for more than twenty years, and Jake himself hadn't been back in fifteen. From all accounts, his father had been in a home the last two years of his life and not living out on the property.

Someone must've been taking care of the animals because they were still there, but no one had bothered to do any upkeep on the house. If he had ever had any affection for the place, the disrepair would have made him sad.

They drove past the collection of tourist shops, which were one major change from when he lived here as a kid. This street had mainly been deserted, and there had been very little value in the properties. Which was, he assumed, how his father had managed to end up with a few of the buildings. And why he had never been able to do anything with them. The place had been a near ghost town back then.

From what he'd gathered since coming back tourism had started to build in the past ten years, along with the restoration of Old Town. Brick that had once been crumbling and run-down was now charming and quaint. Buildings that had been peeling and splitting were now restored, painted bright whites, pale blues and deep reds. Fish shacks that had only ever been for locals were now obviously designed to bait out-of-towners with promises of the freshest seafood.

One little building that he'd remembered as being

empty was now covered in wind chimes, flags and things made of driftwood. It was amazing what paint, new signage and some landscape could do.

He took the main road up out of Old Town, away from the beach. As the road curved inland the pine trees thickened, casting dusky shadows over them, golden sun filtering through the trees and bathing everything in a glittering haze.

Objectively, Jake had to admit the place was beautiful, which was a tough thing for him since it also created a knot of tension in his chest that refused to ease. He managed to find beauty in Seattle, though it had taken a few years of living there to get used to all of the glass and steel. As cities went, there was a lot of nature. And the ocean was still nearby. He didn't think he could live anywhere that wasn't by the ocean.

It wasn't that he spent a whole lot of time beachcombing. He wasn't big on the sand between his toes. It was a feeling of freedom the ocean afforded. He had a vague sense that as long as it was nearby there was an escape. The idea of being landlocked unsettled him. It was akin to being trapped in his mind.

That was one of the reasons he'd always ridden his bike. There was something about it that felt like flying. That felt like escape. What he wasn't used to was riding with another person, and interesting that Cassie's arms tight around his waist didn't feel like restraints. They felt warm, they felt secure.

And it felt like they were escaping together.

Though what Cassie Ventimiglia might have to escape from he had no idea. It struck him then that he knew nothing about the life she'd led since he'd left. He knew that she had opened The Grind two years ago, and that was the beginning and end of his knowledge.

It made him feel like an asshole to realize that. Seemed like he should've asked.

But it wasn't as though she'd asked about him. As far as she knew he had ridden off one day, then ridden back. And nothing had happened in between. In some ways, he was content for people to think that, and in other ways not.

Because he had spent a hell of a lot of years trying to escape the man he'd been. And he sort of wanted people to know he had.

That was the most sobering thing about becoming an adult as far as he was concerned. Riding out of town in a rage, angry at himself, angry at his father. And later realizing that a lot of the shit that had come down on him was his own fault. Of course, the reason he'd been stirring shit up in the first place did come down to his old man.

There'd been no way of pleasing the bastard. So Jake set out to do just the opposite. But that last screw-up had been too much for either of them to overcome. That final altercation breaking bonds that had already been brittle. Shattering them beyond repair.

Cassie suddenly squeezed him tighter, and he looked to the left, spotting a new little row of businesses set back in the trees. Copper Ridge Business Park, as the sign deemed it, was new, or at least less than fifteen years old, which for a place like this meant new. It was almost laughable to call it a business park in his opinion. A row of five businesses that were all connected, and fashioned to look like little white clapboard houses. There were even roses climbing up a freaking trellis. The place was like Mayberry. Again, had he had any attachment to the town, it might've made him smile.

He slowed the motorcycle and turned in, figuring if this wasn't it, he could at least get directions from her here.

When he killed the engine, Cassie got off, tugging off the helmet and shaking out her hair. He couldn't help but admire the way the dark strands shimmered in the sunlight. Yeah, there was no doubt that, physically, at least, where Cassie was concerned he was a goner.

"Thanks." She handed the helmet back to him.

"I take it this is the place?"

"Yeah, this is it."

"How long is it going to take?"

"It shouldn't be long. I just have to drop this stuff off and sign a couple of things. I can get a ride home from Liss. It won't be a big deal."

"I'll wait for you."

"Don't you have things to do?"

"Yeah, honey, I've got a ton of things to do, but leaving you stranded here is not one of them. I'm not in any major hurry."

"Honey, huh?"

"I'm sorry, does the endearment offend you?"

The corners of her mouth turned down. "I'm just not sure what I did to earn it."

"Did you need to earn it?"

"Back in high school you just called me Cassie," she said. "That worked for me."

"Well, I can go back to calling you Cassie if you like."

"It would be for the best."

She turned and walked into the little building, and he crossed his arms and rocked back on his heels. Watching her walk away was not a hardship. There was no doubt that Cassie had an ass he could stare at for days. He wondered idly if she'd had that back in high school, and if he'd just been too much of an idiot to notice. More than likely, though, the years had enhanced her shape.

The Cassie he remembered had been a bit too skinny, but still cute, with large brown eyes that had looked at him like he mattered. Just another reason he'd never gone there back then. Just another reason he couldn't go there now. Hell, he was actively moving toward ruining her life. Which was no surprise, because that was pretty much what he did. Whether he meant to or not. He ruined things. He ruined people.

He could remember sitting in the library with her, studying subjects that made his head hurt, that he didn't care about. But she'd made him want to try, because she'd seemed to believe he could do it. Nobody else had had that kind of confidence in him. Not teachers, not family. And so he had tried for her. Mainly because when he got something right she didn't seem surprised. She just seemed to accept it, accept that what he was doing was simply living up to his abilities. It had been a hell of a thing for a kid who had lived most of his life feeling like everything he did fell short.

He could also remember wondering sometimes, after a word of praise had come out of her mouth, what it might be like to kiss that mouth. What it might be like to kiss a girl who saw more than his bad attitude and motorcycle. A girl who might be into him, not because he was all wrong, but because something about him was right.

He'd dismissed the thought almost immediately. Kissing a girl like her would ruin her. No doubt about it. Not because of who she was, but because of who he was.

Revisiting it now was pointless.

A part of him was afraid that his seventeen-year-old self had had a bit more restraint than his thirty-two-year-old self where she was concerned.

That was sobering.

Cassie appeared a few moments later, a smile on her face when she exited. A smile that faded slightly when she made eye contact with him. Dammit.

And dammit that he cared.

"Okay, I'm ready," she said.

"You have any more errands you need to run?"

"Well, I was going to head over to the Farm and Garden to get some plants for the front window box at the shop. But it's not something I *need* to do today."

"It's not a problem, I'll take you by. I'm assuming it's the same Farm and Garden that's always been here."

"The very same."

He knew the place well, seeing as he'd worked there. Seeing as he'd stolen from the people who owned it. Damn, he had been an asshole. There really was no two ways about it. But he had changed. And maybe it would be a good thing for him to walk in there and let them know that. He felt like he owed that to Mr. Travers.

He wanted him to know that letting a juvenile delinquent off the hook had mattered. That his kindness had amounted to something other than more arrests. Because Jake had gone on to make something of himself. No, there was no pretending he was some kind of tycoon, no pretending he was a millionaire. But he was successful, he owned a house. He was aiming to buy John's mechanic shop. He was responsible, and he had done the right thing since leaving town. It was because of people like Travers that he'd managed that.

He realized just then how grateful he was. He tried so hard not to think of Copper Ridge that he often forgot the good things that'd been hidden here, tucked away behind all the bad stuff. Like light breaking through the trees.

"Put on your helmet. Let's go," he said.

"Are you sure?"

"Seriously, it's no problem. Unless you're afraid of the bike."

A faint dusty rose color darkened her cheeks. "The bike was fine."

"Good to know I didn't scar you for life."

That earned him a smile, and it was genuine. And he felt like the sun had peeked out from behind the clouds. Dammit again.

"Come on, Cassie, let's get your flowers."

CHAPTER FIVE

THE ENTIRE FRONT of Cassie's body tingled. And it showed no signs of stopping. She could blame some of it on the rumble of the bike. On the vibrations of the motor moving through her for the ride out to the Farm and Garden. But intellectually she knew better. The real cause of the tingling was Jake. Was having her legs all wrapped around him, and her breasts pressed against his back while they drove through town.

Really, it wasn't fair. She hadn't had this much contact with a man in too many years and suddenly she was being pressed up against one. A hot one. One she had heard touching himself only a wall away from her just a couple days ago.

There was no way a mere mortal woman could withstand such temptation. And she was sadly a mere mortal, as she was discovering.

She dismounted the bike and took the helmet off, surprised at how comfortable she was with the whole thing already. It really wasn't all that scary. But her mother had drummed into her that motorcycles were vessels of death and if she were to ever get near one she would surely burst into flame.

But it turned out if she *were* to burst into flame it would be because of Jake, not the motorcycle.

Jake took his helmet off and followed her into the store this time rather than waiting outside.

"I thought I might get some petunias." She realized that she was making inane conversation, and she couldn't even stop herself. If it wasn't muffins, it was flowers, and she had a feeling the guy didn't really care about either.

Well, that wasn't true. He'd had some pretty strong things to say about muffins.

"Man, I haven't been back to this place in fifteen years. Which is kind of an obvious statement," he said looking at her, "since I haven't been back to town in that long. And you knew that."

It appeared that Jake was making inane conversation, too. And that gratified her more than it should.

"You used to work here, didn't you?"

"Yeah, for a while. Before I screwed it up. Like I did everything else back then."

"What happened?"

"I stole money from the register. Because I was an asshole." He didn't make eye contact with her when he said that, his expression granite.

"Oh," she said, feeling her heart sink. She didn't know why that bit of information disappointed her. It had happened forever ago. But for some reason, she'd never believed he was as bad as people had said. And she only realized just now that that meant she had thought he wasn't bad at all.

"Are you actually surprised?"

"Okay, I confess I am. I kind of thought your infamy was exaggerated."

"I wish it was. But the fact is I was basically a

ridiculous little cuss. And I deserved most of what came to me."

"I never saw that in you."

"I put on a pretty good show for you. Mainly because you smiled at me, and at that point there were very few people in town who did."

A dark head popped up from behind the counter, and the salesclerk flipped her braid over her shoulder and turned to face them, smiling broadly. "Cassie! What can I do for you today?"

Cassie offered Kate Garrett a smile in return. "I was thinking flowers, Kate. Thank you for asking."

"Who's this?" Kate asked.

Kate wouldn't remember Jake because she would've been a kid when he left. It was easy to forget just how much younger than her brothers she was.

"Jake Caldwell." He extended his hand and Kate shook it. "Currently from Seattle, previously from Copper Ridge."

Kate's dark eyes widened. "Oh! Welcome back, then."

"It's only temporary."

"Well," Kate said firmly, "enjoy your time here anyway. You're visiting Cassie?"

"Not really."

Tension thickened in the silence and Cassie didn't really know what to say. "Just petunias would be great."

"I can grab those for you," Kate said. "How many you need?"

"A couple of flats. Pink and purple."

Kate disappeared out the back, leaving Jake and

Cassie alone again. It was no less awkward with Kate gone.

"I'm not even sure if I should be buying flowers."

"Why is that?" he asked.

"You know, just in case I don't end up keeping the shop."

"Cassie, it's not like I'm selling your business. The building eventually. But you're acting like I'm stripping you of your livelihood or something."

"You might be. You don't know. You don't know what's going to happen."

IT STRUCK JAKE then that he was standing there being the bad guy yet again. He didn't like it, but it was a necessity in many ways. It had nothing to do with Cassie personally, and everything to do with him simply wanting ties cut cleanly. He hadn't asked for this. Hadn't asked to have all of his dad's stuff left to him.

He was too smart to do anything but make the most of it but he was hardly going to fall on his sword for anyone. He wasn't fit to play the role of martyr.

"No, I don't know what's going to happen. And neither do you. This isn't personal, Cassie. I came into all this property unexpectedly and I have no desire to hold on to it. I have a life away from here. And I deserve a little payment for the time I served on the Caldwell family farm." *Do you?* He ignored that thought. He deserved it if he thought he did, right? For all his sins, and yeah, he'd committed them, his dad had plenty of his own.

Jake gritted his teeth and fought against the rising tide of guilt. Guilt over Cassie. Guilt that was as old as the day he left.

Hell, he had a feeling a lot of his guilt was as old as he was.

"Right, fine. I get it, Jake. Things were hard and you don't want to own a piece of this place, and I can understand that. But I do. The Grind is all I have. The Grind and that tiny little apartment above it. I don't want to lose another planter box."

"What do you mean by that?"

"I've already done this, Jake. I've already invested my sweat and energy into a place only to have it taken from me. Those were my flowers, dammit! And he kept them. And she just let them die."

"What are you talking about, Cassie?"

"I spent eight years working on our house. Working on our marriage. And in the end it wasn't permanent. The one thing that was supposed to be permanent and it wasn't."

"You're married?" A flash of heat, of anger, unwanted if not entirely unexpected, shot through him. On the heels of that came the biting realization that the marriage she was talking about certainly wasn't healthy. And a part of him decided very quickly that he didn't much care if she had a husband or not.

Shades of old Jake, and it shouldn't be too surprising considering this place seemed to bring that out in him. Seemed to bring out the worst.

"No. Not anymore. I took my name back and everything, seeing as he had the house."

"How did he end up with it?" He knew it wasn't any of his business, most especially since they were standing there arguing about whether or not he was ruining her life. He had no right to ask for details. No right to get protective and proprietary since he could neither protect her nor keep her.

"We didn't have kids. I didn't have a job. My name wasn't on it."

"Your name wasn't on it?"

"I didn't have credit. He started the process of buying it while we were still engaged. Then of course in the end I was really screwed because I didn't earn any credit over the course of the marriage. I had to move back in with my mother when we divorced. Until I got The Grind and the apartment above it."

"And how did you end up with that?"

"The building was empty, and I noticed. I had gotten a job at Rona's Diner waiting tables so I drove by every day. And every day I imagined making it mine. It isn't like your dad was a mentor, or even a benefactor. I tracked him down and asked him if he needed it for anything and he said it was just sitting there costing him property taxes. So we worked something out that seemed fair. Something I could afford, but that would give him income. It was all sort of unofficial, but at that point he was—"

"In the assisted living place."

"Yeah."

Kate walked back into the room a moment later with a couple flats of flowers on a rolling rack. "Do you want me to just put this on your tab, Cassie?"

"Yeah, that would be good." Cassie wasn't looking at him at all now. He wasn't sure why. If it was because of the whole thing with the coffee shop, the discussion about his dad, or the mention of her divorce. Possibly all three. That would figure, seeing as he couldn't seem to puzzle out how to talk to Cassie.

"Oh," she said, and then she did look at him. "Are we going to be able to get these on your bike? I guess I should've thought of that before we came in."

"We can figure it out."

"Oh don't worry about it," Kate said. "I'll drop them by The Grind on my way home."

"You don't have to do that," Cassie said.

Kate tugged on the end of her braid. "Seriously, no big deal."

"You're too generous, Kate," Cassie said.

"Not even a little." The other woman grinned. "I'm going to expect a coffee for my efforts. Possibly a muffin."

Jake shot Cassie a look, and her mind must have gone to the same place, because she was staring at him, eyes wide, clearly remembering earlier muffin-related innuendo.

Cassie looked back at Kate. "That seems fair."

Jake hesitated for a moment. "Hey, Kate, is Jim Travers around?"

"No, he and Margie are in Hawaii. They come back over the summer. But otherwise they are usually at their house in Maui these days."

"Can't really blame them for that," he said. He ignored the tug of regret in his stomach.

"Definitely not. Someday I'll go to Hawaii and confirm my suspicions that it's paradise. Until then I'll take their word for it." Kate shoved the rack back behind the counter, then grabbed a piece of paper and a marker and scribbled Cassie's name on it, sticking it on the flats. "I'll be by later."

"Thank you," Cassie said.

"Not a problem. See you later."

"Come on," Jake said. "I'll take you back."

"Thanks," Cassie said. "I suppose it was the wrong time for me to rake you over the coals about selling the building. Seeing as you're helping me."

"If you ask me, there is no good time to rake me over the coals. But I might be biased on that score."

She turned and pushed the door open and both of them walked outside into the cool morning air. The wind was just starting to kick up, blowing sea salt and sand in from the beach, mixing with the aroma of pine and bark that surrounded them.

"Possibly. Just a bit." Cassie stuffed her hands in her back pockets and arched her back, the leather jacket parting as she did. His eyes were drawn, helplessly, to the curve of breasts pressing against the thin fabric of her shirt.

He looked away, turning his focus to the thick grove of trees across the road, the ruffling of the pine branches in the wind. "All right, let's go. I have my own work to get to." And he knew he sounded grumpy and ungracious, but he couldn't take the time to rectify it. Because if he did, she might smile at him again. And if that happened he might do the thing he'd been thinking about for days—he might lean in and kiss her. And that wouldn't be good for anyone.

Most especially her.

CHAPTER SIX

JAKE COULDN'T EVEN find respite in the privacy of his apartment. Mainly because he was discovering the apartment wasn't all that private. Oh no, to the contrary, the walls were paper thin and he was very aware of the movements that Cassie was making on the other side of them. He could tell when she was getting into the shower, when she was walking across the living room, and whether or not she was wearing shoes. He found he sort of liked it when she was barefoot, if for no other reason than it meant she was wearing less.

Worse, he was getting attached to the sounds that she made. To not being alone. His house in Seattle was nice, in a quiet neighborhood, with quiet neighbors. He didn't share any connecting walls. And no one ever stayed the night. When Jake hooked up he preferred hotels, and when that wasn't happening he made it so they ended up back at her place. They rarely seemed to mind, and if they did, he just went and found someone else. Clingy wasn't his thing. Sharing space wasn't his thing. Because feelings weren't his thing.

He prized his control far too much.

But there was something comforting about hearing another person moving around so close. Comforting and at the same time disturbing. Especially since what he really wanted to do was storm over to her apartment and eliminate all the space between them. No walls. No clothes.

He hadn't had it this bad in longer than he could remember. If ever. When he wanted a woman he had her, and he never wanted a specific someone enough to cause this kind of trouble. Notable exception: Cassie back in high school.

He had a feeling that was the thing messing with him right now. All that unspent, long-buried desire.

Because right now Cassie Ventimiglia was obsessing his mind, and his body. And it was pretty damn stupid.

Even as he thought of his neighbor, he heard the sounds of her moving around, and then a sharp, shrill squeak. He jumped up from his couch, and ran to his front door without even thinking about it. Probably she had seen a spider. Or something similarly innocuous. But the desire to fulfill the fantasy that was turning over in his brain, combined with the protective instincts Cassie seemed to bring out in him, had him halfway down the stairs before he could even think about it.

He called himself ten kinds of stupid while he walked around to the other side of the little entryway in the back of the coffee shop, and up the stairs that led to Cassie's apartment.

Yeah, he had enough self-awareness to realize that he was looking for any excuse to knock on her door. Which was crazy considering that she didn't like him, she made him feel like an ass, and he knew he couldn't touch her.

His instincts, or his dick, didn't seem to care. Because before he knew it he was standing in front of

Cassie's door pounding on it as hard as he could. He heard a strange thumping sound and then the door swung open and he found himself facing Cassie, who was standing on one foot and holding the other one.

She squinted. "Yes?"

"You sounded like you were in distress."

"Oh. I stubbed my toe." She winced and squeezed her foot then set it back down and straightened. "Did I disturb you?"

"Not disturb per se, but the walls are kind of thin. I don't know if you noticed."

Color flooded her face. "Oh, yes, I have noticed."

Interesting that she blushed when the question came up. It made him wonder if she was thinking the same things he was. It made him wonder if maybe she was listening to what he was doing. If she had been fantasizing about the very thing he was. Tearing the wall down and tearing each other's clothes off.

That was probably wishful thinking. He'd always had Cassie pegged as being a little bit more cautious than that. He'd put her in a box in his brain that was labeled Nice Girl. Whatever *that* meant. He didn't have an exact definition handy, but he vaguely thought it might mean she wasn't the type of girl whose clothes you just ripped off.

"I hope I haven't been too…disturbing," she said, blinking rapidly.

"You aren't that bad." The color in her face intensified. Very interesting, indeed.

"It was really nice of you to come check on me. But I'm fine. I don't think I broke anything, and there's no blood. Just a coffee table that I moved a few days ago.

And now I'm not really familiar with exactly where it is. So the leg got my toe."

"You were rearranging furniture?" He was asking stupid questions now, because he was reluctant to leave.

"Yes. I did a little rearranging." She was still blushing and now he was dying to know why. He wanted to push, and hell, if it was anyone else, he would push. So he was going to push.

"Feng shui?" he asked.

"What…like making a money corner and stuff?"

"Something like that." Except feng shui didn't make you blush.

"I'll have to get a lesson from you in the future, since you seem to know all about it. But in this case I just was moving my couch, so it seemed like moving the coffee table was the thing to do."

"Just looking for a change?"

"Why are you giving me the third degree about the location of my furniture?"

"I'm not trying to."

"If you must know, it's because I can hear you showering when I'm sitting on my couch. And it bothers me." A jolt of something hit him square in the gut.

"You can hear me showering?"

"Yes." She swallowed hard, hard enough that he could see it and hear it. "And I can hear the things you're doing in there."

Heat assaulted him, his face burning so hot he was sure it must be red. Blushing wasn't his thing, but hearing her say that, knowing exactly what he'd done in the shower a couple of days ago, had him feeling like he'd stuck his head into a bonfire.

"Oh." That was all he was capable of saying. He couldn't remember the last time a woman had made him blush, or the last time one had rendered him speechless. But so-called Nice Girl Cassie Ventimiglia had managed to do both.

She tilted her chin up. "Yes, I heard you doing… things."

He cleared his throat and tugged on his shirt collar. She made him feel like a naughty schoolboy. He couldn't remember actually feeling that way when he'd been a naughty schoolboy. "Things?"

"Yes, things."

And then a switch flipped inside him, and he remembered who he was.

He was Jake Caldwell. He wasn't a teenager. And neither was she. He was a guy who got shit done. He didn't blush. And when he wanted a woman he damn well had her. No, he *shouldn't* have Cassie, but there were a lot of things he shouldn't do. And at the very least, he was going to win whatever game they were playing here.

He wouldn't touch her. But he wasn't going to let her direct things, either.

"Honey, I would be very careful about where you take this conversation."

"Would you?" She arched her dark brow.

"Yes, I would. Because if you're implying what I think you are, then you're taking us into dangerous territory."

"I'm not implying anything. I'm saying it."

"You are not saying it. Your voice is thick with meaning, but you said nothing."

She crossed her arms beneath her breasts. "I heard you… I heard you…"

"I'm waiting, babe. Because for all I know you heard me singing 'I Dreamed a Dream.'"

"Do you even know that song?"

"Yeah, I do. I have culture." And he had heard it played over and over again on a movie trailer.

"Well that isn't what I heard. And I think you know it. Otherwise you wouldn't be daring me. Don't deny it, either. I know that's what you're doing."

"Yeah, I'm daring you," he said, taking a step closer to her. "You're right about that. So if you want to have this discussion, let's have this discussion."

"Why?"

"You're turning red, baby. I think you bit off a little more than you can chew."

The color mounted in her cheeks, and he had a feeling that this wasn't a blush. He had a feeling he was witnessing Cassie Ventimiglia entering a full-blown rage. Perversely, the thought pleased him. "All right, Mr. Tough Guy. I moved my couch because I can hear you showering. And I could hear you pleasuring yourself while you were showering." She was breathing hard when she finished, and she was so red she looked a bit like an overstewed tomato.

He gritted his teeth and tried to look casual. "I'm a guy. I'm not going to say I don't do that in the shower."

"Well, I don't need to hear it."

"It bothers you?"

"Of course it bothers me! It would bother anybody. Nobody needs to hear that."

And then, just because he wanted to go to her, just because he wanted to get her to give something away, just because he wanted her to be in hell the same as he was, he pushed further. "It only seems fair that you had to hear it. Seeing as I was thinking about you."

Her mouth fell open and then closed, and then open again. She looked a little bit like a guppy that had been yanked out of the water. A very cute guppy, but a guppy nonetheless. "I can't believe you just said that."

"Offended?"

She blinked a couple of times. "No," she said, standing stunned. "No, I'm not."

"You aren't?"

"No, I'm not offended. I'm not offended at all. In fact, I would go so far as to say I was intrigued."

"You're intrigued. By the thought of me touching myself while thinking about you."

"Yes, I find that very intriguing."

Jake crossed his arms over his chest, all the better to keep from reaching across the empty space between them and hauling her to him. "You really need to be sure this is where you want the conversation to go, baby. Because I have a feeling it could get out of hand very quickly."

"Maybe I want it to get out of hand. And trust me, Jake, no one is more surprised by that than me."

"I don't think you really want what you think you do."

She took a step backward, deeper into the apartment, and he found himself following, like a dog on a leash. He stepped past the threshold, and inside. And he knew that he had made a very grave mistake. His dick, on the other hand, was rejoicing at what it was certain would be a victory.

"If you push me, you might find that you don't like the results."

She lifted her hands. "Or maybe I'll find out I *love* the result." She balled her hands into fists and pressed them against her eyes. "Jake, all my life, I've been a good girl. I know you have no idea what that's like, all things considered."

"Probably not, considering I have a penis."

He was certain that if she had possessed the physical capability she would've blushed even harder. As it was she seemed to have reached maximum capacity. "Oh yes, I'm aware, as we've established. But I didn't mean the gender part. I meant the well-behaved part. The good part. You were always so wild, and you just did what you wanted. You didn't seem to think what anyone else thought mattered. I, on the other hand, am crippled by what everyone else thinks."

Something in his stomach twisted. He didn't like the direction this conversation was going. It was cutting a little bit too close to the bone.

Cassie continued. "You with your tattoos—tattoos when we were in high school. Badass. You and your motorcycle when I didn't even have a car. I just couldn't help but admire that in some ways. I still do. Because I did everything I was supposed to, *everything*. Got married to this guy who was supposed to be great, and we were supposed to have kids. My mother was thrilled with the decisions I made. The guy wore a tie to work. I still didn't win, Jake. I didn't win. Because Allen left me. Or rather, he kicked me out. But either way the end result was the same. He never had kids with me, he wanted to wait. And then he got remarried eight months after the divorce was final and by the time that happened they already had one on the way. Good behavior did nothing for me there. Nothing at all. And right now I'm standing here asking myself what this good behavior has *ever* gotten me."

He'd underestimated her again. He always had. It hit him then the Nice Girl label he'd slapped onto her was just as limiting, just as much a simplistic lie as the Bad Boy label was on him.

She'd been hurt. Badly. And standing here facing that he had no clue how to handle it.

He cleared his throat. "I thought good behavior was supposed to be its own reward."

She exploded, her tiny frame turning into a ball of energy as she paced around the apartment. "Where are my rewards?" She swept her hand around in a half circle. "Do you see them anywhere? I don't see them. I live in an apartment that I don't own, that's going to get sold out from under me, and when that happens I'll probably lose my business, too. I don't have a husband, which frankly is fine, because a bad husband is worse than none at all. But ultimately my life isn't anywhere that it was supposed to be." Her dark eyes locked with his. "I'm tired of being good. I don't want to be good anymore."

"Then what is it you want, Cassie?"

"I want to have fun. I want to be bad. I want the one thing I was too afraid to go after when I was in high school."

"I think you need to spell it out for me, just in case I'm misunderstanding."

Cassie took a deep breath. "I want to be bad, Jake. I want to be bad with you."

CASSIE WAS SHOCKED to the point of being horrified by her own actions. But things had been set in motion, and even though she felt like she was having an out-of-body experience, watching herself say these things, hearing the words come out of her mouth, she didn't seem to be able to control them. She was like a snowball that had started rolling down a hill, picking up momentum, picking up weight. And from her vantage point she could see that she was moving toward destruction and death. But there was no way to stop. Avalanche Cassie was firmly in motion, and she would not be deterred.

This was not her. This was far too bold. But she wouldn't take it back now. Not even if she could.

"Let me get this straight, Cassie. You want to slum it with me?"

Her face burned, her heart pounding so hard she could barely breathe. "I don't really like the way you put it. And sort of."

"You object to me telling the truth?"

"I don't consider you beneath me. So I don't think the term *slumming it* applies. But I do think you're what I need. You're the kind of guy I need."

"Okay, Cassie, let's talk about exactly what you want." Something had changed in his expression, his eyes becoming sharp, dangerous.

"I want... I want you." She could not believe those words had just come out of her mouth. More to the point, she couldn't believe how true they were.

She was a good girl, which she meant in that old-fashioned way her mother would use it. The way that was supposed to keep you out of trouble. Out of a situation like her mother had found herself in.

The truth was Allen was the only man she'd ever been with. And they didn't even have sex until they were engaged. So obviously she had never solicited a guy she barely knew, much less a guy she knew things wouldn't work out with. A guy she wasn't even looking for *things* with. Not things other than sex, anyway.

"What, you want me to bake you a pie? You want me to pay for that last muffin? What *exactly* do you want, Cassie?"

He wasn't going to let her get away with pushing the decision off on him. He wasn't giving her a chance to blame him later, to say it was all his idea. He was making her say it. Making her claim it.

"Sex," she said.

His expression hardened further. "Say it all."

Oh boy, he wasn't going to make this easy.

She took a deep breath, trying to hold on to her nerve. Although there was something to be said for losing her nerve. If she lost her nerve, she could back out. She wouldn't have to tell him what she wanted; she could pretend this had never happened. And she could go back to being the very good, very sexually frustrated Cassie Ventimiglia, who had never once propositioned a man and never would.

The Very Good Cassie Ventimiglia who'd been celibate for three years, and would probably be celibate for three more, and on into eternity because her business ruled her life and she was gun-shy about relationships. Thirty-two, divorced and sexless for the rest of her life.

Either that or she could go play the slots at the nearby casino. Pick up on guys putting nickels in the machine.

Holy hell, if she wasn't careful she wasn't going to

turn into her mother. She was going to turn into her grandmother.

Yes, she *could* lose her nerve. But then nothing would change. She would continue to be the same person she'd always been. She could stand on the other side of life's raging storms, and look back and see herself walking through unchanged, unruffled and the same Cassie she'd always been.

But she had to wonder what the point was of going through a major life crisis if you didn't let it change you for the better. There was none. It was as pointless as being good with no reward. It was as pointless as living what amounted to a nearly spotless life and still having your mother despair of you.

It was as pointless as finally getting up your courage to tell the hot tattooed boy you tutored that you had a crush on him, only to have him disappear the next day.

Cassie had had enough of that kind of pointless. But she wasn't going to change without making the decision to change. And she wasn't going to get her reward if she didn't reach out and grab it.

She was damn well going to grab it.

She took a deep breath. "I want to have sex with you."

He crossed his arms over his broad chest, and her eyes were drawn back to those tattoos on his forearms. They flexed and changed with the tensing of his muscles. Fascinating. And very, very sexy. "Are you sure, baby? You haven't even kissed me."

She swallowed hard. "Well, maybe we should change that."

"You don't even like me."

"Do I have to like you to want to kiss you?"

He reached back and slammed the door shut, walking all the way into the apartment with a determined look on his face.

"Now that you mention it, honey, I'm not sure that it does matter." He approached her, his expression transformed into that of a lean, hungry predator. And she was trembling like prey. But she didn't even care. She didn't want to run. Not even a little bit. She wanted to stay exactly where she was, so that he could catch her.

It hit her then, she would make a terrible gazelle, since she was just standing there waiting to be eaten. But she was wondering right now if she might be a half-decent temptress.

It was total craziness. Utter insanity. And she didn't even care. In fact, she felt like it was her due. She felt like she deserved a bad decision mixed somewhere in the middle of all her extremely logical choices.

Because the simple fact was that though she had made technically right decisions, they had very much turned out to be the wrong ones. Things that had been intended to bring her happiness had only brought her pain. And if things were going to be upside down like that she might as well get an orgasm out of it.

He hooked an arm around her waist and pulled her against his chest. He was hotter than she'd anticipated him being. He was hard, too, a solid wall of muscle, nothing like any other man she'd touched.

Her ex-husband had been thin to the point of being weedy. And bones were hard, but they were most definitely not muscle. She had already learned something new after five seconds in Jake's arms. All male bodies were most definitely not created equal.

He lifted his hand and touched a strand of her hair, winding it around his forefinger. It was a nonsexual act. But there was something about the movement that was more sensual than anything she could remember before.

Another learning experience just two seconds after the first. A touch didn't have to be under the clothes to be sexual. And when a man looked at you the way that Jake was looking at her, it was almost better than skin-to-skin contact.

She was certain of one thing already: this was going to go far and away beyond her level of experience. This was the kind of thing that would change her irrevocably. She didn't have a string of lovers in her past, so there was no way that Jake would blend into the masses. There were no masses. She had a feeling that even if there were she would be facing down the same problem. Jake Caldwell would be unforgettable whether there had been one lover or one hundred. And she had to decide whether or not she wanted Jake to be unforgettable.

Silly girl, he already is.

She knew her smug inner voice was right. Because for fifteen years she had remembered him. Had remembered that touch in the library. Had remembered the way she'd felt when he'd looked at her. For fifteen years she had remembered him and he had never given her reason to.

Tonight he would give her the reason. Tonight he would give her a memory that would make her tremble every time she thought of him

Yes. No matter what, Jake Caldwell would always be unforgettable. But the question was, would she always remember Jake as the one that got away, or would she remember him as the best sex of her life?

She looked at his face, at his dark blue eyes, his sensual mouth. The square jaw rough with dark stubble. He was incredible. He was a mistake any girl would be lucky to make.

Some people went out and got bad haircuts. Not her. She was going to get Jake.

There was no question about how she wanted to remember Jake Caldwell. She wanted to remember him as the only man to ever make her knees shake.

So there would be no losing her nerve.

He released his hold on her hair and moved his hand to cup her cheek, sliding his thumb across the ridge of her cheekbone as he continued to look at her intently. He was the most beautiful thing she had ever seen. More beautiful than the sun setting into the ocean, or a view of the mountains on a clear day. He was more beautiful than a chocolate cake with birthday candles. And that was saying something.

"Are you just going to look at me? Or are you going to kiss me?" She was starting to wonder if Jake was losing *his* nerve. But that didn't seem possible. She doubted Jake was afraid of anything.

"Getting impatient, honey?"

"Yes. I'm a little worried that you aren't."

"I am. Trust me. It might surprise you to know that I've thought about kissing you for a while now. To be honest, I've wondered what it would be like since I was seventeen years old." He brushed some of her hair away from her eyes. "I knew it would be wrong. Because you were a good girl. A smart girl. You were helping me with my math homework, for

God's sake. But that didn't stop me from thinking about it. I thought about what it would be like to lean in and kiss you, right there in the school library. We were the only ones there except for the librarian, and I bet we would've turned her hair a few shades grayer. But it would've been worth it."

"You thought about kissing me?" Cassie couldn't breathe. Couldn't even process what he had just said.

"I thought about it quite a bit. And I'm thinking about it now. But I find the anticipation makes it sweet."

"What, fifteen years isn't long enough?"

He chuckled, the sound rolling over her. "You may have a point." He spread his hand on her lower back, squeezing her tight as he tilted her chin up.

She let her eyes flutter closed and she held her breath, counting down in her mind. In some way she felt like there had been a countdown running on this since they were seventeen. And now it was finally winding down, fifteen years later. And now at three, two—and then his lips met hers.

There was nothing in her imagination that could've prepared her for the reality of Jake's kiss. It was quite simply too far outside anything she'd ever experienced before. His lips were hot, testing for a moment. He simply pressed them against hers and allowed the sensation of touching him in this way to bloom over her. To let the feelings slide over her like melting butter. Slow and warm, growing more liquid with each passing second.

Then he tilted his head, parting his lips, and she followed his lead. He took advantage of the improved angle and slipped his tongue along the seam of her lips.

A shiver started at her core and radiated through her entire body. Her knees were already shaking, and they hadn't even gotten to the good bits. Or rather, she was just going to have to modify what constituted the good bits in her mind. Because not a single part of this had been bad. Not a single part had felt like filler, while he was simply waiting to get to the rest. Every movement was intentional, every one something he seemed to be savoring. She felt desired in a way she hadn't ever experienced before. She felt wanted. She felt needed.

It turned out Jake's lips could say a whole lot when he wasn't talking.

When they parted they were both breathing heavily.

Blue eyes burned into hers. "Tell me again why you want me." It was not a request, but a demand. There was something dangerous in his expression, and she couldn't quite translate what it was. What it meant. She only knew that there was a wrong answer. And that she was afraid she might give it.

"I want you because… Because if a girl can have a wild time, you seem like the kind of guy to give it to her."

"What is this, some bad '50s musical? Find a guy with a leather jacket and he'll show you a good time?"

Her stomach twisted. "Don't be like that, Jake. You know your reputation."

"Yes, I do know my reputation. But I sort of figured you knew more than that."

"Well, I thought maybe I did. But it turns out…"

"I took the money out of the register," he said, his voice rough.

"I'm not upset about that. It was forever ago." She had the strange feeling she had chosen poorly. But what had he wanted her to say? Had he wanted her to say that she wanted him because he was special? Because she'd had a crush on him since she was seventeen and this was wish fulfillment in a way he couldn't possibly understand? Because from the first moment she'd known sex was a thing, she'd wanted him to be the one she had it with? He wouldn't want to hear that. That would send him running screaming from the room. That was the kind of thing that sounded a lot like commitment. Neither of them wanted that.

"So you want a bad boy, is that it?"

She bit her lip. "If you want to put it like that. Sounds a little bit cheesy."

"Why don't we just go with it." There was a hardness to his tone that disturbed her, but the heat in his eyes overtook any misgivings she had.

"I'll go with anything you want to give me."

"Now I like when you say things like that." He rubbed his thumb along her lower lip, then leaned in and traced the same path with the tip of his tongue before dipping it inside her mouth again. The motion was hot, slick and it sent a wave of longing through her that she couldn't control. Didn't want to control. Her stomach tightened, wetness pulling in the center of her thighs. She couldn't remember a kiss ever doing so much for her. In fact, she was sure one never had.

She wanted to tell him that. She decided she would tell him that.

"I've never kissed anyone who is quite so proficient at it." *Great, Cassie. That's how you talk dirty. Throw in some three syllable words.*

A wicked smile curved his lips. "I'm proficient, am I?"

"Well… And sexy. So sexy."

He chuckled, and she felt the weight lift off her chest. Maybe she hadn't made him angry after all. "Just be you, Cassie. I don't want you to be anything but you."

"I don't know if I want to be me. I don't think she really knows how to do this." She laughed nervously, hoping he wouldn't hear just how shaky her voice was.

"You seem to be doing just fine." She tried to look away, and he gripped her chin again, turning her face toward his. "Look at me, Cassie."

She obeyed, keeping her eyes locked with his. "Good girl." He leaned in, and she watched him, watched the intent in his eyes, the desire there. He angled his head and kissed her neck, kissed along the line of her jaw, to the sensitive skin of her throat. She was going to melt. She was going to melt in between all the cracks of the wooden floor, and when he went to sell this place, he wouldn't be able to get a very good price because there would still be particles of melted Cassie lingering in the wood grain.

"Oh, oh, Jake…" She was panting, saying his name, powerless to do anything but beg. Because she was about ready to come just from a few kisses. And that was not like her at all. She was more of a dim lights, flowers, roses, romantic music, forty-five minutes of foreplay kind of girl. She was not an argument, three kisses, climax kind of girl.

Although Jake made her feel like she might be.

Jake made her feel like something entirely new. Jake made her feel like she was drowning. But in the best possible way.

He moved both hands to her waist, tugging her

more tightly against his body, the warmth of his touch seeping through her shirt. It made her feel impatient. Impatient for his skin against hers. And that bit of contentment she felt simply luxuriating in the moment passed. Suddenly, she just wanted it all. Wanted him pressed tightly against her with nothing between them.

She wanted to feel for herself just how different he was in every way. Wanted to feel every inch of his skin, wanted to know if he had chest hair or if he was smooth. She found in that moment she didn't really care what the answer was, only that she got the answer. Because everything about Jake had been perfect so far, and she knew she wouldn't be less disappointed with his body once it was bared to her.

She swallowed hard, and told herself that this was the last of her nerves. If she was going to have one night with Jake Caldwell, the hottest guy she had ever known as a teenager or an adult woman, she wasn't going to waste a moment of it acting like a terrified virgin. She knew the drill. She knew what went where. She'd taken the plunge, and he had said yes. He was kissing her. There was nothing to be nervous about.

"Take your shirt off for me, Jake."

"Getting demanding, are you?"

"I plan on making quite a few demands, actually. I hope you don't mind."

"Not a bit." To prove his word, he gripped his black T-shirt, tugged it up over his head and tossed it onto the floor.

Her heart pumped hard against her breastbone and she had to fight to catch her breath. She had been entirely unprepared for the beauty that was Jake. Yes, no lie, all men's physiques were not created equal. She really hated to do a comparison between Jake and her ex, if only because she hated to think of her ex in this moment. But it was impossible seeing as it was the only other male body she'd been this close to.

Where Allen had been pale, and a bit freckly with ribs instead of abs, Jake was tan and beautifully muscled. He had, to answer her earlier question, a fascinating smattering of dark hair over said muscles. It made her mouth go dry, made her fingers itch to touch.

And so she would. Because tonight wasn't about restraint. It wasn't about sparing herself from embarrassment, or making anyone proud. It was about pleasing herself. And touching Jake would please her in more ways than she could count.

She put her hand flat on his chest, her breath hissing through her teeth as she did.

"See something you like?" he asked.

"Oh, I see so much that I like." She let her fingertips trail over his muscles, relishing the combination of rough, hot and hard. "I used to think about this."

"Did you?"

"Well, kind of. I mean, it's not like I knew very much about this sort of thing back in high school."

"I think I knew too much about it."

"That doesn't surprise me."

"Oh, right," he said, grabbing her wrist and tugging away from his chest. "Because I'm such a bad boy."

"Because you're hot. Unlike me, I'm sure you had a lot of dates."

"Not dates exactly."

She had a feeling the subtext was that he hooked up. If she'd known that back then it would've made him even more impossibly dangerous. It probably would've made her even more attracted to him. Because teenage girl logic. Actually, her adult woman logic, too. Maybe something in her had just snapped. Too much good, too much people pleasing. His entire life was her own personal porn.

It was forbidden, something she would never do. And that was what made his life philosophy so appealing. Human nature. To want what you couldn't have. To be enticed by things you shouldn't be.

"Well, I didn't date, either. Though I mean that in a much less roguish and charming way than you did."

"I'm not sure I was all that charming."

"I beg to differ." She stretched up on her tiptoes, and pressed her lips to his again. She didn't want to talk anymore. She didn't want to do anything but kiss him. Okay, that was a lie. She wanted to do a whole lot more than kiss him. "You charmed me," she said, her lips against his.

"I don't think this is charming. I think this is seduction."

"Either way. Works for me."

She put her hands on his biceps, the utter solidness of him shocking. Without thinking, she patted one of his arms. She felt him smile against her mouth. "What are you doing?"

"I've never felt muscles quite like this before. I like it." Her face heated. "Sorry, I don't think I'm very good at this."

"You are very good at this. I don't think my ego—or my arm—has ever been stroked so thoroughly."

"I'm not very experienced."

"That probably shouldn't turn me on. But it does."

"Well, at this point I don't really want anything to turn you off."

"No chance of that, baby."

He slid his hands down to her hips and around her backside, a bolt of heat spearing her straight to the stomach as his touch moved lower, as he squeezed her gently. An inelegant groan escaped her lips, and she didn't even care. How could she care? Nothing was more important than what she felt right now. Not pride, not ladylike noises.

It suddenly occurred to Cassie that he was doing all of the exploration. And that she was wasting an opportunity. She moved her hands to his back, fingertips tracing a path along the line of his spine, and down to the curve just above the waistline of his pants. She decided not to hesitate, and simply followed her instincts. She pushed her hand just beneath the denim, bare skin making contact with bare skin. She felt him jolt, felt an immense amount of satisfaction as he did.

That she could have such a strong effect on a guy like him was fuel enough for her own ego. Which admittedly at this point was a little bit bruised. Years of indifference would do that. Years of feeling the disconnect between yourself and the person with whom you were supposed to be the most intimate.

It hit her then how little she felt like she had. She hadn't truly had a claim on her husband. Hadn't owned the house. She didn't own the apartment she was in now. But right now, with Jake reacting to her touch the way he was, it felt very much like having something of her own. It felt very much like ownership. And even if it was only temporary, it made her feel anchored in a way she hadn't in years.

He gripped the hem of her T-shirt and tugged it up over her head, leaving her standing there in her plain black bra, the air suddenly feeling slightly cold against her skin.

He cursed, short and sharp and yet more satisfaction bloomed in her stomach. He wanted her. He wanted this.

She made him cuss. That was…immensely satisfying.

"All of it." That was all he managed to get out, the desperation evident in those words fueling her fire even more.

Without pausing to think she reached behind her back and unclasped her bra, throwing it on to the floor before shoving her yoga pants and underwear down, too, leaving her completely naked in front of Jake.

No time for nerves now.

She pressed her body back up against his, luxuriating in the feel of her bare breasts against his chest. His chest hair was rough against her nipples, the contact sending slow waves of pleasure through her, her internal muscles contracting in time with the throbbing of her pulse.

"Jake," she said, barcly able to force the words through her constricted throat. "I want to see you."

He released his hold on her and took a step back, his hands going to the snap on his jeans. And she watched, her attention completely rapt as he pulled the zipper down, then pushed his pants and black boxer briefs down his lean hips.

Cassie's cycs went wide, and she knew she was absolutely telegraphing her thoughts straight to him. But she didn't care. This was for her, after all. That

meant she wasn't obligated to pretend to be more experienced than she was. Wasn't obligated to pretend
to be blasé as she was looking at the most beautiful
man she could've ever dreamed up.

He was incredible, his thick erection enticing in a
way she'd never imagined something like that would
be. Sure, she knew women giggled about big penises,
and size mattering and all of that. But sort of like big
boobs, she'd never figured it was something that might
really matter.

She was changing her stance on the subject.

Of course it wasn't only his blatantly male member
that had her dying to touch him. It was everything.
Muscles, tattoos, chest hair, even his thighs. She had
never given a whole lot of thought to a man's thighs
before. But Jake's were worth thinking about.

"Are you just going to stand there staring all day?
Or are you going to touch me?" he asked, his voice
rough.

"Oh, I'm going to touch you."

She closed the scant distance between them, placing
her hand on his chest, feeling his heart raging beneath
the surface of his skin. She took an extreme amount
of satisfaction in that. In the fact that she had affected
him so strongly. The fact that all of this seemed to
matter to him, almost as much as it mattered to her.

She moved her hand down to his arousal, wrapping
her hand around him and squeezing gently, watching
as his mouth tensed and his eyes closed, as he let his
head tilt back. She watched the tendons in his neck
tighten. She could see his pulse pounding, hard and
fast at the base of his throat, and she leaned in and

flicked her tongue across his skin, tasting his need. The desperation that matched her own.

She flattened her hand over his length, exploring the shape of him, testing his hardness.

"Be careful," he said, his voice a growl, "or this is going to be over a lot quicker than I want it to be."

She moved her hand away from him. "Well, we don't want that." Sure, a small part of her would take pleasure in the fact that she had challenged his control like that. But most of her would just be disappointed to have things end prematurely.

She hadn't had sex in three years, and she was not missing out on it now.

Speaking of that...

"Oh, shit!"

Jake's eyes widened. "Well, that's not something I'm used to hearing at this stage."

"Condoms." She was starting to feel slightly panicked. No, there was no need to panic. There was a store within jogging distance. And her pride honestly had no place in this. She would do a condom dash. She would.

"I've got one," he said.

"Only one?"

"You sound disappointed."

"I haven't had sex in a very long time."

He chuckled and tugged her against him, kissing her deeply. When they parted they were breathing hard. "Why don't you wait and see if you enjoy this time? Then we'll worry about getting more."

"Oh, I am not concerned. About the enjoyment."

"Good."

He leaned in and kissed her neck, then moved lower,

kissing the curve of her breast before sliding his tongue down to her nipple, tracing a circle around it. Her hands flew to his head, gripping his hair, holding him to her as he continued to lavish attention on her body.

He parted his lips and sucked her deep into his mouth, an answering pull of sensation echoing in her midsection. He lifted his hand and cupped her other breast, teasing her with his thumb before pinching her lightly. She tightened her hold on him, lowered her head and rested her cheek against his hair, hanging on tight as he continued his sensual assault. He had her shaking, whimpering, begging… If she hadn't been so lost, she might have been embarrassed.

He raised his head, a slash of darkened color bleeding over his cheekbones, betraying just how affected he was by all of this.

Then his lips crashed down on hers, the kiss deep and hard, his tongue sliding against hers. He gripped her thighs and tugged her up, wrapping her legs around his waist, bringing the damp center of her into contact with his length. She arched against him, trying to ease the ache that was building there. But it wasn't enough.

"Which way to the bedroom?" he asked, his words labored.

"No time. Couch."

He carried them over to the couch and set her down, settling between her legs and kissing her as he slid his hardness through her slick folds. His eyes locked with her own, and a whimper escaped her. He lowered his head and kissed her, taking her lower lip between his teeth and biting her gently, the sensation combined with the motion of his hips sending a white-hot flash of pleasure through her.

"Now. Please now."

"Not yet." He pressed a kiss between her breasts, then one to her stomach. It took her a moment to realize what he intended to do, but when she did everything in her seized up. She had never done this before. But she had fantasized about it.

Oh, had she ever.

He kissed her inner thigh, his wicked blue eyes never leaving hers as he moved closer to the center of her need. He flicked the tip of his tongue over her clitoris, and her hips bucked off the couch. He took that opportunity to reach around and grab her by the hips, pulling her hard against his mouth and deepening the intimate kiss.

"Oh! Jake!" She threaded her fingers back through his hair, not caring if she hurt him. Which seemed a little barbaric, perhaps. But the pleasure he was giving her verged on pain, and somewhere in her muddled mind she thought maybe if she gave him pain, it would verge on pleasure.

He growled roughly as he continued his exploration of her, adding his fingers, sliding two deep inside her, working them in time with his magic tongue.

She wasn't going to last. And if she couldn't, she knew she wouldn't come again. For a moment she felt slightly wistful about the fact that it was about to be over for her. But only for a moment. Because the spiral of need in her was so tight that she knew it had to break. Otherwise she would.

He used his fingers to stroke her in time with the motion of his tongue, and sent her over. Hurtling down into an abyss. For a moment everything was blank, weightless, all of her senses sacrificed on the altar of the pleasure that was coursing through her. There was nothing but this, nothing but what he made her feel.

It was incredible. Beyond a simple climax and into something entirely different. Something that consumed her in a way nothing else ever had. Right now there was no worrying about whether she pleased anyone.

Because she herself was so wholly pleased, she simply couldn't care.

He abandoned her for a moment, leaving her lying spent on the couch, electricity buzzing over her skin. He returned a moment later, and she realized he had gotten the condom and had already seen to protecting them both. He joined her again, kissing her deeply, his hands going back between her thighs, stroking her. She was almost too sensitive, but she didn't want to tell him to stop, either.

Finally, he positioned himself at her entrance, the blunt head of his arousal testing her before he slid in the rest of the way.

She gasped as he filled her, stretching her. It wasn't painful. Not at all. A feeling of complete satisfaction overwhelmed her. He fit so perfectly. He felt so amazing she could think of nothing else.

And she didn't want to.

She cupped his face and kissed him and he began to move inside of her, each measured thrust pushing her back toward the edge. An edge she hadn't thought she would reach again. Not so soon. But this was nothing she'd experienced before. This wasn't just sex, this was Jake. And she should've realized by now what that meant. That none of the previous rules applied. That none of her previous experiences meant anything.

His control started to fray, his movements becoming harder, faster, amping up her excitement to an impossible degree. Each thrust brought his pelvis back against her clitoris, pushing her closer, until she was arching up to meet him, desperate for release.

A second wave broke over her just as he stiffened above her, a hoarse groan on his lips as he shuddered out his own release.

As they lay there on the couch, in the quiet of her apartment, no sound beyond their shattered breathing, three things kept going through her mind.

She'd just made love with Jake Caldwell. He had in fact managed to make her come twice. And she would never be the same again.

CHAPTER SEVEN

OKAY, SO HE was kind of a dick for leaving in the middle of the night. But he had to be out at the ranch early the next day. Or rather, he supposed he didn't have to be, but it made for a nice excuse in his head. And he really needed a nice excuse.

That much was true.

Because without the excuse, he had to face the truth that he needed to leave because he was feeling too many things. Too many damn feelings. He didn't do feelings. He knew madness lay on the other side of his feelings. He wasn't being overdramatic, it was just the truth.

He scrubbed his hand over his hair and grabbed his leather jacket off the hook by the door, pausing and looking at it, thinking about Cassie wearing it yesterday. How it had swallowed her tiny frame and made her look even more petite than she was. And he was done thinking of that. There was only madness on the other side of that, too. He would be redirecting his thoughts now.

He put the jacket on and continued out the door, walking down the stairs and stopping when he reached the landing and saw Cassie standing there at the bottom of her stairwell, looking slightly lost.

"What are you doing here?" he asked.

"I was about to ask you the same question. Since I was looking for you."

"You were looking for me?"

Cassie shifted, her expression adorably sheepish. And when the hell had he ever thought of a woman as adorable? "Well, I've never exactly woken up alone after having sex with a guy."

"Right, well, I didn't have…anything, and we didn't have any more condoms so…" *Right, way to be an asshole, Caldwell. Tell her you couldn't have more sex with her so you left.*

The thing was, he'd needed space. Because while they'd been getting it on he'd been fine. But as he'd been laying there holding her in his arms he kept replaying what she'd said to him over and over again.

He kept hearing her say that she wanted to make a mistake. That she wanted to be bad. And that bothered him in a way he couldn't quantify.

Or hell, maybe he could. Maybe it was because he'd always imagined that Cassie saw more to him than that. And now he could see she was just like every other woman he'd ever screwed. Into the tattoos, into the motorcycle, into the idea that he had some kind of secret bad-boy magic hidden in his wang.

Not that he was complaining, since that got him so laid it was ridiculous, but as he seemed to be getting feelings all over this little interaction with her it was more disconcerting than usual. Again, it was this place. This place and this woman, and all of it made him feel like what he really needed to do was get the hell out of Dodge.

Which was why he'd left her apartment this morning, really. He'd been running. Because he was a coward who'd gotten his feelings hurt. And it was not a nice look on him.

"Sure. Right, condoms." She tucked a strand of hair behind her ear, then clasped her hands in front of her, looking a bit like a nervous little mouse. "Very important. Seeing as I'm not on the…pill. Because of things. Reasons. Celibacy mainly."

"Were you looking for me?"

Cassie bit her lip. "Yes, I was looking for you. Because I don't really do the sex-and-dash thing. And I've decided it's not my thing."

He crossed his arms over his chest. "Then maybe I'm not your thing."

She wrung her hands. "I wouldn't go that far."

"*You* said you wanted to screw around with the bad boy, Cassie. And if there's one thing bad boys are good at, it's a fuck and run. So if that isn't what you want then maybe you need to revise your idea of how you want to conduct your little rebellion. Maybe carrot cake with raisins is more your speed."

"First of all," she said, drawing up to her full height, which put her just beneath his chin, "raisins are awful. A rebellion should be about having fun, and there is nothing fun about eating the lowest form of dehydrated fruit. Second of all, I did say that I wanted a bad boy. But I lied. I think I'm naive, and my idea of what a bad boy is is somewhat skewed. Or maybe I was just being flippant. You're not an asshole, Jake, no matter how much you might pretend you are. Sorry, I guess now your secret is out."

Jake felt the shock of her words all the way down to his toes. "What is it you're saying exactly, Cassie?"

"I don't know!" She threw her hands up above her

head. "I don't know, Jake. The thing is, I feel like I said the wrong thing to you last night. I'm afraid that's why you left this morning." She put her hands back down to her sides, her breathing hard and uneven.

"What, you think you hurt my feelings?" Even as he said the words, dismissive, like they were crazy, he wondered if they might be true. Or maybe hurt feelings was a step too far. But it was just too close to the bone, all things considered.

"Look, whatever I said…"

"Cassie, don't worry about it. This place messes with my head. I was pissed at myself, because I shouldn't have touched you. Nothing can come of this so there's really not much point in continuing, and you said yourself you're inexperienced. You haven't been with anyone in a long time and I took advantage of you."

Her dark eyes flew wide. "Don't feel like that! I mean, I wanted you, I wanted this. I don't want you to go regretting it now because you think somehow I didn't know what I was getting into. I was married for years. It's not like I don't know about sex."

"I know you know about sex, it's this part you obviously aren't too familiar with."

"Maybe the problem is that we're not at the part you think we are."

"What do you mean?"

"I mean, maybe we aren't at this kind of awkward morning-after-we-shouldn't-be-speaking-of-this-let's-never-talk-again moment you think we're at."

"Are you telling me how to do one-night stands?" he asked. "Because I'm more familiar with those than I would like to admit."

She took a deep breath, her eyes going particularly wide. "Last night was really special to me."

"Cassie...don't do this." He wasn't trying to stop her from talking so she wouldn't embarrass herself. No, he was trying to stop her from talking because he was afraid of what she might say. Of what it might make him feel.

"No, you do not get to tell me to stop it! You do not get to control this."

He had never seen Cassie so worked up before. And here she was, all worked up over him. He shouldn't like it, but he did.

"Do you have any idea how long I've lived my life for other people?"

"Probably about as long as I've lived life for myself."

"If not longer! Jake, last night was special to me. Because you're special. When I said I wanted a bad boy, I didn't mean to insult you. I meant that you amaze me, the way that you just did what you wanted. The way you left Copper Ridge because it was the best thing for you—"

"Whatever you do, whatever it is about me that you like, don't let it be that. There was nothing admirable about the way I left."

"What you mean?"

He let out a harsh breath. "Did you think I just left? Did you think I just got it in my head that it was time to skip town, so I did?"

She lifted her thumb to her mouth and started gnawing the nail. "I guess... I guess I sort of did."

"Well, that isn't what happened. I did something really stupid. Like really stupid. Illegal. I am not some kind of figure for you to pattern your rebellion after. You shouldn't admire anything that I did."

"Jake…"

Before his brain could reason it out, his mouth made a decision. "Why don't you come out to the ranch with me?" he asked.

Cassie nodded slowly. "Okay, I can do that."

"I'll just get your helmet from my place."

Jake turned slowly and walked back toward his apartment. He wasn't in a hurry to get to the ranch. After this she would understand who he was, and why he'd had to leave. And anything admirable she had seen in him would be destroyed. And no matter how much he knew it had to happen…he was in no rush.

CASSIE LEANED AGAINST Jake's back as he maneuvered the motorcycle over the back roads that lead to his father's property.

Last night had been a revelation for Cassie. She had felt uninhibited in a way she'd never felt her entire life. She hadn't done anything to please anyone but herself. And still she'd somehow managed to please Jake.

Waking up and finding him gone had put something of a dent in that confidence. But regardless of whether he'd been able to establish a physical distance, there was no emotional distance. Not really. There was a bond between them, no doubt about it. No matter that he'd shown up to Copper Ridge without so much as a smile for her, from the moment she'd seen him again she'd known it was still there.

It was a strange sensation to be so certain of something. To feel like she wanted to hang on to something. She'd realized something this morning as she was lying in her empty bed, missing Jake and wishing he hadn't left. She'd realized that she had never fought for anything. Lord knew why. But she hadn't. Maybe it was because of the way things had been with her mother.

She hadn't felt like she had the right to fight with her, because she'd always known that her existence had made her mother's life difficult. Oh, Maria Ventimiglia would never say that, and she never had. But she implied it in new and interesting ways all the time. From the time Cassie was about six years old she could remember the story of the one man her mother had loved. The story of how he had wanted her to choose between having a child and having him. And Cassie had always known what the choice had been. Because she was with her mother, and her mother didn't have a husband.

That was why her mother had always put so much importance on making sure she got married before she got pregnant. Why Maria had always put so much emphasis on the need to find a husband. Because when you were a working single mom finding one was nearly impossible. When you'd had your heart ripped out by the father of your child, who wanted you to make an impossible choice, you knew how precious that relationship was.

So Cassie had felt obligated to make her first relationship work. To give it the respect her mother wanted her to give it.

Her mom had been instantly attached to Allen, and in fact still was. Cassie had never felt like she had any other option but to follow that relationship to its conclusion down the altar. And she could see now what a mistake it had been. But she had simply gone along with the path it was easiest to walk.

And when Allen had wanted a divorce, she had complied. She hadn't even fought for her damn house. Who did that? Eight years of marriage, and she had simply walked away. She hadn't asked him for counseling, hadn't asked him to keep trying.

The sad part of that was that she had loved him enough. But she was starting to wonder if she had loved herself enough.

Spending a few years alone was an interesting thing. She'd had the benefit of starting a business, of fighting her way through financial uncertainty, of making things happen for herself. Of being with a man simply because she wanted him, not because he was an ideal prospect for future husband, or someone who would make her mom proud.

Those experiences had changed her, and were changing her still.

And when she realized all of that this morning, she had also realized that she was prepared to stand and fight for Jake.

Because she wanted him, because the feelings that she'd always had for him had never truly gone away, but had only been dormant.

And he had brought her out here to discourage her. Of that she had no doubt. But he was about to discover that she was a lot stronger than he was giving her credit for.

She hoped she was about to discover that she was a lot stronger than *she* had ever given herself credit for.

It occurred to Cassie as the motorcycle pulled into the property that she had never been to Jake's family ranch. By the time she had started doing business with his father, the older man had been in a nursing home. So she wasn't certain what exactly she had expected. But it wasn't what she saw. The house was run-down, old cars, tractors and other farm implements littering the lawn in front. Slowly corroding, halfway between a man-made creation and dirt at this point.

There were wire fences, with chickens running through gaping holes, and goats wandering around in the muddy enclosure. All of the foliage had been stripped within a two-foot radius around the fence, compliments of the voracious hoofed creatures.

"Wow." She tugged off her helmet and dismounted the bike.

"Yeah," he said, following her lead, his boots sinking into the mud. "It's basically a shithole."

He sounded almost ashamed, and she didn't want him to. She wanted to make it better. "It's really not."

"No, Cassie, it is. You don't need to be nice. It wasn't all this bad when I was growing up. But things have really fallen apart since."

"I just imagined, since your father owned other properties in town…"

"Yeah, you imagined that this would be nice. That we had money or something."

"I'm starting to realize how little I knew about you."

"Which is what I've been trying to tell you."

"Well, stop *trying* to tell me, and just tell me." She looked at the man who last night had become her lover. She felt inextricably linked to him, and she would be lying if she said it was because of the sex. Because she had felt inextricably linked to him since she was seventeen years old.

He had always been there. In her heart, in her mind. She had always been drawn to him, fascinated by him. And now that they'd slept together that pull had only grown stronger.

She looked around, searching for something to say, since he was not responding to her prompt. "So, you've been fixing the place up?"

He chuckled. "Why? Can't you tell?"

"Not really."

"It's a testament to how bad it looked before. I don't really know who was taking care of the animals, but obviously someone was. Now that I'm here they seem to have stopped. So I've been managing them."

"This is where you grew up?"

"Yeah, unhappily." He put his hands on his lean hips and looked around. "I never missed it. I never missed it once after I left."

"And you were going to tell me why you left." She took a step out of the muddy patch and to the side. She fixed her eyes down on the green, stepping on a weed that popped, a milky substance oozing out of the stem.

"Yes, I guess I was."

"Are you still going to tell me?"

Jake was silent for a moment, then he took a deep breath. "Look at me again."

His request was firm, loud in the otherwise silent front yard. She obeyed. "Why?"

"Because I want to see you looking at me one more time before you lose your respect for me."

"Jake, being perfectly honest, you've come here, endangered my livelihood, had sex with me and left my apartment before I woke up. If that hasn't damaged my opinion of you, I think it's safe to say nothing will."

He looked away from her, a muscle in his jaw ticking. "You say that, but you don't know."

"No, I don't know. So stop with this mysterious crap and just tell me."

"It's in the bad-boy handbook. We're supposed to be mysterious and brooding."

"Yeah, well, knock it off. We both know you don't particularly like the label, so stop living up to it."

"I haven't lived up to it. That's the thing. I'm not the same person I was when I left here. I've gotten a handle on my shit. I'm not just going off half-cocked, letting my anger bleed out on everything. That's what I was doing back then. My version of managing my temper was to release it and let it savage whatever got in my way. There's nothing sexy about that. Nothing attractive about it. I needed to get punched in the face, I did not need to get blow jobs as a reward for my bad behavior."

Heat prickled her face. "Get a lot of those, did you?"

"A few," he said, deadpan.

She cleared her throat. "You've got a handle on your anger now," she said, looking at him, at the rage that was evident behind his blue eyes. It was funny he was saying that, because she felt like he was still angry. Felt like there was an endless well of it inside of him that he'd simply covered up. But it was leaking out, escaping, maybe because of where he was, or maybe because she had gotten too close to his emotions. For whatever reason she was more conscious of it now than she ever had been.

"Yeah, I've had a handle on it. I got out. I did what my father said I could never do. I got a job, I kept it. I earned the trust of the owner of the business. I learned a skill. I'm a mechanic, and I'm a damn good one. I know that for a lot of people that wouldn't seem a big achievement, but for a kid who was told he would never do anything but serve jail time? It's huge. When I left, I found something I could do. I found a way to be constructive. There's a whole lot of power in learning a skill."

"I imagine there is. I own a coffee shop, I'm not going to look down on you because you're a mechanic. I respect it."

"Yeah, *I* respect it. I don't especially need anyone else to. My dad never would have, he owned land. That was somehow better than anything I could ever live up to."

"What did your dad do to you?"

Cassie thought of her own mother, of how fraught their relationship could be at times. Though she had to admit, her mother probably wasn't aware of how difficult it was. Her mother excelled at manipulation, at guilt, and creating a running tally of debts owed. She rarely shouted, but she would cry, get upset. And for Cassie that was a lot more damaging than a screaming match.

"Doesn't matter. After my mom died I just don't think he could figure out what to do with me. I was about twelve when that happened. I'd never been close to my dad, but it only got worse. We didn't grieve together, because he didn't grieve. And as a result neither did I. At first he just stopped paying attention to me, so I would do stupid shit to make him look in my direction. And eventually the neglect turned into resentment. I couldn't do a damn thing right in his eyes. Not my chores, not my schoolwork. And I admit, I didn't do any of it particularly well. I had a hard time in school, I was never going to graduate at the top of the class—you've seen my work so you knew that."

"It isn't that you weren't smart, Jake. That stuff just isn't easy for everyone."

"I know that, objectively. Now, as an adult. But as a kid? I just believed him. I was dumb, but I couldn't do anything right. And since I could never do anything right anyway, I decided I might as well embrace it. So I was always pushing things. Always trying to make him angry, because he was always angry anyway. The more I pushed it the angrier he got, the angrier he got the angrier I got. And eventually I stopped trying to control it. So we would have shouting matches, and that never ended well. Usually with me getting punched in the face."

"Jake," she breathed, feeling like all the air had gone out of her lungs. "That's not okay."

"I know it. I know." Cassie's stomach tightened, anxiety coursing through her, pain wrenching her chest. "What happened, Jake?"

"The night after you and I studied in the library, I came home. He was pissed about something, something I had done wrong on the ranch. Something I had missed because I had gone to get some extra tutoring, because I was failing school. Which was just typical. Because I couldn't do anything right. I couldn't do the chores right if I was trying to do school right, but if I was smarter I would've been able to just do school, instead of needing all that extra help."

Jake shook his head. "I was so angry. So fucking angry. I couldn't do a damn thing right for him. He told me to go out and check on the wheat field. So I did. I went out there with my lighter and my cigarettes, and I thought to myself it would be so easy to just smoke the place. To make all my problems go away. Because if the ranch wasn't there, I wouldn't have to take care of it. I wouldn't be able to fail it. And I just did it. I didn't have any control over my emotions. I didn't have any control over my impulses, and I threw the lighter and the cigarette down the field. I watched it burn, Cassie."

Cassie put her hand over her mouth, careful not to interrupt him. Careful not to make a sound.

He continued. "I regretted it pretty quick, but by the time I tried to put it out, it had gone too far. There was nothing I could do. Nothing I could do but watch my anger burn out of control. I didn't leave. I was thrown out. My father told me he never wanted to see me again because of what I'd done. So I got my bike and I left. I never came back."

Cassie pictured Jake as he'd been. The long, lean boy she'd known, with a chip on his shoulder and a reputation she'd always assumed was misunderstood. And she realized that she had been doing him just as much of a disservice as everyone else. Other people had written him off, while she had been looking at him through rose-colored glasses. Both things had prevented people from seeing what was actually going on with Jake. Some people had made him a villain; she had made him a fantasy. And all the while no one had seen the boy as he was. No one had seen that he needed help. That he was drowning, in hurt, in grief and in rage.

"Oh, Jake, I'm so sorry."

He took a step back from her. "Why are you apologizing to me?"

"Because I should've seen, I should've asked you. Should've talked to you. I was so busy fantasizing about making out with you that I never stopped to see you as a person. And I did the same thing last night. You're not just a fantasy, you're a human being. And I didn't see that." She took a deep breath. "I didn't see past myself. What I wanted."

Jake laughed, the sound bitter, echoing off the canopy of trees. "Most men wouldn't complain about you seeing them as a fantasy, honey."

"But you know what I mean, Jake."

He looked down. "I guess I do."

"I'm sorry."

"Don't apologize to me. What I did was inexcusable. I cost my father Lord knows how much money, unless he got the insurance to cover it. But probably not, seeing as it was arson."

"You don't even know?"

"No, I don't know. I left, and I never came back."

"Because he told you to."

"Yeah, and I was looking for any excuse." He let out a long breath. "Don't try to make me the victim here. I was the bad guy."

Cassie scrunched her nose. "It's funny, I thought of us as opposites all this time. I looked at you and I saw a guy who had the kind of freedom that I envied. My mother always made me feel guilty. Like she had sacrificed everything to have me. And she did, Jake. In fairness, she did sacrifice to have me. So I felt like I had to live my whole life to please her. On the surface we seem different, but if you really look closely I think we're the same."

"Why? Did you set your mom's kitchen on fire?"

"We both had people who wanted something from us we didn't know how to give. I changed myself. I did everything I could to be the person my mom wanted me to be, even if I didn't want the things she wanted. I wanted to own a business, I wanted to go to college. But my mom made me so conscious of the importance of finding a man and getting married, and not ending up like her, that I did that instead. Without even realizing that was what I was doing." She was only just now fully realizing it.

She bent down and picked a dandelion, snapping the heavy yellow head from the stem before she continued. "But it wasn't me. It wasn't right. I don't even think I loved him. Not really. I loved the idea. I loved the idea of finding someone, and having this idyllic family life that my mother had always wanted, but couldn't give us. I wanted to give that to us. And then when push came to shove and he didn't want to be married anymore, I didn't even know how to fight, because I had always just gone along with what other people wanted for me. Then I was standing there, a failure in my mother's eyes. And it didn't even matter what I thought, how I saw myself, because it had never mattered to me before. I think we are just the same. Your father wanted something from you, but instead of bending over backward to try and do it like I did, you flipped him the middle finger and did everything you could to rebel against him."

"That's basically us being opposites."

She laughed even though she didn't find any of it particularly funny. "Except, if you think about it, both of us were just living for other people. Neither of us were doing what we wanted. We were reacting to the things other people told us. What do you want, Jake? What do you want from life?"

He rubbed the back of his neck before dropping his hand and making eye contact with her again. "I have what I want. At least I had it. I just want to go back to Seattle, I want to buy the mechanic shop, and I want to keep living." He took a deep breath. "I've got a handle on everything now. Coming back here just stirs it all up."

"Probably because you don't actually have a handle on it."

"I do. I just need to get away from this place."

"And what would you do in Seattle, Jake? Once you have your mechanic shop, then what?"

"What kind of question is that, Cassie? What will you do? Are you going to keep living to please your mother? Are you going to run your coffee shop and try to find a new husband? What are your goals?"

"My goals? I'm good with figuring out who I am. Apart from all of this. Apart from expectation. I've already started. I have my business. Right now, I have you."

"Not for long."

Okay, so she'd overstepped here. She'd been feeling...brave. Not herself. And she'd said something dumb. Damn, that hurt. Even if it was true. And she knew it was. She didn't expect this to be a forever thing. She knew she couldn't keep him for very long, but that didn't mean she wouldn't miss him when he was gone.

"I know that, okay, Jake? I've been married before. I don't really want to go there again. Not just now. Now when I'm still getting everything together."

"Is there a point where we're supposed to have it together?" he asked. "Because if so, I seem to have missed it."

"I intend to someday. I'm tired of settling. I'm tired of settling for my mom's dreams. I'm tired of just accepting what gets lobbed at me. I think I deserve more. Don't you?"

"Do I think you deserve more? Hell yeah. Do I think I do?" He squinted and looked off into the distance. She wondered if he was looking toward the field he'd lit on fire. "I think I deserve what I worked for. I don't really think I deserve much else."

And she could tell the subject was closed now. That she'd pushed things much further than a one-night stand should be allowed to.

"Do you want to show me around?"

"That is kind of why I brought you here. I was going to show you the field I burned. He never grew anything in it after that. At least, it doesn't look like it. Still a bunch of ash." He swallowed hard. "Sometimes you just can't undo stuff. Sometimes you can't fix it."

"Do you wish you could fix things with your dad?"

"I don't know. Our relationship was what it was. I doubt he ever changed."

Her heart felt like it was splintering, for him. For the rift he would never have the chance to heal.

He walked up the porch steps, and she watched one of them bow beneath his weight, and she followed carefully to avoid the one that was compromised. He unlocked the door and she trailed him inside. The inside of the house smelled stale. It looked clean enough, but as she walked across the wooden floor she could see that there was a film of dirt on the wood, could see where Jake had walked when he'd come in on previous visits.

"Are you going to clean all this yourself? Are you going to get someone in to help you?"

"I don't know. I'm trying to find the line between how much work I can miss, and how much money I want to fork out. Basically, I'm sacrificing vacation days that I never take to be here. So at this point I'm not losing money. But I'd really like for this venture to be an asset, and not a drain. So there's only so much I'm willing to invest."

"That makes sense." She thought about their previous conversation. "And you want to use the money you get to buy the mechanic shop you work at."

"Yep."

"Why is that so important to you?"

"Because it's what I've been working for."

"And you only want what you worked for."

"Makes sense, right?"

"I suppose so." She stuffed her hands in her back pockets and walked deeper into the room, looking at all the furniture, the dusty Afghan laying across the dusty couch. It was such a quiet space. And she had a feeling it hadn't been when Jake and his father had lived here. "Is it weird to be back?"

"You have no idea." His voice was rough. And all she wanted to do was reach out and touch him. Offer comfort. But she didn't know if she should. Didn't know if he would feel like she was invading his space. Or take things further than he wanted to.

"So you've never thought about staying?"

"I can't stay here." Blue eyes clashed with hers. "There's nothing for me here."

I'm here.

She left that unsaid. Because hadn't he just told her that she wouldn't have him for long? He made it very clear that this wasn't permanent. One night hardly meant forever. And she knew that intellectually, but it didn't stop her from wanting more. The ache that was building in her chest wasn't based on logic. It was based on that connection that had always been there. That had never been uprooted, no matter how life had tried to dig at it.

"Well, did you ever wonder why he left it to you?"

His hollow laughter filled the room, and he put his hands in his pockets and leaned back against the wall, resting his head against the cracking plaster. "I've done nothing but wonder that since I came back." He cleared his throat and lowered his head. "The old man told me never to come back. So why the hell would he leave it to me? I would've thought he'd be more likely to leave it to you. Or to some vagrant. Or a drinking buddy." Jake shook his head. "I have no idea why he picked me. No fucking idea."

"Do you think the reason is important?"

"I've never treated anything the old man did like it was important. Why should I start now that he's dead?"

"I suppose that's a good question. You know, I never knew my dad." She didn't know why she was telling him this. She didn't waste a whole lot of time worrying about her dad, or lack of one.

"I suppose that means you're going to tell me I should appreciate the one I had."

"No, I don't think that at all. I just think crappy parents have a lot to answer for."

He laughed again, and this time it was much more genuine. "Now on that I absolutely agree with you."

"So, can I help you today?"

"It's your day off, Cassie. I hardly think you should spend it scrubbing out this place."

"I want to. Jake, let me do this for you."

"Why do you want to do anything for me? I thought I was just your rebellion."

"My rebellion can take a backseat. For today I can just be a friend helping another friend. Two people who have something in common hanging out together."

"Is that something in common that they really like getting in each other's pants?"

She had a feeling he was trying to be offensive, but instead she was flattered that he wanted to get into her pants again. "Sure, that. And the fact that we're both trying to make lives for ourselves outside of what people told us was possible. Outside of what people told us we should want."

"All right, Cassie. I'll accept your help. But only because I'm in no position to do otherwise."

"You flatter me so. Now where can I find a mop in this place?"

BY THE TIME Cassie was done cleaning she could hardly say the place sparkled. If anything, the house seemed like it had been brushed over with a patina, leaving a dull, well-worn look to everything. But it couldn't be helped. In some ways it was charming, especially now that there wasn't a layer of dust covering every available surface. Baby steps.

Jake had been outside all day, throwing junk into a Dumpster that he'd had the disposal company bring out to the property, and making arrangements for the bigger things to be hauled away. He was also working on finding homes for the animals. By the time they got on his motorcycle and headed back into town, they were both on the brink of exhaustion.

About halfway there, it started to rain. The sky seemed to break apart as cold water poured out over everything, fat drops hammering the two of them as they rode on.

By the time they reached the apartments, they were both soaking wet, and Cassie was saying a prayer of thanks for face guards. They dismounted the bike and she tugged off her helmet, shaking out her hair, the damp ends splattering the leather jacket.

Jake turned to face her. "Thanks for your help. I really do appreciate it. I know sometimes I have a hard time showing it. But I think now I'll go ahead and pay for that muffin you dropped on the floor."

A crack of laughter burst from her lips. His displays of humor were so rare, so few and far between that they always shocked and delighted her. "Well, your generosity is appreciated. I fear the lack of revenue from that muffin was really going to affect my bottom line for the month."

"Hey, the hazards of owning a small business."

She smiled at him, and he smiled back. Such a simple thing, but it made her heart squeeze tight. Made her stomach flip over. "We're still standing in the rain," she said, her words sounding a little dazed. Because she was a little dazed. By this. By him. By whatever was happening between them.

He looked up, raindrops falling on his face, roll-

ing over the bridge of his nose and down his cheeks.
"So we are."

"Do you want to go inside and get dry?"

"Just a second."

JAKE DIDN'T OFTEN act on impulse, not anymore. But
something about Cassie seemed to bring out a side of
him he had long repressed. And tonight, he was acting on impulse. Again.

He wrapped his arm around her waist and tugged
her against him, relishing the feeling of her soft breasts
pressed against his chest. Then, before he could think it
through too much, before she could protest, he brought
his lips down on hers and kissed her.

Her lips were soft, wet from the rain, tasting like
salt air, sex and Cassie. He dipped his tongue into her
mouth, sliding it against hers, feeling her shiver beneath his touch.

She was so hot. So perfect. Everything he could ask
for in a woman, and then some. He had never wanted
like this, or if he had, he certainly didn't remember.
And if he couldn't remember, the feeling couldn't have
been this strong.

Because this kind of desire would stay with him,
just the way a rainy afternoon in the library studying
math had. Memories like that should've faded, and
yet they hadn't. Cassie was too vibrant. When he was
touching her, when he wasn't touching her. It was like
holding life in his hands. Not just something alive, but
the very essence of life. Warmth, beauty, air. Everything a person needed. Everything they could possibly
want. And he knew without a doubt he didn't deserve

to be holding her. But he was. For now, for as long as he could, he would.

And it didn't matter that it was raining. Or maybe it did. Maybe it was the rain that made the two of them together feel possible. That made this feel fresh, and new. Maybe it was the rain made him feel different, like he could have this. If only for a moment.

He wanted to push her up against the side of the building and take her there. Right there on the main street of Copper Ridge. He wanted to stake a claim on her, when he had no right to do that. He wanted to shove his control to one side and simply do as he pleased.

Dangerous. Those thoughts were dangerous. And right now, he didn't even care.

He managed to wrench himself away from her, his body protesting, his brain driving the boat for a moment as he tried to convince himself that they needed to move this somewhere a little more private.

"Let's go back around to my door," he said.

He didn't want to walk through the coffee shop with her, not now. That desire was in complete opposition to the one he had only a moment ago. To the fantasy he'd had about taking her outside so that everyone would know she was his. In reality he knew he couldn't do that to her. He couldn't link her that closely with him in public.

Because in the end, he would be leaving. And Cassie had to stay. Cassie was the one who would have to deal with the fallout of having a fling with him. And he wouldn't do that to her.

He had a feeling he wouldn't be able to leave her

entirely unscathed, but on this score, he would protect her.

"Okay, I'm not going to argue."

He grabbed hold of her hand and started to lead
her to his door, fumbling for the key and opening it
as quickly as he could, his fingers clumsy, numb from
the cold rain.

He waited for her to walk inside before he slammed
the door shut behind them, making sure it was locked.
Then he turned to her, his heart pounding heavily. "My
hands are cold."

She pulled her shirt up over her head and gave him
a defiant look. "I don't care."

"Maybe we should go upstairs instead of standing
here in the entry. I don't have condoms."

"Well, the condom thing I do care slightly more
about. But, happily for you, and for me, I was not actually just getting out of bed this morning when you
ran into me here."

"What were you doing?"

"I was coming back from the store. Where I got
these." She dug into her big purse and produced a
box of condoms. "Which is…you know, a lot of them.
Slightly ambitious. Especially considering you disappeared on me after…but I thought just in case. I'm an
optimist."

He laughed, completely amazed that he was able
to be both this turned on, and amused. "A little bit.
But I like it."

"I'm glad. Because I don't think I'm going to suddenly transform into a smooth-talking siren."

"I wouldn't like it. Because then you wouldn't be
you."

Her dark eyes, which had been sparkling with humor, suddenly took on a glossy sheen. "I don't think anyone's ever said anything like that to me before."

"Anything like what?"

"Like… Anything that made me feel like being me was an asset."

His heart squeezed tight, and he hated those who had come before him. The people who had been in her life before this moment, for having her around all those years and never saying just how special she was. And then he hated himself, for realizing it back when they had been in high school, and never saying it then. Because someone should have. This woman should know how special she was.

"I need you to be you. I don't think you can possibly know how much." He shouldn't have said those words. And yet, he couldn't keep them to himself, either. She needed to hear them, but it should be from a better man. From a man who wasn't going to leave her, who wasn't going to put her business up for sale to serve his own interests.

Are you still going to do that, you prick?

He didn't really have a choice. It had nothing to do with her, it never had.

But everything right now was about her. Everything. He felt like he was being kept alive by her very presence, which was a strange and terrifying sensation. And also one he didn't particularly want to lose.

He didn't understand it, either. But what he did understand was the hum of sexual attraction that burned beneath the feelings that were swelling in his chest. He couldn't do anything with the feelings even if he'd wanted to, so he figured he would just follow the sexual attraction. That he knew. That he could deal with.

It was all they could ever have.

And since she'd been forward-thinking enough to buy condoms, they could have it right now.

He took her into his arms and kissed her deeply, gripping the clasp on her bra and undoing it with one hand before moving deeper into the entryway.

She pulled away from him, her eyes wide. "You're very good at that."

"I've honed some very specific skills over the years. If your transmission needs replacing, I'm your guy. If your bra needs removing…I'm pretty good at that, too."

She blinked rapidly, a smile curving her lips. "What else are you good at?"

He pushed her back against the wall, kissing her neck. "What else?" he whispered. His lips were close to her ear, so close he couldn't resist biting her gently. "I've been told I really know my way around a woman's body." He lifted his hand and cupped her breast, squeezing her nipple between his thumb and forefinger. And suddenly, thoughts of all of his previous experience fled from his brain. The words he'd been about to say drying up on his tongue. Because no other women mattered. "I suppose that doesn't matter. The only thing that matters is that I know my way around your body."

"I don't have any complaints."

"What do you like?"

"You."

He kissed her cheek. "I'm flattered by that, honey. But I really do want to know."

"I… I liked what you did in the apartment last night. No one has ever done that for me before."

"What? No one has ever gone down on you before?"

Color flooded her cheeks. "Well, technically now someone has. But before that…"

"How long were you married to that asshole?"

"Eight years."

"Something was seriously wrong with him."

"Didn't really think much about it. That's the hazard of inexperience, I suppose."

"It's not a hazard of inexperience, it's the hazard of sleeping with assholes."

She wrapped her arms around his neck and kissed him, tugging at the waistband of his pants. He helped her get his jeans and underwear off, then ripped his shirt over his head when he realized he was standing there in nothing but a black T-shirt, probably looking a bit like a dick.

She didn't seem to mind.

He unsnapped her jeans and made quick work of the rest of her clothes. Then he stopped for a moment, trying to get a handle on his breathing, and just enjoyed the feeling of being skin to skin with her, every inch of him touching every inch of her.

"There is something I do have experience with." She met his eyes, a determined glint in them.

"Oh really?"

"Yes, and you asked me what I liked. Well, I can't say I've particularly liked this in the past. But I'm feeling inspired. And I think we should follow bursts of inspiration."

"Do you?" he asked, arching one eyebrow upward.

"Sure. If I hadn't followed my inspiration for this

coffee shop I would still be living with my mother. Inspiration is a good thing." She extricated herself from his hold and lowered herself to her knees in front of him. He felt like he'd been slugged in the stomach. The vision of Cassie, kneeling before him, her brown eyes locked with his, was something out of the fantasy he'd never even dared let himself have.

"Cassie," he said, his voice rough.

But whatever he had been about to say was cut off, lost to him completely when she wrapped her hand around the base of his cock and leaned in, flicking her tongue over the head. She tightened her grip on him as she took him more deeply into her mouth, the edge of her tongue sliding down his length.

He laced his fingers through her hair and fought the urge to let his head fall back. He wanted to watch her. Wanted to watch this. The sight of her lips around him was enough to push him over the edge now.

And if that wasn't enough, the physical sensation had him ready to beg for more. Her heat, the slickness. But it was only an echo of what he really wanted. Where he wanted to be.

"Okay, Cassie, I'm going to need you to stop now." He could barely force the words out through his tightened throat.

She moved away from him, her eyes glassy, her expression dazed. "Did I do something wrong?"

"No. You're doing it a little bit too right. And I don't want this to be over yet."

He reached into her purse and pulled out the condom box, tearing it open and pulling out a plastic packet that he made quick work of. While he rolled it on to his length she stood, her eyes fixed to him, like he was a particularly decadent dessert.

He couldn't say he'd ever had a woman look at him quite like that before.

Part of him wanted to stand there and enjoy it. But a much bigger part of him wanted to be inside her thirty seconds ago, so he decided to forgo the pleasure of being stared at.

He pressed her against the wall, gripping her chin and kissing her deep while he took hold of her thigh with his other hand and tugged it up over his hip, opening her damp center to him. He pressed the head of his cock against her entrance and tested her before sliding the rest of the way in, gritting his teeth in a valiant attempt to keep from exploding.

"Fuck." He said the word more like a prayer than a curse.

He flexed his hips, thrusting hard, and a rough sound escaped her lips.

"Too hard?" he asked, concerned that he was asking too much of her.

"No." She put her hands on his butt, encouraging him to keep going. "If you stop, I might kill you."

"You wouldn't."

"I will poison your muffin."

"You're ruthless, baby."

"I am now. Ruthless about what I want. And I want you."

He withdrew from her, then thrust deep. "The feeling is mutual."

And then talking was impossible, because he was lost in the sensation of being inside of her. Lost in his need. His need to be consumed by her, to consume her. His need to have everything. All of her.

He buried his face in her neck, bracing himself as his climax started to build, as it began to overtake him. He didn't want to finish first. The other selfish guy who took what he wanted without a care for her satisfaction. He wanted to be different. He wanted to be better. He wanted to wipe all the memories she had of her husband away, and replace them with memories of him. Of course, he needed to be worthy of that, and he wasn't certain he was.

His limbs began to shake, his blood roaring through his veins. He slipped his hand between her thighs and rubbed his thumb over her clit, desperate for her to find her release. He stroked her, once, twice, and felt a shudder wrack her body, felt her internal muscles pulse around his cock.

That was all he needed. He let go, her name on his lips as he found his own release, as it overtook him completely.

He rested against her for a moment before withdrawing, looking around the small entry area. "No trash can?"

"No." She laughed.

"What's so funny?"

"Nothing is funny, really. Just…great."

His heart started thundering faster in his chest, a feat he hadn't imagined possible, considering it was still raging from his recent orgasm. "I am going to need a trash can, though," he said looking down.

"Oh! Of course. Well, you can come up to my place and use mine. And we have a few uh…left, and we can use the rest of those."

Heat streaked through him. "You're very ambitious."

"It's a new thing I'm trying. High standards."

"I like the way you think."

"I'm glad. Because I don't just set goals, I meet them." She smiled at him, her determination and enthusiasm infectious.

He marveled at the difference in the way they approached life. She was breaking free. Uncovering all of the things she had kept buried for so long. In contrast, when he had left town, he had foreclosed on his feelings. Boarding them up, and leaving them vacant. Making sure he couldn't access any of them again.

Because when he opened himself up, bad things escaped. He envied her in some ways. Most of all he regretted the fact that she needed a man who was open to her, too. And he could never be that for her.

But he could be with her now. And if that was all he could get, he would take it.

CHAPTER EIGHT

CASSIE HAD NEVER been so happy in her life. She was just focusing all her energy on not facing the fact that that happiness was a fantasy, and not reality.

Because Jake wasn't going to stay in Copper Ridge. Jake wasn't integrated into her real life. Her freedom was confined to the bedroom.

Well, that wasn't strictly true.

They had thoroughly explored their chemistry in several different rooms. Kitchen, living room, her bedroom and his. Not to mention the entryway to their apartments, which she could no longer walk through without remembering what it had been like to be pinned up against the wall by Jake while he thrust into her, hard and deep.

She smiled happily and put the lid on a paper cup, turning and handing it to Lydia, the president of Copper Ridge's Chamber of Commerce. The other woman was on her phone, but offered a broad smile and a finger wave as she took her coffee and walked back out of the café.

Suddenly, Cassie was overwhelmed with a feeling of sadness. Which was strange considering just how happy she'd felt a moment before. It was something to do with standing here in the coffee shop, not knowing how long she would have it. Not knowing how long she would have any of the things that meant the most to her. Jake among them.

He really was important. He was becoming essential.

But it was different than things had been with her husband. With Allen, it had been about maintaining a certain type of life. It hadn't ever been about him specifically, and she was sort of ashamed to realize that. To admit it to herself.

Being married to him had been about realizing an ideal, an ideal she realized…well, hadn't been ideal. At least not for her. It hadn't been about love, it had been about changing herself so she could be more acceptable to the people around her. And being with Jake wasn't like that. She didn't care what anyone thought about her and Jake. Granted, no one knew about her and Jake yet, but she already knew she wouldn't care.

But if she wanted Jake, in any capacity besides the temporary, it wasn't going to be a smooth path. It was not going to be the path of least resistance, nor one that earned her approval.

She didn't care. She realized right then that being with Jake was going to mean sacrificing that sweet, nonconfrontational comfort she prized. Interestingly, she didn't think anything she'd ever done had been sacrificial. Yes, it had been to please other people, but it had been about her own comfort. Not just about theirs.

She was afraid of confrontation, afraid of making people angry at her, because then they might not want her anymore. She'd gotten angry about losing her house. Her flowers. Her husband. But she hadn't fought for any of it. She hadn't even tried.

But Jake was changing that, had been from the mo-

ment he'd come to town. She'd pushed against him almost immediately. Had fought back, had demanded
what she wanted.

And she liked that. Wanted to keep doing it. Wanted
to keep being strong.

The revelation was shocking enough that it took
her a few minutes to realize she was staring straight
through Ace Coleman like he wasn't even there.

"Oh." She blinked. "Hi, Ace. Did you need your
Red Eye?"

"Yeah, late night last night. Another late night tonight."

"The life of a bartender." She started a double shot
of espresso and filled up a medium-size coffee cup
while the shots were running. Then she dumped the
shots in the cup and put the lid on. "Here you go."

She took his money and made change on autopilot,
still considering what she might be willing to do. What
she might be willing to sacrifice.

She looked around the coffee shop, weight settling
on her chest. She knew everyone in here. Knew everyone by name. And when tourism picked up later
in the spring there would be strangers for her to meet.

She would miss the building if it were sold. But it
occurred to her that without a doubt, she would miss
Jake more.

And just like that she realized that her decision
was made.

WHEN JAKE GOT back from the ranch that night he had
a surprise waiting for him on his doorstep. It was
his very favorite kind of surprise. A Cassie-shaped
surprise.

Over the past two weeks she had become an essential part of his day. He didn't leave at night anymore after they were finished making love. He stayed. Mornings had become something wonderful, instead of something to be dreaded.

Because he no longer woke up to a blaring alarm clock, cold sheets and bone-deep exhaustion. No, he woke up to a blaring alarm clock and the warm, curvy woman in his arms.

And now she was here waiting for him when he was ready to drop dead from exhaustion after working on cleaning up the junk around his dad's old property. She was here, looking like home, and rest, and everything he needed right in that moment.

She had a habit of doing that. Looking at him like he was important. Like she saw all kinds of good things that no one else ever had. She smiled at him when she was helping him deal with ranching responsibilities— and when he was helping her bake scones for the coffee shop, because it really was the least he could do with all the help she'd given him.

Not a reserved smile, either. A real smile. One that made him feel like he could do no wrong.

He didn't think he deserved it, but he'd damn sure take it.

"Well, aren't you a sight for sore eyes."

She smiled, and he felt like it was a tally in the relatively vacant win column on the score sheet he kept of his life. "Am I?"

"Very definitely." He stepped past her, leaning in and dropping a kiss on her lips before unlocking the front door. "I need to get cleaned up a bit, though. Then maybe we can have some dinner."

"Okay." Cassie was vibrating with energy, even more than usual. It was one of the things he liked best about her. She had a lot of enthusiasm for what she was doing with her life, for life in general, and it only seemed to be growing.

He stripped his shirt off and threw it on the floor, wandering into the bathroom and removing the rest of his clothes before turning the shower on. It was an interesting thing having someone waiting for him when he got home. Something he hadn't ever missed, because he never had it. Something he realized now was most definitely missing from his life.

Don't go getting attached to it. He turned the water to the shower on and waited for it to get warm before he stepped inside.

He heard the bathroom door open, and saw Cassie's silhouette through the textured glass. He could tell that she was naked, and immediately his cock started getting hard.

"I figured, seeing as you have me now, I would make sure you knew you didn't have to pleasure yourself in the shower." She opened the shower door and stepped inside, all smooth skin and gorgeous curves.

"Pleasure myself, huh?"

"Well, what would you call it?"

"Nothing fancy. Just a little jacking off."

She worried her bottom lip, looking like she was considering the words very carefully. "Jacking off. Serviceable. Definitely descriptive."

He wrapped his arms around her and kissed her nose. "I will never understand how you can make my cock so hard it hurts and make me laugh at the same time."

"I don't know. I can only say that I'm honored." She kissed his lips. "Honored both to make you laugh and to make your cock hard."

"Nice girl Cassie Ventimiglia, talking dirty to me in the shower."

"Nice girls know how to have fun, too."

"Yes, we're smashing stereotypes all over the place lately."

"No more talking." She kissed him again, this time deeper, moving her hands over his chest and around his back, down to his ass.

"Demanding."

She nipped his bottom lip. "What did I just say?"

His erection pulsed, arousal flooding through him. If she wanted to play this game, he was not going to stop her. She moved away from him, revealing the condom packet in her hand. She opened it slowly and positioned it on the end of his length, rolling it on.

"Foreplay is great," she said, "but we don't need any of that right now."

He was not going to argue. He reversed their positions, pressing her against the wall as he thrust deep inside of her. He kept his eyes open, trained on hers. It was a surreal thing, being here with her now, when just a few short weeks ago this had been nothing but a fantasy. It had been his own hand on his cock, not her tight, slick body.

It was real now, she was real. And it was better than he ever could've imagined.

Need built between them, each thrust bringing them closer and closer to the peak. She clung tightly to his shoulders as he rode her hard, and when they reached it, they reached it together.

They stood there, sated, and he didn't want to move away. He wanted to stay inside her. Wanted this moment to last.

"Oh, Jake." He loved it when she did that. When she said his name like that, like it was her own personal revelation. "Oh, Jake, I love you."

CHAPTER NINE

Wow. SHE HAD really said it. She meant it, so she didn't regret it. But she did sort of regret that Jake was looking at her like she'd grown another head. That was not the typical postcoital expression she was used to getting from him.

"Aren't you going to say something?" she asked.

They were still standing underneath the water, reminiscent of that day in the rain. But she didn't feel triumphant right now; instead she felt a sense of foreboding.

"What is there to say?"

"Well, *I love you, too* is typically the desired outcome of that kind of declaration, but I can't say I was really expecting that. Though I was expecting a little bit more than the angry face you're giving me right now."

Jake opened the shower door and got out, grabbing a towel off the rack and running it over his chest. "You knew this wasn't permanent."

"Yeah, I knew it. But I decided to go full rebel and not play by the rules. I fell in love with you."

"How is that even possible?"

"How is it not possible, Jake?" She followed him out of the shower, grabbing the towel out of his hands and running it over her own body, leaving herself mostly damp.

"I don't even know how to answer that."

"Well, fair enough because I don't know how to answer your question."

"I feel like I did a pretty good job of making a case for the fact that I'm kind of an asshole."

"I have yet to see a whole lot of evidence of that." She should've known he would be like this. Really, she should have.

"Did you miss the part where I burned down my father's fields?"

"Nope. Fresh in my memory."

"Then you must realize that you don't make any sense."

"Okay, so let's just stop this right now. I love you, and you're not talking me out of it. So you can stop trying."

He picked his jeans up off the floor and put them on, zipping them carefully. "Did you forget one little problem?"

"What problem?"

"I'm going to sell your coffee shop. I'm endangering your livelihood." He stared at her hard, and she didn't say anything. "I'm not staying here."

"I know. I thought… I was thinking that if you want to, I mean, that is if you want me to, I would go back to Seattle with you."

His face went blank, his frame stiff. "You want to come back to Seattle with me?"

"Yes. I do."

"What the hell is wrong with you? You're just going to drop everything and come with me?"

"It isn't like that." Cassie took a deep breath. "I was thinking about it and I realized that the worst thing I do, and I do it over and over again, is play it safe. I do things that make other people happy so that I don't have to take chances. I don't have to make mistakes, or struggle. And I especially don't have to deal with the consequences. Because it's all someone else's fault. Well, I'm tired of that. I want to take a chance. And I want to take it with you."

"Are you sure you aren't just changing the narrative so you can revert to type?"

That barb hit its intended target, sent a bit of insecurity running through her. "I'm not." And she knew she didn't sound all that confident. But she wasn't used to this. Wasn't used to confrontation, wasn't used to holding her ground.

"You sound real certain."

"Well, what's the point either way?" She was feeling angry now. "I mean, you're going to put me into a precarious position anyway once you leave. I might as well take a chance on this."

"Oh, so you want to come with me because I'm forcing your hand? I've never been so flattered."

"That isn't it. You're just making me mad." She swallowed hard. "It's always been you, Jake. Always. Back in high school and now. I almost took a chance then, but I missed it. I missed my chance. I knew I couldn't miss it this time, not because I was afraid. I started to say something that night in the library and I changed my mind, I let fear get the best of me. And I lost my opportunity for fifteen years. I was not going to lose this opportunity, too."

Jake turned away from her, his broad, muscular

back filling her vision. Then everything blurred, tears filling her eyes. Because she knew this was the end. She knew he wasn't going to soften, wasn't going to make his own declaration of love.

Declarations of love didn't go this way.

"I'm not sorry I said it." She wouldn't be sorry. She would not be sorry for her existence anymore. For taking up space. For being the choice she often feared her mother wished she hadn't made, for being a disappointment to her husband. "I'm glad I said it. I'm glad I took the chance. And I hope years down the road when you look back on this you'll wish you'd taken the chance, too. You'll wish you were as brave as I was. Tough, tattooed Jake Caldwell, too afraid to take chances."

Jake turned around, his expression fierce. "You think that's it? You think I'm afraid to take chances? Maybe I'm just too damn smart to make the same mistakes more than once. I know what happens when I give free rein to my emotions. Shit burns, Cassie. And so do all of my relationships." He pushed his hands through his hair. "I am not the guy you give things up for."

"Maybe not. But I'm the woman who takes chances for herself. Because I deserve to try for happiness. I thought I deserved to try for this."

"You deserve a hell of a lot more than me."

"Only because you don't really see yourself, Jake. You were so angry because all anyone ever saw you as was a bad boy. A screwup. But you don't see yourself as anything more. You're your own biggest enemy."

"Maybe so. Or maybe I just see myself clearly."

"I've never fought for anything before. I just kind

of let things happen. I'm fighting now. I want to fight for you. I love you, Jake. There, I said it again. I officially have no pride."

"I can't love you back."

Cassie's eyes filled with tears, her chest so heavy she thought she might fall to the ground, thought she might never be able to get back up again. So she took a deep breath, used all her strength to stay standing. "Okay, then."

"Cassie…"

"There's nothing you can say to make it better. So don't even try."

"I wasn't going to."

That almost made her laugh. "Of course not. Were you going to rub it in?"

"I don't know. I don't know what I was going to say."

"Well, I'm going to say goodbye. There's only so much my ego can take. This was a great growth experience but I can't say I'm eager to stand around and marinate in it. Please don't come buy your muffin from me tomorrow. I hope wherever you do buy one, it has raisins in it."

She put her clothes on as quickly as possible, not looking at him again. Ignoring the fact that her T-shirt was sticking to her wet skin. Then she walked through the apartment and stormed out the door, only then realizing that she'd left her shoes there. Oh well, it was too late. Those shoes were dead to her. She would have to get new shoes.

A sob wracked her chest, and tears started spilling down her cheeks. She scrubbed her forearm across her face, but it didn't stop the tears from falling. She had a feeling nothing would.

She felt like the world was ending, and she hadn't felt that way when she got divorced. But then, she'd already known this was different.

Because Jake was her choice. Jake was the one thing she'd stuck her neck out for. Jake was the one thing she'd taken a chance on. Jake had been her decision, and her decision alone. And the failure of that was all hers.

The heartbreak was all hers, too.

She knew from past experience that what-ifs could consume you, could keep you up at night with the possibilities of what might have been. But, standing here, with absolute certainty, didn't feel a whole lot better right now.

She only hoped it would take fewer than fifteen years to get over Jake this time around.

But she wasn't overly optimistic.

BY THE NEXT morning Jake had two things: a hangover and a plan.

He was a little bit happier with the plan than he was with the hangover, but he imagined it was par for the breakup course. He wouldn't know; he didn't think he'd ever been involved in a breakup before. Not calling a woman you were sleeping with the morning after didn't count.

This was more like an official breakup. He could tell, because he felt like wolves had burst through his chest in the night and savaged his innards. He'd felt a similar pain at other times in his life. When his mother had died, and when his father had made him leave the ranch. Heartbreak, maybe. Or just plain old grief.

Either way it sucked.

But he couldn't ask Cassie to give up her life here for him. He'd lied to her last night when he told her he couldn't love her. But he'd told her the truth when he said he wasn't the kind of guy worth giving up a life for.

All he had to do was look at the evidence of his past to prove that. He'd never done anything but screw things up, had never done anything but give the people he cared about grief. He'd never been able to be good enough for his father. Disappointment was all he ever saw reflected in the old man's eyes.

It would kill him to watch the love in Cassie's eyes transform into that. Slowly, over the course of years, he was certain it would. Because his relationships had never gone any other way.

So it was decided. He was going to leave. He would turn over the cleanup of the property to someone else, and he didn't care if that cut into his profits. The other thing he was doing was signing the building that housed the coffee shop over to Cassie. He wouldn't be out anything. Not out of pocket anyway. Sure, he would have to get a bigger loan to buy the mechanic shop, but that didn't matter. The building only had value because of Cassie's business. It only had value because of the work that had gone into restoring Old Town. He hadn't been a part of that. But Cassie had been. She was the one who deserved to reap the rewards.

He was back out at the ranch for one last visit. One

last time to look around. To yell at some demons. To rage at things that couldn't be fixed.

That was how he found himself standing at the edge of the field. The dirt in front of him was still a mix of ash and soil, and nothing more. Unsurprisingly, there were no answers here. He didn't know why he'd bothered. He didn't know what he'd been looking for. Or maybe he did. He'd been looking for answers, but there was nothing here but ghosts. Nothing here but memory.

There was nothing new at all. The time for getting answers was over. His father was dead; they could never reconcile. Jake could never scream at him and ask why nothing he'd ever done had been good enough. Jake could never say he was sorry.

The time for all of that had passed. And he'd been hiding.

So many things left unsaid.

That made him think of Cassie again. Mostly because everything made him think of Cassie, but partly because of what she'd told him about that night in the library. And how she'd almost said something to him then. That was the night he'd almost kissed her. But instead it was the night everything had gone to hell.

Yes, his past was littered with things left unsaid. Kisses left ungiven.

You're just doing it again. Repeating the cycle.

No, it wasn't the same. He was making a conscious decision to turn away from her, because it was the best thing for her.

Maybe you could stop running?

He was ready to kick his inner voice in the balls.

He didn't have anything for himself here. Nothing but shitty memories.

He turned away from the field and headed back toward the house, walking up the porch, purposely stepping on the board that flexed beneath his weight. He pulled open the screen door, and went inside.

He wondered what other people felt when they came home. If they felt a sense of belonging. If they felt happy. All he felt was like he was being crushed beneath something. Beneath too many words that could never be spoken. Beneath the mistakes he could never fix.

He walked up the stairs, each one creaking beneath his feet. They had always done that. In a weird way it was kind of comforting. Familiar.

There was a stack of papers on the desk in his dad's room that he wanted to grab before he left. Just in case it had personal information. Here there were some report cards and other personal documents of his and he didn't really want to leave them behind for whoever ended up inhabiting or cleaning the place.

Their existence was as inexplicable as the old man's decision to leave him the property. He didn't know why his dad had kept them. He'd thrown Jake away quickly enough. Why not the papers documenting his life?

He pushed open the door and picked the papers up from his father's desk, shuffling through them. He'd meant to do this weeks ago but he'd simply looked at it all and taken the first few sheets off the pile, then left it.

He sat on the edge of the bed, kicking up a cloud of dust as he did. He flipped through documents, absorb-

ing himself in the past. In receipts and shitty grades.
In notes from teachers.

And then, somewhere in the middle, was an envelope with his name on it. Another report card maybe.
He tore the envelope open, his stomach tightening
when he did.

It was a letter.

Jake,
If you have this letter I'm probably dead. No
getting around that fact. I started a few of them
years ago and never sent them. So I imagine
the only one you'll end up with is one you find.

I wasn't a good father. But you know that. I'm
not good at apologizing, either, but I owe you one.

I'm sorry. It doesn't seem like enough. Because I said a lot of other things when you were
growing up that should never have been said.
And *I'm sorry* doesn't take them away.

I can't think of a better way to show you that
than to leave everything with you. I know I said
you couldn't handle it, but I was wrong. I don't
know what you've been up to all these years but
I know you did good.
Dad

Jake's hands were shaking when he put the letter
down. There was no explanation there. No grand answers. No declaration of familial love, but then, that
just wasn't in his dad's nature.

But there was something better than that.

His dad had trusted that he'd turned out okay. Had
trusted that he could leave all of his properties with

him, and that he wouldn't make a hash of it. Had trusted he wouldn't burn anything down.

He looked around the room, and things suddenly seemed different to him.

He wished his dad had sent the letters. And Jake wished he had come back at some point while his father was alive. But he'd been afraid. He had been afraid that he wouldn't be able to fix it. Afraid that no apology would ever be enough. It would've been. He realized that now. On both sides, *I'm sorry* would have fixed a lot of things. Talking would've fixed a lot of things.

He had been planning on riding out of town today. Had been planning on leaving today much the way he'd left fifteen years earlier.

But he wasn't going to do that now. He wasn't going to leave things unsaid. Not again.

Fifteen years ago he'd been nothing more than a scared boy. Running away from mistakes he'd made, letting someone else's words dictate how he felt about himself. Dictate who he was going to be. He'd spent all that time away licking his wounds and trying to become worthy of something. Anything.

And he'd come back trying to show them. Show them all that he'd changed when what he'd really done was hide.

But he had someone who thought he was worthy already. And that was worth more than a mechanic shop in Seattle. It was worth more than anything. And if it wasn't too late, he had to see if he could prove that to her.

Something Cassie had said was moving through his mind, over and over again. She hadn't been brave enough to fight. Because she'd been too afraid to fail. And that was what he'd been doing, for the past fifteen years. All under the guise of being a better man. He had convinced himself that what he was doing was protecting the world. From his anger, from his emotions. But what he had really been doing was protecting himself. Selling himself short.

Well, he wasn't going to do that anymore.

He wanted Cassie Ventimiglia, and while he wasn't entirely certain any man could be worthy of her, he was going to go and get her.

Because without her nothing mattered. Without love, nothing mattered.

CHAPTER TEN

CASSIE WAS EXHAUSTED by the time her shift ended. Emotionally and physically. She loved working in the coffee shop, and the only thing she ever would have traded it for was Jake Caldwell, but that didn't mean it didn't take its toll.

Making coffee with a broken heart was especially taxing.

She walked out from behind the counter and was about to turn the sign in the window when she saw a very familiar figure walking toward the door. She froze, unsure of whether she should scamper back behind the counter and hide, or if she should jerk the door open and fling herself into his arms. Probably she should find a middle ground. She wasn't good at middle ground with Jake.

No, considering they'd gone from bickering to her telling him she loved him in the space of only a few weeks, it was pretty clear middle ground was not a place they could inhabit.

Since she couldn't decide on a course of action, she was sort of standing there staring like a deer caught in the headlights. And it did not take long for him to notice her.

"Crap crappity crap," she said under her breath.

And Jake just kept moving closer. He pushed open

the door and came face-to-face with her, his blue eyes intense.

"I have something to say to you."

"I hope it isn't more mean things," she said. "Because I'm kind of over that."

"No, and I'm sorry there were mean things. Any mean things. You didn't deserve mean things."

"I know," she said, her heart thundering heavily.

"I think I had a revelation."

"Well, this should be interesting." She crossed her arms beneath her breasts, trying to stay immune to his apology, trying not to melt. Trying to look casual, and not like she was dying to hear the words he was about to say. Really, when people had news to deliver, they should just get to the point instead of making a big song and dance about it.

"I went back to the house this morning. I was going to leave. I had made my decision. I was going to pay someone to finish cleaning up the property, and I was going to leave this building to you."

Shock speared her in the chest. "Jake, I never wanted charity. I never wanted you to give me the building. I wanted to buy it."

"I know. I know you didn't want anything unreasonable. But I wanted to leave it to you. Because this is your blood, sweat and tears. This is all your work. The reason the building matters is because of what you've done. You should be proud of yourself."

She felt a warm glow in her chest. "I am."

"Good. I'm glad about that. But I changed my mind."

"Jake, this is pretty close to being mean. You said you weren't going to be mean."

"You can still have the building. It's just that I decided not to leave."

"What?" The warmth was growing now, spreading through her, and it felt an awful lot like hope.

"When I went back to the house today, I was going through some paperwork that I knew I needed to take care of before I let anyone else in. I found a letter from my dad."

All of the breath rushed out of her body. "What did it say?"

"The long and the short of it? He apologized. And I realized that we could have been spared a lot of years of hurt, if we hadn't been such idiots. There are a lot of mistakes that can't be fixed, a lot of hurts that can't be erased completely, but *I'm sorry* is a pretty good Band-Aid. I wish we would've at least tried to put it on there."

"I don't need an apology from you, Jake."

"Well, that's good, because I don't want to give you an apology. Well, I do. But that's not all I want to give you."

She took a deep breath. "What do you want to give me?"

In response, he took a step toward her, gripped her arms and pulled her toward him, dropping a kiss on her lips. It was deep, hard and short. Over way too soon.

"I'm a little confused now," she said.

"I love you."

Her mouth fell open. "Say it again."

"I love you, Cassie. I did last night when I sent you away, when I told you I couldn't love you. I was lying because I was afraid. And like you said, because I didn't think I was worthy. I'm still not sure I am, but I want more. You're the bravest person I've ever known. You're overcoming things instead of letting them own you."

He took a deep breath. "I thought if I left Copper Ridge I would escape all of the bad shit in my life. But all of my demons came with me because they weren't really about this place, they weren't really about my dad. They lived inside of me. I've spent a long time just trying to get by. Protecting myself from wanting anything too badly. Because I didn't want to be hurt again. I loved my dad, and he rejected me. I messed things up. And I've spent all these years afraid that I would do something like that again. Afraid that if I ever loved anyone all it would do was push them away. That they would find out I wasn't good enough. And Cassie, the last thing I wanted was to see your love for me turn into indifference, or worse, contempt."

"That's never going to happen." She hurt for him, for the pain he'd been through. For the pain they both had been through. "I saw you. Even then."

"I think it's kind of amazing that you did."

"We've always had a lot more in common than we realized."

"I don't want to be safe anymore, not if it means being alone. Not if it means not having you."

Cassie looked into his eyes, at the sincerity there, at the love. No one had ever looked at her that way before. Like she was everything they could ever want. It was exhilarating, and terrifying. And she wanted it to last more than anything. "What about your mechanic shop? I don't want you to give up anything for me. I know what it's like to be responsible for crushing somebody's dream. I worry that my mother always regretted choosing me over the man she was in love with. I don't want to be in that position with you."

"First of all, you're the only choice. That's all there is to it. Second of all, I can open a mechanic shop anywhere. It was never about that, really. That was a thing that I could pour myself into, that didn't cost me very much in terms of my emotions. I wanted it, I worked for it. But it only mattered because it gave me something to do that wasn't dealing with my shit."

"I can kind of understand that."

"Well, it would figure. Since you were about as emotionally messed up as I am."

"Hey, I've been working on myself for a couple of years now. I'm a little more advanced than you are."

He laughed. "I suppose you are."

"What are you going to do?"

"I figured we could break down the partitions between the apartments. Live up there. You could continue to run The Grind. I could assist. I've learned how to make scones. Maybe I'll open a mechanic shop. Right here in town. And if your car breaks down, I will be here to help."

"A live-in mechanic… That is tempting, Jake, I won't lie."

"I thought it might be."

She chewed her thumbnail. "Are you worried about your reputation? About what people will think of you? I mean, we don't have to stay here. We can go anywhere you want."

"No," he said, his voice firm. "This is your home. And mine. I want to stay here. Anything else would be running. And I don't really care what anyone else thinks. I have changed. And I can prove it to them. I'm not afraid to do that."

"I'm so proud of you, Jake. I really am."

"Are you afraid of what people might think of you being with me? Of what your mother might think?"

She laughed. "Unfortunately, it's not even a very fair test. My mom will just be happy I'm with someone. As far as she's concerned relationships are the holy grail. And as for everyone else? They'll learn to love you. Otherwise I won't serve them coffee. And I'll save all the muffins for you. All your detractors will be muffinless."

"That's a pretty intense threat."

"And I mean it. You're mine, Jake Caldwell. You aren't a bad boy, you're my man. My very good man. And I'm proud of you."

"And you, Cassie Ventimiglia, are most definitely your own woman. And I wouldn't have you any other way."

"I love you, Jake."

"I love you, too, Cassie." He took her into his arms and kissed her, long and deep, the kiss they should've shared fifteen years ago. "Even if it came a little late, I'm glad it happened." He had obviously been thinking the same thing.

"Maybe it didn't come late. Maybe it came at just the right time."

"That's right. I think maybe we both had to go on a journey before we were ready to meet here."

"If that's the case, then you're just in time."

He brushed his hand over her cheek, and she went ahead and let herself melt. She wasn't going to hold back. Not with him. "That's good to know. I don't have a white horse. I have a Harley and I'm not exactly a white knight…"

"I'm fine with that. I like you with an edge. I'd never ask you to be anything different."

He tightened his hold on her, his blue eyes intent on hers. "In that case, are you ready to ride off into the sunset with me?"

Cassie leaned in and kissed his cheek. "I'm ready to ride with you forever."

Jake smiled, a true smile that she felt all the way down to her toes. "Forever sounds just about right."

EPILOGUE

PEOPLE HAD BEEN complimenting Cassie on her engagement ring all day. It wasn't getting old. She doubted it ever would. This time around was so much different from the first time she'd gotten married.

Because this was Jake, and there was no one like Jake. And because Cassie finally felt like herself. Which was a much better place to be in when you were pledging yourself to someone forever and ever.

The past six months had been the best of her life, no question. Business at The Grind was booming, they'd set a date for their wedding, and Jake was about to open his very own mechanic shop.

Happily, it hadn't taken any time at all for the citizens of Copper Ridge to accept that Jake Caldwell was most definitely good people. If her stamp of approval hadn't done it, Jake's work ethic most certainly had.

Well, and some of it probably had to do with the fact that he was smoking hot. Even though he was taken, it didn't mean that the women in town didn't enjoy getting their car worked on by the best-looking mechanic in a hundred-mile radius. Possibly in the entire world. But she might be biased.

Though she didn't think so.

The door to the coffee shop opened, and a familiar but elusive face walked in. Unlike his brother Eli, Connor Garrett was rarely around these days. He rubbed his hand over his beard and approached the counter, stuffing his hands in his pockets. He looked like he had lost weight.

It was no secret that the past couple of years had been rough for him.

"Hi, Connor, what brings you in?"

His gaze landed on her left hand. "Engaged?"

Classic Connor, not very talkative.

"Yes, recently."

"Congratulations. Nice when you find that special someone." His voice was gruff, definitely not projecting much joy. But she couldn't say she blamed him.

"I would say so. What can I get for you?"

"Just a coffee. I'm meeting Liss here in a little bit to discuss some business things."

"Oh, she helping you with some accounting for the ranch?"

"No. If everything goes smoothly, we're going to be renting out one of the houses on the property to be used as a bed-and-breakfast."

The idea of more lodging right near town definitely appealed to Cassie. The Garrett Ranch was a couple of miles inland, but it was close enough that a B and B on the property would probably benefit The Grind.

"That's a great idea, Connor!" She handed him his coffee and he took it with a curt nod.

"It's not a bad one." And she had a feeling that was the friendliest remark she would get out of him.

He turned and walked to a table, taking a seat and busying himself by staring fixedly at the table's surface, not making eye contact with anyone.

The door opened again and Jake came in, covered in grease and wearing a broad smile.

Cassie leaned over the counter. "Kiss me, but don't touch me."

"You don't ask for much, do you?" He leaned in, careful to let only their lips touch and nothing else.

"I do. I ask for a whole lot. At least I do now."

"And I'm so glad you do. Because if you hadn't, Cassie, I would've let you get away. You were the braver of the two of us. You have no idea how happy I am about that."

"And you have no idea how happy I am that you are ready to stop running."

"That's right, honey. The only running I'm going to do from now on is going to be to run toward you."

She'd always lived in Copper Ridge. From the moment she was born, and she couldn't imagine ever living anywhere else. But it was Jake that made Copper Ridge truly feel like home.

Because he was here. And he had her heart. Now and always.

* * * * *

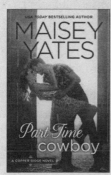 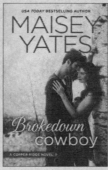 

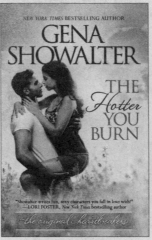

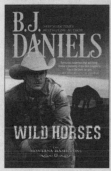
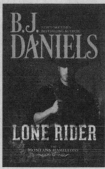
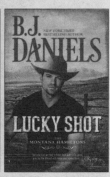

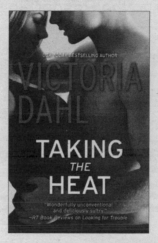

MAISEY YATES

| 78842 | BROKEDOWN COWBOY | __ $7.99 U.S. | __ $8.99 CAN. |
| 77959 | PART TIME COWBOY | __ $7.99 U.S. | __ $8.99 CAN. |

(limited quantities available)

TOTAL AMOUNT	$ _____
POSTAGE & HANDLING	$ _____
($1.00 FOR 1 BOOK, 50¢ for each additional)	
APPLICABLE TAXES*	$ _____
TOTAL PAYABLE	$ _____

(check or money order—please do not send cash)

To order, complete this form and send it, along with a check or money order for the total above, payable to HQN Books, to: **In the U.S.:** 3010 Walden Avenue, P.O. Box 9077, Buffalo, NY 14269-9077; **In Canada:** P.O. Box 636, Fort Erie, Ontario, L2A 5X3.

Name: _____
Address: _____ City: _____
State/Prov.: _____ Zip/Postal Code: _____
Account Number (if applicable): _____
075 CSAS

*New York residents remit applicable sales taxes.
*Canadian residents remit applicable GST and provincial taxes.

HQN™

www.HQNBooks.com

PHMY0815BL